Across the Stars

By: Jay DeMoir

DeMoir Publishing
An Imprint of House of DeMoir Productions

Also by Jay DeMoir

The Wives Series:
The Wives
Journey to Freedom

ISBN-13: 978-1794038653

ACROSS THE STARS

By: Jay DeMoir

DeMoir Publishing
An Imprint of House of DeMoir Productions

Edited by Mrs. MeMee of DeMoir Publishing
&
RaKesha Gray of RGEdits
Cover Art by LaNorris Allen

This novel is dedicated to every human being out there who has ever had a dream. A dream can only begin when you write it down with a pen.

Acknowledgments

This is book #2 for me and soooooo much has occurred since I released my debut novel "The Wives." I'm so grateful for the help of my momager who's not only helped to manage this new arena as a novelist, but also taken on the role of one of my editors. I'm eternally grateful for my greatest cheerleader. Also, special shout out to my older brother, LaNorris, who brought my characters to life for my cover! You're the G.O.A.T! Lastly, special shout out to Ms. Gray! Ra, thank you soooo much for coming onboard to help edit! Glad to have you on the team.

When it comes to the creation of this particular book and subsequent series, I just want to thank any English/Creative Writing teacher out there. We inspire the next generation daily when we expose them to narratives, amazing characters, and the authors who created them. I take pride in my journey as an English Language Arts/Creative Writing teacher and the growth in my own scholars.

I'd also like to take this moment to thank everyone who has opened his or her wallet and used their hard-earned money to purchase a copy of my books. Without you, my works wouldn't be circulating. So, THANK YOU, from the top, middle, and bottom of my heart!

Jay DeMoir

Introduction

Picture it: it's 2004, you're in a cramped middle school Creative Writing classroom, and your instructor tells the class that you all are going to write a story.

Imagine that all the kids look confused and their eyes grew wide with horror at being told they're going to write a story.

One kid shouts out, "Writing stories and books are for old people!"

Another kid raises his hand and the teacher calls on him. The kid adjusts his glasses and asks, "How?"

The teacher grins, turns to the white board, and begins to write the different parts that make up a story.

The kid that asked that question would grow up to become Jay DeMoir.

In the fall of 2004, I sat in that classroom and realized that I was about to put pen to paper and come up with characters. That short story assignment Mr. Moore gave us eventually became this novel. That day, the floodgates of my imagination were opened and I've been writing ever since.

At that moment, I was given an outlet to express myself. I could allow my mind to run wild and escape from the real world.

"Across the Stars" was originally a six-page short story that became a pretty sizeable manuscript and eventually birthed ten sequels. And now, here we are *fourteen* years later publishing that very story!

Welcome to the universe of Zedo Jeta, an unlikely hero that lives in an alternate reality parallel to ours.

This is the story of one such person being transformed, over time, to fulfill his purpose. This is the true beginning...

Chapter 1:
The Deconstructulator

ೞ

They said that it would be the chance of a lifetime. They told me everything would change. They told me that I would be better than any normal human being. They told me that I was weak, human, and they would make me stronger. Guess what?... They lied.

My name is Zedo Doreem Jeta, but most people just call me Zedo or Zee. I joined the force (Secret Agency XII) in 1989. I was fourteen at the time, and I woke up in 2020.

What do you think I look like? Do you think I'm tall or husky? Do you think I'm muscular or slender? Do you think I'm white or a member of another group?

Does it really matter?

I'm sure you'd like to know, but I'm not going to tell you. Right now, it doesn't matter. All you need to know is I'm a guy…and I was innocent.

When I first joined the army I lied about my age. I'd forged my documents after running away from the orphanage I'd been placed in.

At least in the army I'd be able to make money and would be somewhere safe.

After enlisting, I was asked by a sergeant to join a black-ops division. I agreed and became the prime subject of a program. After finishing basic training, I was shipped from the military and placed in the hands of one of our numerous black-ops agencies.

I had no family, no one would miss me, and I guess that's what made me the ideal candidate.

Boy, was I in for a treat! That's sarcasm, folks.

When I arrived at Secret Agency XII in Michigan, I realized I wasn't the only teenager here. Dozens of operatives were around my age.

My life was about to change, and I had no one that would miss me. If anything happened to me, I'd just become another number.

The program I was placed in was led by the fringe science department of Homeland Security. Secret Agency XII was an organization that invented special machines, weapons, and focused on fringe science and the paranormal.

The experiment I'd been attached to was tasked with producing organic weapons: the world's first super humans; humans gifted with supernatural powers.

I was only supposed to be in the program for thirty-six months. However, something went wrong.

General Devon Merota, a highly respected official, led this agency.

I was told by our scientists that the Earth we lived on was actually one of many. We live in an alternate reality that runs parallel to many others. Sometimes these realities merge and complicate things. But for all intents and purposes, let's just focus on *my* reality. We'll call it "Reality Z" (my name's Zedo after all).

The job paid well and I was as happy as a glorified Guinea pig, to a certain degree… In retrospect, I'm sure they knew I was just a kid, but who cared about an orphan right? The answer is no one.

It was the year 1990, Winter was here and it was freezing cold in Michigan, where Secret Agency XII was based. I woke up in the abstract structure that was the base and started the same routine that I had followed for a year. I got dressed and went to the lab. Lab assistants came to me and prepared me for another round of tests. I was overwhelmed with emotions. For some reason, this day felt different. The energy in the air was different.

After I changed into my form fitting lab suit, one of the scientists showed me the Deconstructulator, and that was when I realized that the difference I'd sensed was this machine.

The Deconstructulator, a highly sophisticated machine that reconstructs your DNA pattern and adds to it, kind of reminded me of a hair dryer—the hard hat kind that you sit under.

This machine was placed on my head and strapped on. The assistants checked my vital signs and everything else like they did the day before.

It was business as usual in Lab 29.

A mysterious Russian doctor named Burton moved into the lab. He had a terrible reputation, known for his quick temper and heavy drinking. I'd also heard that he was only working for the agency to work off his debt to the country. He was a glorified hostage for all intents and purposes, but a brilliant hostage at that. But to me, he just seemed dangerous.

Burton had been a known enemy of the state—a terrorist of global proportion— and I couldn't understand for the life of me why he'd been allowed to work for our division.

For whatever reason, we didn't see eye to eye. I was typically more sarcastic than normal around him. He saw me as a major threat, a smart aleck that if unleashed into the world, would turn on the U.S.A and the world as a whole.

But what did he care? *He* was a threat to the world!

The brown haired, wrinkled skinned, hellish-looking doctor gave me an evil smirk and waved goodbye. The assistants cleared the deck and moved to the observation platform as an automated countdown began.

The tests were about to commence. But something wasn't right. Burton watched me, glancing at me over the top of his horn-rimmed glasses.

No, I couldn't let this test start. My heart began to race, and I felt my anxiety levels rise.

Suddenly, the Deconstructulator came alive. I yelled for help and my cry caught the attention of nearly everyone in the lab.

Without full clearance, Dr. Burton slammed his sausage fingers on several buttons and alarms began to blare. I felt energy course through my body and I screamed.

The entire lab shuddered and the Deconstructulator exploded. It sent thousands of volts of electricity to my brain.

Somehow it triggered something deep within me. I felt energy move through my veins and something came alive in me that day.

All around the lab machines exploded, circuits shorted, and a pipe burst, causing water to spill into the lab—causing further destruction. Chaos ensued.

The moment the Deconstructulator exploded, two things happened. One, something came alive inside of me. But you already knew that. The second thing that happened was that energy had overloaded my nervous system and the power of the explosion had caused me to fall into a coma for what I believed was *thirty years*...

Chapter 2:

The Awakening Offer

ೞ

The day the machines blew up was the last time I saw the light, well it's the last time I saw anything, until 2020...

I woke up, terrified, and connected to a ventilator. I gagged and as my vision cleared, I realized that I was still in the lab. Had no one moved to get me help?

How long had I been unconscious? So many people were around me. I realized I was in a cylinder-shaped tank filled with water and felt claustrophobic. I didn't know what was going on. I could hear my heart thumping in my ears. All I knew was that I had to get OUT of there!

I began to kick the glass and as I did so, I tore off the mask that had covered my face. But as water rushed into my mouth I didn't panic. I realized I could *breathe*!

I slammed my fist into the glass. I hadn't expected anything to happen, but the glass began to crack.

That finally caught the attention of the lab aides in the room. The glass of the tank shattered and water flooded the floors— hitting circuits and causing explosions.

Great! I'd caused more damage. Someone yelled out and people ran away from me. Alarms blared and I covered my ears. All my senses seemed heightened.

It felt nice to smell and breathe on my own again. My muscles were sore and I stumbled out of the tank. I tried my best to avoid the broken shards of glass.

People were shouting and running all around. I looked at my body. I was only dressed in a pair of black compression shorts. My body looked more defined, yet pale and my black hair had grown into a shaggy mess.

How long had I been unconscious? I looked at my hands but didn't have time to investigate.

Security arrived on the scene and shouted into the disarray. They began to shoot.

I ducked behind a machine and wondered why they'd opened fire on me! I was just a kid!

It was at that moment that I noticed that I felt different, *stronger*.

I remembered being under the Deconstructulator, the increase of power and the change of my body, but mostly I remembered the explosion.

I lifted my right hand and felt energy awaken within me. It wanted to come out. My body wanted to protect itself. I tried to use a power and to my surprise, something happened. I unleashed a green beam from the palm of my hand and it hit one of the many guards dressed in all black.

My eyes grew wide with shock. "Oh, shit!" I yelled, looking at my hands. I hadn't expected that. I also hadn't expected my voice to sound as raspy as it did.

I decided to call the beam a "si' beam"—I just came up with the name.

Another guard rushed towards me and tackled me. I slammed into a computer server and snatched a wire from it, sending sparks into the air. Whipping the cable about, I firmly held it in my hand and stabbed the guard.

He screamed and then I seized him by the throat. "Where am I?" I asked him. "What happened to me?"

The guard didn't reply and just strained against me to break my hold on him. I threw him across the room and into the wall— amazed at my strength and how far I'd thrown him.

But I didn't have time to marvel at becoming some guy jacked up on steroids. I leapt into the air and amazed myself. I didn't fall, instead my body propelled me upward.

I laughed aloud as I zoomed around the lab. It felt so natural, but I'd never flown before.

The guards continued to fire rounds at me and I dodged the bullets. I grabbed a steel chair as I moved through the air and hurled it at a window, shattering it, and without looking down, I jumped.

Outside, the fresh air slammed into me like a freight train. The night was dark, but the world looked so different.

My focus slipped and I fell to the ground. I slammed into the concrete and groaned. Surprisingly, nothing was broken. I had changed.

I looked around and saw holographic billboards and cars zoomed by on repulsor lifts—hover cars?? What year was this? It quickly became clear to me that it wasn't 1990 anymore. Clearly, I'd been unconscious for far longer than I'd imagined. For me, it had seemed like just yesterday.

I ran like I had no tomorrow. But, did I really? I had nowhere to go, no one to turn to. What could I do?

I heard police sirens and quickly turned into an alley and found clothes in a dumpster. I gagged at the smell, but I needed clothes. I cringed as I slipped into the clothes and wished I had shoes, but that was a problem that would have to wait until later.

Now, I was on the hunt for shelter.

It was around this time that my stomach began to growl; I was starving.

Lights from helicopters shined all around. My heart pounded in my chest. I couldn't believe the uproar. Was I that important? Why was all this necessary? Why did they want me back?

I was in need of assistance and I was fearful of my surroundings. This wasn't the world that I'd left behind.

I knelt to the ground and picked up chips of gravel. As I stood to my full height, I realized that I could feel energy in the gravel—I could sense it. It was hard to explain, but as I moved the gravel around in my clammy hands, I could swear those chips of earth *moved*!

"Oh, boy," I sighed. Shaking my head, I realized that whatever Burton had done had indeed awakened something inside of me.

I wasn't human anymore. I was a super human, and by the looks of things I had several abilities.

I recalled not drowning in the water; I'd been able to breathe in the tank without the ventilator. I'd flown across the air with relative ease and now here I was making rocks float a few inches above my palm.

I'd been gifted with the ability of elemental manipulation—I could control air, water, and the earth. I was pretty sure I could control fire, too, but I hadn't experienced that.

As cool as this was I was still unable to comprehend the sheer magnitude of the situation.

When I thought it was safe, I left the alley. I knew I wouldn't be captured.

Just when I thought I was in the clear, I was spotted by a jelly donut eating police officer.

"Hey, you!!" the officer cried, reaching for his radio.

I turned around and ran towards him. I couldn't let him call for help. I didn't want anyone to find me. But it was too late; the sirens I'd heard earlier were heading my way.

I ran as hard and as fast as I could and ducked into another alley and hid. I breathed heavily against the wall. As they ran past me I climbed the ladder beside the dumpster and moved onto the roof. God, what had I done to deserve this?!

Unfortunately, I wasn't alone. Was I going to have to fight again? A man stood on the roof dressed in all black with a leather coat and dark sunglasses. Why was he wearing sunglasses at night?

His skin was olive toned and his hair was rustled by the breeze.

I knew that I was going to have to fight, I could feel it.

"Don't be alarmed," he said, holding his hands out towards me to show he wasn't armed. "I can help you. I know who you are, Zedo."

My eyes grew wide! "How do you know my name?" I asked, my voice still raspy, yet quivering from the pain my body was experiencing. I was thirsty and hungry and running on fumes. My body hadn't been awake long enough to be at full strength.

"Come," he said turning towards the door on the roof. I swallowed hard and considered my options. When he realized that I hadn't moved, he looked over his shoulder. "I'm not going to hurt you, Zedo. You can trust me."

But could I really?

I sighed and followed him. I didn't have another choice. We descended the stairs that led back into the building, which seemed poorly lit. We moved in silence but there was one screaming question that I had that needed an answer.

"What year is it?" I asked.

"The year is 2020," he replied without looking back at me.

I froze in my tracks, shocked, and quickly did the math. I'd been in a coma for THIRTY years!

We went through many doors and one after another, they slammed shut behind us. It seemed as if we'd gone down ten or twelve flights of stairs.

"Where are we going?" I asked.

He ignored my question and instead gestured at the doors. "They are security locked. No one can enter without the special access codes."

We came to a lab. It was gigantic, filled with many gadgets and devices. Immediately, I froze.

Memories began to flash before my eyes. Labs made me uneasy, that much was for sure. It was not too long ago that I'd escaped from one.

I stopped at the entrance of the lab. I couldn't do this.

"I don't even know who you are. How am I supposed to trust you? Who are you?" I asked, fear growing in my heart.

"I'm not going to hurt you, Zedo. Like I said, you can trust me. Now come in before the blast door closes."

I stepped into the lab and the black blast door slid into place.

He removed his knee-length leather jacket and threw it over the back of a chair before he sat down. I moved towards the computer station he sat at and was surprised that the screens were flat instead of bulky as I remembered.

"I am Jonathan Sorelle. I was one of the assistants assigned to your project in 1989. We were friends in the Agency..." He paused and looked over his shoulder. "You don't remember me... *do you?*"

I didn't answer. I'd never seen this man a day in my life. We couldn't have been friends in the agency. I'd only interacted with a hand full of people that weren't scientists and lab techs. The only people I remembered were Darren and a girl I'd had the hots for: Rose. I wondered where they were now.

"We need to analyze your powers and techniques. Please come." He showed me to a table and put this small round orange and red machine on my head, I jumped. Pushing him back, I moved from the machine.

Jonathan held his hands up in mock surrender. "I'm trying to help you, Zedo."

"How'd you know where to find me? It's no coincidence that you were on that roof. Did Burton send you?"

He frowned, creases forming in his brow. He scratched his chin, causing light to catch in his mingle gray beard. "I'm trying to help you. I knew one day you'd wake up. I wanted to be in the best possible place to help you when that day arrived. How I found you doesn't matter. All that matters is that I found you before the police did. I remember the Deconstructulator. I was there that day. Let me help you, Zedo."

I exhaled and my shoulders relaxed a bit.

"Don't worry...and try to relax. I won't put you back into a coma." He grinned.

I tried to relax, but I didn't trust him… not fully. Yes, he offered me sanctuary, but I didn't know this man.

Jonathan circled around me. "Now we thought that you were a normal human, but we were very wrong. Your powers weren't activated." He moved to a small computer. The screen glowed on his face. "You can fly and control the elements."

He confirmed what I already knew. When I didn't say anything, he looked at me and nodded.

He turned back to his computer and stroked the keys. "The beam you attacked the guard in the lab with is called a si' beam. It comes in different colors and shapes depending on the element you use."

"How'd you know I hit a guard with a beam?" I asked.

He stroked a key and a screen above us came to life. On the screen was surveillance footage of the lab. "I've been monitoring that lab from here since you fell into a coma. Nearly everyone that worked in Secret Agency XII at the time was fired. I've been a freelance agent since."

"Can you help me?" I asked as I climbed off the table and moved away from the machine. "I need to know why Burton tried to kill me."

Jonathan ignored me so I crossed the room and grabbed his arm.

He looked at my hand on his forearm. "Ow," he groaned, pulling away from me. "You need to keep your strength in check. I need that arm."

"Seriously, Jonathan. Will you help me? I need answers."

After a moment of thinking, he exhaled and nodded "Yes, Zedo, I can help you...but there is another." Then he looked at the clock on the wall. "We must leave now, Zedo."

"Where are we going?"

He grinned. "Dinner."

As if right on cue, my stomach growled and we both laughed. Jonathan moved through the lab and touched a keypad near a set of steel doors. Elevator doors swung open and we moved onto it. As the elevator doors closed, the lights in the lab began to flicker off.

The elevator stopped on the sixth floor and we moved into a corridor lined with doors. Jonathan lived in a co-op building. But then how was he able to have a secret lab in the basement? I doubted the co-op board knew about this. I doubted anybody else in the building knew about the lab either.

Finally, we arrived in front of a door that had been painted light blue, which vastly stood out among all the red painted doors that lined the white hallway. He pulled out a key and looked at me. "It was my wife's idea to paint the door a different color. She wanted us to stand out." He rolled his eyes, shook his head, and slid the key into the slot. As we moved into the apartment, he announced our arrival.

"Jonathan Ismay Sorelle, you're late!" yelled a voice.

"Zedo, this is my beautiful *young* wife, Saray," he said, as we moved into the kitchen. There, before the stove, stood a middle-aged woman with brunette hair piled atop her head in a messy bun.

"Zedo?" she said, glancing at me and smiling. She turned her eyes on her husband. "That name sounds so familiar. Jon, is he the coma child?"

Jonathan glanced at me and looked apologetic. He kissed his wife on the cheek. "Yes, dear, but we don't say 'coma child' in their faces," he whispered to her.

"Sorry, dear. Where are my manners?" She moved across the kitchen and hugged me. I smiled and awkwardly returned the gesture.

Jonathan moved around the tight kitchen and kissed each of his kids at the dinner table. He moved to my side after he'd spoken to his brood.

"These are our lovely children: Carly, Jonathan Junior, Sarah, twins: Daniel and Daniella, and the last one is Joey. Ages 14, 13, 11, 9, and 6." Jonathan grinned with pride.

"You've been busy," I said under my breath and then waved at the children who eyed me curiously. I guess I didn't look much older than them. I hadn't aged a day since I'd fallen into my coma.

He put his hand on his wife's belly as she moved to his side. "This little girl on the way will be named Ju Kay."

I realized Saray wasn't fat. She was pregnant. Saray removed the hand of her husband from her belly. "Please don't call her that, Jonathan."

We sat down at the fairly large oak table and Saray brought us two white glass plates. It would be my first meal in decades.

After dinner Jonathan took me to see someone named Nicolas…

Chapter 3: Nicolas Martin III and the Team

We rode in silence as we moved through the streets of Michigan. I marveled at how much the world had changed in thirty years. I couldn't believe how much I'd missed. I wondered if I'd stay frozen in my teens forever, though I was technically in my mid-forties by now.

Jonathan's Lamborghini Diablo was superior. I liked its sleek design and it purred beneath us as we moved through the streets.

Eventually we arrived at a three-story, abandoned Victorian house. I raised a brow at Jonathan and wondered why we were here. There were no signs of anyone living there. The house was dark and covered in vines though it still carried much of its beauty. The house was pale green, but I'm sure the color had once been vibrant.

We moved through a fence that was rusted and twisted in on itself.

Jonathan turned off his sports car's headlights and slowed down until we eased to a stop just before the concrete steps that led to the veranda of the mansion.

Across from where we'd parked was a running three-tier fountain that had eroded with time.

As the suicide doors slid open, Jonathan and I climbed out and I wondered what this mansion must've looked like in the good old days.

Jonathan ignored my curious glances as we headed up the steps and moved onto the veranda. He looked over his shoulder as if half-expecting that we'd been followed. Turning back towards the front door, he knocked on it in a triangular pattern.

Moments later the door opened with a loud creek. No lights shone from within. A chill ran down my spine.

I heard the whirring of circuitry and soon a droid made of rusted gold parts appeared, opening the door wider. My eyes grew wide as I took in the droid. Its head was oblong-shaped, with two white glowing eyes and a slit for a mouth. The droid wore a bronze colored metal wig that was cut in a sharp bob that was reminiscent of the 1920s style women had worn.

"Follow me," she said and I was surprised at how soft and feminine its voice sounded. But I guess I shouldn't have been surprised. Technology was sure to have advanced since I'd fallen into my coma.

Jonathan and I followed the droid to a large room that was bare except for a chair next to the fireplace. The fireplace was lit and the red-orange flames illuminated much of the room. I was surprised I hadn't seen smoke from the chimney.

The droid turned her white eyes on me and cocked her head, as if taking me in. When I caught her looking, she faced front and moved towards the chair, which was facing away from us.

I remembered when department 3-0-4 was designing protocol droids for everyday people. I guess I'd just never fathomed the day when they'd be in use.

The droid motioned for us to stop and then she moved twelve feet forward and approached the chair.

"Master," the droid said, bowing at the waist.

"Who was at the door, Shaylo?" asked a low, husky voice—obviously male.

The droid—Shaylo—gestured with her hands. "Jonathan Sorelle has arrived and has brought with him"—the droid looked at me again and I felt a twinge of unease as she gazed at me a little too long then snapped her head back towards the chair—"a guest. For some reason, I cannot identify his guest. There seems to be no record of him in my internal database."

The man in the chair rose to his feet and turned to face us, revealing an elderly man dressed in a red turtle neck and slacks. He grabbed his cane, which was leaning against the arm of his chair, and moved towards us.

"Hello, there, Nicolas," said Jonathan, remaining at my side.

The man named Nicolas ignored Jonathan and moved towards me, squinting as if trying to get a better look at me.

I subconsciously took a step back as he came closer to me.

His lips parted and his wrinkled face shifted to one filled with realization. "*Zedo*? Zedo, is that you?"

I froze. He knew who I was. I looked at Jonathan, and he grinned. "Zedo Jeta, I'd like to introduce you to Nicolas Martin III."

I extended my hand and the old man shook it. He then turned to the droid. "That will be all, Shaylo."

"Yes, sir." The droid exited the room, disappearing into the darkness.

"It is a pleasure to meet you, Zedo. I've seen you in the lab, many years ago, but…" The man trailed off and turned back to his chair and moved towards it.

So, this mansion wasn't abandoned, just occupied by this recluse.

Jonathan moved to intercept the old man before he could sit down. "Nick, Zedo needs to find Burton." He glanced at me. "Nick used to be an intelligence officer for Secret Agency XII. He was one of the best trackers in the agency."

"Keyword: *was*," he said, taking a seat in his red sofa chair. "I'm retired now, Jonathan, and I have been for decades now. I'm not as young as I used to be."

I remained standing where I was. Jonathan looked at me and beckoned me over. I swallowed and moved to the chair and stood in front of the old man. He wouldn't meet my gaze so I knelt in front of him and forced him to look at me.

"Sir, I need to find Burton."

Finally, Nicolas spoke. "Burton, ay?" He scratched his white beard. "I haven't heard of that name in some time."

I wondered how old he was. He seemed senile to me and his eyes kept glazing over, as if he'd lost focus. When he didn't speak for a moment, I glanced at Jonathan, who just shrugged. Nicolas's eyes were baggy and he looked weary, as if life had drained everything he'd had.

I placed my hand atop of his, shocked at the difference between my smooth skin and his wrinkly one which showed signs of age spots and varicose veins. Nicolas turned his gaze on me.

"Zedo?" he said, his eyes growing wide with shock, as if this was his first time seeing me. "My *God,* you're *awake!*"

I forced my agitation aside. Jonathan had brought me to a demented member of the baby boomers' generation.

"Please, sir, can you help me find Burton?" I asked.

His eyes filled with fear. "He's the *devil!*"

And just like that, he began to tell us about all of Burton's activities since 1990. Nicolas had been keeping a file on Burton all these years in case a day like this had arrived.

It turned out that Burton was a highly wanted criminal these days. He was arrested and imprisoned after what had happened in the lab but had managed to escape after murdering the guards assigned to his solitary confinement cell. To this day no one knew how he'd escaped a maximum-security prison. It must've been an inside job.

Burton went on to commit acts of terrorism, including attacking the UN. Around 2004, he emerged with a newly formed syndicate of zealots bent on world domination.

Nearly every intelligence agency in the global community was looking for Burton, but to no avail. He'd gone off the grid a few years ago.

Secret Agency XII was closed, until further notice, a little after I was placed in a coma. Several investigations were launched and many lost their jobs, Jonathan and Nicolas included.

Nicolas had Shaylo bring us his file on Burton which was comprised of Burton's known hideouts, a list of all his crimes, and the charges the UN had brought against him.

As Jonathan and I turned to leave, Nicolas stopped us, and handed me a single sheet of folded paper. I opened the paper and discovered it was a list of contact information for people that could help me in my vendetta.

I thanked him for helping and we said our goodbyes. The droid showed us to the door and placed a metallic hand on my shoulder. Jonathan moved to the car, oblivious, as Shaylo's eyes locked on mine. "Good luck, Zedo Jeta. The galaxy needs you to rid it of this evil."

My brow creased in confusion, but that was all she said before she closed the door in my face. I turned towards the car and moved down the steps and wondered what she'd meant.

Everyone knew that we weren't alone in the universe. Even Jonathan had told me that there were planets beyond our solar system that had been discovered and had life on them. But did the droid mean that Burton had caused problems on other planets too?

By the time we returned to the Sorelle home, it was well after four a.m. Though we were exhausted, we pushed on and hurried to the lab.

Jonathan handed me something called an 'iPhone' (*wow!*) and I called the people on the list. After I told them who I was and confirmed each person's identity through Jonathan's databases, I arranged a meeting at a warehouse in Illinois (Jonathan's idea; he had contacts in the state).

The ones that Jonathan and I would be meeting with were: twenty-four-year-old Mona Lisa-Flynn, twenty-year-old Gonzo Daniels, fifteen-year-old Jordan Flynn, and thirty-year-old Cassandra.

Each member of this newly formed "task force" had once been a subject in other Secret Agency programs. They turned out to be super humans, but the projects were to enhance their powers. However, in my case, the project had been to generate powers, but unknowingly, I was already gifted. But by the time that knowledge was discovered, it was too late.

Days later, we met in Illinois...

The warehouse was a car manufacturing plant, but also served as a front for a black ops division of the NSA.

Jonathan and I arrived in his Lamborghini, dressed like father-and-son in matching black outfits.

Next to arrive were Mona Lisa-Flynn and her half-brother, Jordan. Mona looked like a super model with olive skin and long flowing auburn hair pulled back in a sleek ponytail. She wore an aqua, Klein blue, and fern vintage Diane von Furstenberg sleeveless scarf dress with nude sling-back heels, which I felt was overdressed for a meeting of former weapon's subjects.

Contrastingly, her half-brother wore jeans and a red t-shirt, his shaggy brown hair hanging in his face.

The next to arrive was Gonzo Daniels, a man of Hispanic descent with dark, tousled hair and a finely built body. He wore a simple outfit as well, black jeans paired with a form-fitting shirt that showed off his muscles.

Last to the party was the mononymous Cassandra, a Romanian woman who'd been a subject in Secret Agency VI's program. She wore a black and white Carolina Herrera number, with a black blouse over a pair of white wide legged pants. A belt was wrapped around her mid-section. Paired with a sensible shoe, she looked ravishing.

Apparently, these women were dressed to kill.

Jonathan stepped into his role as moderator and started the meeting. We quickly introduced ourselves and then I took the floor, explaining to everyone what I was expecting of them. We discussed our individual roles and made plans to bring Burton down.

"I just want him to pay for what he did to me," I said.

"To all of us," corrected Mona. I nodded in agreement. He'd turned all of our lives inside out, but none worse than mine.

Jordan barely said a word, but he was up to bringing Burton down.

"He must die by our hands," Cassandra said, her accent thick. "Burton has done much evil." She ran a hand through her blonde hair.

"Let's get a move on, then," Gonzo said, rubbing his hands together. Though I didn't know these people well enough, yet, I could tell that despite what Burton had done to him, Gonzo had retained his jovial personality. We'd be fast friends in no time.

I gave them Jonathan's information and instructed them that we'd meet at his lab in 48 hours.

Two days later, we regrouped and Jonathan, who would act as the team's handler, gave us all gadgets and other materials we'd need. Cassandra had come up with our first lead and we were going to check it out. I'd never been a field operative during my time in the agency, and neither had Jordan, but we were all ready.

Suddenly, the phone situated above Jonathan's super computer rang. Jordan, who was closest to it, moved to answer it. Only Jonathan's family had access to the line.

As Jordan picked up the receiver, it exploded—sending a rippling effect through the lab that caused a secondary explosion.

Debris rained down and I was hurled across the room— slamming into a locker.

Cries rang out and smoke filled the air, activating the sprinkler system.

"Jordan!" cried Mona as she rushed across the lab to where he'd been standing.

Everyone was fine, but for a few bruises and scratches, save Jordan, who'd been closest to the blast. He was bleeding from a huge gash on the side of his head. He was also missing an ear.

I rushed to his side as an alarm began to blare. Jonathan looked around and a blast door slammed over the elevator.

Gonzo's arm began to glow as he called energy to the surface.

"There's no way someone could've gotten into the lab!" Jonathan cried.

"He's on to us," said Cassandra, looking around. She caught sight of the security cameras. "Kill the cameras!"

Gonzo threw his arm forward and hurled an energy blast at each of the eight cameras in the lab.

"Am I going to be okay?" Jordan asked, trembling as his body went into shock. Mona grabbed his hand and I moved to the elevator, trying to get the blast door to open.

Jonathan knocked me out of the way and put in the access code.

"We've got to get him out of here," Mona said, fear gripping her heart.

We rushed to the emergency room and Jonathan headed upstairs to check on his family.

I was worried. Either Burton or one of his operatives had infiltrated the lab…or someone in the group had.

"Jordan is in a lot of pain, but we are doing what we can to save his inner ear function," a doctor told Mona after Jordan had been in surgery for a few hours.

I turned to the others and nearly at the same time we said, "Burton."

"Spies?" asked Gonzo.

"How else would he know?" I asked. I had a very bad feeling about this.

"How did he know where to find us?" Mona asked.

"It's likely we tipped him off the moment we started pulling information on him," answered Cassandra.

After hours of surgery, a doctor informed us that Jordan's emergency surgery was completed to the best of their ability. His right eardrum had been destroyed and his jaw would need to be reconstructed once he was stable, but he'd live…for now.

I called Jonathan. "We need to pay Nick another visit."

"We shouldn't pull him into this, Zedo," he said, his voice filled with agitation. "It had to be someone in the group."

"I'm not so sure of that. Let's just pay Nick a visit. It all started with him…"

When we got to Nick's the door didn't open when Jonathan knocked. Shaylo never arrived.

Jonathan placed his palm on a panel next to the door frame and a biometric scanner appeared. He placed his palm on it and it glowed green. When the door still didn't open and the panel turned from green to red, I knew something was wrong and so did Jonathan.

Fearing the worst, Jonathan kicked down the door and made sure that no one saw us. Jonathan drew a pistol from his hip holster and moved into the house. I followed him and Cassandra and Mona were behind me. Gonzo took up the end, igniting his right hand in a yellow glow of energy that crackled like fire.

Mona scanned the area with a small flashlight and while she did so, I noticed that the fireplace was out.

I was worried and so was Jonathan. "Nick?" he called out.

Gonzo stepped on something and it cracked. Mona shinned her flashlight on Gonzo's foot. It was Shaylo's head—one of her eyes were missing.

"Nick!!" Jonathan cried, running up the grand staircase and heading to the next level.

"Spread out," I ordered.

The others moved through the house and I headed upstairs, my heart racing. We searched the house franticly.

Within a few minutes, we discovered that Nick wasn't here. We knew something was wrong.

Shaylo had been Nicolas's only companion. Someone had broken the droid and likely kidnapped Nick.

Suddenly, a loud screech sounded throughout the mansion. Jonathan lifted his pistol and we all moved closer together, raising our hands in anticipation of a confrontation.

I tried to call upon my powers, but I hadn't used them since escaping from the lab. To be honest, I didn't really know how to use them—how to bring them to bare. I'd have to ask Jonathan about that, but now wasn't the time.

I looked at Gonzo and his other hand began to glow with energy as he generated another energy blast. He was prepared to fire the energy blasts at any moment. Mona lifted her fist and angled the flashlight around the dark corridor.

Another screech echoed through the empty, dusty house.

"What *is* that?" Gonzo asked.

"We're not alone," I said, my voice strong.

Suddenly, from above, we heard other screeches join the initial one. Footsteps, like a herd of rhinos, echoed across the ceiling, followed by chittering. ***Something*** was coming for us!

"Run, it's an ambush!" Jonathan cried.

As we turned to run, the sound of footsteps grew louder. I looked over my shoulder, but didn't see anything. Suddenly, smoke filled the mansion. I coughed and covered my mouth with my forearm.

"Tear gas!" Cassandra screamed.

A thick screen of smoke filled the mansion and through the haze I caught sight of something horrible.

Fuzzy, black creatures were moving towards us with alarming speed. Through the smoke I could see dozens of red, glowing eyes. Finally, my eyes focused on one of the creatures. It was about four feet tall and skittered across the floor on eight legs, like some sort of overgrown spider. As it opened its mouth, revealing rows of sharp teeth dripping with saliva, the creature screamed—filling the mansion with its banshee-like cry. The other beasts opened their mouths and screeched as well. There had to be hundreds of them—stampeding through the mansion and headed directly towards us.

"¡Dios mío!" exclaimed Gonzo, frozen in place as the horde continued to move towards us screeching.

"Let's move, people!" yelled Jonathan as he opened fire on the horde. Cassandra took off and Mona was right behind her. Gonzo launched two of his yellow energy blasts into the thick of the group and one exploded on contact—killing a beast. This only seemed to anger the rest of them.

Jonathan grabbed a handful of my shirt and yanked me along, forcing me to move. Finally, I gained control of my own body and began to run.

As we neared the entrance, a second horde of the creatures intercepted us, blocking our way.

Mona screamed as one of the beasts lashed out at her.

I threw an arm forward and felt power course through my body and exit through my palm—another si' beam flew out of my palm and slammed into the beast, knocking it across the room.

Cassandra pulled Mona to her feet as Gonzo tried to clear a path for us.

"There's no way out!" cried Mona, growing frantic as the horde began to close in on us. Had Burton sent these monsters to kill us?

"There!" I yelled, catching sight of a secondary staircase that led to the second floor. As one, we made a mad dash towards the stairs.

"Go, go, go!!!" Gonzo yelled, forcing the women to move faster.

"They're gaining on us!" Jonathan added, as he loaded another magazine into his pistol. He stood his ground on the staircase and opened fire before being washed away by the horde.

No one heard his muffled cries as several of the beasts sank their claws and teeth into his flesh.

The darkness of this building mixed with the terror I was feeling of being chased by these beasts was getting to me. And so, we ran!

Once our feet touched the second floor we kept moving up, heading towards the attic.

Amid all the chaos, Cassandra noticed that Jonathan wasn't with us anymore.

My eyes grew wide with concern. "He was right behind me!" I yelled, gesturing down the corridor we'd just come from.

"We've got to keep moving!" Gonzo said.

"I'm not leaving him behind!" I told them. But just as those words escaped my lips, the first of the beasts turned the corner and howled.

We took off running and I felt my eyes sting with hot tears. I couldn't believe I'd abandoned Jonathan after everything he'd done for me.

We could hear the horrendous shrieks, and the shrieks echoed through my body and I felt the physical pain of it—like nails being pierced into my rib cage.

I couldn't bare it any longer; I turned back and headed in the direction of the screams.

Gonzo grabbed me and held me back. "It's too late, Zedo! He's gone! He sacrificed himself so we could keep going!"

"Jonathan!" I yelled.

"We couldn't go back if we wanted to," Cassandra said as tears filled her eyes. Her blonde hair was disheveled and her mascara was smeared as she dabbed at her eyes.

"Let's move," Gonzo said, taking over. He pushed me ahead of him and I ran down the next hall. Nicolas's house was like a giant labyrinth.

Suddenly, human cries sounded and we turned. It was Cassandra. They were taking her... they were *killing* her. We watched in horror as the jaws of one of the beasts closed around her legs. She screamed and thrashed.

"Help me!!!" she yelled, her face turning red as the monster ripped her apart. Another latched onto her arm and chewed it to shreds.

"Hold on!" I yelled, grabbing her free arm and attempting to free her from the grasp of the demonic creatures.

"I can't," she cried and then she let go.

I screamed and watched as they ate her alive.

Mona yelled and pulled me back as one of the demons jumped at me. She kicked it, her heel slamming into one of its eyes, causing it to howl in pain.

"The attic, come on!" Gonzo yelled to Mona and me; we were all that remained.

As we reached the attic, Gonzo slammed his shoulder into the frame and it flew open. Mona and I ran past him and he slammed the door.

"Find something to block the door!" Gonzo yelled as the first demon slammed into the door, nearly knocking it off its frame.

Mona and I moved a desk in front of the door and then started throwing anything we could find against it. That wasn't going to hold them for long.

I was filled with dread as sweat rolled down my face and my chest heaved in and out.

There was another loud thump, and we all jumped.

"They're coming for us!" Mona yelled, scrambling away from the door.

Gonzo looked around the attic, looking for something else to throw against the door. "It's not going to hold them much longer! They must all be at the door by now."

I stared at the door, picturing Jonathan and Cassandra's remains among the horde. My heart sank. We weren't going to get out of here alive.

Mona ran to the sole window in the attic and pushed back the curtain. She swore to herself and I heard Gonzo yell that it was boarded up.

As he yanked at the planks covering the window, light poured into the attic. Suddenly, something in the corner caught my eye.

I brushed sweat slicken hair from my face and moved to the object that had caught my eye. As I moved closer, I yelled and took a step back.

My eyes took in the sight of Nick's head and torn torso. His face was frozen in disbelief—his dead eyes pierced my soul.

Mona wrapped an arm around me and tried to get me to look away. Just as she did that, the door gave way and the monsters hurried in and began to swarm.

I wasn't going down without a fight. And it was at that moment that my powers came to my aide, fueled by my anger, my pain…my *rage*!

We fought for our lives, we really did.

Suddenly, I heard wood snap and I realized that we were in for something terrible. I glanced down in between striking one of the demons and realized that the floor was cracking under the weight of so many bodies being in the attic.

"The floor! The attic is going to give way!" I yelled.

Another crackling sound turned us into statues. My eyes dropped to a second crack in the floor boards.

Seconds later, the crackling noise resumed as both fissured, expanded, and then forked. My breath snagged in my throat.

The floor gave way, spilling the three of us and the beasts onto the second floor of the mansion.

Objects from the attic fell with us, and just as we slammed into the second floor, it gave way, too. We screamed as we came closer to the ground floor.

Suddenly, the house began to collapse in on itself. I broke through debris and caught sight of more creatures rushing towards us from the other half of the broken estate.

I pulled Mona out of the debris and Gonzo moved to his feet, limping. We had to get out of there. Two of our companions had died.

I spat blood and felt tears on my soot covered face.

"We can't just leave their bodies here," said Mona, between breaths.

"I doubt there's anything left of them," replied Gonzo.

"Let's get out of here before they kill us, too," I said somberly and we made a run for it, heading towards Jonathan's Lamborghini that remained untouched, despite all the chaos that had ensued inside Nicolas's mansion.

We climbed into the car with Gonzo behind the wheel.

"Clearly Burton knows we're onto him," Gonzo said as he drove at dangerous speeds. Mona looked out the rear window and watched as beasts spilled into the street but didn't follow us.

"We can't afford to back down, now," I said.

"What are we going to say when we get back to the hospital?" Mona asked as she faced forward, dusting herself off.

I shrugged. "Maybe they won't notice we're covered in dust, sweat, and scratches." The three of us rode in silence and my thoughts turned to Jonathan's wife and kids. A lump began to rise in my throat and I swallowed hard.

Poor Mrs. Sorelle would be left alone to raise all of her kids by herself.

When we returned to the hospital, all had changed. The doctors told us that Jordan had not survived the night. While in recovery, he'd made a turn for the worst. We had been through a painful night and now this.

Mona could not handle the loss of her younger half-brother. She broke down and Gonzo awkwardly tried to comfort her.

People were eyeing us curiously. I'm sure we all looked like crap.

"We need to get out of here and get cleaned up," I whispered to the others.

"Where will we go?" Mona asked, drying her eyes. "Jonathan's lab has been compromised."

"Let's just find a motel for the night," Gonzo said, moving towards the elevator. "We'll shower, get a good night's sleep and figure things out."

"I want to go back and get Jonathan's body," I told them. I didn't need their permission, but I didn't want to go alone either.

"Let's do it," Gonzo said. "I doubt those monsters will come out during the day."

The next morning after we got ourselves together, we headed back to Nick's. Despite knowing we shouldn't have gone back, I wanted to retrieve Jonathan's body for his family.

He'd helped me and they deserved the closure.

The carnage was even worse in the daylight. There were no signs of police. Clearly, they hadn't been notified, but then again, no one lived within twenty miles of Nick's mansion.

We couldn't find Cassandra's remains, but found the blood-spattered boots she'd been wearing. There were no signs of Jonathan.

After searching the rubble for any clues and coming up with nothing, I headed back to Jonathan's apartment and delivered the news to Saray. She was utterly devastated and my heart broke for her.

Chapter 4:

The Dark Warrior Attacks

03&0

It had been four months since the deaths of Jonathan, Cassandra, and Jordan and now the month of May has arrived. Spring was in full swing, yet, sorrow still weighed heavily on our hearts.

We still couldn't believe that Burton had caused this. Now more than ever, we had to destroy him. Unfortunately, no new leads had turned up.

Mona, Gonzo, and I went to Jonathan's lab and salvaged what we could. Saray had the codes and allowed us to enter his lab. After the explosion that had ultimately taken Jordan's life, there wasn't much to salvage.

Afterwards, the three of us took Gonzo's F-150 and headed to Virginia. Mona lived there. She made us lunch at her apartment and then we talked about which base we would check out first.

By noon the next day, we were on the move again. Since we were already in Virginia, we figured it would be best to search Burton's hideout that wasn't too far from Langley.

"So, Zedo," Gonzo began as he sat in the backseat of Mona's vehicle. I looked over my shoulder after he called my name. "Aren't you at least curious to know what all you've missed out on since coming out of your coma?"

"Gonzo," Mona said warningly, glaring at him in her rearview mirror. He shrugged.

I chuckled nervously. "I mean, yeah, sure...I guess. I just haven't had much time to think about it. I mean, it's been a little crazy since I woke up."

"Thirty years is a long time," he said. "That's a lot of catching up to do."

"You two weren't even thought of yet," I pointed out.

Mona grinned, but I could tell it was a sad grin.

Gonzo pulled a sucker from his jacket pocket and threw the wrapper out the window, drawing another glare from Mona. He popped the lollipop into his mouth and shifted in his seat. "Think about the movies you've missed! Once we finish all this vendetta business, I've got to show you some movies."

I'd always loved movies. I turned in my seat. "What movies?"

"There's Titanic, such a classic, and then I'll show you Star Wars and—"

"I've seen Star Wars," I interjected.

He cocked his head. "You have *a lot* of catching up to do! You missed the prequels and a bunch of sequels!" My eyes grew wide and he grinned. "This is going to be fun. And after that, I'll have to start exposing you to the Marvel movies."

Mona let out a shout of glee. "They were game changers!"

"You like superhero movies?" Gonzo asked her, shocked.

She grinned. "They're the best kinds of movies!"

"Black Panther is still one of my favorites!" Gonzo told her.

"They're part of the reason I joined the agency," she said. "I mean, look at us."

I laughed. "We're far from superheroes."

Gonzo frowned. "You think?"

"Sure, we have powers," I clarified, "but we're not out to save the world."

Mona grew somber and shrugged. "Don't be so sure about that. We're out to kill Burton. He's done a lot of evil in the world."

"Probably the whole galaxy," added Gonzo.

"Hmm." That was all I could say. I leaned back in my seat and the others grew quiet. Were we really superheroes? I was just after revenge...but what did I know?

A few hours later, we pulled up to a seemingly long-abandoned building comprised of rusted gates, three floors, and broken windows. I told Mona and Gonzo to be prepared for anything.

When Gonzo jumped out of Mona's Lexus, gun shots rang out and he was struck several times. The impact hurled him into the air and he slammed into the Lexus, denting it.

Mona threw her hands in the direction of the shots and released ice beams from her hands.

So that was her power, I thought to myself as I pulled Gonzo out of the line of fire.

But as I leaned him against the driver's side of Mona's car, screeches filled the air.

My heart sank and I knew what that sound meant. As I stood up, I realized we were surrounded by at least, forty of those creatures that we'd encountered at Nick's.

"Not again," Mona groaned, lifting her hands and firing ice beams from her fingertips.

While Gonzo was trying to conserve his strength, Mona and I fought for our lives. I called energy to me and hurled si' beams into the fray.

Suddenly, time froze. Creatures were caught in mid-attack. One of my si' beams hung in mid-air as one of Mona's ice beams was lodged into the eye of a beast.

She and I looked around but saw nothing. What happened?

"Did you do this?" she asked. I shook my head.

She looked up and gasped and I followed her line of sight and caught sight of someone falling from the sky. He'd leapt from the roof—he was probably the sniper that had shot Gonzo.

I looked over my shoulder and caught sight of Gonzo, he hadn't frozen either. He still wheezed and tried to apply pressure to his wound, which was still gushing blood.

The man was dressed in black battle garb. He seemed to slow his descent and landed silently, unhurt. As he moved towards us, I moved closer to Mona.

He wore a niqab that only showed his dark eyes. I wondered why. I'd never seen a man wear one before.

Mona's auburn colored hair rustled in the wind.

The man raised his arm as he moved closer to us and when he spoke, I was surprised to find he didn't speak Arabic, but rather some ancient language I'd never heard of.

I glanced at Mona and she shrugged slightly, keeping her hands pointed at him.

"Do mahak' yi nok?" he asked. He repeated the sentence again when our expressions remained puzzled. Finally, he sighed and spoke in English. "Why are you here?"

"We came to find Burton," Mona said.

"Do you know him?" I added.

The man cocked his head and looked at me. "I am Ardet, his dark apprentice and right-hand man."

"We don't care who you are," Mona replied. "Where is he?"

"You wish to speak to me with disrespect?"

"I didn't stutter," she replied, crossing her arms over her cleavage.

"He isn't here."

"Then where is he?" I asked, taking a step forward.

When the man didn't answer, Mona exhaled sharply and lifted her arm. "I've had it with this clown."

"So be it," he said. He pointed a hand at the building and I felt the earth shake beneath my feet. Mona yelped and took a step back as the ground opened beneath us.

Before our eyes, the building exploded as Ardet lifted himself into the air and gestured. Grit and debris poured down all around us.

As the remaining parts of the building began to collapse to the ground, the cinder blocks of walls buckled, ground themselves together, and crumbled.

I stood very still, mesmerized at his display of power.

He turned in the sky and his eyes glowed red. I heard Mona gasp at my side.

"Leave now," he warned, "before I do *that* to your insides." When we didn't move to flee, he laughed and began to lower himself to the ground. "Little boy, you shouldn't go searching for things you aren't ready to confront."

"You don't know what I'm ready for."

He moved towards us and I prepared myself to fire a si' beam. "You think you can beat me? You think I'll let you bring harm to my Master?"

I didn't answer, because I wasn't sure I dared tell a lie right now, and a lie was all I really had. I was barely aware of my powers and didn't have the slightest clue what I was truly capable of. As a matter of fact, I didn't know what Ardet or Burton were capable of. But I wasn't going to back down now.

I needed answers, and I needed Burton to pay for what he'd done to me…What he'd done to others.

Without warning, Ardet lashed out and moved with such speed that we were caught off guard. He slammed a fist into the pit of Mona's stomach—knocking her into the side of her car.

I watched helplessly as Mona rolled to her hands and knees and spat blood.

"Not my car," she whined, more upset about the damage than her body.

I moved forward and threw a punch but missed. He was much too fast for me. I fired a si' beam at him and missed. My palm ached. It weakened me; it was painful using my powers. I was in desperate need of training—like Luke Skywalker.

Where was my Obi-Wan Kenobi? I was already down a Han Solo and Leia was down for the count, too; both bleeding out on the sidelines.

Suddenly, he seized me by the throat and squeezed—***hard***! I gagged and tried to fight him off but couldn't.

 I locked eyes with him and he frowned. "Die, boy," he spat.

I tried to kick him but failed. I needed to be free. I need air. I needed my POWERS!

I called energy to me and it came without me fully knowing how I'd summoned it. The sky grew dark and I felt something stir inside of me. My eyes glazed over as I stared at the dark clouds.

Ardet frowned and squeezed harder. At that moment, my body took over.

I felt the air on my skin and the hairs on my arms rose. I moved the air—causing a gale force wind—and then pulled something from the sky.

I called lightning. A purple blast of energy erupted out of the clouds and struck Ardet in the chest—hurling him across the field. I fell to my knees, gasping for air.

Mona rushed to my side and placed a hand on my shoulder. She was electrocuted and flew backwards, screaming as she did so. She skidded to a stop next to her car and I jumped to my feet.

I looked at my hands and saw electrical currents rippling across my skin. I could control aspects of weather, too??

"What *am* I?" I said, scared of my own power.

"You're pure greatness!" I turned to see Ardet striding towards me. "You're everything the master envisioned you'd be."

I suddenly felt light headed. Using my powers was taking a toll on me. As I fell, Gonzo caught me. I hadn't even heard him move.

"We're in this together, to the end," he struggled to say, his breathing labored.

It started to rain and I forced myself to stand. Gonzo spat blood and tried to move towards Ardet but I held a hand out to stop him.

"Make sure Mona's alright," I told him. "I can take him."

Ardet laughed and lifted himself into the air and flew off. I recalled the first time I'd flown. I closed my eyes and imagined myself lighter. As I began to float, I focused on Ardet, and soon I was zooming off after him.

Somehow between trying to fly and getting the rain out of my eyes, I'd lost him. But as I turned around, there he was. Or rather, there his fist was as it slammed into my jaw—knocking me back down to the ground below.

Mona was rising to her feet, pushing her wet hair out of her face. She caught sight of Ardet and moved her hands through the air—freezing rain droplets and hurled them at him.

He dodged her attempt and Gonzo moved into the fray, hurling an energy blast of yellow plasma at him.

Ardet waited until the blast was inches away and then he simply slapped it aside.

Gonzo's jaw dropped in shock and he looked at Mona. She looked just as worried.

I charged forward and was hit in the stomach by an invisible force. Just as suddenly, I was picked up off the ground and swung in midair.

"How do you like the air?" Ardet toyed. "You're not the only one with gifts. Perhaps you weren't worthy enough for the master. Maybe that's why he needed me."

So Ardet was a telekinetic, too? How many powers did this guy have?

I sucked in air as I fought off the urge to vomit as I continued to spin in the air.

Ardet dropped me without warning and flew towards my friends, but I beat him to them, knocking him aside.

"Are you guys alright?"

"We're fine," Gonzo lied.

"Zee, kick his Jon Brown hind part," Mona said.

"Yes, ma'am, grandmother," I replied, grinning. "Get Gonzo in the car."

"I'm fine!" he shouted. I ignored him and turned back to Ardet…but he was gone.

The rain slowed and I wondered where Ardet had disappeared to. I searched the skies. Maybe we'd live to see another day after all.

I moved to search the rubble, but there wasn't much left to search. But then again, if there was nothing there to begin with, then why was Burton's dark apprentice there to attack us?

There were so many questions, but we didn't have time to find answers for them. Gonzo was still bleeding out and growing paler by the minute.

We took another friend to the hospital, except this time, we stayed. I wasn't going to let him die on my watch.

Chapter 5:

A New Day and Sunrise

ೞ೫ೲ

When I woke up the next morning, I felt calm and relaxed. Gonzo and Mona were still asleep so I decided to go for a walk. I needed some alone time to mull over the events of the past twenty-four hours.

I saw the golden sun rising in the distance. I felt warmed by the sun's rays and a sense of calm washed over me. Everything was going to be alright. In reality, I knew nothing had truly changed, however.

I stayed out for a while, collecting my thoughts. Clearly Burton was dangerous and if he had super humans on his side like Ardet, we were in way over our heads.

I barely had control over my powers and needed training. But who could I turn to? I'd grown up in the foster system. I didn't have a family. I didn't have friends. The government had basically become my family when I lied my way into the agency. But of course, I hadn't pulled one over on the government. They'd known everything.

My life had been nothing to them. My life had been nothing to Burton. But my life meant something to me.

And I wanted my revenge, but now that I'd had time to think, I needed proper training. I'd never been a field agent. This was my first time actively in the field and I was clueless and scared out of my wits.

Was I really ready to take Burton on?

I eventually returned to the hospital to find Mona beside herself with worry. "Where the hell have you been?" she asked, rushing to me as I turned onto the hallway Gonzo's room was on.

I stopped in my tracks and looked behind me, suddenly feeling awkward. "Who me?"

"Who else, genius?" She sighed. "I was worried. I thought Ardet had come back and finished you off."

I chuckled nervously and ran a hand over the back of my neck. "He's not ready to take me on again."

"Yeah, right," she sarcastically replied. "Seriously, Zee, I was worried."

I grinned and nudged her shoulder. "I didn't know you cared so much."

She blushed and looked away, tucking a strand of auburn hair behind her ear. Did she like me?

"I just wanted to make sure you hadn't gotten yourself killed. We still have a long way to go before this is over." She turned to head back into Gonzo's room, but I placed a hand on her forearm to stop her.

She looked at me and for a second I was lost in her beautiful green eyes. "What's wrong, Zedo?"

"Mona, I'm not really sure how to say this, but…I haven't the slightest clue as to what I'm doing."

Her eyebrows shot up. "What do you mean?"

I let a nurse pass by before I continued. I lowered my voice, a little embarrassed. "I mean, I only realized I had powers when I woke up from my coma. I don't know how to control them or—"

"What?!" she shouted. I immediately shushed her. "Zedo, are you kidding me? You have us going against Burton and his crazy crew and you don't even know what you're doing?"

I gestured with my hands trying to get her to stop interrupting me, but she wouldn't. "Mona, I want Burton to pay for what he did! He deserves to die."

"I agree with you on that, but Zedo, you showed a massive display of power yesterday and if you don't know what you're doing…" She trailed off. I bit my lower lip, waiting for her to continue. She exhaled. "That could be very dangerous for the rest of us. You could harm yourself, not to mention me and Gonzo. You're powerful, Zedo. But raw power isn't enough." She exhaled. I could tell she was frustrated. "I can't believe Jonathan didn't warn us." Her eyes grew unfocused as her thoughts turned inward.

"I'm sorry I didn't tell you."

She finally looked at me and simply nodded. "Well we need to get you some training. You handled Ardet, but you're a little rough around the edges." She grinned and walked down the hall, away from Gonzo's room.

"Where are you going?"

She glanced over her shoulder and flashed a smile. "You're taking me to breakfast."

I found myself smiling and had almost forgotten that I had dimples.

Across from the hospital was a quaint little diner. Mona and I slid into a booth and talked about how we got into the agencies we'd once been a part of. Soon a waitress brought our orders and I munched on toast, bacon, and pancakes.

Was this a date? Was this like my first *real date?*

After telling me about her past, Mona told me she'd been assigned to another mission right before the original team had been assembled by Jonathan.

She was an understanding and caring person underneath it all, that much I could tell.

Content in her company, I found myself focusing on the curve of her lips, the way she ran a hand through her hair, the way she smiled… and I was thus lost in her beauty. She was truly a beautiful woman; auburn haired with glowing green eyes that seemed to change colors with each passing day.

When it was my turn to talk, I told her of the deconstructulator and how Burton caused me to miss out on the years of my youth; and how he caused me to fall into a coma.

I tried to recall life before the accident, but there wasn't much to tell. I didn't want to depress her with the details.

———————————————————

After breakfast we went to the graveyard to see Jordan's tombstone. We'd brought flowers. This was turning out to be an unconventional date, not at all how I'd imagined my first date would be, but I didn't tell her that.

"Burton will pay for this," Mona said as she sobbed.

I placed a reassuring hand on her shoulder and she looked up at me from where she knelt on the cold ground.

Through her teary eyes, I could see so much hurt. Mona was in agony. I could relate.

Squeezing her shoulder, my lips parted and I spoke to her. "Burton will pay for it *all*. He will answer for every crime he's committed…. I promise you that."

———————————————————

When we returned to the hospital, it was well after six.

Gonzo was awake and laughing at what was on the television. We were both in utter shock. "Gonzo, you're awake!" exclaimed Mona, running to his side and hugging him.

I smiled from afar and nodded at him. I was pleased.

Gonzo groaned and winced inside Mona's embrace. "Not so tight, okay, sheesh."

Mona pulled back and threw her arms into the air in mock surrender. "Sorry, sorry, I just can't believe it. It was like you were dead, but not dead, alive... but not alive..."

Gonzo rolled his eyes. "I get your point, you're happy to see me."

As Mona chuckled in reply to Gonzo's remarks, the phone rang.

The room grew silent as we looked at each other. "No one has this number," Gonzo said.

I clenched my jaw. This couldn't be good.

Mona reached for the hospital phone and cleared her throat. "Hello?"

"Come to Carey Creek at one o'clock tomorrow. We'll be waiting." The other end went dead.

Mona froze as she processed what had just happened. After a moment, she hung up the rotary phone and had a confused expression on her face when she turned around to look at Gonzo and I.

"Mona," I started, "what is it?" I rose from where I sat at Gonzo's bedside and moved towards her.

"It was Ardet."

My blood began to boil. How'd he find us? Mona turned to look out the window. Was he nearby? Maybe on the roof looking at us through the scope of a rifle?

I could hear my heart thumping in my ear as anger welled up inside of me. I clenched my fists and suddenly they burst into flames. Mona yelled and Gonzo jerked backwards in his hospital bed.

I took a step back, amazed and terrified at the same time. I began to hyperventilate.

"Zedo!" Mona shouted.

"I didn't do it!"

"You had to, Amigo! Put it out!"

"I don't know how!" I shouted. Suddenly, the fire began to move up my arms. I yelled but didn't get burned. It just felt like a warm breeze on my skin.

"Mona, do something!" Gonzo yelled. "Do something before he sets the fire alarms off!"

Mona rushed to her feet and tried to douse the flames with one of Gonzo's sheets. But the sheets caught on fire. She stomped the flames out and reached for a good old-fashioned fire extinguisher, but as soon as the foam stopped blasting, fire erupted from my fists again and began to crawl over my entire body like vines wrapping around an abandoned house.

I could feel other things happening inside me—energy churning, feeding the flames. I turned and tried to shake the flames off, but that wasn't helping me.

Mona was attempting to throw water on me from the restroom, but that barely helped.

Fire was always virtually unstoppable in its natural form, like burning houses or causing destruction, but if this remained unchecked, I'd singlehandedly destroy this hospital.

I tried to stop panicking.

"Focus, Zedo!" Mona said as she moved in front of me. "These are your powers! Control them, don't let them control you!"

I closed my eyes and tried to focus on stopping the fire from spreading. The flames licked my clothes and my hair, but neither of them burned. As I focused internally, I could feel my other abilities stirring, too.

I think I might have screamed, but I'm not really sure. My body dripped flames and I could see my reflection in the window of Gonzo's room—a pillar of fire, looking like some demon out of a movie.

My curly black hair fluttered in the flames, but didn't burn.

Suddenly, I caught Mona's reflection in the window as she reached for the fire extinguisher and mumbled something. She raised the extinguisher and my eyes grew wide as I turned to face her.

"No!" I yelled. But that was the last thing I did as in the next second she knocked me over the head with the fire extinguisher and the darkness took over.

I woke up in the backseat of Gonzo's F-150 with my head throbbing. As I sat up, a wave of nausea overtook me and I immediately rolled the window down and emptied my stomach.

"Good morning, sleeping beauty," said Gonzo from the passenger seat.

I groaned and rolled the window up. "How long was I out?"

Mona refused to look at me as she kept her eyes on the road. "Twelve hours."

I looked out the window. Were we not going to talk about what had happened in the hospital? Was I a risk to us all? I didn't really need to ask that question. I already knew the answer.

Of course, I was. I couldn't control my powers.

As I gazed out the window I took in the sights and realized we were in the country somewhere, moving off the main road. "Where are we?"

"We're headed to Carey Creek," Mona answered.

I looked at Gonzo and frowned. "Shouldn't you still be in the hospital?"

He chuckled and I could tell he was still in pain. "After you torched the room, flame boy, we couldn't stay there."

"But you're still healing!"

"Don't you think he knows that?!" Mona said sternly. I could tell she was livid. "We didn't have a choice."

Gonzo turned in his seat and looked apologetic. "Don't worry, Zee. I'll be fine."

I nodded and sat back. We rode in silence until we arrived at Carey Creek. It seemed to be abandoned, with a little pier on the end that was missing planks.

I wondered why Ardet had wanted us to meet him here.

Mona pulled the truck to a stop and we all climbed out.

"Do you think he's here?" Gonzo asked, swallowing hard.

"Why don't you just ask him?" said a voice behind us. We turned and there, floating in mid-air above the water, was the dark warrior.

But this time, he'd decided to dress in white battle garb and once again, a niqab covered his nose and mouth.

Floating beside him was a horrible looking woman in a matching white battle garb. Scars covered her face. Her skin was stiff, cracked, and flaking.

She glared at us and seemed to be rather deformed. She pointed at Mona. "I want to take her first."

Mona rolled her eyes. "Of *course*, you'd target the pretty one first."

The woman clenched her jaw and the skin on her face cracked some more.

This led to the fight at the Creek of Carey...

Chapter 6:

The Battle at Carey Creek

CR&O

Ardet moved from the water and lowered himself to the ground. The woman followed suit. He opened his hands in welcome. "I'm so happy that you were able to make it." He glanced at Gonzo. "How are the wounds?" he asked sarcastically.

Gonzo moved to engage him, but I stopped him—placing a hand on his shoulder to pull him back. "Easy, buddy. He's baiting you." I removed my hand from his shoulder as he relaxed.

"You're going to pay for what you did!" Mona yelled.

"I doubt that very much." He turned to the woman beside him. "Allow me to introduce my associate, Estella Monroe."

"Another of Burton's apprentices?" I asked. "Why does he keep sending you to do his dirty work?"

Estella looked at me. "You're not worthy enough to even glimpse the sole of his boots."

"At least not yet," added Ardet. I could hear the grin in his voice. If only I could see his face.

Without warning, Estella launched a blue fire ball at us.

We split up and ran. It slammed into Gonzo's truck—destroying it.

"Not my *truck*!!" exclaimed Gonzo.

Mona shrugged. "Welcome to the totaled car club."

Gonzo growled and hit Estella with a yellow energy blast and she fell from the sky with a BANG!

"Take a rest, you could hurt yourself," she teased as she picked herself off the ground and dusted herself off.

Gonzo dropped to one knee; the attack was too powerful for his weak body. Mona moved to his side. "Easy, Gonzo," she whispered as she kept her eyes on Estella.

"I'm alright, Mona. I'm just a little flushed," he replied, out of breath.

I released several si' beams, pushing them through my fingertips, and one struck Estella's face.

She grabbed her face and fell to the ground, screaming.

I flew to my teammates. "Are you guys okay?" I asked, turning my attention from them, then back to Ardet and Estella. Ardet hadn't moved, but Estella was already recovering.

Estella howled in anger and threw her arms forward, hurling a teal colored blast from her eyes at us. The force of the blast tossed us into the air like rag dolls and we fell into the lake.

I moved towards the surface, but Gonzo wasn't moving! He was unconscious! And Mona was sinking, too. I swam as fast as I could to reach Gonzo.

I remembered that I could control water; it was an element after all. I moved my free hand around in the water and forced the current to change, brining Mona to my side. I strained with the effort as my lungs began to burn.

Once Mona was close enough, I swam upward, but was pushed back down. I'd hit a barrier!

Had Ardet covered the surface with some sort of force field? I couldn't breathe!! And I knew Gonzo was fading fast. Mona still hadn't come to, either.

Was this our final moment? Would we live, or die?

I didn't want to die, and I couldn't let Mona and Gonzo die, either. I kicked and kicked, trying to keep us close to the surface, but it made no effect. I started to black out. I tried to stay alive.

As I looked up, I saw Estella and Ardet were laughing above the surface where they floated.

I felt like giving up. The edges of my consciousness were turning dark. I drifted downward. I was dying. This couldn't be happening...

Suddenly, we were pulled from the water by a powerful force!

I gasped for air and my two friends rolled to a stop on the shore. I got up and revived them, scared that it was already too late. But as they started to cough up water, relief flooded me and I stood up.

I looked at Ardet; I could feel his eyes trying to look deep within me, as if searching for something. Then, he attacked me, flying towards me—arms outstretched.

I fought dirty now. I fired a si' beam into the side of Ardet's neck as he tackled me. He yelled in pain and released me, skidding to a stop as he slammed into the dirt.

I landed on my feet and caught sight of Gonzo and Mona engaging Estella. The three of us tried to kill the atrocious duo.

I called power to bear down on Ardet and forced the winds to respond to my touch—I pulled a swift wind across Carey Creek and Ardet tried to plant his feet. His clothes rustled fiercely in the gale wind. He was losing ground.

I moved across the creek towards him with relative ease. The elements were on my side.

I held a hand up and called fire to my fist. It instantly responded, hungry! My fist burst into flames and Ardet took a step back—unbelieving. I could see fear in his eyes. As the fire tried to move down my arm, I spoke silently to it.

Easy there, tiger, I thought to myself. I recalled Mona's words: "*Control your powers, Zedo. Don't let them control you.*"

I hurled a fire ball at Ardet and he tried to dodge it, but I curled the air around him and the fire ball slammed into his chest—hurling him into the side of a tree.

His strength was finally failing him, an effect of holding the barrier over the water for too long, no doubt.

As I called more fire balls to rain down on Ardet, I felt the anger inside me stretch its massive paws. The beast within was waking, and that scared me a bit.

On and on we fought. The day was gone and night had arrived.

Sweat soaked my clothes with the strain of calling on my powers so heavily. I backed down to regain my energy, and I flew away.

Mona and Gonzo turned towards the sky, watching me.

"Zedo!" Mona yelled. Estella tried to follow, but Mona fired an ice beam into her calf, pinning her to the ground.

Estella's screams echoed into the night.

I needed a lot of ground, more ground, and there'd been no time to tell them. Ardet lifted himself into the air and chased after me.

Suddenly, I heard Gonzo yell out and as I turned back towards Carey Creek, I caught sight of Mona fainting.

I angled back towards the creek, but Gonzo flew off with Mona in his arms. Maybe it was for the best. I couldn't expect them to fight all my battles, but I had expected them to keep Estella busy.

I guess I was on my own now. I turned in the sky and shot off, forcing the air to propel me forward faster and faster.

Estella zoomed through the sky, nearing her partner's side.

I had no idea where I was heading, but I needed time to think, and as long as they chased me, that was fine by me.

Ardet raised a hand to the sky and the night grew pitch-black. It started to rain, and he loved it; making it harder for me to see him, to defeat him.

"It has to end here so I can kill Burton," I said to myself.

This was all about revenge; I couldn't let myself forget that. I stopped flying and punched Ardet in his face as he came soaring through the sky. He yelled in agony. It caught him off guard.

As I flew down, Estella grabbed me. She blew me away with a punch I called the twister; because she twisted her fist then hurled it at me. I fell to the ground and skidded to a stop, knocking down a tree or two.

My ribs ached and I gasped for air. She'd knocked the wind out of me.

I didn't want to fight without my full strength, but I didn't have a choice. Had Mona died? Is that why she'd fainted? Or was she just too weak?

I needed them.

Suddenly, I couldn't breathe. What was happening to me? I turned in the grass and caught sight of Ardet and Estella landing. Ardet had a hand extended towards me. He was telekinetically choking me.

Chapter 7:

My Mystery

CShD

I felt as if I had no destiny. My future was long lost…. Or was it? I couldn't return to my natural state of mind. It was not my place.

If I had no place to go, where would I go? Would I live or die?

Would I kill Burton? Would Estella and Ardet leave? Would they take me away? Would Ardet kill me as I lay there, squirming on the forest floor—clawing at the ground as I tried to break his telekinetic hold?

Would I remember my life and history?

I was filled with fear. I was scared. My future was no more and I knew nothing about my past.

My feelings weren't hurt, but I felt sorrowful. I needed peace.

Had the sun set for me on this day? Would the moon rise and tell me goodnight? Would I end? Was this my conclusion?

I felt a deep darkness fall over me. I stopped fighting the darkness. I stopped thrashing and relinquished control of my life.

Had I just *died*?

I screamed in pain, but nothing came out.

What was happening to me?

Tears I longed for would not come.

There was no shadow to see. There was no light to comfort me, no warmth to console me.

There would be no sunshine. There would be no dew on the morning grass, no birds in the trees screeching.

Where had my life gone? Had it ever truly been mine?

Was this the other side?

If this was the afterlife, I wanted to go back. There was no color, only dark. There was no sound, only a deafening silence.

Where was Saint Peter and the pearly gates? Where were all the angels and stuff?

Suddenly, I gasped for air and awoke to find myself covered in snow.

Where was I? My vision was blurry, but I knew what snow felt like. I knew what the bitter cold felt like on my prickly skin.

"Where am I?" I asked myself, or rather croaked. My voice was hoarse, my throat was awfully dry.

As my vision cleared, I realized I was on a mountainside. How had I gotten here?

Chapter 8:

The Passing of Estella

༼ʒઠ༽

I blinked and everything changed. I jumped back, startled to find that I was back at Carey Creek! As fast as I had left, I had returned. What had happened? Where had I gone?

I knew what to expect since I'd seen it in the darkness.

"How could I see in the darkness?" I asked myself.

Gonzo and Mona landed at my side.

"Where were you?" Mona asked worriedly.

I frowned. "I don't know," I replied baffled. "I thought you two had left." They looked puzzled. "Where were *you*?! I saw you and Gonzo fly off! You two left me."

Gonzo and Mona looked at each other and then back at me. "What are you talking about, Zedo?" asked Gonzo, trying to keep his voice even. "We never left..."

Shock filled me.

Had I hallucinated? Had I blacked out? *Were those visions?* I wondered.

Estella swooped down, interrupting my thoughts as Ardet flew towards us. I had no time to deal with a deformed demonic apprentice outcast like Estella.

I lifted my hand and called fire to my palm. The fire came with ease, as it had before. I quickly poured more power into it and then forced it to slam into Estella's chest and then *through* it.

Mona gasped and Ardet took a step back.

Estella stopped in her tracks, her mouth frozen in an 'O' and then she exploded into flames, blown away to the point of no return. I didn't know I had that kind of power inside of me.

As Estella's remains—which were now particles of ash—fluttered to the ground, Ardet lifted himself into the air and flew off without another word.

I let him go because I knew deep down inside that he would be back. They always come back. Evil can't help but retreat, regain their strength, and come back.

And when Ardet finally reappeared I'd be ready to end his life just as I'd ended Estella's.

Mona, Gonzo, and I leaned against a fallen tree trunk in an attempt to regain some portion of our strength.

"We need to regroup," began Gonzo. "We need to come up with a plan…and get out of here."

I nodded.

"I agree," added Mona. She wiped the sweat from her brow and sat up. "Burton is just going to keep sending his flunkies after us."

"And let's face it, guys," said Gonzo, "we're not really ready to take him on."

Mona and I said nothing. I guess neither of us wanted to admit that on some level Gonzo was *right*.

Since Gonzo's truck was a shell of its former self, we had to head back to civilization on foot. Eventually, we made our way back to Mona's posh apartment only to find that it had been ransacked.

"They know where we stay," Mona said in disbelief as she moved through her apartment.

"Of course, they do," Gonzo told her. "Burton used to work for the government remember? He probably still has friends in high places. Not to mention that his crime syndicate could have access to all kinds of information."

I said nothing. There was still too much on my mind. I still didn't know if I'd died, or if I'd had some sort of vision of the future. When I thought of it, I felt chilled to my core. Something about that experience was definitely off.

Not only could I control the elements, but I could also control the weather? There was so much I didn't know about myself and my powers, not to mention the world around me. Everything had changed.

"Salvage what you can, Mona, but we can't stay here," I said, my voice low and thoughtful. She looked at me and nodded.

As she moved through the apartment grabbing anything left of value, I began to fall into my thoughts.

I had no place of my own since I came out of my coma in January and Gonzo was a nomad, too.

There was no turning back now. Burton was on to us.

"Burton is doing everything he can to stop us," Mona said.

"But why?" Gonzo asked.

I turned to face them. I knew the answer all too well. "He's scared of us. He knows we're coming for him."

Gonzo smiled. "Well let's give him something to truly be scared of then."

I grinned and then moved across the room to Mona. "I'm thinking Gonzo and I should head back to Michigan and look over Jonathan's lab again. Maybe we'll find something we overlooked. Will you meet us there when you finish up here?"

She pulled me into a hug and I relaxed as her body pressed against mine. I hugged her back. "Be careful, Zedo."

As we pulled apart, I locked eyes with her. "Don't worry. We'll be fine. Just don't take too long."

Gonzo and I crossed the country and eventually arrived at Jonathan's apartment in Michigan. Along the way Gonzo filled me in on more things I'd missed in the thirty years I'd been in a coma.

More solar systems and galaxies had been discovered and there was life beyond Earth. We weren't alone.

Scientists had also discovered that alternate realities existed. They were also working on ways to travel through space quicker, cutting down travel time between planets from years to a matter of hours. That was amazing.

I couldn't believe all the advances in technology and I hoped that one day I'd have time to experience life again. I would never be normal, but I'd enjoy life the best I could once all of this was over.

I also wanted to see what it was like to travel across the stars. There was so much to see and so much to do. I'd fallen into my coma before my 15th birthday. I was ready to *live*, but I couldn't until I had Burton's head on a silver platter.

Mona met us in Michigan a day later and the three of us went to visit Saray together.

Saray and the children welcomed us back. She'd been awfully lonely since Jonathan's death. Thankfully, she gave us access to Jonathan's armory and there we found a host of vehicles and technology.

I grinned to myself and rubbed my palms together. We were back in business.

I wondered why Jonathan hadn't told us about the armory before. He'd only showed us his lab. The armory would've been useful when we'd visited Nick's mansion and had encountered those beasts.

If it hadn't been for Saray telling us, we never would've known about this vast cave filled with DARPA-like technologies.

Chapter 9:

The Trader

ॐ

Unfortunately, during our inventory of the armory, we found information in Jonathan's lab that was quite disturbing. On a simple laptop that Gonzo had come across was an email account that had been left open.

In those emails were instructions on leading us back to Nick's and other incriminating messages. The email that stuck out the most to me was an email filled with dummy locations for bases.

"He made it all up!" Gonzo exclaimed.

I was speechless. I swallowed hard and wondered how long my friend had been working for Burton! How had we missed that? How did we not catch that?!

It became clear that Jonathan had never really been my friend. He'd been keeping tabs on me for Burton. No wonder he'd been the first person to find me after I'd come out of my coma!

I clenched my jaw and felt utterly betrayed.

Gonzo kicked a chair over. "He played us. We *believed* him! I've known Jonathan for YEARS! He used to be friends with my handler!"

"When I first met him, he offered me shelter." I shook my head and removed the watch he'd given me before we'd gone to meet Nicolas the first time. I slammed the watch into the ground and the parts flew apart.

Gonzo knelt and picked up a small piece that pulsed with a red light every few seconds. "It's a tracking device!" he yelled. He touched his forehead and swore. "We've got to call Mona!"

"He's been tracking us," I said, shaking my head in disbelief.

As soon as those words touched my lips the spider-like monstrosities from Nick's place appeared from the shadows and Ardet stood among them. I heard Gonzo swallow hard and I took a step back as Ardet floated across the air, landing in front of me.

I looked at the ceiling, considering if I had enough time to save Saray and the kids. Was Mona with them?

Ardet spoke, as if reading my mind. "Don't even try it. She's dead," he said. "They all are."

My eyes grew wide. Was Mona among the dead, too? "Why?" I asked through clenched teeth.

Suddenly I heard a crash and Gonzo and I turned to catch sight of Mona moving through the hoard of beasts—hurling ice beams at them.

Ardet held up a hand to keep the creatures at bay. Mona moved towards us and glared at Ardet. "You sent those beasts to kill innocents."

So it was true. He'd killed Saray and her children. Even if Jonathan had betrayed us his wife didn't deserve to lose her life and neither did the kids.

Ardet shrugged and took a step towards the three of us. The arachnid creatures began to surround Mona, Gonzo, and I, boxing us in. "I had to tie up some loose ends."

"I knew you were a monster, but why kill innocents?" Mona asked, keeping an eye on the creatures as they snarled at her and crept closer.

Ardet gestured with his hands, pointing at the laptop. "So, you found out my little secret? It took you longer than I'd expected."

"What?" I said, a sinking feeling hit me in the gut as I began to put the pieces together.

"You thought I was dead." He reached for the veil that covered his face and pulled it away.

My eyes grew wide in shock and the others gasped. "*Jonathan*?" Mona and Gonzo said at my side.

I couldn't even speak. I felt like such a fool.

"My *real* name is Ardet Udakarre. I lived a double life, but not anymore. With my family dead, I can live free. I can serve my master wholeheartedly."

My blood began to boil. "You killed them: your wife and your children... your own *children*!"

"I'm an agent of The Shadow, an apprentice of the Master. We are encouraged not to have connections with people until we reach the rank of Shadow Master. Until then we cannot control how our attachments affect us. They cause us to be weak and—"

"The Shadow?" I asked, looking at Gonzo then Ardet. "What's that?"He just stood there, glaring at me. I faintly recalled seeing that name in one of the reports Jonathan—well Ardet—had given to me "What's The Shadow?!" I asked again, growing angrier the more he waited.

He smirked. At that moment, I knew he wasn't going to tell us.

Was *'The Shadow'* the name of Burton's crime syndicate?

Gonzo spoke and it pulled me from my thoughts. "How did you pull it off, the body trick? We saw your corpse. We thought you were dead."

"Robotics, dear friend. They're the thing of the future. I created a robotic replica of myself." He stopped for a minute and stroked one of the beasts at his side as if it were a mere pet and not a vicious demon. "I saw everything. I controlled each and every move." Ardet looked me square in the eye. "I helped create you, Zee. I helped Burton plot to take you. He hadn't meant to put you into a coma. He'd initially planned to kidnap you and raise you as his personal weapon…He saw so much potential in you."

My heart sunk at this revelation. I wasn't a slave able to be stolen. I wasn't someone's property. I was a human *being!*

"I've been in place since before the Deconstructulator…and this is the thanks I get? You come to me and attack the blessed Father when instead you should be *joining* us as he intended."

"You're insane if you think I'd ever join Burton! He took my life away from me!"

Ardet smirked. "*No*, my friend. He gave you *life*."

Mona pointed her hands at Ardet and generated ice beams. I reached for her. We didn't want to attack Ardet until we had all of the information we needed. Gonzo moved to intercept her.

"You killed Jordan!" Mona yelled. "You killed my brother!"

Ardet looked at her and cocked his head. "Yes…yes, I did kill him, and the others. But I'm not the only one that's hid something from Mr. Jeta."

"What is he talking about?" Gonzo asked.

"Do you want to tell them, or should I?" Ardet grinned. He was enjoying this.

Mona looked at me. "I'm sorry, Zedo, but I'm a special agent from Secret Agency VI," she said, drawing her gold and blue star shaped badge from the inside of her jacket. "We've had our suspicions of Jonathan for a while now… but this has confirmed my worst fears. Jonathan is evil... and a member of The Shadow."

"The lies!" I shouted. "The lies!"

The arachnids snarled and howled, responding to my anger. Ardet held up a hand, holding the creatures at bay.

"You could've told me the truth, Mona. This entire thing—all of this—was a trap to get to Ardet! You used *me*. You used us," I said, gesturing to Gonzo and I.

"You aren't the only one with a mission, Zedo! This goes beyond just US! Burton is a galactic enemy wanted by several governments! When my agency found out about your escape from the lab, they tasked me with tracking you down and confirming Jonathan's involvement."

"See, Zee, they want to take you in," Ardet said.

Confusion filled me. Was anyone truly on my side?

"They want to control you. They want you to be their weapon. But my master—my *leader*—Burton, can help you." Ardet stretched a hand towards me. "Join me."

I shook my head. "Regardless of her actions, Mona isn't the enemy here. *You* are."

Did he use us to see how powerful we were? Was it to see if we could make it through hard times? Had Burton asked him to test us? To eliminate us?

Ardet pointed at us and the arachnid demons crept forward. The three of us backed up.

I quickly lowered my voice. "Gonzo, I'm going after Ardet, he's going to pay."

"We can handle it, Zee," Gonzo said.

"I'm sorry, Zedo. I didn't intentionally try to deceive you."

"That isn't important right now," I told her. "Our survival is all that matters right now." I couldn't look at her; I was utterly disgusted by her. She was no better than Ardet. She'd lied and manipulated me, just as he had.

The creatures instantly lashed out at the wave of Ardet's hand and Gonzo attacked, punching one in the chest. "Go, we can handle it!" he shouted.

I called energy to myself and hurled fire at several of the demons—burning them to a crisp. I yelled, forcing flames from my palms to clear a path through the demons as Ardet began to retreat.

He flew towards the exit and I chased after him, hurling flames at his back until I knocked him out of the air. His body slammed into the ground and he slowly got up, instantly brushing the flames off. Before I could reach him, he flew off again.

Ardet blasted a hole through the wall with a burst of telekinetic energy and flew out into the night.

I had no time to waste. I lifted myself into the air and raced out and into the night. But as I soared into the sky, I couldn't find him.

He'd just vanished into thin air.

Suddenly, Ardet came out of nowhere and slammed his fist into my jaw. The blow knocked me out of the sky and I fell into unconsciousness just as I slammed into the rooftop of a nearby building.

———————————————

I awoke atop a mountain. The sun was rising and the wind chilled my soul as snow flew about in the strong wind. This was the same mountain from that weird dream—vision?—I'd had during the confrontation with Ardet and Estella. Had I seen my future?

"Where am I?" I asked myself. My forehead throbbed and the frigid temperature chilled me to my core.

How long had I been unconscious?

I tried to fly, but the atmosphere was too thin. So instead, I slid down the mountain and dodged a couple of rocks.

I was over being angry and I was more than pissed off. Now it was time to reach out and touch my rage. I needed to go on a rampage and I needed to be deadly.

A bloody massacre, I thought.

I was prepared as I slid down those icy, freezing, snowy slopes.

My adrenaline was pumping. I would be prepared for my next encounter with Ardet. The question was: would he be?

Chapter 10:

The Mountain

CRXO

I don't know how long I had been on that mountain, but for however long it had been was too long. I was frustrated beyond belief. I didn't know where I was, however, I knew who had put me up here.

I tried to fly again and I still couldn't.

"What is going on?" I asked myself as I only grew more upset.

I ran down the slope and tried once more. I fell and crashed into a boulder and hit my nose—it began to bleed.

I tried to use my powers to blast through the boulder, but nothing happened but a small si' beam that barely dented it.

"What's happened to me?" I said aloud. What was wrong with my powers?

I grew feeble, I hadn't eaten, nor had I had a drop of water to drink.

I began to meditate, centering myself day and night for eight days. I was completely at peace with myself as I slowed my heart rate to keep my hunger and thirst under control. I also needed to regain enough strength to access my powers.

When I opened my eyes on the ninth day, I remembered that I had to destroy Ardet. I had only just started my way back down the mountain when Ardet suddenly appeared.

"Hello, Zedo. I started to get worried. I thought you would never wake."

He landed and threw a punch, but I dodged it. In the next moment, I began to race down the side of the mountain. I needed to gain some distance between the two of us.

I needed to be able to fly, which meant heading down the mountain. While I had been in my state of meditation, I gained a new understanding of my body and the powers I had access to. Sure enough, I was gifted with the ability to control the elements, but I also had the ability of atmokinesis—the ability to manipulate the weather.

I had more power at my disposal than I knew. I just didn't know how to channel it. I needed someone to teach me. If Ardet was an apprentice to Burton, then surely, I could find someone who was willing to train the good guys.

But right now, I had other problems to worry about.

As I ran down the side of the mountain, gravity began to take hold. I nearly fell a few times, but at the last instance, I reached out with a hand and called upon my ability to manipulate the earth. The ground beneath my feet shot up and supported me. I grinned to myself and used my hands to propel me forward as the earth beneath my feet fashioned itself likes skis and allowed me to move faster.

I felt Ardet closing in the distance between us. I gestured with my hand and a fissure opened in the ground. As Ardet landed, I opened another, trapping his leg. I spun to face him and gestured with my hand, closing the fissure.

He shouted, screaming in agony. In the next instance, I turned to leave, heading back down the mountain.

"You can't leave me here!" he cried.

"I can…and I **WILL**!!" I shouted over my shoulder. I had no desire to help him. I told myself I'd come back one day and see if he was deceased. Maybe he'd cut his leg off with a burst of energy so he could escape, but I doubted he'd cause himself that level of pain.

When I realized where I was—which happened to be the Sierra Nevada Mountain range—and arrived back in civilization, I made my way to a rest stop and cleaned myself up in the sink.

But on the mountain, it had snowed. What in the global warming hell was going on? Had my presence caused the weather in that area to change? Or was it truly the climate?

I began to search for Mona and Gonzo. After mulling over ideas of where they'd be, I decided to check the cemetery back in Virginia. Surely enough, they were there and stood before Jordan's tombstone.

Mona was mourning and Gonzo comforted her with a pat on the back. "Sometimes it's good to cry. It's part of the healing process," Gonzo told her. I had to admit that I was a little jealous of Gonzo at that moment.

"Is this all for me?" I asked, knowing full well that it wasn't.

"Zedo?" The two turned to see me and they rushed towards me.

Mona hugged me. I grinned to myself and took her scent in. She smelled heavenly.

"We were so worried about you. Where did you go?" Gonzo asked.

"Never mind that, how are you? Are you all right? Are you hungry?" asked Mona.

My teammates took me to a nearby diner and Mona apologized for her deception and I forgave her. I couldn't stay mad at such a beautiful woman.

I filled them in on the events that had occurred in the mountains. But, much to my surprise, Mona told me I'd actually been MIA for several weeks and not days.

I couldn't believe that I'd survived in the wilderness for that long. Gonzo paid the bill and we headed to the parking lot where Mona's rented vehicle sat gleaming amongst the plain cars.

Suddenly, an object slammed into the ground in front of us. Gonzo's eyes grew wide. "Grenade!" he shouted.

We turned to take cover, but the grenade exploded, hurling us into the air and through the glass of the diner! As I hit the floor of the diner—shrapnel raining all around—I blacked out. I hated being human.

Chapter 11:

Lester Burton & the H.I.T.S.

ଔଔ

I had no idea how long I was out. I wasn't sure of much at that time. When the blast hit, it was swift. We had no time to react.

I woke up and looked around. Gonzo and Mona were on either side of me inside tanks filled with water. I was surrounded by water, myself, and then the flashbacks hit me. All of a sudden, I felt like I was back in the lab! I was Burton's prey.

I had another regulator on and I tried to break out, this was too much like the lab in which I'd awaken in. I began to panic and I could feel my heart racing, *beating* against my rib cage. The glass of the tank was very thick, like temperate glass. I couldn't break through.

Frantically looking about, I noticed that Mona had started to gain consciousness. She was startled. I could hear her screaming. Next to her, Gonzo was struggling against the glass, too, pounding his fist against it.

I glanced around; we were in a humongous laboratory. There were computer systems, machines, and other gadgets.

Three people dressed in white lab jackets began to observe Mona. She began to kick at the protective glass.

Gonzo stopped hitting the glass and seemed to seize in the water.

I had to do something. We were in danger.

I called energy to myself and forced my powers to awaken. I could control the elements. I could control the water in this vertical tank. The water responded to my control and I flexed my fingers. As I moved my hands back and forward, the water responded, hammering against the glass until it began to crack—spiderwebs spreading through the glass. But still, it didn't shatter. I wasn't going to give up.

I didn't know where we were, but I was going to get us out of here.

Two different observers moved closer to Gonzo's tank and one pressed a keypad on the tank's side. Gonzo's tube lowered itself to the floor and floated over a drain in the floor. The bottom of the tank opened and water gushed out, drained through the floor. Gonzo remained suspended in the center of the tube, and was still having a seizure.

The tube quickly turned horizonal and a section of the glass slid away. One of the people in lab coats reached for his arm as another readied a syringe.

I yelled, slamming the water against the glass. The lab tech jabbed the syringe into Gonzo's arm and he relaxed. It was most likely a sedative. The techs quickly set up a central line and hooked Gonzo up to an I.V. I watched helplessly as they began to pump his body full of drugs and placed his mask back on him.

A taller observer went to the keypad and the stretcher slid back into the tank and turned vertically. Water filled the chamber and he began to float.

I grew tired and relaxed in my tank. My powers had failed me. I looked at Mona and she looked worried.

"Well, well, well. Who do we have here?" a voice in the distance rang out. Descending a stairwell in the center of the lab was a man dressed in an all-black suit. My eyes grew wide and Mona did a double take—quickly looking from the man to me and then back at the man.

He looked so much like me, but yet totally different. It was my face, but wasn't. My eyes, but not quite. The difference wasn't something you saw…it was something you *felt*. Where I'd always sensed good energy from around Gonzo and Mona—their auras perhaps—whoever this man was reeked of dark energy.

While my skin was a medium beige color, his was olive toned. While my hair was black, thick, and curly, his was sleek and black. While it's safe to say I was biracial, he clearly was not.

As he walked down the stairs, a shadow seemed to creep over my soul, a darkness that could potentially blot out the sun if we'd been outside. Something about him was evil. I sensed darkness in him.

Things were about to turn from bad to worse.

"Zedo Jeta, Mona Lisa-Flynn, and Gonzo Daniels." He clapped his hands and grinned. "It is *truly* an honor to have you here in my state of the art laboratory."

"Who are you!?!" I asked, pulling off my mask. I didn't need it to breathe. I manipulated the water to pull oxygen from it and fill my lungs. "Why are we here?"

"I am Lester Burton. I am not *the* Burton you seek, clearly.... I am my father's son, born in 1975..." He turned his dark eyes in my direction and studied me. I didn't, *couldn't*, hold his gaze. Something didn't feel right.

I didn't believe him. Who in their right mind would have sex with a monster like Burton, let alone have a baby with him??

Mona banged against the glass of her tank and Lester Burton looked at her. "Please stop, dear."

I was utterly puzzled. What was going on here? Was he studying us? Was he experimenting on us?

Well, I wasn't about to sit around and find out.

I called energy to myself and unleashed an electrical surge from my body, all the while shielding myself.

However, nothing happened. I was baffled.

Lester Burton shook his head. "When will you learn? I studied the machinery they used years ago and created more advanced devices. I know *all* about you and your gifts so I was able to make unbreakable equipment. You can't win here. Just relax and let me do my work."

"And what is your work?" Mona asked, her hair floating about her face.

"Let me out!" I demanded, ignoring her. I was starting to feel claustrophobic.

Who was this man?

He claimed to be the son of Burton, but was he really? As I studied him, I could see few features that resembled Burton.

"You're not a threat to me in there, Mr. Jeta. You're nothing... just an animal."

I looked at him, it sounded so familiar. Maybe he was Burton's son after all. I glared. "You're going to let me out."

He gazed at me, waiting for something to happen, and grinned. "I doubt that very much."

I yelled, forced energy through my palms, and forced the water to slam against the central crack in the tank. I began to slam the water into the same spot like a battering ram.

Finally, it shattered—water spilling out. I leapt from my tank and Lester took a step back—surprise etched on his face.

I hurled a si' beam into the side of Mona's tank. The keypad exploded in a shower of sparks and the tank opened, spilling water onto the lab floor. Mona jumped down and landed.

"Get Gonzo," I told her, refusing to take my eyes off Lester. He snapped his fingers and guards dressed in black military uniforms filled the lab.

"So you work for the government?" I asked.

Lester looked me square in the eye. "I work for The Shadow."

There was that name again. I heard shattering and assumed it was Mona freeing Gonzo from his prison. Guards aimed their weapons at them and Lester held up a hand to stop them from opening fire.

Water from the tanks overflowed and roamed freely through the lab touching circuits and causing sparks to fly and things to explode.

Mona moved to my side, Gonzo limping next to her—groggy but beginning to wake.

I hadn't moved an inch. "You attacked us at the diner." It wasn't a question, I knew it was him.

"I did," he replied anyway. "And I killed every person that witnessed your abduction as well." I heard Mona gasp at my side and I swallowed hard.

"You cannot win, Mr. Jeta. You never will. We are more powerful than you can ever imagine."

"What exactly is The Shadow?" Mona asked.

He looked at her and smirked. "We are *power*."

A chill ran down my spine. I didn't doubt him. I felt truth in his words.

"We are everywhere…not just on Earth. Our hands extend to several galaxies. We will always come out on top."

"Las x zed ya!" Mona yelled in a language I'd never heard before. She blew him backwards with a beam of ice. Just then, chaos broke out as the guards opened fire.

Mona dove for cover, pulling Gonzo along with her. I spun and called upon my inner flames and emitted fire—hurling flames all across the lab. The flames slammed into equipment and all around. The lab began to burn.

"Don't harm them!!" I heard Lester yell.

"We need to get out of here," I told Mona.

"Where the hell are we?" Gonzo asked, suddenly alert.

"Get us out of here, Jeta!" Mona ordered as she hurled ice beams at several guards. But the exits were covered.

However, I recalled when I'd first awaken in the lab months prior. I looked at the ceiling and grinned to myself. I rose to my feet and began to move the air molecules in the room—spinning them faster and faster, whipping up a breeze until it turned into a gale wind that hurled people around the lab. I lifted the three of us into the air and caught sight of Lester holding onto a railing.

He screamed out, his eyes filled with rage. "Jeta! I'll find you, Jeta! You can't run from me!"

As I lifted us towards the ceiling, I reached out with a hand and blew a hole through the roof. Debris fell to the ground—hurling dust into the air.

Arriving on the roof, I felt the howling wind against my skin. The night was dark and filled with clouds. There was barely a sliver of moonlight to illuminate the city, but I could tell we were in the center of a metropolis. Chicago, maybe? But I wasn't for sure.

My clothes were soaking wet and I was freezing. The wind slapped me in the face, and yet I knew we needed an escape route.

"The guards are coming!" yelled Mona as she turned towards me, her long, wet hair blowing in the wind.

"Jump!" Gonzo yelled, grabbing her by the arm and leaping off the ledge.

I smiled, lifted myself into the air, and jumped off the ledge, leaving the guards on the roof.

I rushed past them as they free fell and used my aerokinetic abilities to grab them and pull them closer. I quickly gestured with my free hand and forced the air upward and lifted us into the sky.

Mona laughed, filled with glee as we flew towards the clouds. I moved closer to them and grabbed Mona's hand. It would be a shame if I lost control and she plummeted to her death; she was the only one who couldn't fly. As she intertwined her fingers with mine, I felt heat begin to race.

She looked at me, smiling. Sure, there'd been girls in the agency before my coma, but never one as beautiful as Mona. I immediately felt nervous and I could feel my palm grow sweaty as she held my hand.

She made me nervous. I was a teenager when I'd fallen into my coma, and even though I'd lost thirty years of my life, I still felt like a kid. All of this was new to me. But at that moment, I knew I had a crush on her. This was probably the worse time to think about that, but I couldn't help it. And maybe she had a crush on me, too.

I had to break our eye contact though. She was distracting me and I needed to focus on keeping us airborne. I looked down and caught sight of the city below. I was amazed at the sight of the world beneath us.

It's crazy how we were running for our lives, fighting enemies, and out for revenge against Burton but below us, life seemed to be going just fine. To me, that seemed…odd.

As I looked at the world below, cars moved through the streets, pedestrians strolled along the sidewalks, coming in and out of shops with hands either full of shopping bags or empty. I caught sight of a few people jogging in the dark.

Below me, everything was business as usual for everyone…everyone but the three of us. Mona, Gonzo, and I had been agents of black ops divisions. We'd never known *'normal.'*

In that moment, Mona released my hand and my thoughts were pulled back to the present. I looked at her and her eyes fluttered.

"Mona?" I called out over the howl of the wind as we flew perhaps 20,000 feet above ground. Without warning, she fell, having moved out of my area of control.

"Mona!!" Gonzo and I yelled.

I dove for her, and for a moment, I forgot about Gonzo. But suddenly, he was zooming past me! He didn't need me to keep him in the air.

Suddenly, out of nowhere, a figure dressed in all grey appeared, and flew towards Mona at an incredible speed.

My eyes grew big. "NOOOOOO!!!!"

The figure caught her and we chased them—him?— swirling through the sky. I hurled a si' beam forward, but missed, and tried to speed up.

I raced through the air and Gonzo was right behind me.

The person put their left hand up and the space around it turned black and suddenly Gonzo couldn't move, covered in black rope. He began to fall towards the ground—hurtling head over feet.

I looked towards the earth and then back at Mona's kidnapper. I couldn't let Gonzo die, but I also couldn't let Mona be stolen from us.

My heart dropped. I had to save Gonzo.

I'm sorry, Mona I thought to myself. I hoped she'd forgive me.

I dropped down and grabbed Gonzo and tried to free him from his prison, but it vanished the moment I caught him.

When I looked up, the person was gone.

We landed in a field just beyond the city's limits and I exhaled sharply, trying to slow my racing heart.

Gonzo inhaled sharply.

"Who the hell was that?" he asked. It was a rhetorical question, so I ignored it.

"Let's pay Ardet a visit," I said. The person—whoever it had been—was covered in battle garb and their face had been hidden.

Ardet was the only person I knew that fit that description.

"You think that was him? I thought you said—"

I shrugged. "Maybe, I don't know, Gonzo. I just know that we have to save Mona and stay off Burton's radar; *both* Burtons..."

"Isn't Ardet dead?" Gonzo asked, bewildered.

"I stuck him in a mountain, he should be… But I have a feeling he's still alive. Come on."

I took off running and then reached for energy—propelling myself into the air. Seconds later, Gonzo was at my side and we flew upward and onward.

We flew to the mountain and found Ardet still stuck in the fissure that I'd left him in. He was ghostly pale and thin—almost skeletal.

"Stay back, stay back!" he said weakly. His voice was raspy.

I walked towards him. "Relax, Ardet. We just need some information. We don't want any trouble."

"Zedo, I think you already made that clear," Gonzo said. He leaned closer to me and tried to whisper. "Why didn't he just cut his leg off and get out of here?"

"My powers didn't work up here for a while," I replied. "Maybe his don't either."

I yanked Ardet out of the mountain and he screamed, his leg hanging beneath him limply. "You're going to tell me everything I need to know! Understood?"

He nodded and I dropped him to the ground. He clung to his broken leg. "Alright, alright. Just don't hurt me." His breath smelled like death and he looked the part—sickly and frail and reeking of body odor.

"What do you know about Lester Burton?"

"Speak," I demanded.

"I just know that he is fulfilling his aging father's dream. That is all he wants to do, to please his old man."

Gonzo shook his head. "Ardet, you know more then that."

Just then, a black device was thrown towards us, and it exploded. We were hurled into the air and then we tumbled down the jagged, icy slope.

As Gonzo and I recovered from the attack, I ran back up to find Ardet. I found him under the snow. I reached for him and picked him up, only to discover that it was only his head.

I dropped his head in disgust and ran my hand through the snow, wiping his blood off.

"What do we do now, Zee?" Gonzo asked.

I thought for a moment and wondered how much things had changed in thirty years. "Does the world still have libraries?"

Gonzo laughed and then waved a hand. "I don't mean to laugh at you, man. I just sometimes forget that you've been in a coma all these years. Yeah, man, we still have libraries. What do you want to look up?"

"We need to know more about our enemies. We need to know what we're up against. *I* need to know what we're up against."

"Well we can just use the internet and figure that out."

I frowned. "The *what?*"

After we gathered ourselves from the loss, we went to the library. I was still shaken up from what had happened just three hours ago.

Ardet had been killed, blown apart by a grenade. Someone didn't want him talking, least of all to us. Now, more than ever, I knew that I had to find out what was going on.

Gonzo sat and I stood behind the oak chair, overlooking the computer. I was amazed at how much technology had changed in thirty years. These computers were sleek and tiny and didn't require the use of a mouse. All you had to do was touch the screen to get things to work.

They seemed to be made by a fruit company, but I didn't see the irony in naming a device after an apple.

Gonzo tried to show me how to work the internet, but now wasn't the time to try to teach me. He easily navigated the sites and pulled up something called 'Google' and searched for Lester Burton.

Several of the searches came up with articles on his deeds— mostly he was linked to acts of terrorism. Among most reports was a reference to 'The Shadow' but still no one dove into exactly what it was. Maybe no one really knew the scope of the organization, at least not on Earth.

We moved our search to the world's most wanted criminals. At number fifty was Lester Dwayne Burton. At number thirty-nine was Ardettinay Salvis-Slay. Dr. Burton was currently listed at number fifteen.

"Look up their personal files, Gonzo. Can you hack into any of the government databases or something?"

Gonzo went to work on hacking through the databases and networks, disabling firewalls and accessing the government documents. "Alright. Give me a few more seconds and I'll be able to access the documents... Almost there." Gonzo bit his lip as he focused. "Now we're talking," He pulled up the first document and quickly scrolled through the document until he found something useful.

"Dr. Henry Otoowa Burton... 1984|87 went on a large-scale killing spree after his second project "Caleb" was shut down by the government. This document was recorded in Moscow, Russia."

"What else does it say?" I asked, eager to learn more.

"Okay." Gonzo tapped the screen and scrolled down. "In 1990 he put a teenager in a coma during a failed black ops experiment."

"They're talking about me," I said, looking over Gonzo's shoulder as I read the paragraph that discussed my case. "So, the whole time they knew I was a teenager?"

"Looks like they didn't care," Gonzo replied. "They needed a guinea pig. But you weren't the only minor experimented on."

I was going to ask him what he meant but shook my head. I didn't really want to know the extent of the agency's treachery.

"In 1992, he resurfaced after breaking out of a highly sophisticated prison. He infiltrated several prestigious government bases and stole classified documents. Thereafter, he was charged with several counts of rape, treason, conspiracy, and aggravated assault upon his capture in late 1992....In the spring of 1993, he was extradited to the U.S. to answer for his crimes but broke out of a supermax prison...How he managed to do so is classified." Gonzo exhaled sharply and ran a hand through his hair. "This is one twisted dude. The United Nations have been trying to locate him ever since."

"Is there any recent information on him, anything within the last six months or so?" I began to pace, my thoughts racing. "There has to be something."

Gonzo stroked the screen's virtual keyboard and shook his head again. "He seems to have gone off the grid."

"Who's next?"

"Ardettinay Salvis-Slay aka Ardet, bka Jonathan. In 1998 he was captured and imprisoned for murder in the second degree. Sometime in April of 1999, he escaped and went on a killing spree that lasted until 2002. He killed over seventy woman, thirty-eight men, and seventeen children. When he was captured in November of 2002, he was sentenced to death by guillotine—ouch—but managed to escape after a trio of powers manifested."

"Wait, so he only received powers eighteen years ago?"

Gonzo frowned. "That doesn't make any sense. Most super humans receive their powers at the onset of puberty. I mean, sure some people's powers are latent, but Ardet was a full-grown man by that time."

I nodded and gestured with my hand as I started to pace. "Keep reading."

"Upon being captured in 2005, Ardet was taken to an undisclosed underground base. By August of 2006 he was the prime subject of a government project, code named 'H.A.D.I.' The terms of this agreement simply specify that Ardet agreed to become the subject of this project in lieu of a death sentence. At the conclusion of the project, Ardet discovered that the bargain had not been upheld, and was still sentenced to death. Thus, he used his powers to overpower agents, guards, and even other super humans that had been tasked with guarding him and broke out of prison in February of 2010. He's been on the run since then."

I shook my head. What was the government thinking letting known criminals run projects and be subjects of them? I didn't understand it whatsoever, however, none of that mattered now. It was all in the past, and only the present mattered. Ardet had been on the loose for ten years, and he'd been the first person to find me when I'd come out of my coma.

Sometime during the ten years he'd been free, he'd teamed up with Burton, perhaps even before then. Ardet had been Burton's apprentice but had died at the hands of an assassin.

But now, things had only grown more complicated since Lester—Burton's son—had appeared.

I shook my head again and attempted to pry myself from my thoughts. "Lester Dwayne Burton... let's have a look shall we?"

The full picture was beginning to form, but it wasn't clear yet.

Why were they all after me?

What had I done that had earned me a spot on their hit list? *I* wanted Burton dead, it shouldn't have been the other way around…right?

Gonzo stroked the virtual keyboard and accessed a file on Lester. "In 1987, at the age of twelve, he joined his father's new order and Russia-based mafia. In 1990 he was tried for murder and found guilty. In 1994 he was broken out of jail during a huge jailbreak, most likely at the hands of his father's followers. From 1996-2001 he murdered sixty-four major drug lords, seizing power from each of their organizations..."

"This is chaotic. I still don't understand how Burton was able to get a position in the agency. This doesn't add up. Why would Secret Agency XII employ a mad man like Burton?" I couldn't fathom the sheer complexity of it all.

"Do you think your coma was planned?" Gonzo asked. "Sure, the agency was a black ops division, but maybe there's something else there. Who knows, maybe it was even a front. Maybe you were working for the bad guys."

A chill ran down my spine. "That isn't possible. I saw military officials and—"

"Who said military leaders couldn't be crooked?" asked Gonzo.

Gonzo had a point. "I only knew what I was supposed to know. Nothing else, nothing more...And I was a kid, so I didn't ask questions. I was young...and naïve."

"You shouldn't have even been there," Gonzo said, closing the files and hiding his digital footprint as he did so. Gonzo might've seemed ditzy at times, but he was quite bright.

"So what now, boss man?" Gonzo asked as we left the library.

"We should look for Mona. I just don't know where to start."

Out of nowhere, I heard a voice inside my head. It was as though the voice was calling out to me. I stopped walking and my eyes grew unfocused as I turned my focus inward to identify the voice in my head.

"What is it, Zee?"

I shushed him and closed my eyes. The voice seemed distant at first, as though it were an echo. Then, the voice grew louder and louder, sounding truer and truer. Suddenly, my mind hummed with clarity.

Help, help! screamed a female voice in my mind.

My eyes flew open! It was **MONA**! I gasped. I could hear her in my mind! Did I possess the ability of telepathy, too?!

Mona, is that you? I thought back.

Zedo! I didn't know if this would work, but I'm glad to hear YOU! Please, hurry!

Where are you, Mona? We'll come get you!

She sounded exhausted, but even her thought-voice sounded strained and she was panting, as if her mind was just as exhausted as her body. *Zedo, I've been taken to New Hampshire! I-I don't know exactly where but—*

"New Hampshire!" I exclaimed out loud.

Gonzo looked at me and frowned. "What are you talking about?"

I ignored him and closed my eyes again, focusing on the telepathic link between Mona and me.

Zedo, please, I'm scared! Help me! They're coming!

The link suddenly ended and I felt a jolt of pain on my cheek and jerked to the side. I'd been slapped, but Gonzo hadn't moved. My eyes grew wide. Whoever had Mona had slapped her and I'd felt the effect of it, too.

Clearly a telepathic connection was stronger than I'd imagined. But how was Mona able to contact me? We were nowhere near New Hampshire! If telepathy was being added to my roster of powers, it shouldn't have manifested this strongly. I was suddenly scared of myself.

I possessed elemental manipulation, atmokinesis, and now telepathy! My first power was already stronger than most folks' abilities and when I realized I could control the weather, too, that had been a surprise. But now I was able to hear peoples' thoughts, too? I was overwhelmed.

I looked at Gonzo and wet my lips. "New Hampshire," I said. "She's in New Hampshire."

His eyes grew wide with shock. "How do you know that?" And so I told him. He laughed aloud when I finished. "Zedo, that is *amazing*! Do you know what this means?" I shrugged and my face twisted into an expression of utter confusion. "Zedo, telepathy is just what we need right now! A super human with telepathy can psychically perceive the thoughts of others, but you already knew that. I'm just amazed that you could hear her at this distance. In addition, one can psychically perceive the presence and location of subjects by tracking their minds, at will."

"So you're saying I should be able find her through her thoughts?" He nodded. "But I don't know how."

"Focus, man." He looked around the parking lot. The day was growing late. The library would be closing soon. "Look, let's go back in until you can pick up her trail. There's no better place for peace and quiet than a library."

We headed back inside and found a quiet corner to sit in. I closed my eyes and Gonzo tried to help me focus. I reached out with my mind and thought of Mona, while whispering her name aloud.

Zedo? She finally thought back.

I opened my eyes. "I hear her!"

Gonzo inched closer to me. "Now follow her!"

I closed my eyes again; it seemed to be the only way I could use my power. If I physically closed my eyes I could shut out the outside world and focus internally. Hopefully one day that would change.

Mona, we're coming.

Hurry, Zedo!

We headed outdoors and Mona's thoughts began to form a trail in my mind. It was like I could see a mental map with Mona's thoughts lighting the way.

In my mind's eye I saw a map of the United States. It seemed to float amongst a dark abyss.

As I closed my eyes tighter Mona's thoughts linked with mine and created a path outlined in red that headed up the east coast leading to New Hampshire.

As I followed the trail that Mona had telepathically left for me, I called on my senses; all five had been amplified since I'd awakened from my coma and realized I was a super human.

Hours later, we pulled up to the gate of a seemingly abandoned warehouse.

"She's here, somewhere," I told Gonzo. He pulled our transportation away from the gate and turned around. "What are you doing?"

"We can't just park here and knock on the door. They'll know who we are. We need to go in stealthy."

"How Gonzo?"

He grinned. "We'll land on the roof."

And sure enough, Gonzo pulled the stolen vehicle we'd 'borrowed' into an alley near another abandoned building and we took to the sky.

Gonzo and I flew upward until we merged with the clouds and then came down on the roof of the warehouse I'd identified.

"They've left the roof unguarded," Gonzo said, ducking down.

"Or they pulled back when we pulled up to the gate," I told him. Why hadn't we stopped sooner?

I looked for a roof access and found an iron door. It had been left wide open. Someone had *definitely* been on the roof. Gonzo and I slowly descended the stairs and entered the warehouse.

The building was dark and dusty and I could hear the skittering of tiny feet on the concrete floor—probably rats or some other vermin. I stretched out with my mind but detected no other thoughts.

Mona? I telepathically called out, but no answer came.

"Let's split up," I said. "I don't think anyone's here."

And sure enough, after we searched the warehouse top to bottom, it was empty. The warehouse was utterly empty.

However, we found blood on the floor in a central area on the bottom level.

I found a shredded piece of Mona's clothing nearby. "They tortured her," I said aloud, but not to Gonzo…just to myself, acknowledging the blood.

"But why?" Gonzo asked, approaching me. "It doesn't make sense. She doesn't know anything…really, none of us do."

I ignored his question and posed one of my own. "If I felt that someone was about to come after me, what would I do?"

"If it was me, I'd leave the city," Gonzo answered. "Find another hideout…or return to the main base."

"You're a genius!" I headed towards the exit. "They couldn't have gotten far! Her blood is still fresh!"

I rushed back to our stolen ride, Gonzo right behind me.

"Maybe they figured out that she'd telepathically contacted you? Maybe they knew we were on the way?"

I ignored him again as we climbed into the car. Gonzo slammed the gear into reverse, spun the car, shifted into drive, and zoomed off. We quickly made our way to the nearest main road and headed towards the city limits and sure enough, there they were: two black SUVs.

I closed my eyes and focused on accessing my telepathic gifts. *Mona,* I called out.

I caught sight of someone in the backseat of the closest SUV moving in their seat. I squinted and realized it was Mona! The drivers of the black trucks sped up.

Gonzo sped up and slammed into the rear of the SUV. I rolled down my window and climbed out of it. I called the air to me and flew towards the lead vehicle. In mid-air, I gestured with my hand and forced the wind to slam into the side of the first vehicle. The brute force of the hit slammed into the vehicle and flipped it over several times.

The second vehicle slammed on its brakes and lost traction, flipping horizontally on its side until it came to stop on its roof.

As the SUV came to a halt, Gonzo stopped his vehicle and rushed to yank open the driver's side door. He pulled the driver from the wreckage and slammed his fist into his face, knocking him unconscious.

I landed and hurled a si' beam at another door. I reached into the SUV and found that the other three lackeys in the car were dead.

Mona squirmed against her constraints and I reached for her. I pulled Mona from the car and removed the gag over her mouth.

"Thank God it's you, Zedo!" she exclaimed as I freed her hands. I freed Mona Lisa-Flynn! *I* did!

She wrapped her arms around me and squeezed tight. I wrapped my arms around her and felt my heart swell.

"What took you so long?" she asked as we pulled apart.

I chuckled and wiped the sweat from my brow.

Gonzo moved towards us and hugged Mona. "Are you okay?"

She nodded, growing teary-eyed.

"Let's go," I said and moved towards the car that now looked worse for wear. "Were those Lester's men, Mona?"

Gonzo and I opened the doors to the car and were about to get in when we noticed Mona wasn't with us.

We turned to see a red faced and teary-eyed Mona. She had cuts and bruises and looked disheveled, but I couldn't figure out what was wrong.

"Are you hurt?" I asked as I moved closer to her.

"What's wrong?" Gonzo asked.

She didn't answer.

"What's wrong? You can tell us," I said, moving closer to her. I reached out to touch her and she jerked away.

"Just get me to the hospital," she said, and refused to meet my gaze. She moved past us and opened a car door, sliding into the backseat.

I watched her go and suddenly sensed pain. Tears flowed down her cheeks. Just then, my telepathy activated itself on its own and I realized that it was worse than that. She felt violated...she *had been* violated.

I cringed and felt a shudder run down my spine. They'd raped her.

Suddenly, Mona looked up and locked eyes with me through the windshield. "Get out of my head, Jeta!" she yelled aloud and I jumped.

Gonzo looked at me. "What did you do?"

"I didn't try to! I can't control it all the way, yet."

"Never read someone's mind without their permission!" He moved past me and got in the car, cranking it.

"I didn't mean to!" I climbed into the passenger's seat. I turned in my seat to glance at Mona. She looked away. "Honestly, Mona, I didn't mean to pry. It was an accident. I—"

"Just shut it, Jeta," she said, her voice cold. "Gonzo, get me to the nearest hospital, **now**."

Gonzo nodded and pulled away from the scene, leaving the wreckage and corpses on the road.

I faced front and gazed out the window. I couldn't imagine what she was going through. I'd never been kissed—that I could remember—let alone had sex. I was a virgin in every sense. I couldn't imagine being forced to have sex with a stranger, let alone raped as violently as it seemed she'd been.

Just from the brief thoughts and memories I'd seen and heard…she'd been traumatized.

I tried to force the thoughts aside as Gonzo drove onward. We rode in silence for nearly an hour until Gonzo pulled up at an emergency room entrance.

Mona climbed out of the car before Gonzo came to a complete stop and headed inside without waiting for us.

"Maybe we should ditch the car, too?" he said. "It's bound to be linked to those SUVs once someone comes across them."

I nodded, not sure what I should say. I felt bad for invading Mona's privacy, but it was honestly an accident. I was still learning to control my powers. I hadn't had proper training like they had.

Mona was checked out, and I couldn't help but feel sorry for her. She didn't want to be around us and so Gonzo and I simply waited in the waiting room until she was admitted into the hospital. At that time a nurse came to retrieve Gonzo and I. Mona had requested our presence.

The nurse had told us that she didn't want to be left alone in her room.

Finally, a little after midnight, as Mona lay in her hospital bed—her back to us—she parted her lips and spoke. "Thanks for finding me," she whispered.

Gonzo and I looked at each other, unsure of what she'd said until she repeated herself in a stronger voice.

She rolled over in bed and eyed both of us from where we sat in our chairs at her bedside. "Thank you for killing those bastards, too."

"You're part of the team," Gonzo said. "We wouldn't leave you hanging."

She grinned, but it didn't reach her eyes. She was sad...and there was no hiding it.

I apologized again and she waved the comment off. "I just want to rest right now." And with that, she rolled over and fell asleep.

Three days later, we were heading to Vermont. Mona didn't want to discuss what had happened to her, and all we could do was offer our support.

Along the way, we decided to stop at a roadside motel for a good night's sleep. I was in desperate need of a shower. Mona booked three rooms on a credit card and then handed me a room key. Without another word, she moved past us and headed into her room.

I looked at Gonzo and he shrugged. We headed towards our rooms and I excused myself as I almost bumped into a housekeeper that was coming out of a room.

"So, do you want to grab a bite to eat, Gonzo?" I asked. "I'm starving." When he didn't reply immediately, I looked over my shoulder and caught sight of Gonzo flirting with the young housekeeper. She blushed and swatted at his hand playfully. He reached out with a hand and stroked her unkempt hair, grinning at her.

I sighed. "Gonzo?"

He looked up from the woman's face and waved me off. "I'll catch up with you later." He looked at her name bag. "Marisol is going to give me a tour of this room."

"How about a tour of *your* room?" she asked, smiling.

"That works for me." Gonzo grabbed her hand and led her down the hall to the room next to mine. I shook my head and slid the hotel key into the slot.

I moved into the room and began to strip. I inhaled sharply and took in the sweet scent of the room. I was surprised that the room smelled pleasant…it was a motel after all.

I wish I had a clean set of clothes. But instead, I grabbed a bar of soap, moved to the bathroom sink and filled it. I removed the stinking, sweat-encrusted clothing and undergarments that had virtually stuck to my body after days on the road. Then, I plunged the clothes into the sink and began to scrub them.

The water soon turned murky. I allowed the water to drain from the sink then filled it again to rinse the clothes. Afterwards, I hung the wet clothes in the room's closet so they could air dry. That would have to do.

I moved my naked body back into the bathroom and turned the shower's dial until it could turn no more. I moved into the shower and the hot water caressed my skin. I exhaled in pleasure and began to remove the caked sweat and grime from my skin.

Through the thin wall, I could hear a man's—Gonzo's—voice and then water gurgling as he turned on his own bathroom faucet, as if to draw a bath or shower. Then I heard the maid giggling. My eyes grew wide! These walls really were thin.

I scrubbed under my arms and then rinsed my armpits; the smell grew more pleasant. I then leaned closer to the wall, water drumming down on me as I now stood directly under the shower head. I tried to concentrate on the sound, but it was hard to hear. Then, I heard more giggling and Gonzo laughed aloud and then there was a loud splash…and another. As if two bodies were in the bathtub instead of one.

There was a silence for a while. I turned off my shower and began to dry myself off. Suddenly, I heard more splashing, gasps, kissing sounds and laughter. I flushed as I realized I was eavesdropping a little too hard. I moved the towel over my hair to dry it and left the bathroom as I heard a series of sharp moans, first from the maid and then from Gonzo.

My eyes grew wide and I rushed into the bedroom. They were having *SEX* in the tub! I just couldn't believe it. But then, a moment later, I was laughing. After all we'd been through since we'd created this team, I guess Gonzo needed to blow off steam just like anybody else.

I wondered what that was like. I'd never had sex, let alone kissed a girl.

But then again, I couldn't help but wonder why Gonzo was having sex. I mean, how could he, after what had happened to

Mona? Our friend had been raped, and here he was hooking up with some maid he didn't even know. We had enough problems. We needed to concentrate on our plan. We needed to concentrate on finding Dr. Henry Otoowa Burton. We needed to think ahead.

Maybe it just bothered me because Gonzo was the first real friend I'd had since we'd been brought together. Maybe I was just jealous that he was having sex and I didn't even know what that was like. It was none of my business though, right?

I moved to check and see if my clothes were dry and then realized that I controlled the elements. I grinned to myself and placed a hand on my wet shirt and jeans. I focused and pulled the water droplets from the clothes and gestured towards the bathroom. The water drained from the clothes and I forced it into the bathroom sink. Smiling at myself, I moved on to my undergarments and repeated the process.

I touched my clothes. They were dry, not warm, but at least they were dry. I pulled on my clothes and headed to the door to search for food. As I opened the door I heard the faint sound of groaning bedsprings.

So, they moved from the tub to the bed, I thought to myself. I closed the door and headed down the hall to Mona's room. Maybe she'd want some food, too.

Twenty minutes later, Mona and I sat at a table in the diner across the street from the motel, waiting on our food to arrive. We made light conversation about the weather and a few other mindless topics. But soon, we grew quiet and it felt awkward. I sighed, unable to avoid the elephant in the room.

"Mona…are you alright?"

She sighed and made a shooing motion with her hand. "Leave it alone, Zedo."

"I'm sorry…I just wanted to make sure that you were okay. I'm worried about you."

She smiled sadly at me. "I appreciate the concern, but I really don't want to talk about it."

Just then, Gonzo slid into the booth next to me. "What did I miss?" he asked, seconds before he grabbed Mona's cup and took a sip of her Pepsi. Mona cocked her head and looked at him, her eyes squinting in confusion.

"Welcome back," I said, trying to avoid the tension that was sure to follow. "We can plan the next move while we eat. We're out of here first thing in the morning."

Just then, a waitress brought our food. Gonzo reached for one of my fries and I swatted his hand away. Mona grinned.

"I have contacts in Vermont. We could head to their location, lay low for a while, and maybe you could get some training in, Zedo."

I looked at him. "What do you mean?"

"As a teen, I spent time at the Haszeem Institute of Technology and Science—H.I.T.S—a training facility that not only teaches super human youth how to control their powers, but also teaches them applied sciences. I spent most of my teens there before I enlisted in the agency and became a spy."

I shrugged. "I don't see why not. Sounds like a pretty cool place."

The next morning, we hit the road and headed to Vermont. Once we arrived at the institute, my mouth dropped in awe. According to Gonzo, this place had taught him about computers and information technology and had set him up for a career in I.T. This place had also taught him how to control his energy blasts and how to fly. His parents had sent him here to find his place in a world that was still hesitant about people with powers and Gonzo had blossomed into the person he was today.

He was the first of our little team to receive his powers naturally and without enhancements.

I gazed in growing wonder at this great campus, vaster and more splendid than Gonzo had described. It was simply beautiful. The buildings were made of glass and designed in such complex ways that it must've taken years to construct. There had to be about twenty or so buildings that I could see.

We arrived at a large golden gate, where guards stood dressed in grey robes. In their hands were glowing rods.

"Who are they?" I asked.

"They're Lightway, members of a paramilitary organization of super humans," Gonzo replied, grinning. "They've pledged their lives to protect others and only use their abilities for the greater good."

"So, they protect the school?" I asked.

"They protect the world," Mona told me. I looked at her.

Just then, Gonzo pulled up next to one of the guards and rolled down the window. "Hi, my name is Gonzo Daniels. I used to be a student here."

The guard was an African American man with hazel eyes and broad shoulders. He seemed very tall and powerful. He looked at Gonzo and then peered into the car at Mona and myself. "Who are they?" he asked, his voice deep and rich.

"They're with me," Gonzo replied. "They're both super humans, too."

"It's okay, Lee," said the second guard—a female with brunette hair—as she moved towards the car. "I know this trouble maker," she said, grinning at Gonzo.

I suddenly wondered if he'd slept with her, too.

The guard named Lee looked at her and nodded. "You'll vouch for him then?"

She nodded and moved to the driver's side. "It's been a long time, Gonzo."

"Indeed, it has, Robyn."

"Professor JR and Dr. Jerome will be pleased to know you're back."

Gonzo waved her words aside. "I'm not back, Robyn. Just passing through."

She nodded and gestured at the other three guards at the gate. "Let them through." The other guards and Lee moved to comply.

Gonzo nodded at the woman named Robyn and drove through the gate. We drove down a winding road and passed several glass structures. Most of the buildings were shaped like letters. I realized that some were dorms and others were halls that housed classrooms.

"This place is *amazing*!" I exclaimed.

Gonzo chuckled. "I loved it here. Would've turned out differently if I hadn't been a student here. The agency changed me, but this place taught me how to hold onto my humanity."

Students roamed the grounds, moving between classes. It all looked so normal. Clearly, I had a lot to learn about people like me…super humans. I assumed we were feared by the world, but I guess not.

There was so much I didn't know. Maybe after I killed Burton, I could find happiness in learning more about who I was…and maybe try to build a life for myself. After all of this was done, maybe I'd go back to school. Maybe I'd become something more than a government experiment.

Already it seemed that word of Gonzo's return had reached the ears of those who knew him because as we pulled up to the administration building, a group of people were already standing on the steps waiting to receive us.

A man of about fifty, dressed in business casual clothes and a lab coat smiled broadly and extended his arms. I assumed this was

Dr. Jerome. He was about 5'9'' with salt and pepper hair cut close to his scalp. Beside him stood a matronly woman with hair pulled back in a bun. She wore a pale blue ankle length dress and pearls hung about her neck. Behind them stood about ten or twelve others.

Gonzo parked the car right out front and climbed out of the car, beaming. Mona and I exited soon after but he was already in the embrace of the man. Others moved close to welcome Gonzo.

As Mona and I approached the steps, Gonzo turned to us. "I'd like to introduce you to my friends." He gestured. "Mona Lisa-Flynn and Zedo Jeta, I'd like to introduce you to Dr. Jerome and Professor JR."

"Janice Rogers," the woman said, introducing herself. "But call me Janice, dears," She grinned at us as she pulled Mona into a hug then moved to me. I shook the doctor's hand and then Mona did as well. "My husband and I run the facility," she added.

"Why, yes, we do," said Dr. Jerome. He clasped a hand on Gonzo's shoulder. "Gonzo was one of our brightest pupils."

Mona looked at the professor. "So you kept your maiden name, good for you."

Janice laughed. "Oh, no, dearie. My husband just doesn't use his family name. He prefers for the children to call him by his first name."

"But I won't let them forget I'm a doctor," he said. He clapped his hands together. "Come, come, let's get inside, shall we?"

The doctor, professor, and students welcomed us with open arms to H.I.T.S. They gave us a tour of the grounds and showed us old footage of Gonzo during a training session when he was fifteen.

After the tour, we sat down for dinner at the Rogers's personal home on the grounds.

"So what brings you back to the institute, Gonzo?" Janice asked.

"Just passing through. We're in the middle of a mission." He took another bite of food into his mouth and chewed.

"Well, you three should get a decent night's sleep."

Of course, we stayed. We needed someplace to crash and take a breather from our task.

That night, Gonzo knocked on the door of the cramped dorm room I was staying in. "I'm going down to see Dr. Jerome. Would you like to join me?"

Dr. Jerome had once been Gonzo's mentor, that much was clear. But I think it was more than that. I think Gonzo saw the doctor as a father figure.

"No thanks. Go on without me," I replied.

"You sure? I thought you might want to train."

"I'm beat, but go, enjoy yourself. Have a good time, Gonzo."

"What are you going to do?"

"I might go down to the main gate and speak with those Lightway. They seemed pretty interesting."

He chuckled. "I don't think they'd be too keen to hear about our mission, Zee. Revenge really isn't their thing."

I nodded, understanding immediately.

And with that, he disappeared.

My mind was racing. This place was alive and filled with super humans. I wondered what the rest of the country was like. Were there other places like this? Maybe art institutes or something? Were super humans at large accepted? Were they ostracized?

There was so much I needed to learn—wanted to learn. I was craving knowledge. Life was so much bigger then just my need for revenge against Burton.

A moment later, there was a knock on my door. I was pulled from my thoughts and I climbed out of the twin sized bed. I opened the door and there stood Mona. I was kind of shocked to see her.

She smiled at me. "Hey, handsome. Are you hungry?"

I grinned and my heart fluttered. She called me '*handsome.*' "Sure," I said. She motioned me to follow her and we made our way to the dining hall within the dorm. I was surprised to find it full of students, especially at this late hour. We grabbed some food and I paid for it with a few bills from a wallet Mona had given me months ago. She grinned, noting that I still had a bunch of cash left over— she'd given me a few hundred dollars shortly after we'd met. She said she'd figured I'd need some money to get started.

We took a seat at a table near a window and dug into our meal.

After a moment of eating in silence, Mona looked at me. "I've really enjoyed being here," she said after swallowing a bite of food. "It's so peaceful here. I haven't been this at ease in a long time."

I nodded, understanding completely. "Everyone seems comfortable. These kids are just like us, but they feel safe."

"They don't know treachery and espionage or military experiments."

I nodded, agreeing with her. "They get to be normal teenagers," I added and then took a sip of water. I suddenly envied all of the kids around us. "I wonder what that's like...to be normal."

She bit her lower lip, as if hesitant to speak. I looked at her, sensing she wanted to say something.

"It's okay, Mona. You can talk to me. What is it?"

"You know...I was thinking. We don't *have* to do this. We can stop here."

My eyes grew wide with shock. "What? Are you kidding me?"

She held up her hands in mock surrender. "Just hear me out, Zedo. We're chasing Burton and he knows we're coming after him. But what if we stop? What if we just let it be? I'm starting to think that getting revenge isn't necessary anymore."

"Mona, Burton had people kidnap you. Burton put me in a coma! He took my life from me. You don't have to come with me. Gonzo doesn't either, but *I* need this." Suddenly, I felt my anger get the best of me and hot tears stung my eyes. "I have to kill Burton, Mona! I have to!"

Suddenly, eyes were on us in the dining hall. The room had grown eerily silent. Mona looked around, slightly embarrassed.

I exhaled sharply and lowered my voice. "I have to do this, Mona...I have to. I'll never be free of him otherwise. He took thirty years from me...I have to take his life."

"But you're *alive*, Zedo." She took my hand and I looked at it, surprised. She intertwined our fingers and I moved my eyes from our hands to her face. "You survived, and now you get to pick up the pieces. You can't get those years back, but you've been given a second chance to live. So *LIVE*, Zee. You can make new memories, do something different this time...I joined this team because I needed to seek redemption, but...I'm starting to have a change of heart." She shook her head and I swallowed hard. She slowly removed her hand and stood up from the table. "I'm still a member of this team. I made a vow, but I'm just letting you know, we don't have to do this anymore. We can change our minds. *You* can change your mind."

And with that, she turned to walk away, leaving me alone with my food and my thoughts.

After she left, I sat at the table, pushing food around my plate. I suddenly felt self-conscious. I could feel people's eyes on me and my telepathy told me that they were wondering if I was crazy or something.

Sure enough, I rose from my chair. It skidded back and drew more looks. I lowered my head and left the room as quickly as I could, murmurs filling the air as I passed tables.

I headed back to my room and threw myself onto the bed.

Eventually, sleep claimed me, though sometimes I suffered from insomnia. I was often scared to sleep, it reminded me too much of being in a coma.

However, after today, I was exhausted and sleep easily claimed me. Fortunately, I slept soundly until…I began to dream…

I felt like a fly on a wall. It felt like I was viewing things from far away. All around me people hustled and bustled in a corridor. I felt myself following them, but I wasn't in my body. It felt like I was watching something that had already happened, or would happen…Maybe it was happening now? I couldn't tell.

As I moved with the flow of traffic, I felt myself move down a corridor. Suddenly, I came near a window. I gazed out and found that the Earth hung far below me.

How could Earth be below me?? Was I on a ship?

Just then, I realized that the people hustling around the corridor weren't just normal people, they were officers. I was aboard a vessel. I noticed that a man with a white uniform was coming my way. He wore medals on his uniform and was in the dress of an admiral. His face was twisted in a frown, as though he were concentrating on something.

"Get out of the way!" he yelled. As he drew closer to where my 'dream body' felt it was, he waved a hand around. "Move, move!" Others in the corridor moved and he shifted from a brisk walk to a trot.

Something was wrong. I had to follow him. My 'dream body' trailed him and we rushed into a large room that I realized was the bridge.

"I'm here, my lord," the admiral said, bowing before a metal-like chair that vaguely resembled a throne. When the admiral rose to his feet, he wiped beads of sweat from his forehead. At the admiral's side stood Lester Burton! His head was lowered as he cowered before whoever sat in the throne chair, which was most likely the commander's chair.

I turned my 'dream eyes' towards the throne and strained. The person in the chair was dressed in a dark cloak with the hood pulled down, casting his face in shadow. I knew it was a man because he had a mustache that was filled with mingle grey hair.

"What took you so long?" Lester said, turning his head to take in the admiral, but he quickly dropped his gaze as he realized he stood before the throne.

"I'm sorry, my lord. I was delayed. I'd only just been notified that you were aboard The Maverick ten minutes ago."

"The lord arrived eleven minutes ago," Lester informed him. "He teleported aboard the ship and—"

"Silence!" boomed the man on the throne. My 'dream eyes' suddenly grew wide as I immediately recognized that voice. It was BURTON!

Burton rose to his feet, his face still hidden by the shadow cast by the hood. His cloak was black and his sleeves were billowy.

Wait, Lester said that he'd teleported aboard?? Burton had POWERS?! I wondered what else he could do besides move instantaneously from one place to another without physically occupying the space in between.

Burton descended the stairs that led to his throne and Lester and the admiral stood their full height and moved aside so he could pass between them. Burton moved to the center of the room, with Lester on his right and the admiral on his left.

The bridge was circular, with bright monitors glowing and data creeping across the screens as dozens of officers worked. Holographic monitors projected images in midair. Burton moved towards the largest of these displays which currently displayed an image of the Earth in its fullness.

Burton raised a hand, pointing at the planet. "Where is he now?" A chill ran down my spine as I realized he was talking about **me***.*

Lester glanced at the admiral, who raised his eyebrows—he didn't know. Lester rolled his eyes and took a step closer to Burton. "He's in Vermont." Lester looked over his shoulder at an officer at a nearby terminal. "Magnify." The officer nodded and the holographic projection of the Earth shifted and grew more detailed as it zoomed it—zeroing in on the state of Vermont. Lester exhaled and rolled his eyes. "Isolate our target, you idiot!" The officer stroked a few keys and the image shifted again. "Magnify!"

"Magnifying, sir," the officer said, his voice trembling.

Now the image showed an aerial view of the Haszeem Institute of Technology and Science. "He's here, my lord," Lester said. "He's at H.I.T.S."

"At least it isn't a Lightway training academy," said the admiral.

Lester turned and glared at him. The admiral shrugged. "H.I.T.S. is guarded by Lightway, but it isn't a stronghold of our enemies. We've been tracking Jeta and his friends, Father. What would you have us to do?"

"Draw him out," said Burton. "I believe it's time for another test."

The admiral cleared his throat and took a step forward. "My lord, what is our goal here? Why are we tracking this kid?"

Lester and every person on the bridge suddenly stopped and stared at the admiral like he was insane, which he obviously was. The eerie silence enveloped the admiral and he swallowed hard.

Burton turned to face him and took a step closer—the admiral took a step back. "**Don't** question me," said Burton, his voice cold. The admiral swallowed hard. "Do you understand?" The admiral nodded. "Leave me."

The admiral turned and headed towards the exit. Burton stretched out a hand and flames leapt from his palm, consumed the admiral, and burned him alive. Lester recoiled from the flames. The admiral's screams filled the air and several droids that stood sentry near the doors moved towards the burning body.

The admiral collapsed to the floor, dead. *His body began to turn to ash.*

"Get his body out of here!" Lester ordered. He pointed at officers nearby. "Get back to work!"

The officers around the bridge got back to work.

Lester turned back towards Burton. "I will draw him out, Father."

"Yes," said Burton, turning away from Lester and gazing out the massive viewport, taking in the view of the Earth. "Zedo is destined for greatness...we must put him on the right path."

Lester's jaw clenched. "Yes, you've said that before, Father. I've lived in his shadow for years."

Burton held up a hand to silence him. "Leave me, boy," he spat. "Bore someone else with your insecurities."

Lester recoiled at the retort, bowed, and turned to leave. He stepped over the ashes of the admiral as he fled the bridge.

Chapter 12:

Burton's Letter

CRThBO

I heard a scream and was roused from my sleep. My heart hammered against my ribs. What kind of dream had that been? Who'd screamed?

Then, as I heard footsteps run past my door, I realized that the scream hadn't come from my dream, but from the here and now.

"*Mona*," I said, my eyes growing wide. I tried to slow my heart rate, but to no avail.

I jumped out of bed, pulled my clothes on, and hurried to Mona's room.

Gonzo was already there as well as others who hung in their doorways trying to see what all the racket was about.

Dr. Jerome and Professor JR entered the corridor, wrapped in robes.

"What's going on?" asked the doctor as the professor tried to get students to move back, giving us space.

Mona turned to face us, a hand pressed to her mouth.

In her hand was a blue envelope. "It's a letter..." she said. She turned towards me and I took it from her hands as her lips parted. "It's from Burton," she added.

Gonzo sucked in a breath.

I swallowed hard as my hand ran across the envelope. It read *'From Burton With Love'* across the front.

Dear Zedo Jeta and Company,

My father and I have grown tired of your games. We found the bodies of our henchmen on the road, left for buzzards to consume their corpses. I hope you won't mind yours being done the same. We have a special treat waiting for you three.

Yours truly,
Lester Burton

"The letter was nailed to the door with this knife," Mona said.

She handed me the knife. I looked at Gonzo and nudged my head in the direction of the children gathering in the corridor. Gonzo looked at Professor JR and she understood immediately.

"Alright, children, back to bed," she said, shooing them away. "Everything is alright. Back to bed."

The children began to murmur and shuffle back to their rooms.

Dr. Jerome moved towards us. "Why are you really here?" When I didn't answer he turned to Gonzo. "Tell me the truth."

"We were laying low," Gonzo told him.

Dr. Jerome's lips parted. "What have you gotten yourself into, Gonzo?"

"We should leave," I said.

"How did they know where we were?" Mona asked. I looked away. Now wasn't the time to tell them about my dream. It had felt so real, and maybe it was real.

"It doesn't matter," said Gonzo. "All that matters is that they know we're here. We're not safe. Zedo's right. We should leave."

"What are you running from, son?" asked the doctor, moving closer to Gonzo.

Gonzo looked at Dr. Jerome. "Darkness."

———————————

We took showers and fled into the night, hitting the road. Professor JR had instructed us to leave our vehicle and take something called an 'Uber.' It was something like a cab service.

I didn't know where we were going, but wherever we were headed…it would be far away from here. We'd put everyone at the Institute in danger, and we shouldn't have.

We bid farewell to Professor JR and Dr. Jerome and we were on our way. Mona instructed our driver to head to the airport. There were plenty of cars in the parking garage at the airport that we could steal.

Forty minutes into our trip, I sensed a mind nearing us as thoughts flooded my mind—first hazy and then clearer as the person drew near. I gazed out the back window and realized we were being followed by someone on a motorcycle.

I sensed danger! "Get out, now!" I yelled.

"What?" Mona said, shocked.

"Now," I said, my voice stern.

The three of us hurled ourselves out of the taxicab and rolled onto the concrete. We got out just as the car was being shot at.

Suddenly, the cab came to a screeching halt and the driver jumped out of the car, opening fire.

Gonzo moved his arms about and fired an energy blast that swept our would-be killer off his feet, punching a hole through his chest—killing him almost instantly.

Mona and I jumped to our feet and prepared to attack the person riding the motorcycle that had seemed to appear out of thin air. The person on the motorcycle aimed their gun at us again and opened fire.

I whirled my hand and forced the air to turn the bullets aside. They slammed harmlessly into trees nearby.

"Can't even trust the drivers now," Gonzo said, moving beside us. I looked over my shoulder and caught sight of the driver's smoking corpse.

"I want answers," I said, looking at the cycler as the vehicle neared us. Suddenly, the rider of the motorcycle leapt from the mount and the vehicle slid across the road shooting sparks into the air.

The rider somersaulted in midair and landed—bent low. They wore a leather jumpsuit and it became apparent that it was a woman by the way the jumpsuit accentuated her curves.

As the rider stood, she removed her helmet and revealed a mane of jet-black hair and the features of a woman...rather a young girl. She couldn't have been any older than sixteen.

In three swift moves, the girl had closed in the gap between us. She hurled the helmet at Mona and she took the full force of the hit to her face. Mona howled as she fell backwards and blood gushed from her nose.

Our assailant was fast, that much was certain, and she was talented. Her agility displayed that, if nothing else.

I threw myself forward, lashing out, but she flipped back. As Mona picked herself up off the ground, I threw a punch, and then another, but the assailant dodged.

Gonzo moved to Mona's side.

The woman kicked at me and I jumped back, giving myself distance. However, the next time she kicked, I was ready. I grabbed her leg and Mona jumped over me—kicking our attacker in the back with her heels.

The leather-wearing girl slapped me with her gloved hand and landed. She grabbed her back and glared at Mona then turned her eyes on me, hair cascading over her shoulder.

I pulled the air around us closer and she came flying into my embrace. I grabbed her by the shoulders and squeezed, shaking her as I did so. "Who are you?"

She spat in my face.

I wiped the glob of saliva off my face. "Who are you?" I asked again, enraged by the level of disrespect this girl showed. I drew a hand back and ignited it in flames. The girl's eyes grew wide with shock.

"My name's Tempestt."

I threw her to the ground. "Who sent you?" I asked her. She simply glared at me, her chest heaving in and out. "I won't ask again." I raised my hand and prepared to throw the fire ball at her.

"You already know who," she answered, her voice cold.

"Let's just kill her and get on with it," Mona said as she moved towards us. "Chances are, Burton will send more like her."

Tempestt glared at Mona and I wondered why this little girl had been sent to attack us. She was a teenager. Surely Burton had known she couldn't take us.

"Maybe we should tie her up, beat the crap out of her, and see if she talks," said Mona.

"Bite me," the girl replied. Tempestt leapt to her feet and Mona lashed out, but in a swift move, Tempestt slammed her right fist into Mona's jaw and the left into her rib cage.

Mona fell sideways and I gasped. It had all happened in a matter of seconds.

Mona fell into Gonzo and Tempestt turned to flee.

I suddenly felt energy well up inside of me—hot in my chest—and then it exploded outward as I threw both of my hands forward. Eight lines of flames flowed from my fingers and shot across the space between the girl and me. A split second later, a scream followed in the flames' wake.

Tempestt tucked and rolled, swatting away the flames as they burned through her leather gear. I lifted myself into the air and flew towards her and Gonzo and Mona ran down the road following beneath me.

Tempestt rolled on her back and pulled a gun from her ankle holster and shot me; I gasped and fell from the sky.

Mona caught me, screaming my name. Tempestt jumped into the air and kicked at Gonzo, who was trying to seize her. She knocked him aside.

As she hit the ground, she ran to her customized motorcycle—lifted it off the ground, mounted it, and then rode off.

Gonzo came to my side and inspected my left shoulder, where blood slid down my arm. I only had a flesh wound from the bullet. "You okay?"

I nodded, breathless.

"That little bitch!" exclaimed Mona. She pressed a hand against the wound and I yelled out.

Running over to the car, Gonzo grabbed the man and tossed his dead body aside.

"Hop in, we're going after her," Gonzo said. I looked at Mona and she smiled. We were off.

Gonzo climbed out of the driver side window and I grabbed the steering wheel, surprised that he'd climbed out the window without a word.

Wind whipped Gonzo's hair as he leaned out the driver's side window and fired yellow energy blasts at her back tire. Tempestt swerved but dodged the energy blasts.

Gonzo swore under his breath and dropped back into his seat. He stopped the car and it came to a screeching halt; and we ran.

Gonzo flew over me and went ahead of us. My arm throbbed, but I ran on.

"These heels are killing me," Mona whined.

"Come on," I said, short of breath. Mona threw her right arm forward and hurled ice beams at Tempestt. One beam caught the back tire and Tempestt was thrown from the motorcycle and shrieked.

I hurled flames forward and the fire formed a circle around her.

Gonzo landed in the middle, ahead of me and Mona. "*Tsk, tsk,* tsk," he said, wagging a finger at her. "You've been a bad girl."

Tempestt snarled and attacked him furiously, throwing her fists at him, and then pulling them in to block his kicks.

Mona froze the fire and it turned to ice. She broke her way in and I followed with my hands crossed behind my back.

"Give up," I said as Mona grabbed the girl, yanking her by the arm.

"Never!" Tempestt snarled, yanking away from Mona and trying to hit her. Mona blocked with her forearm and then kicked, her heel striking the teen's rib cage.

Tempestt cried out as pain coursed through her body and fell into the wall of frozen flames behind her.

I moved towards her and held a si' beam in stasis before her. I stretched out with my mind and heard her thoughts. She was terrified! She hadn't really wanted to do this, but she needed the—

"*Money?*" I said, my brow creasing in confusion. She froze under my gaze and seemed to relax, trying to catch her breath. "You were forced into this?"

"Zee, what are you talking about?" Gonzo asked.

I couldn't take my eyes off Tempestt. She swallowed hard and tried to stand up straight. "Sh-She isn't a follower of Burton..." I moved closer to her, trying to touch her mind with my telepathy, but now that she knew I could read her mind, she was fighting me. "What did they take from you?" I asked her.

She looked at me and I saw fear in her eyes. "*Everything*," she confessed.

The four of us stood in the center of the frozen flames and I began to question her.

Burton had sent members of The Shadow to kill her parents when Tempestt was five. She'd been pulled into his service and trained in martial arts and wet work to become an assassin and mercenary. She was made into a weapon of The Shadow.

Tempestt told us that Burton had vowed to pay her $300,000 a piece if she killed us. He had also promised her *freedom*. Freedom from his influence and freedom from the life he'd given her.

How could she not see that it had been a lie? He would never let her go. She would forever be his slave until the day she died.

But, with money like that, Tempestt felt she could survive. She said that she'd planned to run after the money had been deposited in her off-shore accounts. She was going to get out.

Practically an orphan, the girl was simply looking for a way of life that would provide her with comfortability.

"I hate to say this, but…I believe you," Mona said in disbelief. I looked at her and shrugged.

I looked at Tempestt and wondered if I would've ended up like her had Burton succeeded in the experiment that put me in a coma. I was starting to wonder what his true goal for me had been…Maybe he wanted to make a great weapon? Maybe he wanted to use me as a tool to give himself more power?

"You're coming with us," I told her. When her eyes grew wide, I held my hands up, palms out. "I'm extending an olive branch. I *think* you should come with us."

Gonzo nodded. "If you're going to run from Burton, you might as well join the team that's going to kill him."

That made Tempestt smile. She placed a hand over her mouth, trying to hide it. Something in me told me that she didn't smile very often. At that moment, Tempestt glanced at Mona, as if wondering what her vote would be.

Mona sighed and ran a hand through her auburn hair. "I already said I believed you when you said you were a tool of Burton's. Don't push it." Mona turned and walked to the wall of ice and gestured with a hand. The ice began to melt and she walked out of the circle.

As I turned to follow Mona, I suddenly sensed a threat to my well-being in the immediate vicinity: *DANGER!*

"DOWN!!!" I yelled as I sensed a surge of power.

"Redis!!" someone yelled. We split and the ground exploded in a cloud of concrete and asphalt. Someone had launched plasma bolts at the ground—aiming for us.

I looked around, but I saw no one. "Take cover!" I yelled as I pushed myself to my feet.

"Where?!" yelled Gonzo, firing up an energy blast. "We're in the middle of nowhere."

Another explosion sounded in front of us, tossing us into the air. I slammed into the road and skidded to a stop, pain exploding in my chest as the wind was knocked out of me.

"Burton had me followed!" Tempestt said. "He said that if I didn't finish the job than someone would take care of me."

"And by that he meant kill you," Gonzo told the child. She nodded.

Just then, a man dressed in all black appeared out of thin air, a katana in his hand. My eyes grew wide, but before I could react, Gonzo hurled an energy blast at the man.

"Zedo, we can't just leave her here," Mona said. "She's an enemy of Burton now…just like us."

I looked at Tempestt. She was just a child, yet filled with so much hatred, confusion…and fear. I nodded. "She's with us," I replied. "We'll protect you."

Tempestt nodded. "I don't need your protection, but I'll join you. I'm not some helpless damsel."

"Fair enough," I replied.

Yes, she would live to see another day. I couldn't kill a child, even though she'd blindly tried to kill me.

I raised a hand towards the sky and a cloud moved towards me, turning from white to gray. I focused and called a single bolt of lightning from the sky that slammed into the body of the man with the katana.

He screamed as he fried—electricity making his weapon glow. Smoke rose from his body as he collapsed—dead.

Tempestt's jaw dropped in surprise as she looked at me.

"Let's move," said Gonzo, heading back towards the car.

I turned from the body without a second thought and wondered if Tempestt would truly be useful. I wasn't sure if she was friend or foe, if she'd deceived me with her thoughts or was truly genuine…but I was about to find out.

We piled into the car of our deceased Uber driver and Gonzo drove off, heading towards the sun, which was beginning to set.

Chapter 13:

On the Run Again

෬෬

By early morning we decided to pull over and get some rest. Gonzo pulled into a plain motel off the highway and we checked into two rooms.

A few hours later, we rose and decided to regroup, but first we'd decided to grab breakfast. There was a rundown diner down the road from us. Deciding to save gas, we walked with Gonzo hovering above us, complaining that his feet still hurt and he didn't feel like walking.

"Gonzo get down from there," I said.

"Why?" he asked.

"You're drawing attention to us, you idiot!" Mona said.

I turned to make sure no one saw him and caught sight of something heading towards our direction, a cloud of smoke trailing behind it.

"What is that?" I asked, pointing.

The others turned around and Mona's eyes grew wide. "Is that a torpedo?"

"Take cover!" Gonzo yelled, moving towards Tempestt as I grabbed Mona. Mona shrieked as the torpedo sped towards us. Seconds later, the torpedo slammed into the asphalt and exploding, hurling debris into the air and tossing us aside. Dust filled the air and I began to cough.

Mona pushed me off her—I'd tried to cover her body with my own—and rose to her feet. "Why is someone always trying to kill us?!"

"Better question," Gonzo said, "why do they always try to kill us before or after we eat? Is nothing sacred?"

I turned to see Gonzo floating above our heads, Tempestt just below him.

I caught sight of a black SUV down the road and a man stood in front of the vehicle dressed in all black and shades, a torpedo launcher propped up on his shoulder. He yanked off his shades and his jaw dropped in shock.

Yes, we survived, I thought to myself. I clenched my jaw and watched as the man opened the driver's side passenger door, threw the launcher inside, and rushed to climb into the SUV.

I glanced at Tempestt. Now was as good a time as any to test her loyalty.

"Tem. Mona." And that was all I let move from my lips. In the next moment, Tempestt took off running down the road, Mona a fraction of a second behind her.

"Tem?" the girl yelled over her shoulder. "What kind of a nickname is that?!"

Gonzo flew off without being instructed and I took to the air, right behind him.

Ahead of us, the SUV peeled off and rushed down the road.

Mona leapt into the air and stretched her arms up and Gonzo grabbed her by the hand. Mona released one of Gonzo's hands and stretched towards Tempestt.

"Trust me!" shouted Mona.

Tempest took her hand and Gonzo lifted the two women twenty feet off the ground. As he sped towards the SUV, the two women locked arms.

"Now, Gonzo!" Mona yelled and he swung them towards the vehicle. Tempestt and Mona spun through the air and landed atop the SUV's roof.

Tempestt let out a yelp as she lost her footing, but Mona grabbed and steadied her seconds before she fired an ice beam into the SUV's roof.

The vehicle swerved, trying to knock them off the roof. Tempestt moved to the edge of the roof and slammed one of her heels into a window, shattering the glass.

Just then, someone within the SUV opened fire, blowing holes into the roof.

Mona flipped off the SUV and landed crouched low. Tempestt followed suit and landed at her side. Mona threw both her hands forward and hurled ice beams at the vehicle's wheels, freezing the back tires.

The truck skidded and then flipped end over end and it landed on its hood, bursting into flames. Tempestt recoiled from the explosion.

Gonzo and I landed behind them.

Another vehicle, a silver Lexus ES, came into view, coming from the direction of the diner we'd intended on going to. Two Lexus LF-LCs—one red and the other blue—moved beside it, forming a "V" shape.

Several heads appeared from the windows of the three vehicles and began to open fire, black automatic weapons in hand.

I released several si' beams as Gonzo hurled energy blasts.

"We're sitting ducks here!" said Mona, looking for cover. And she was right. We had nowhere to hide. Maybe that's why they'd chosen to attack us out here.

More than that, our stolen vehicle was back at the motel.

I closed my eyes, stretched out with my right hand, and focused. I reached down with my mind, touching the earth.

"Zee, what are you doing?" asked Gonzo. I could feel his eyes on me, but I didn't reply.

I felt the earth beneath my feet and called upon my ability of elemental manipulation to coax the ground to respond to my commands. Suddenly, the ground began to open up. The others took a step back as a crack in the ground began to spread around me.

I slammed my right hand into the ground and all along the road, the ground began to open up until the cars came to a screeching halt, but it was too late. The fissure had reached them and they were swallowed up by the earth.

I clapped my hands together and the ground closed up, only showing a slight break in the road.

I heard a gasp behind me and turned to see Tempestt with a hand over her mouth. I wiped the sweat from my forehead and realized that the three of them stood frozen, eyes wide. Was that fear I detected on their faces?

Were they afraid of my powers?

An explosion shook the ground and I looked at my feet. The vehicles must've exploded below the surface. An aftershock spread through the area and leveled the diner and the motel in the distance.

Car alarms in the parking lot were set off, filling the air with a chorus of blares.

"We should get out of here before someone spots us and calls 5-0," Gonzo said.

"I agree," Tempestt added, moving down the road, evading my gaze as she moved towards the remains of the motel. Gonzo moved after her.

Only Mona remained behind, looking at me. A breeze rustled her hair and she brushed a strand aside.

"Y-You killed them…all by yourself," she said in a voice just above a whisper. I didn't know what to say. Yes, I did…but I had to. They were after us.

What was she getting at?

I'd saved us.

But I'd also been responsible for leveling the motel and the diner…Innocents had probably been killed, because of *me*.

She walked past me and headed towards the carnage I'd created—smoke rose from the remains of the diner, joined by the chorus of car alarms, and screams.

We were tired, dirty, and hungry, but had to get a move on. When I arrived back at the destroyed motel, the others had already climbed into the car.

I climbed into the back beside Tempestt and Gonzo pulled the vehicle out of the parking lot. I could feel the tension, but there was nothing I could do about that.

Using my powers had drained me and I was exhausted.

Eventually, the lull of the tires going round and round began to relax me. I leaned against the cool glass of the window and drifted off to sleep.

I awoke to a brilliant light beaming through the windshield. Mona and Gonzo had their hands raised, trying to shield their eyes from the blinding light. Then came a roar so loud that it resonated in my skull.

What was that? The sound was terrifying! It had roused me from my sleep. Beside me, Tempestt was screaming!

"What's going on?" I yelled.

Suddenly, something slammed into the car and then we began to roll. Glass shattered and our screams filled the air.

I only knew one thing: one moment I was asleep, and the next some blinding light was washing over us and something had struck the car. Now I lay dazed amid debris—I'd been thrown from the car.

My body ached all over. I coughed and pain racked my body. I turned my head and caught sight of the smoldering wreckage. My thoughts were fuzzy and I tasted blood.

Mona, I thought to myself. *Gonzo*.

I hoped they were alright.

Tempestt. She was an afterthought; she'd only just recently joined us. I hoped she was still alive.

Were they all in the car still, or had they been thrown from the car, too?

The blinding light returned, followed by that eerie sound.

I screamed, pain overwhelming me. The light grew brighter, washing over me until it erased the world from my consciousness.

I opened my eyes and found myself in a bed—a *hospital* bed.

I didn't know how I'd gotten there.

I was baffled…and worried. My vision began to clear and as I observed my surroundings, I found myself frozen with dread as I realized I had a visitor.

Lester Burton was sitting in front of me dressed in dark jeans and black shirt. A leather jacket hung over the arm of his chair. He smoked a cigarette, which I was sure was banned from hospitals.

When he realized I was awake, he put his cigarette out on the table in front of him. "Ah, you're awake." He clapped his hands together and grinned. "Good. I'm glad."

"What have you done?" I asked him, trying to shake my grogginess.

"I didn't do anything that would harm you...yet."

"Where are my friends?" I asked him, utterly confused. I still didn't know how I'd gotten here. Something wasn't right.

But if Lester were here, was I truly in a hospital? Wouldn't someone have recognized him? He was a wanted criminal after all.

Maybe I wasn't in a hospital at all, but a medical bay in one of his facilities.

I felt my body go cold as my thoughts raced.

Lester sighed and rose from his seat. "Gonzo's resting. Mona's in recovery, as well. Tempestt, on the other hand, is in surgery."

My eyes grew wide. "What happened? What did you do to them?"

Lester began to pace. "You all were in a car accident."

"What car accident? We were never in a car you *lunatic*!" But just then, I recalled that we had gotten back into the stolen vehicle. Gonzo had been behind the wheel before I'd drifted off. But I didn't remember an accident. Had I slept through that, too?

Everything seemed so fuzzy…

And then, the memories came rushing back. I gasped aloud as my mind was overloaded with memories of being thrown from the car and—

Lester jumped up and grabbed me by the collar of my hospital gown. He pulled a pistol from the small of his back and pressed the nozzle to my forehead. My heart began to race.

"Don't ever disrespect me," he whispered, his mouth close to my ear. I could feel his breath on my neck. "My father may think the world of you, but your life is in my hands." He threw me into my pillow and placed his gun back in the small of his back.

He moved to a counter across the room and reached for something, I couldn't see what, and then he moved back to my bed side. "Now, be a good boy and be still."

Then, he revealed a syringe and stabbed me in the chest before I could even yell or resist him.

Chapter 14:

Visions of the Past

ೞ೫ೞ

I felt groggy and anxiety gripped my heart...Pain coursed through my veins.

I opened my eyes and found myself enveloped in pure darkness. I couldn't move, I couldn't speak, and I couldn't see.

I knew my eyes were open, but there was nothing to see.

Suddenly, the darkness exploded in blinding light and then vivid colors appeared from nothingness. I found myself floating among the colors.

I let go of my conscious mind. I simply let it all fall away and was immediately overwhelmed by all the vivid colors as they washed over me.

As I let go of my conscious mind, something took its place. That '*something*' was energy. It surged through my body like electricity then poured out of my fingertips in a wave of light.

The light merged with the display of colors and then shifted, forming images before me. Suddenly, the light and color began to shrink until it formed a rectangle about nine feet tall and five feet wide.

I saw my reflection in the rectangle and realized that the light and color had formed a mirror of sorts.

I moved closer towards the large mirror, but now only light reflected on its surface. The rest of the area I was in was once again pitch black—devoid of color, devoid of life. Only me and the mirror existed now.

As I moved closer to the mirror, I no longer saw myself but now I saw a picture, but it was moving. Maybe it was a film? Was this mirror projecting a visual now? Was I seeing the past? The present? Perhaps it was showing me the future?

I moved closer and the image grew clearer.

Suddenly, I was sucked into the mirror and merged with the pictures. I tried to scream, but only colors came out of my mouth. My body grew transparent and I merged with the moving pictures.

Sound buzzed in my head and I realized that I was hearing music. The song '*Half Breed*' by Cher played on a large radio that looked out of date. It was at that moment that I realized I was viewing the *past!* But *how?*

I was able to watch the memory, but I was stuck in place and there was no sound.

A tan skinned toddler dressed in overalls over a yellow shirt and hard bottomed shoes on his small feet moved into focus as he walked across green grass. The boy had dark, curly hair and currently had his thumb in his mouth. He stood in the backyard of a house that bore the signs of the architecture of the 1970s.

A man with skin the color of mahogany and a small afro with a goatee moved towards the boy and the toddler grinned and reached towards him with two stubby hands. The man lifted the child into the air.

He had to be the boy's father. He wore malachite-colored pants with this skintight yellow t-shirt and a striped vest.

Then, an older woman possibly in her late 60s came through the sliding doors with another little boy that looked similar to the one that the father placed back on the ground. This boy was also dressed in overalls, a yellow shirt, and white shoes. The woman placed the child on his feet and he ran to the father.

*The two boys were **twins**—fraternal but twins!*

The woman, dressed in a purple outfit, ran a hand through her mingle gray hair and grinned. Her heart fluttered at the sight of her son with his children.

At the same time, a car pulled into the driveway, a 1978 Honda Civic by the looks of it.

A fair-skinned woman, probably in her early 20s, stepped out of the car in a tailored black-striped suit with her long curly brunette hair flowing down her back. She closed her car door and in the backyard, the elderly woman turned to face the noise.

The father looked up, as well, and his face shifted from one of happiness to one of contempt.

The father led his twin sons in the house, his mother trailing behind him, and then he stepped out of the front door to confront the woman.

An argument broke out between the two young parents, but words couldn't be deciphered from the distance.

The elderly woman moved outside to break up the argument, but the younger woman pushed her aside with such strength that the elderly woman flew back and slammed into the front door of the house. Clearly, this fair skinned woman was a super human.

The elderly woman's son glared at the woman then rushed to his mother's side. The young woman stood there, her face etched in horror at what she'd done! She covered her mouth in shock and tried to move to help, but the man swatted her away and then helped his mother inside and locked the door.

The young woman began to beat on the door. Neighbors began to peek out of windows and step onto their porches— wondering what all the commotion was about.

The man moved his mother into the living room and hurried to a nearby rotary phone as the twin boys moved into the room. One began to cry and the other patted him—confused.

The man picked up the phone and dialed 9-1-1. Outdoors, the woman was still banging on the front door. She began to dent it with her fist.

She kept glancing over her shoulder, shouting at neighbors that watched her from a distance. A pair of the neighbors went back indoors and locked their doors while another set closed their curtains.

The woman snarled and slammed her fist harder into the door—trying to burst through it.

The elderly woman sat on the couch and her face twisted in fear. She turned her head and caught sight of the twins. She pulled the one that was crying into her arms. "Zedo, I've got you."

Suddenly I woke up. I looked around, drenched in a cold sweat. Wiping my forehead, I tried to slow my heartbeat. I was panting as if I'd been running at full speed. I was still in the hospital, but where was Lester?

As I tried to slow my breathing, I stretched out with my senses. I needed clarity.

What had I just seen? Was that my ***PAST!?!?***

Had I just experienced a vision of my past? Had Lester injected me with something that had activated a new power in me? Was I now gifted with the ability of retrocognition—the ability to view the past?

If I now had the ability of retrocognition, it came with limitations. When I'd been struck with the vision of the past, I'd become oblivious to events in the present. I'd also been forced into a trance, which had left me vulnerable to harm.

But how had Lester known I possessed that ability? And more than that, did I have more powers hidden in my blood?

Was that why Burton had experimented on me? Had that been what my project had truly been all about, creating super humans with multiple abilities? Or were these my natural abilities?

I was so ignorant! What did I really know about the black-ops agency I'd signed up for?

I exhaled sharply, finally starting to calm down. I tried to rise from the bed but found both of my hands were cuffed to the bed rails. My eyes grew wide and I strained against the handcuffs.

I needed to know if I was still in Lester's custody or in an actual hospital. But if I was in an actual hospital and not a Burton facility, why'd I been placed in handcuffs? Had I been arrested for attacking the motel and diner?

Just when I was about to yell out for help, the door opened and a nurse entered.

"Are you alright?" she asked, dressed in white scrubs, her blonde hair pulled back into a ponytail. "We were afraid you weren't going to wake. Do you need anything?"

"Water. I need some water," I answered. My throat was dry and my voice cracked when I spoke.

The nurse nodded and then disappeared—vanishing into thin air. I gasped: shocked! She had powers, *too*??

I was definitely in a facility then and not a normal hospital. Surely, super humans didn't just roam around freely…did they?

When she returned moments later, she appeared out of thin air with a cup in hand. I drank the cool, refreshing water and thanked her.

"You can teleport," I said, more of a statement than a question.

She grinned and nodded. "Are you going to be okay?" she asked, taking the empty cup.

"I'll survive. Thank you." She turned to leave, but I called out to her. "Where am I?"

She cocked her head. "You don't know?" I shook my head and she turned to exit the room, using the door this time. Why hadn't she answered my question?

I turned my head towards the window and realized that the room wasn't just dark, but it was also dark outside: night. How long had I been in my dream-state under the influence of the vision? What had Lester done to me?

"Where am I?" I asked no one. I was utterly baffled…and worried about everyone else. Where were they? Was Mona alright? Was Gonzo? Tempestt?

I moved my hands and realized I should've asked her about the handcuffs.

I exhaled and relaxed into my pillow. I closed my eyes, trying to calm myself, but was sucked back into the vision.

I gasped and when I forced my eyes open, I was back in the past—merged with the vision.

The fair skinned woman began to kick at the front door as the much older woman screamed out in fear, clutching the twin boys to her bosom.

It became clear that the younger woman was a deranged person that had an explosive temper.

The man tried to calm the cries of his confused, wailing twins.

The absurd mother moved around to the side of the house where a wide glass window was. She slammed her fist into it and the glass shattered. The woman threw her hair over her shoulder as she forced her way into the house.

The neighbors could hear screams.

The father grabbed the twins from the grandmother and tried to hide them in a closet.

The mother went into the elaborate kitchen and discovered the sharpest, deadliest knife she could find!

Smirking, she twirled the knife in her hand and walked into the living room. She held it up, preparing to strike.

"May God forgive you," the grandmother said, closing her eyes—accepting her fate. The mother stabbed the paternal grandmother as she cried out loudly.

"Mother!" yelled the father. In the next moment, he charged across the living room and tackled the mother of his sons. The woman dropped the knife and slammed into the ground.

She yelled, but quickly threw her ex off of her. Climbing to her feet, she opened her suit coat, revealing a shoulder holster with a silver handgun sitting in its place. She drew her gun and fired two rounds at the grandmother for good measure—once in the chest and once in the head.

Beneath her, the father lay frozen—his eyes on the corpse of his mother. "You're a MONSTER!" he shouted.

The woman cocked her head. "You really think I don't know who you are?"

She moved closer to her ex-bedmate and he scrambled to his feet and then took a step back.

He shook his head and his eyes began to glow as he pulled energy from the air and prepared to attack. "You can't take them, Kelly. They're **mine!**"

"They're mine, too." She raised her gun and aimed it at his chest.

Fear was etched on his face. "Kelly...don't do this!"

She swallowed. "Goodbye, Troy." She pulled the trigger and shot him four times. His body crumbled to the floor, blood spilling onto the wooden floor.

A cloud of black energy lifted from his chest and the woman named Kelly watched as the energy floated upward and disappeared through the ceiling—vanishing into thin air.

She moved across the room to stand over her dead ex and began to wail, tears falling.

The police arrived, circling her—demanding that she drop the gun. An officer, with the last name 'Wright' on his name plate, kicked the handgun out of her hand and pinned her on the ground.

"Spread out!" yelled another officer and three others began to search the house.

Two people from the coroner's office arrived and removed the corpses from the house in body bags.

At that same moment, a male officer, last name Dale on his name plate, located the twins in a dark closet, screaming.

The deranged woman—Kelly—was carried off swearing and kicking. "No! One day! One day he will return! You have to burn the body! Please, no! My children!" She fought against her restraints as an officer tried to drag her out of the house. "I have to protect my children! You can't do this! You don't understand! I need to protect my boys!"

I woke from the vision, screaming. The restraints dug into my wrists, but I pulled hard and ignited my fists into flames. The handcuffs melted off in time and I jumped out of bed.

I felt the tug of my I.V. and yanked it out. My blood began to flow from the opening in my arm, so I pressed a hand to it then moved to a nearby sink and grabbed a towel—replacing my hand with the towel.

I wiped the sweat off my brow and moved my hand through my damp hair.

So, I was biracial. That much was clear. I'd always felt that, but now I was sure of it. My father was black; my mother was white. My dad's name had been Troy and my mother's name had been Kelly. Well, maybe her name was *still* Kelly? I didn't know if she was dead or alive.

I'd seen their faces and had heard their voices. But what was more mind blowing was the fact that I had a *brother—a **twin!***

I'd had a grandmother, too. I'd had a FAMILY! But my mother had taken them from me. She'd murdered my father and paternal grandmother.

I wondered where my twin brother was now. Was he older than me or younger? My mother had robbed me of a life with him.

She was the reason I'd gotten put into the system as a ward.

She was the reason I'd entered the agency.

She was the reason why I'd ended up in Burton's grasp and had fallen into a coma.

This was all Kelly's fault!

I thought and thought about what I had just seen, but right now I needed to find the others and get out of here.

Suddenly, I heard a faint *POP* and turned to find the nurse standing behind me. I lifted my hand to attack, but she quickly jabbed something in my neck.

My eyes grew wide as I felt the sting of the needle. Suddenly, I grew groggy and my legs turned to jelly. I felt my consciousness slip and as I fell, she caught me.

"Let's get you back to bed, Mr. Jeta."

As I lost consciousness, I wondered what had led my mother to kill my father. She'd been screaming that 'one day he'll return!' Who was she referring to? And what was that black substance that had rose from my father's body?

When I woke, the sun was peeking through the hospital blinds. I sat up, groaning and rubbing my forehead.

The door to my hospital room opened and the young, golden haired nurse entered. I sat up a little straighter, watching her hands.

"I'm not going to let you dope me up again," I told her. "You can't keep me here."

"You can leave now," she said. "I was just instructed to keep you here until you saw what you needed to see."

I threw back the covers and rose from the bed. I felt lightheaded and swayed. "You were instructed by who?"

When she tried to move towards me, I held up a hand to stop her.

"No, I'm fine. Where are my friends?"

"Well, they're here and doing fine. But the young lady— what's her name?"

"Tempestt?"

She nodded. "Yes, *her*, well she isn't doing well."

"What's wrong?"

"I'm not at liberty to say at this time, sorry." She turned to leave and then stopped in her tracks. "I should find you some clothes, we threw away the ones you arrived in. They were filthy. Stay here, I'll bring you a fresh set of clothes."

The door closed behind her and I began to pace the room. I moved towards the window and peered out of it.

Everything seemed to be normal outside of my window, but I felt uneasy.

The nurse had been instructed to keep me here until I'd seen what I'd needed to see…But who had told her to keep me here?

Had it been Lester…or his father?

Did Dr. Henry Burton have a hand in this?

The nurse brought me clothes, surprisingly in my size, and a pair of black boots. I got dressed and went to find Mona. She was resting; and her food tray was beside her bed, empty. I figured I'd wait till she was awake.

When I went to see Gonzo, he was in a deep sleep, as well.

When I went to see Tempestt, she had been pulled into yet another surgery! Clearly, she'd been more banged up than I'd been led to believe.

I explored the hospital, which turned out to be a public hospital in the middle of nowhere, and sat in the lobby for a moment. I bowed my head and prayed for the young, black-haired teen.

Still perplexed by how we'd ended up in a car accident, I went back to Mona's room. I took a seat at her bedside and watched the monitor that showed her heart rate. I watched the line go up and down.

I then realized that there was a second monitor attached to her. There was a band around her midsection and this monitor detected numbers a lot faster than the average heartbeat.

Did Mona have *two hearts?* As I gazed at the monitors, I realized something was off. As I rose to my feet, I realized that she didn't have two heartbeats…She was connected to a fetal monitor.

My heart sunk. Mona was *pregnant!*

I swallowed hard and moved to the nurses' station down the hall. I lied and told them I was Mona's boyfriend and they confirmed that she was indeed connected to a fetal monitor.

Mona was *pregnant*!

I wondered if she was alright. But then, I realized that it had only been a few weeks since she'd been raped by Burton's goons.

A heartbeat wouldn't have been able to be detected, yet. My eyes grew wide as realization dawned on me. That meant that it had happened before then, possibly even before the formation of our team.

Mona must've been involved with someone back in her other life. Did she have a boyfriend? A husband?

Thoughts flooded my mind as I realized that there was a man in Mona's life…I didn't have a chance.

Pushing thoughts of Mona aside, I headed to the nurses' station to get an update on Tempestt. I told the nurse I was her brother. After she told me she'd been pulled into recovery, I exhaled a sigh of relief, and headed to the garden level to take in some fresh air.

Flashes from the vision came to the forefront of my mind.

I had to know about myself. I needed to know where I'd come from; who I'd come from. I suddenly craved to know my family.

When I woke from my coma, I only lusted for revenge, but now…things were different. Maybe Mona had been right. Back at

H.I.T.S. she'd said that perhaps we could have more…Perhaps this was a sign?

There had to be a reason why I'd received that vision of the past.

Maybe Mona had been right. Maybe we didn't have to do this anymore. What had it brought us besides death? We'd lost half the team in the very beginning, been betrayed by Jonathan, and Mona had lost her brother.

I had been driven by my desire to find Burton and kill him— take away everything that he'd taken from me. However, things were changing.

I kneeled down beside the blue roses and took in their scent. I closed my eyes and wondered if maybe my vision now took precedence over revenge.

Going after Burton had caused us nothing but pain. We'd lost so much and Mona had ended up getting sexually assaulted. What had we accomplished beyond forging a friendship?

This road was dangerous.

Or…had Lester triggered the vision to throw me off his father's trail?

That vision had left an impression on me… It wouldn't go away, and that feeling led me to believe that maybe I needed to follow the new path set before me.

Maybe this vision of my past was what I needed to focus on?

New emotions seemed to come in waves.

I recalled that I had allegedly been born in Ann Arbor, Michigan. At least that was what my foster parents had told me when I was 9, after I'd asked them about my family.

I remembered my name. How could I remember that but nothing else? My life before the age of five was lost to me. Perhaps the trauma of my past had forced me not to remember?

My memories only went as far back as five. Perhaps I needed to find someone who could unlock my memories before then?

I rose to my feet and moved back into the hospital.

I couldn't leave my team at the hospital to discover my history… Could I? It was urgent, though. But is my life more important then revenge?

They'd nearly died because of me…and now, Mona was pregnant. I couldn't put her unborn child at risk.

I needed time to myself to figure it all out. Perhaps I needed to let go of my need of revenge to find who *I* was…Who was *Zedo Jeta*?

My mother might've murdered my grandmother and father, but I had a twin brother somewhere out there. Maybe I could find him. Perhaps I had aunts and uncles out there. But if I did, why hadn't they rescued us from the foster care system?

I shook my head. No, if I had family, they would've taken us in…right?

I headed back to the nurse's station on Mona's floor and asked for the golden-haired nurse. Someone had told me her name was Jayne.

Sure enough, Nurse Jayne appeared moments later. I realized that she didn't hide her powers. People knew she could teleport.

She grinned at me gestured with a nod of the head for me to follow her down the hall.

"I need to go," I told her.

She nodded. "I figured you might."

"Did Lester tell you—"

"I don't work for him, Mr. Jeta," Nurse Jayne told me. She clenched her jaw.

I frowned. If she didn't work for Lester then who did she work for?

She held a chart in her hand. Gazing down at it, she spoke. "Go find your answers…I'll keep an eye on your friends…at least until they check out."

I nodded. "Will you tell them that I'm sorry, but need to do this?"

"They're secret agents," she replied. "I'm sure they're used to being abandoned."

I looked at her, shocked. "How'd you—"

She waved my words aside. "It's fine, Mr. Jeta. You don't owe them anything."

But the truth was, I *did*!

I had to say goodbye. I couldn't just disappear. So, I headed to Gonzo's room. But sure enough, he was resting. I caught sight of his coat, which had been hung over a chair. I moved towards it and patted the pockets.

Sure enough, I came across his wallet and borrowed three hundred dollars from Gonzo's coat pocket. He had held out on us. How could he? Mona had been forking over money to fund our mission.

I wanted to say goodbye to Tempestt, then decided against it. Though she was a lot like me, I didn't truly know her.

Then, there was Mona, but I couldn't bring myself to say 'goodbye.'

As I left the hospital, I began to walk. Clouds had moved in to create an overcast sky.

As I got a little further down the road, it began to rain. What was I doing? I didn't have a vehicle, I was getting soaked, and had no idea where I was going.

The person I'd been before was gone. Anger and hatred had been replaced with longing and curiosity. I needed more than revenge. I needed to *belong*.

I lifted myself into the air and flew off. The rain slapped against my face, but I didn't mind. I looked down and caught sight of rain forming puddles, sending ripples through the gathering water.

Ripples were everywhere.

One droplet changed the size of the puddle.

One droplet changed things…and that's what the vision of my past had done.

It had changed *everything*.

As I flew through the rain, my mind began to wander…

I moved down a well-lit corridor, two soldiers were accompanying me—one in the front and the other behind me. They led me to an elevator and then we made our descent into the earth.

I watched the numbers on the elevator as we moved further down until we arrived Level -10. I frowned. That was strange for an elevator. But as I stepped off and saw the rugged earth around us, I realized that the -10 meant we were ten floors underground—ten floors below street level.

My heart began to race as we stepped off the elevator and I was led through a series of doors until we arrived at a blue one. There was a security pad next to the door and the soldier in front of me pressed his hand to it. The panel glowed green.

"Access granted," said a female voice.

I heard a faint clicking sound and then the blue door slid open, disappearing into the wall.

"Step in, please," said the soldier.

"You aren't coming with me?" I asked.

He didn't answer; he didn't even look at me. I moved beyond the doorway and the blue door slid back in place.

"Hey!" I yelled, but of course, no one was there. There was no glass window in the door, so I couldn't see behind me.

Suddenly, I was scared. Where was I?

I didn't think this was how it was supposed to be. I'd enlisted in the army, but...

I turned and there, in the hallway, stood a man dressed in a shirt and tie and slacks. A lab coat was pulled over his attire. He wore horn rimmed glasses and had a salt and pepper beard. His eyes were nearly obsidian and his lips were thin—slits really.

"You must be Zedo Jeta?" he said, his voice thick with an accent.

I nodded, suddenly wary of the man that stood alone in the corridor, waiting for me. "Yes, sir."

He grinned and extended his hand. He was probably fourteen feet in front of me, which was ironic because I was fourteen. I guess he'd expected me to move towards him. I forced my shaky legs to obey and closed the gap between us.

I had no business being here. I was a teenager. I had no business signing up for the military. I had no business forging documents that said that I was older. But I had no other options.

I was tired of the foster care system. I was a runaway and needed a life on my own.

I shook the man's hand.

"I'd like to welcome you to Secret Agency XII. We're going to be spending a lot of time together." He dropped my hand and turned to walk down the hallway. "Follow me, please, Mr. Jeta." He moved down the hall and then stopped, turning to face me. "Where are my manners? My name is Dr. Burton."

"Nice to meet you, sir," I replied, my voice low.

I followed him without question. I realized at that very moment that my life was no longer my own. I swallowed hard, trying to force the bile back down.

We arrived at another door. This one was red. The doctor looked at me and grinned. "Behind this door is your future, Zedo."

He opened the door and we moved inside. I gasped instantly. Before us stood a massive training facility the length of a football field.

Soldiers—both men and women—battled one another in what appeared to be a training exercise. Some were armed with assault rifles and ammunition. Others were equipped with weapons similar to katanas but they glowed with multi-colored lights.

Dressed in battle garb, these soldiers looked more like fighting machines then people.

Bullets flew across the field as soldiers battled one another. Screams filled the air along with blood and gore.

This was a live fire exercise.

I felt the vomit try to come up again. I took a step back, but the doctor turned and looked at me.

*"Don't be frightened, Mr. Jeta. **You** joined the agency. This is what you signed up for." He nodded towards the field. "We build warriors here."*

I was terrified. *I was just a kid! I didn't know what I was getting into. I didn't want to die! I'd only seen guns on tv. I'd never seen someone get shot before. This wasn't real! This couldn't be real!*

Dr. Burton glanced down and I followed his line of sight. Directly below us was the medical bay. I watched in horror as a doctor tried to revive a soldier covered in blood while another tended to a screaming man with an amputated arm. Blood was everywhere.

I kept swallowing hard; I refused to vomit in front of the doctor. I wondered if he was head of the medical staff or…

"I'm not ready to die," I admitted, before I realized I'd said it.

Dr. Burton took a step towards me. "Then don't get killed." I closed my eyes and tried to steady myself. I felt a hand on my shoulder and looked up to find the doctor staring at me. "Your training begins tomorrow. As of today, you are a junior operative at Secret Agency XII. You will have basic training during the day and report to the lab in the evening. Lieutenant Roth will assign you a barrack and provide you with a schedule. I will introduce you to him. To your comrades you are now Agent Jeta. To **me**, you are the future."

I had no idea what he meant. I didn't know what to say. He removed his hand from my shoulder and then turned to leave the training facility. I followed behind him.

"I thought I was Private Jeta? I thought I was joining the army or—"

"You have been selected for something so much bigger than just the armed forces." That was all he said. He led me through the *facility and dropped me off in a little office where Lieutenant Roth sat behind a desk.*

The lieutenant was a young white man with close cropped hair. He wore a black uniform. The lieutenant was a man of few words and quickly showed me to my assigned barrack.

I noticed there was a small chest at the end of my twin bed within the barrack. I wondered what clothes and trinkets I'd put in the chest. I only possessed the clothes on my back.

As if hearing my thoughts, Lieutenant Roth said, "You will receive three uniforms. Take care of them. They should be delivered within the hour. The shower is down the hall; it's a community shower."

Was I going to be a spy? Was I going to be a warrior for the government?

This had all seemed cool at first, but I'd seen army movies. This was nothing like that.

My heart sunk and I suddenly had a very bad feeling about this, but there was nothing I could do.

I'd already signed my life away.

The sound of thunder pulled me from my thoughts and I slowly lowered myself to the ground. That was when I'd first met Burton back in 1989. So much had changed since then.

He hadn't seemed like a monster then…but everything had changed just like how things were changing again.

I shook my head and moved off the road and into the forest. The rain had slowed and I found a hollowed tree to sleep in. I was suddenly reminded of the old days, when I was a runaway. I'd slept in the woods many nights.

The tree that I'd dozed off in wasn't very comfortable, but I felt safe. When morning came, the fog was somewhat thick, but I traveled through it.

My cold hands were in my pockets as I walked, silently…alone.

I walked past a sign that read 'Welcome to Springfield, Illinois.' I guess I'd crossed more miles then I'd originally thought.

I wondered where I should start. Should I return to Michigan and start searching for my family there?

I was still tired. Perhaps sleeping in the tree hadn't been a good idea after all.

I flagged down an Audi A5, but it didn't stop. I wondered if hitchhiking was still illegal. I flagged another vehicle and was surprised to see that it was a vintage Peugeot 407.

"Where are you heading?" the driver said, rolling down the passenger side window. He was the grandfather type with powder white hair and kind eyes.

"Michigan," I replied without thought. I guess all roads would lead there sooner or later.

"What for?" he asked, still coasting beside the road as I walked alongside his sleek vehicle.

"Family emergency," I lied.

The man nodded. "I'm not going that far, but I'm going far."

"That's good enough for me, sir." I got in, thanked him, and he drove off.

His car smelled of peppermint candy and smoking pipes. As we headed down the road, I put his age around 65.

He was loquacious but I didn't mind. I was just thankful for the ride. I was too tired to fly and my stomach was empty. I was running on fumes.

The money I'd taken from Gonzo was heavy in my pocket, but I didn't want to use it yet.

"... I'm from Alabama, but I live in Washington D.C," the man said as he continued to ramble on. "I'm just here on business."

"That's nice," I replied, glancing out the window.

"So, are you a runaway?"

I looked at him. "Why do you say that?"

He shrugged. "A young fella like you? You can't be any older than thirteen or fourteen."

I grinned to myself. I was technically forty-five, but still had the appearance of a teenager. My body had been frozen in time since I'd fallen into my coma. I still didn't understand that.

"No, sir. I'm not a runaway."

He nodded and his eyebrows shot up; he wasn't buying it, but didn't press the matter. "Oh, I almost forgot. My name is John Valzo-Dupre." Grandfather John scratched his gray beard and I noted the age spots on his wrinkled skin. His stomach touched the steering wheel and his breathe smelled like body waste, despite the smell of peppermints in the air. He wore a checkerboard shirt with a brown sleeveless jacket. His pants were khaki and his hat sat on the dashboard near the radio tuner.

"Nice to meet you, sir."

He grunted and then exhaled sharply.

"What is it, Mr. Dupre?" I asked annoyed.

"The tank's nearly empty. I was hoping to get to the next town before I ran out, but—"

"I'll go and fetch some." The car rolled to a stop and I climbed out. I wondered what it would've been like to ride with my own grandfather, wherever he was.

I wondered if John's grandkids got annoyed at his rambling. I ran from the yammering driver with the smelly breath that had almost hindered me unconscious.

After a while, I flew and stopped in a nearby town. I caught sight of children playing in the huge grassy yard. They were playing tag.

"Billy, I'm going to get you!" cried a little girl as she laughed and chased a little boy.

I wondered if my brother and I had grown up together, if we'd have played tag. The children laughed and raced around the weeping willows. I smiled and walked on.

I wondered where my twin was now…

I reached the edge of the state line and took to the sky. I soon passed the 'Welcome to Wisconsin' sign.

I soon came to another small town and could go no further without food or water.

The money I'd taken from Gonzo was burning in my pocket. I searched for food but as I crossed into town I collapsed.

I jumped up, startled out of my sleep.

I didn't know where I was or how I'd gotten here. I laid in a bed, dressed in a new set of clothes and I was clean.

That meant that someone had touched my body, but who?

I didn't like that. I looked around the room and jumped when I caught sight of a man leaning against the doorway.

"Good morning, I am Doctor Edward Wong."

Not another doctor, I thought to myself.

He looked to be in his early to mid-30s. He wore a simple tunic over blue jeans and his hair was black and closely cropped.

I threw back the covers and climbed to my feet. "You washed me and changed my clothes," I said, more of a statement then a question.

He nodded. "You were unmolested."

I had to take his word for it, but he seemed to be harmless. I decided to be honest. "I am Zedo Jeta."

The man moved closer and I got a better look at his face. Though he had Asian features, there was something else there, too.

"Where am I?"

"Michigan."

My eyes grew wide. "But I just crossed into Wisconsin just yesterday…"

He began to laugh. "That was four days ago. You've been out cold since then."

I didn't understand. "So, you found me unconscious on the side of the road and just decided to kidnap me? I—"

"Oh, you're awake," said a feminine voice. The man called Edward Wong turned. I looked at the door, as well. A young woman stood in the doorway with a food tray in her arms.

Edward's jaw clenched. "Seay', not now... he's tired."

"But, papa!"

"Not now!" he said firmly. The teenager nodded and left. She was around my age and dressed in a white dress. She also possessed shiny, dark hair.

Edward Wong turned to face me. I took a step back. "I'm so sorry. Seay' has been bringing you food every day, though you've been unconscious till now. She's been waiting for you to wake."

"Why did you bring me here? What kind of sick doctor are you?"

"No, no, no, you misunderstand. We found you in the dirt. You were unconscious and we found you directly next to a sign that read 'Leaving Wisconsin.' You needed hydration and rest," he told me. "My daughter and I brought you to our home, I set up an I.V. for you—"

"Why not just take me to a hospital?" I asked, wary of him. This didn't make sense. I only remembered entering Wisconsin…not leaving it…

"What kind of doctor are you?" I asked.

He grinned. "A good one."

And with that, he turned to leave the room then seemed to think of something and stopped in the doorway. He looked over his shoulder. "I'm sure you'd like something to eat? Perhaps we can talk over dinner?"

Dinner? I wondered. *What time was it?*

I nodded and followed him. The house was small, a three-bedroom cabin in the woods. I was still on edge, but I decided to go with it. I needed food.

"Why did you bring me here?" I asked after swallowing a bite of food.

Seay' looked at her father, but Edward wouldn't meet her gaze. She looked at me, tucked a strand of black hair behind her ear, and spoke. "You're just like us…"

I cocked my head. "What do you mean?"

"Seay'…" said Edward, warning in his voice.

Seay' dropped her head and ate her food. I looked at the "doctor," wondering what he was hiding. "Wait, are you super humans, too?"

Edward sighed and pushed his plate aside. "Yes, we are."

My face twisted in confusion. "How'd you know I was one?"

"We smelled it on you," Seay' said under her breath.

"To your room," her father ordered. Without a word, she left the table and headed to her room. I heard the door slam. I took a sip from my cup and then looked at Edward.

"Why don't you want her to talk to me?"

"You're a stranger and she's my daughter. I'm very protective of her."

"Then why bring me here?"

He shrugged. "You're a kid. We found you on the side of the road, unconscious. I was going to leave you there, but she said she sensed you were a super human... We couldn't leave one of our own to die."

"*How* did she sense it?"

"My daughter is gifted with the ability of power detection. She can sense the presence of supernatural abilities in others. Sometimes she can even decipher the type of power someone has and its intensity."

"Wow."

"She's gifted, but young. We stay in the woods for many reasons, but one is to keep her under the radar. A few years back, the government started collecting super humans with certain abilities. I'd imagine that her gift would come in handy. I couldn't have her taken from me. I wouldn't survive."

I nodded, knowing full well what it was like to be the government's property.

Edward Wong rose from the table and grabbed the empty plates, placing them in the sink. "You can stay the night but come morning you must leave."

"I can leave now. I don't want to cause any trouble."

"I'm sure you could use a good night's sleep."

"According to you I've been sleep long enough."

Edward turned towards me and grinned. "I can tell you're running from something."

"I'm running *towards* something."

"Even so, stay the night and rest up. Come morning you head out. The woods can be a dangerous place for a kid at night."

"I'm no kid, mister."

He shrugged and left the dining room, leaving me with my thoughts. I heard his bedroom door close behind him and decided to head to the guest room.

So, the country was full of super humans, maybe even the world. But why was the government collecting them? Perhaps they were building an army? More weapons? Maybe Secret Agency XII and others like it had succeeded in their missions.

I'd been in a coma for thirty years and in that time, everything had changed....

The next morning, I woke to find Seay' sitting at the edge of the bed. I jumped.

"I didn't mean to startle you," she said as she took a step back. "I'm Seay'."

"I'm Zedo." A sat up in bed and eyed her wearily.

"Where are you from? How did you manage to travel without company? What kind of name is Zedo? Where does it originate from?"

"Whoa, whoa, what's with all the questions?" I ran a hand through my disheveled hair. "It's too early."

"It's after seven. It's late. But I apologize for the questions. I was just interested. I didn't mean to offend you. Papa doesn't allow company."

I understood why so I took pity on Seay' and decided to talk to her. She asked about my powers and how long I'd had them, and I was honest. We talked for more than an hour.

I enjoyed her company after all.

Seay' was very fascinated with outsiders. She had never been outside of Michigan.

The sound of tires on gravel reached our ears and she looked out of the window. "Oh no. I have to go, now! My father's home." She ran out of the room.

I heard a creak; I only assumed that it was the front door, and then I heard Edward's voice. Seay' welcomed her father home.

I guess he sensed that she had done wrong because he said, "Seay', why were you in the guest room?"

"I wasn't."

"Seay' Bonnet Wong, why were you in that room!?!" he yelled.

I heard a slap that sounded like thunder, then Seay' shrieked and fell to the floor.

I jumped out of the bed, outraged. Seay' started to constantly scream and I heard hard punches being given.

"Stop, papa! Ahhh!" Seay' cried with tears in her green eyes.

I dashed into the living room and hurled Dr. Wong off her and across the room. Edward slammed into the wall and collapsed, leaving a dent behind.

"Stay away from me!" Seay' cried, recoiling from my touch.

I couldn't believe it. She didn't want my help. She cowered away from me and crawled across the room to her father's side.

I blew the door open with a si' beam and dashed out. I looked both ways, not knowing where to go.

So I pushed off the ground and flew off.

I caught sight of a hospital, entered, and went to the front desk. I grinned to myself, thinking of the friends I'd left behind. We'd always ended up in hospitals.

It was only right that I be at one now. At least this time, I wasn't hurt.

"May I help you?" the white woman at the reception desk asked dryly.

"Yes, ma'am. I need to find my records."

She refused to look up from her computer as she spoke to me. "Well, you have to go through United Affairs."

"What is United Affairs?" I asked.

She rolled her eyes, but still refused to meet my eyes and began to recite a speech. "Formerly known as Social Services, U.A. is an international company that holds all records of every human. Here, in the states, United Affairs has access to all the records of every human in the United Stated of America. United Affairs has a location in every capital city."

"Thank you so much, ma'am."

She grunted a 'you're welcome' and I headed to a nearby phone booth. Even phones had changed. This station had a screen and a touch pad to dial the number.

If every state possessed a United Affairs location in every capital, then I needed to travel to Lansing. So, I used the hospital's phone and called United Affairs.

I made an appointment with a gentleman by the name of Lewis Sashar. Departing from the hospital, I made my way to Lansing.

The next day, I came to a humongous building that had a huge blue spinning globe on top of it. I couldn't believe how tall it was. The title "United Affairs" orbited the globe.

I shook my head at the opulence and walked in. At a reception desk stood three men—identical triplets—dressed in security guard uniforms.

"May—"

"—I—"

"—help you?" the triplet guards asked, each saying a word with the third triplet finishing the question.

I grinned to myself as I looked upon the faces of the identical triplets. *What a peculiar way of speaking,* I thought to myself.

"I have an appointment with a gentleman by the name of Lewis Sashar."

The first man nodded and the second stroked the keys of the holographic keyboard before him. The third guard viewed the holographic screen and wet his lips. This time they spoke in the opposite order with the third man speaking first. "Lewis Sashar is—"

"—on the forty-fifth floor."

"Take the elevator up then—"

"— take a left, then go straight, and he's the first door on the left side."

"Thank you," I said, amused by the exchange.

I quickly made my way to the elevator across the lobby. I boarded the glass elevator and up, up, up I went. The people below soon looked like ants.

When I reached the forty-fifth floor, I got off and followed the directions. Arriving before Lewis Sashar's door, I took a deep breath and opened it. I moved inside and frowned when I realized that less than four feet away was a second door.

I was about to find out who I was. My heart raced, hammering against my rib cage. I reached out with my right hand, balled up my fist, and knocked on the door.

"Come in!" said a voice beyond the door.

I turned the doorknob and entered. The desk before me was covered in documents. The leather chair behind the desk was turned away from me, facing the window. I could hear the clicking of keys; he must've been typing.

"Hello, Mr. Sashar. My name's Zedo Jeta. We talked the other day."

"Yes, yes, please sit." The chair still hadn't turned. I nodded and took a seat, waiting patiently until I had his full attention.

Moments later, the chair swiveled around and Lewis Sashar placed another document on his massive desk.

Lewis Sashar appeared to be 40-something with ear length chestnut hair. He wore a multicolored shirt and tie with a suit coat and dress pants. I glanced at the edge of his cluttered desk and caught sight of an ashtray.

"So, what can I do for you?" Mr. Sashar asked as he rose from his seat. He buttoned his suit coat and moved around to the front of his desk and leaned against it, mere feet from me.

"I need to know about my family. I need to know who they are, just everything."

"Do you not have contact with them?"

I held his gaze. "I was an orphan."

He nodded. "Well, we're going to need proof of your identity—for verification purposes, of course—and you'll need to fill out a couple of forms." He reached back and grabbed a stack of papers off his desk and handed them to me. "It will take about four business days."

My eyes grew wide with shock as I took the form. "Four days just to fill out some forms?"

"Yes, sir." Lewis crossed his arms over his chest. "For all I know, you could be trying to kill whoever you may be looking for. Therefore, we require this paperwork to better verify your identity, in addition to requesting I.D."

"I just came out of a coma! I don't know anything."

"A coma, wow!" he said, his voice dripping with sarcasm. "When?"

I rose from my seat. "Don't worry about that. I just needed to know who I was…where I'd come from."

"Well, I just can't give you information. Plus, it's going to cost you. I'm going to need proof of something."

"Oh. Well thanks for your time." I turned and reached for the door.

"Giving up so easily?" he asked from behind me.

I looked over my shoulder. "Sir?"

"Fill out what you can, and we'll go from there. As far as payment, we can work that out as well."

"Thank you, thank you so much, sir!" I said excitedly as I moved across the office to shake his hand.

"Um, you can let go now," he said, his face twisting in annoyance.

"Oh." I released his hand, left his office, and headed to the elevator.

"Wait!" I turned and caught sight of Mr. Sashar moving down the hall.

"Yes, Mr. Sashar?"

He stopped a few feet from me. "How old are you, kid? Thirteen?"

I thought about it for a moment. Though I was technically about his age, I still had the outward appearance of a teenager. Why not go with it?

"Fourteen, sir," I lied.

"Jesus Christ!" he exclaimed, running a hand through his hair. "You're the same age as my Cassie." He looked at me. "That's my daughter. We shouldn't even be having this conversation. The law requires a person to be of age before we even release sensitive information to them, but..."

"I don't want to cause problems, sir."

He waved the comment off. "I'll take care of it." He reached into his pocket and pulled out his wallet. My eyes grew wide. "A kid like you shouldn't be out in the world all by himself. I know protocol dictates that I call CPS and have them to reunite you with your foster family, but—"

"I don't want to go back there!" I said, trying to put a little fear into my voice. That would never happen. I was a grown man trapped in the frozen body of my teenager self.

"Here is seven hundred dollars, which should help you get back on track." I took the money and thanked him. "Take care of yourself, kid, and come back when you've completed the forms, alright?"

"I will. Thanks again, sir."

I took the elevator. Down, down I went.

I got off and the triplets at the front desk said 'goodbye.' I headed outside and hailed a cab.

"Where to?" asked the driver as I climbed into the backseat.

"Take me to the edge of the city."

We rode in silence and he dropped me off at the city limit, just before the sign. I paid him and waited until he was out of sight.

I closed my eyes, reached deep down inside of me—causing my powers to awaken. I felt the air around me began to shift and I began to lift myself into the air.

I was always amazed when my powers worked.

I headed into the clouds and headed across the country. I didn't want anyone to see me, in case it drew attention to me.

I avoided planes as much as I could.

I had the forms I needed to start the process of finding my family, but right now, I felt I was needed by my *other* family. I was ready to get back, back to my team... and back to Mona.

Chapter 15:

Got You Now

CREW

I returned to the hospital and surprisingly my teammates were still there. Mona was waiting at the entrance, as if she'd known I was coming back. She wore a black top over jeans with a bolero blue jean jacket and finished the look with a pair of boots.

"Mona!" I grinned. "You're awake! I—"

She slapped me and my face turned with the hit.

"Ow!" I shouted, shocked.

"Where in the world have you been, Zedo Jeta?"

"I had to take care of something from my past."

"You killed Burton without me?"

"No. I'm trying to find my family," I answered, rubbing my cheek, still in shock. "I took your advice and tried to focus on something other than revenge. I told the nurse to—"

"Yes, Nurse Weirdo gave us the message, but still…" She crossed her arms over her plump breasts and exhaled. "That was impersonal, Zee. After all we've been through…you shouldn't have left us like that. We deserved better than that."

I nodded. "I'm sorry. I wasn't trying to abandon anyone, especially you."

She turned and headed into the hospital. I followed her. "So, you went after your family? You know who they are?"

She led me to the elevator and we entered it, heading up.

"No, I don't know, yet, but if I fill this out"—I showed her the forms—"I will be one step closer to finding out."

"What made you want to find them?" she asked, walking off the elevator as we reached the eighth floor.

"I had a vision of the past, I think."

"That is amazing, Zee."

I shook my head. "It is, but it *isn't*. My powers are growing. They're all so different from one another and it's all been happening within the past few months. It's a lot, Mona. It's almost overwhelming. I have to focus just to keep them under control."

"But you're doing it, Zedo. So far so good."

I shrugged. "If you say so." I explained to her what Lewis Sashar had told me about the forms. I then told her about Edward Wong and his daughter.

Mona couldn't believe that the massive stack Sashar had given me would take four days to fill out. She asked me why Lewis hadn't given me an electronic copy. Then she asked if I thought Dr. Wong worked for Burton.

I told her I didn't think he did but who really knew. It was all too strange.

"Well, we're all doing okay here. I was discharged a few days ago. Gonzo was moved to the sixth floor the other day."

"How's Tempestt?" I asked.

"Your friend just got out of surgery, sir."

My eyes grew wide. "She's *just* getting out?"

Mona rolled her eyes. "No, genius. She's had to have multiple surgeries since you vanished. She suffered a lot of internal damage. She's been recovering. I was going to take you to see her, but—"

"No, that would be great."

She nodded and we turned the corner. A nurse exited Tempestt's room and we gazed through the window. Tempestt had been wrapped up like a mummy.

We moved into the room and I moved to her bedside where she could see me. "Oh, Tem. Are you alright?" I asked, then thought better of it. Of course, she wasn't alright.

"Hi, Zedo," she said, her voice hoarse. I sat next to her for a while, catching her up on things. She told me about her surgeries and forty minutes or so later, I rose from my chair to head to check on Gonzo.

Mona moved towards Tempestt and helped her sit up for her to take a drink. As I watched Mona act on maternal instinct, I wondered if she was aware that she was indeed pregnant.

I grinned to myself, sad but content. She'd had it rough, just like Gonzo. She deserved a happy ending. We all did.

I left the room and went to find Gonzo Daniels. When I came into the room, he was just coming from the restroom. I heard the toilet flushing and he appeared, limping into the room—his leg wrapped in a cast.

"Hey, you," I said.

He jumped, startled. "Dude, you scared me!" I moved across the room and we embraced. "Buddy I'm so glad you're back."

He turned away and limped towards his bed.

I pulled a chair beside the bed and we conversed.

"I'm so glad you're here so I can get out of this dump," Gonzo said. "They won't let us leave, which is illegal!" Then he looked at me. "Do you know how we ended up here? I…." his words trailed off as though he had fallen into deep thought.

I shook my head. "My guess is as good as yours. At first, I didn't remember ever being in a car, but Lester paid me a visit once I was in the hospital." I could tell Gonzo wanted me to fill him in, but I waved it off. I didn't want to share everything that had happened. Though he was my friend, I wanted that to be between just Mona and me.

"Get dressed," I told him.

He frowned. "Where are we going?" he asked.

"Just get up," I told him, rising from my chair.

I waited as Gonzo hopped around the room to grab his clothes and change.

As we left the room, I realized I shouldn't have shut him out. He was part of the team, and there was nothing going on between Mona and me—we were just friends.

So, as we headed to Tempestt's room, I told him about United Affairs. I also told him about my vision.

We went back to Tempestt's room and Mona was in tears. *Hormones*, I thought to myself.

We gathered around Tempestt's bed and for a brief moment, we felt like a family.

Suddenly, I sensed a change in the air. My senses flared and my telepathy kicked into overdrive. Something was wrong.

"What is it, Zee?" Gonzo asked, looking at me.

"We've got trouble," I told them. I couldn't explain it, but as thoughts began to overlap in my mind, I knew that something was off.

I closed my eyes and tried to focus and slowly the voices began to retreat.

"What trouble?" asked Mona, rising from her seat.

My lips parted and one word escaped them. "Burton."

"What now?" Tempestt asked.

The phone in the room began to ring. We all jumped; startled. Mona glanced at me and I nodded. She moved towards it and reached out for the receiver.

"Hello?"

"Mona Lisa-Flynn," came a distorted voice.

"Who is this?"

"You *know* who this is."

She looked over to us, her eyes wide. She mouthed "*it's him.*"

I wondered if she meant Lester or his father. I stretched out with my mind so I could hear Mona's thoughts and confirmed that it was Lester on the other end.

"I see you," the voice said, growing colder. She turned to the window. I felt her thoughts screaming with alarm, the pressure building in my mind.

"Where are you?" she asked, her voice turning hard with a bit of an edge to it. She squinted into the distance when she suddenly gasped. Her eyes grew wide in disbelief. "GET DOWN!" she screamed.

Gonzo moved to Tempestt and pulled her off her bed. Mona and I threw ourselves to the ground seconds before a missile came through the window and exploded.

We were thrown through the opposite wall—smoke and debris filling the air. Alarms began to blare. My head throbbed and there was a ringing in my ear.

I coughed and wondered why he'd attack us in a hospital. Then I shook my head as I rose to my feet; I knew why. He didn't care about the loss of life. Lester was a monster just like his father.

Screams filled the air and I caught sight of a fire breaking out. Across the room, I heard moaning and realized it was Tempestt. I moved over debris towards where she and Gonzo laid sprawled across the floor, under a piece of the ceiling.

Sparks flew everywhere and I wondered where Mona was. I got my answer a second later when she pushed a door aside and climbed into view.

"Are you two alright?" I asked.

Gonzo eyed Tempestt worriedly and slightly shook his head.

"Gonzo, stay with Tempestt. Mona, let's go!" I moved towards the hole in the wall we'd been hurled through and headed back into the one we'd been in. A hole had been punched into the side of the wall where the window had been. Smoke rose from the singed edges of the wall where the missile had struck.

I looked around, wondering where the missile had come from then glanced at the parking garage across the street. On the top floor of the garage, a black clad figure tossed a missile launcher aside and made a run for it.

"Mona, let's go!" I yelled again.

Mona looked at me with her face etched in utter horror. "These boots are *Fendi*, Zedo! I can't run in these."

"Come on!" I told her, annoyed.

She groaned and moved to my side, pulling her auburn hair into a ponytail.

A black mustang sped off below us at street level —burning rubber.

I grabbed Mona and jumped from the hole in the wall. She screamed, startled by our sudden fall. I called the wind to bend at my will and I softened our fall as we neared the ground.

The black mustang sped down the street and we ran after it.

"Mona, take out the tires!" I ordered as I lifted myself into the air again and flew after the car.

Mona threw both hands forward and hurled ice beams at the back tires. Ice hit the wheels but they didn't freeze. The tires emitted such heat that the ice nearly melted.

Mona snarled and threw her arms behind her. She fired ice beams at the ground and propelled herself forward—using the ice to keep her suspended in mid-air as she faux-flew towards the assailants.

I was surprised that she could propel herself with ice.

Mentally punching myself for being distracted, I added more speed and closed the distance between the mustang and me.

I landed on the roof of the vehicle and steadied myself with the wind, then back flipped onto the hood of the car. The car swerved—the driver startled by my sudden appearance.

I yelled and slammed my fist into the windshield. The glass shattered and I reached inside to seize the driver by his neck.

Mona hurled ice beams onto the back on the mustang. It jerked and came to a screeching halt. I yanked the driver out of his seat and tossed him into the air and he slammed into the concrete. Blood flowed from his head onto the ground.

From his place in the passenger seat, Lester Burton cackled like a deranged man. I wondered how Lester had moved from the roof of the parking garage to the car in less than a few seconds.

"Got ya, Lester," I said frustrated and fed up.

"No, no you don't," he said and suddenly his face was hard as stone—a darkness in his eyes. "I've got *you*."

"Zedo, watch out!" Mona cried.

I turned around and jumped into the air.

Just then, Lester jumped out the car and fell to his feet. Another car, a black mustang GT, had launched a missile. It slammed into the car and exploded, shooting flames into the air.

I ducked, pulled air molecules tight around me, and formed a shield. The air rippled around me. I slammed my eyes shut as chunks of the car bounced off my shield.

As the flames receded I rose to my feet and rushed to Mona's side. She pulled a piece of shrapnel out of her thigh. Tossing it aside, she glanced at the blood that oozed from the wound.

Across the road, the driver of the mustang GT put out his hand. Lester dashed to the car and grabbed it, being pulled in seconds before the car sped off.

Mona moved to chase the car, but I held out a hand to stop her.

"I've got this." I flew upward and lifted my hand to the sky. The clouds grew dark and I focused on my powers. Energy crackled and I felt my powers stir. I called down a lightning bolt and it landed in my palm.

I swirled it around and it grew—changing from white light to a faint blue. I yelled as the sting of bolt grew and then hurled it down the road and into the mustang.

The mustang burst into flames. I flew towards the vehicle and landed. Mona moved towards the car. I tore the door off and yanked the driver out. Lester leapt from the vehicle and made a run for it.

The driver was dead and I allowed his body to slump to the ground.

"Zedo, he's getting away!" Mona shouted, pointing at Lester.

"I won't let him get away. Go get Gonzo."

She turned and without a word, threw her hands back and propelled herself back towards the hospital with a burst of ice.

I turned to chase Burton but was caught off guard as a helicopter materialized out of thin air. It was sleek and was definitely something out of the future. Then I realized that when I'd fallen into my coma, that the world had moved on. Surely, technology had as well.

This helicopter was black and silver and its blades were made of pulsing energy.

Several men in black armor leaned out of the helicopter's sliding door and aimed their weapons at us but didn't fire. One reached down to pull Lester aboard.

As I moved towards the helicopter, it lifted off the ground, flew off, and disappeared before it reached the clouds.

My jaw dropped, astonished at the technology. I swore under my breath.

Where had it gone?? I couldn't even hear it!

Turning, I lifted myself into the air and flew towards the hospital.

When I arrived at the hospital, Mona and Gonzo were already waiting for me—stolen vehicle in tow.

"Where's Lester?" Mona asked. I told her how the helicopter had appeared out of thin air. She nodded and they climbed into the car, Mona behind the wheel.

Gonzo eased into the front seat. "We have to leave Tempestt behind, for now. Our friendly nurse will watch after her until we return."

"We can't leave her behind," I told them. "We have to get her. We're leaving the state and we won't be able to come back. The authorities might want to question us after the attack on the hospital."

I glanced around at all of the emergency personnel rushing around. Flashing lights were everywhere, from the police cars and fire trucks.

"Where are we going?" Mona asked as she eyed me through the rearview mirror.

I looked out the window as Gonzo climbed out of the car to retrieve Tempestt. "We're going to Michigan."

"Zedo…" Mona began, and I knew she was going to challenge my decision. "Lester just attacked us. If that isn't a sign that the Burtons aren't going to give up, then I don't know what is. Now isn't the time to find your family. We need to go after them. We need to—"

"Weren't you just telling me that maybe we could stop? You told me that we could be different! You told me that I could choose *life* instead of revenge!"

She bit her lower lip and I could see she was about to retort.

Then, I decided to tell her about Dr. Edward Wong and his daughter, Seay'. I told her about how they lived in fear of the government taking Seay' away because of her powers. I told her how Edward feared for his life and his daughter's future.

We lived in fear of Burton and had decided to seek revenge, but what would that do? Burton was the head of a syndicate we really didn't know the full scope of. If we cut the head off the dragon, how could we be sure that another wouldn't sprout up in his place?

Soon, Tempestt and Gonzo appeared and he helped her climb into the stolen vehicle. Luckily, the truck was big enough to give everyone space.

Tempestt winced as Gonzo laid her on the back seat next to me. Of course, she hadn't been discharged, but we couldn't worry about that now.

"So, what's the plan, boss?" Gonzo asked.

I opened my mouth, but Mona beat me to it. "Michigan," she said.

I glanced at her and she quickly looked away—clearly displeased.

As Mona drove away from the hospital, I wondered how she was doing, knowing that she was pregnant and all. I hoped that the baby was all right and it hadn't been hurt.

Eight hours later, we pulled into a rest stop. Gonzo helped Tempestt out of the truck and to the restrooms. I turned to Mona whom was looking out the window. My legs were stiff and I needed to stretch, but I needed to talk to Mona first.

I cleared my throat. "Um, Mona?"

"Yeah?" She turned to look me in the eye.

"How are you?"

"I'm fine, Zee," she said, giving a nervous chuckle afterwards. "Just a little tired. I agree with what you said back at the hospital. We have the right to choose, but—"

"No. I mean how are *you*... with the child?"

Her eyes grew wide. "How'd you—?"

"I was there when…" Mona lowered her head and I frowned. "Mona?"

"Zedo, while you were gone—" She stopped and placed a hand over her mouth. Tears filled her eyes, but she wouldn't let them fall. She immediately wiped her eyes.

"You didn't do it, did you?" I tried to not let the sound of judgment fill my voice, but it still came out judgmental.

She looked at me, furious. "I had no choice!"

"I'm on your side!" I threw my hands up in mock surrender. I didn't know the first thing about having a baby, let alone sex. Who was I to tell her what she should do with her body?

Beyond that, I was a guy! I had absolutely **NO** right to make that decision for a woman.

"I am in no condition to have a baby," Mona said, but I could tell she wasn't saying it to me. She was trying to convince *herself*. "We're on a mission. I can't stop now; we're too far into this."

"We could have stopped if you'd wanted to," I told her, my voice low. I looked at her and she seemed to diminish before my eyes. She seemed so torn up about her decision to have an abortion. I wondered if she regretted it?

Had she been in love with the father? Where was he now?

But none of that mattered. She needed my support now. I couldn't see her letting Gonzo hold her hand through that.

Then, it hit me! She'd been *alone*! My heart began to break for her.

"I'm sorry you went through that all by yourself. I should've been there."

She waved the comment off and dabbed her eyes; a few tears had escaped. "I'm a big girl, Zedo. I'm fine."

Then something else dawned on me. "Wait, I wasn't gone that long! And you were using your powers back there! Mona, you aren't healed! What are you thinking?! Isn't that dangerous?"

She unbuckled and climbed out of the truck. "You aren't my father, Zedo! I don't need you to lecture me!" She slammed the door and walked off.

I followed her. "Lecture you?! Mona, I'm trying to *help* you! You and your child are much more important than Burton…"

"Well it doesn't matter now! There's no baby!"

"What about the father?" I asked.

"What about him?" She turned and crossed her arms over her breasts. I could see fire in her eyes. She was furious, to say the least.

"Mona, please. I'm just trying to be here for you."

"His name was David Connor Williams. He was twenty-seven."

"*Was?*" I asked.

She seemed to melt just then and looked away from me. "Yeah, *was*. He's dead now…" She once again lowered her head.

"You didn't kill him, did you?" I asked, in a calmer tone.

"No, Zee! Of course not!" she shouted, furious all over again. "What kind of monster do you think I am?! I loved him! We were going to get married in six months. We didn't know that I was pregnant. But when Jonathan contacted me, everything changed! David was murdered hours later and I assumed it was Burton's way of warning me to stay away! But then I couldn't! I needed to avenge David's death!" She exhaled sharply and began to cry.

I reached out to touch her, but she knocked my hand away.

"If I'd known I was pregnant, I wouldn't be on this team." She shook her head. "That's a lie. I still would've joined. I had a new reason to kill Burton, but…"

"Mona, I-I'm so sorry. I didn't know."

"Of course you didn't know! I was a secret agent! It was my job to keep my private life secret! If your enemies know your weaknesses—"

"They exploit them," I finished, nodding.

"I miss him so much, but I couldn't do this without David."

"You felt that if David wasn't alive to enjoy this child then you shouldn't have it?"

She shook her head, rolling her eyes as she did so. "No, that's not why I had an abortion. I didn't, I *couldn't*, raise a child on my own. I just couldn't. I'm not maternal. I just lost the love of my life. Then I lost my brother. There was too much going on in such a short time. I just needed everything to stop."

"You could have put the child up for adoption, Mona."

She looked at me, wiped her eyes, and then turned to walk away. "This discussion is over."

Tempestt and Gonzo soon returned and shortly after they climbed back into the truck, we were on the road again. After about three hours I noticed we were beginning to be followed by a Ferrari 575M Maranello.

"Mona—"

"I see it," she said, glancing out her rearview mirror.

I suddenly felt thoughts pressing against my own—the familiar pressure of my telepathy activating against my will. I sensed malice and knew who was behind us.

Behind us, the Ferrari 575M Maranello began to float off the ground, as though on repulsor lifts—an anti-gravity technology that allowed vehicles to hover. The headlights disappeared and miniature cannons appeared in their place.

My eyes grew wide as I sensed danger a second before we were attacked. "Down!" I yelled.

The cannons were loosed and fired bursts of energy-rich gas that had been converted to a glowing particle beam that upon impact could melt through targets.

"Blaster cannons!" yelled Gonzo, pulling Tempestt down as blaster bolts pierced the truck, shattering glass.

Mona twisted the wheel and the truck swerved. I grunted as I was thrown about.

"Can this truck float like that car can?" I asked, twisting around in my seat to see the Ferrari gaining on us.

Without a word, Mona pressed a button next to the gear shift and I heard a faint humming and felt the vibration through my feet. In the next instance we began to float. I looked out the window and caught sight of our tires disappearing and were replaced by cylinder pods that lifted us into the air.

Behind us, the blaster cannons kept firing, hammering us with blaster bolts.

Suddenly, I heard a loud popping and the truck flipped over. Our screams filled the air as we flipped end-over-end and headed towards the ground.

"We're going to crash!" Gonzo yelled.

I tried to call my powers into play, but it was too late. We slammed into the ground and landed bottom up.

Panting, I fired a si' beam at the door and it flew off its hinges. "Is everyone alright?" I asked as I began to climb out.

"Help me with Tempestt," said Gonzo. Across from me, Mona was kicking the remaining glass out of her window and began to crawl out of the wreckage.

As we moved away from the totaled truck, we found nine figures across the road.

Standing in all black were eight men and a few feet before them stood Lester. His shoulder length, midnight black hair was down—rustled by the wind. They were lined straight across, weapons in hand.

"Lester," I called out as I took a step forward. "We've got to stop meeting like this." I pulled a shard of glass out of my forearm.

Mona placed Tempestt on the ground and then she and Gonzo moved towards me.

Lester grinned. "Hello, Mr. Jeta." He looked past me and glared. "Hello, Tempestt."

I moved to block her from sight. "You don't speak to her. Speak to *me*."

Lester smirked. "You're such a cocky little thing." He eyed Gonzo and Mona. "I'm surprised you two are still alive." He snapped his fingers.

Without a word, the men rushed towards us and the three of us—Gonzo, Mona, and I—simply kicked the first three in their faces.

As we landed on solid ground, the three goons fell before us. The others skidded to a stop.

"Don't just stand there!" shouted Lester. "Kill them, you fools!"

Tempestt was trying to get up at this point. I didn't know what she could expect to do. She was still in a leg cast and had a sling on her left arm.

Lester pulled two pistols from shoulder holsters and aimed at us.

We spun and flipped out of the way. Mona and Gonzo did cartwheels and I somersaulted and landed behind Gonzo.

Lester pulled both triggers, trying to shoot us. I moved about, doing whatever I could to dodge the bullets and rushed over to my teammates that, by now, had regrouped.

Lester struck several of his goons by accident and yelled.

"We're still outnumbered," said Gonzo.

"I'm going to level the playing field," I told him. Rising to my feet, I moved from behind the truck—the only cover we had—and moved to where Lester could see me.

His remaining goons aimed, but Lester held a hand up to stop them. "Are you surrendering to me, Mr. Jeta?" he asked.

"You know I can't do that. Why don't you just leave, Lester? You don't have to die."

He chuckled and began to speak, but I shut his voice out. I closed my eyes and reached deep down inside of me and then reached outside of me and into the Earth itself. I reached for *power*.

It came slowly, but surely. Instead of using that power to attack, I let it gather inside of me until I felt it reach overwhelming levels—like a sink that was beginning to overflow.

I held the power in place.

All of my powers responded differently. I felt warm and safe now. It was nothing like the energy I felt when I pulled power for the weather or fire. Using my elemental powers to affect the earth or air felt less seductive than the destructive flare of fire or the unpredictable wrath of lightning.

With earth and air, it was more soothing, caressing even; like mother Earth was responding and sharing her gifts with me.

I was going to manipulate the earth but then I remembered the last time I'd done so. I recalled the horror on my friends' faces when I'd destroyed the road and the diner, killing innocents as well as those sent to attack us. I didn't want to scare them, but I also knew what needed to be done.

I reached down and slammed my fist into the earth, releasing my power with a yell and burst of energy. Chunks of earth shot up and lava followed, bursting forth like geysers. I heard shouts fill the air.

Forty feet in front of me, Lester fell to his knees and crab walked backwards until his back was against a car door. Fear was etched on his face as he eyed the geysers of lava. Then, he looked at me and glared.

I rose to my feet and called upon the might of my powers. I heaved the chunks of earth higher into the air and yelled—the strain of holding this much power making my head throb. I forced the chunks down, driving them into the ground crushing Lester's goons and causing an explosion from the brute force of energy being displaced.

The explosion emitted a brilliant flash of light. The blinding light was followed by an aftershock that knocked me off my feet and into a boulder left behind.

I slammed into the boulder and cried out in pain. Falling to the ground, chaos ensued all around me. Yet the blinding light grew brighter still. There was ringing in my ears and my vision grew spotty.

There was just...*light* and *pain*.

Then, there was *darkness*. It always ended in darkness.

Chapter 16:

Any Way You Can

❧

I didn't expect to open my eyes ever again. The pain of using that much power, plus the pain of hitting a boulder at full speed was just too much. Something felt broken. But somehow, despite an explosion and chaos and lava and dead goons, I'd survived.

I opened my eyes and found myself floating in a transparent bubble of shimmering energy surrounded by boulders covered in flames, smoking vehicles, and carnage.

I was bleeding from a gash in my side, my left arm had been dislocated, and my right ankle throbbed. My vision began to clear and I realized I was lying in a pool of my own blood; a pool that had gathered in the bottom of the transparent bubble. My jeans were partially soaked and my shirt was torn to shreds.

I heard sirens, but faintly.

Where was everyone?

As I took in my surroundings, I only saw destruction. *I* had caused this.

I tried to stand but found it impossible.

I hadn't created this bubble of protective energy, at least I didn't think I had.

So, if I hadn't…then who had? Someone had saved me, but who?

Mona could only emit ice beams, as far as I knew, and Gonzo was only able to fly and emit yellow-shaded energy blasts. Could it have been Tempestt? I knew she was a highly skilled martial artist and assassin, but was she a super human as well?

Something moved, out there in the chaos—in the rubble—in the smoke and flames. I watched as a figure moved through the smoke and soon became clear. My heart froze.

It was Lester Burton. He held a hand forward, his fingers stretched. His black suit was covered in dirt, his hair was dirty as well, but his eyes were clear. His eyes shone with rage; his face twisted in a snarl.

"You thought you were going to kill me, did you?" He laughed aloud, but there was no joy in it. "You thought I was going to let you die, too? My father wouldn't allow that. I kept you alive. You can't even control your powers, you just knock things about. You should thank me for saving your life!"

"No one asked you to."

"My father would—"

"I don't care about your father! He's going to get what's coming to him!"

Lester froze and dropped his hand to his side, but he didn't release me from the force field he'd encased me in. "You really want him dead?" He took a step towards me then stopped. "You don't even understand." His voice was low.

What was he talking about?

I quickly took in my surroundings. I didn't see the others. Had I killed them?

Oh, God! Where are they? I thought to myself.

As he moved towards me, moving over rubble, I realized that he was injured, too. He limped and pressed his free hand against a wound, which was also in his side.

Lester now stood just a few feet from me. "You don't know what he did for you."

"*Did for me?!* Are you **MAD?** Your father tried to kill me!"

Lester shook his head. "You're an idiot, Jeta! My father *freed* you!"

My eyes grew wide. "What are you talking about? You weren't there! You don't know! You didn't see the look in his eyes when he—"

Lester held out a hand. "Come with me."

Just then, he released his hold on the force field and I crumbled to the ground. I screamed out upon impact. Lester watched me with icy focus as I rose to my feet.

"I'm not going anywhere with you," I snarled. I winced as pain shot through my body. My ankle was definitely twisted. I held my shoulder and wondered if I could pop it back in place.

A hot breeze rustled Lester's dirty clothes. "I can't make you. You have to come on your own free will."

I dusted myself off and took a step forward, wary of my sprained ankle. "The answer is **no**."

Lester sighed and dropped his hand. "I'm keeping you alive for *him*. Other than that, I'd kill you now. I'm tired of testing you."

I blinked, confused. "Testing me? What the hell is going on?"

Suddenly, a blur rushed by and tackled Lester. Lester yelled and was thrown backwards. Beams of ice came from the opposite direction.

I turned and caught sight of Mona. She leaned against a chunk of debris, arm outstretched. At her side stood Tempestt.

"Gonzo!" I yelled, going after him and Lester. As I moved through the debris, I caught sight of Gonzo, but he stood alone.

"He's gone," Gonzo said, touching his lip—it bled now. "He just vanished into thin air."

"Well, that was close," Tempestt said from behind me. I turned and caught sight of her wiping her face.

"Zedo, you could've killed us," said Mona, her voice low but clear. She was seething.

"I didn't try to…I just—"

"Can't control your powers," she interjected.

"So, where to now?" Tempestt asked, looking from one person to the next and changing the subject. I looked at her, silently thanking her for saving my neck.

"Any suggestions?" I asked, doing the same.

"Let's... go to my house," Tempestt suggested, her gaze moving to the sky as the last word left her lips. She frowned. I turned my gaze towards the sky and caught sight of a single vulture looping about. She shook her head and then looked at me. "We can regroup at my house."

Mona shrugged and Gonzo clapped his hands together. "Sounds good to me," he said.

"We'll have to fly," I added as I glanced at the truck, which had been torn apart.

"Where do you live exactly?" Mona questioned.

"South Carolina."

"Well, that's a-long-ways from here, young lady," Gonzo said with a thick, put-on southern accent.

"Let's get going," Mona told them.

"But you can't fly," Gonzo pointed out.

She rolled her eyes. "Thanks, genius. You and Zedo can. You'll just have to carry us."

I raised an eyebrow. I'd get to carry her? Just then, she moved towards Gonzo and my heart sank. I should've known she wasn't going to let me carry her. She was still royally pissed off at me.

"We'll have to fly low," Gonzo said as he heaved Mona into the air.

"We'll only need to fly until we can get close to civilization," Mona told him. "The second we're near a parking garage, we're stealing a vehicle."

I exhaled. "Must we be thieves as well as vigilantes?"

She ignored me and Gonzo lifted himself into the air. Tempestt limped towards me. Her arm sling glowed for a second then was reduced to dust. I took a step back and she grinned. "It's okay, Zedo. My arm's healed now." She flexed her once broken arm. "That's how tech works, now. When you're injured, they wrap it in accelerated healing garments and when your bones have mended, they melt away."

I nodded, curious. So much had changed.

Tempestt glanced at her leg cast. "I'd give this one another day or two before it pops and melts, too." She moved towards me and circled about.

She quickly grabbed my shoulder and popped it into place before I could protest. I opened my mouth to scream as pain wreaked havoc on my body. But as quickly as the pain had come, it left.

I exhaled sharply and touched my shoulder. It was back in its socket. "Much better," I said, nodding my thanks.

She grinned and jumped into my arms and I caught her. "Let's go."

I grinned and lifted us into the arm.

We reached Virginia a few days later, after having stopped a few times to rest and eat. Tempestt hotwired a mid-sized SUV and we made our way to Norfolk.

By the time we arrived in Norfolk, Tempestt had fully regained her strength and was back to being her old self.

Since I had more then enough money with me, I treated my teammates to brunch.

Afterwards, we settled into a motel to shower, change, and rest. We were all in need of showers and I for one, was ready to crash.

Mona and Tempestt headed into one room and Gonzo and I headed into the other.

I threw my clothes into the sink and let them soak before I climbed into the shower and turned the dial as far as I could.

That evening, we were supposed to meet in the lobby and then head to dinner, but Mona and Tempestt were late. I was quickly growing weary of motels and hotels.

As I headed outside to see if the vehicle was back, I caught sight of the girls coming through the motel's doors with at least five bags.

"Um, ladies," I called out, crossing my arms over my chest.

"Zee," Mona said, busted. She skidded to a stop and Tempestt tried to hide her bags behind her back.

"Where'd you get the bags?" I asked, raising an eyebrow.

"What bags?" said Tempestt. Mona nudged her in the rib and she cried 'ouch.'

"We went to this boutique down the road," Mona answered, locking eyes with me.

"Wait, wait. Where did you get the money?" I asked.

"I don't know about Mona, but I used my credit card," Tempestt said as she shrugged. "I'm not broke."

Mona's eyes grew wide. "I didn't know you used your card! I told you to use cash!"

"Do you know what you've done?!" I shouted, louder than I'd intended.

Silence filled the air and heads turned to look at us. I hadn't realized that the lobby was full of bystanders.

Tempestt frowned; she didn't get it. "No."

"You're a paid assassin, but sometimes I forget that you're still a kid. You just led anybody that's looking for you or us straight to us," Mona said, glaring at the girl.

"They can track card transactions," I told her, running a hand through my curly hair.

"Oops," Tempestt said, biting her lower lip.

"Oops?" I repeated.

"Sorry, Zee. I wasn't paying attention. I was just enjoying the experience."

"Sorry won't save our lives if Burton tracks us here," I told her, shaking my head.

"She said she was sorry. We'll pack up and get out of here before Burton has a chance to back us into a corner." Mona moved closer to me. "Lighten up, Zee," And then she pecked my cheek.

I blushed, and the two women rushed past me and up the staircase, giggling.

I tracked them with my eyes and watched them until they disappeared onto the second floor and headed down the hall.

Had she simply kissed my cheek to shut me up?

I touched my cheek and it felt warm. I could tell I was still blushing.

Going back to my room, thoughts of Mona filled my mind. I was furious with Tempestt and her lack of judgment, but then, I couldn't stay mad at her. Mona had glared at her and I'm sure she'd give the teen a piece of her mind in time, but overall, she'd kissed my cheek.

Was that a sign that she liked me?

With auburn hair and beautiful eyes that seemed to change, she was a sight to behold. Her lips were full, and she always smelled so good, but there was more to her than just her looks. A fashion fanatic like most women, she kept up with all of the latest styles, yet wasn't shallow. I didn't know if she'd adapted that as a past cover with the agency, but regardless I liked it.

I liked that she kept herself up, even when we were on the run. I liked that she was classy and yet had a bit of an edge. More than that, I just *liked* her…But I wondered if she liked me.

I didn't have much experience in that department and I was too embarrassed to ask Gonzo.

Then my thoughts turned to Tempestt. She was the exact opposite of Mona.

With jet black hair and a slender build, Tempestt possessed a charming personality and a good heart despite spending much of her formative years under Burton's thumb. But beyond that, what I felt for her was different. She was like a sister to me.

Even when she'd attacked us I felt a kinship to her. We instantly connected on a level that even I didn't truly understand.

Perhaps I saw a little bit of myself in her.

I rolled over in bed and forced my eyes to close and tried to turn my brain off.

If we weren't going to get dinner then I'd relax. Lord knows I needed my sleep.

Chapter 17:

<u>Nothing New</u>

☙❧

The sun peeked through the curtains and I realized it was morning. I left for breakfast in the lobby and decided to go for a long walk afterwards to clear my mind.

Unfortunately, Gonzo had wanted to tag along. But truly, I guess I didn't mind. He ended up being a welcome distraction to keep my mind off Mona.

Gonzo had so much to talk about. He told me all about his childhood growing up in New Mexico with four brothers and two sisters. This was the most personal conversation we'd had since we'd first met.

His parents, both from Mexico, always wanted a big family and came to the States shortly before Gonzo's birth. Once he started talking about the family he'd left behind, the flood gates burst open. He began to recall fond childhood memories before he'd been sent to the institute and before he'd joined the agency that had changed his life forever.

I grew a little jealous hearing about his family when I had no recollection of mine. I reached into the pocket of my jeans and pulled out the family papers I'd received from United Affairs. I began to read the document that I needed to fill out in order to find out more about my family. There were thousands of questions. I did my best to answer what I could. It was extremely hard to do that when I barely knew anything.

After two and a half hours, I had only completed thirteen questions.

Eventually, Gonzo realized I had stopped listening and had left me to work on the forms. I soon completed thirty-seven questions and decided it was time for a break.

I returned to the hotel and headed to my room, avoiding Mona's room. I needed some time to sort out my thoughts. After hearing about Gonzo's childhood, I was left wondering what mine would've been like if my mother hadn't murdered my father and grandmother...I wondered what life would've been like if I hadn't been put in the foster care system and thrown away like yesterday's trash.

After pouring over those forms, I felt drained and decided to catch a nap. I'd left instructions with Gonzo to wake me when the ladies were ready to leave. We couldn't stay here much longer, especially after Tempestt had used her credit card.

We probably should've left immediately when I'd found out, but we hadn't...

The second I seemed to drift off into a dreamless sleep, I woke to Gonzo's hands shaking me. When I started to question why he'd shaken me awake, he put a finger to my mouth.

It was an unmistakable warning. I went still, my heart froze and then began to beat faster and faster and adrenaline pumped through my veins.

I fought my way back to full alertness and Gonzo removed the finger from my lips but kept an index finger over his lips. He wanted me to stay quiet.

The room was dark. How long had I been asleep?

As I looked around I caught sight of Mona. She knelt next to the wide window. The curtains were drawn, blocking the outside world from view. Tempestt stood close by, up and on her feet, hands clasped around a small black blaster. Their eyes were on the door. Her leg must've finished healing overnight because the leg cast was no longer on it.

I slowly rose to my feet, trying not to make a noise. Everyone was quiet, too quiet. I didn't know what was going on and I was scared to ask, but I felt terror well up and could sense the fear in the air.

Suddenly, I realized that maybe Burton had located us and had sent his son and goons after us. I wasn't going to be Burton's guinea pig again—his slave, his experiment—and I wasn't going to let my friends suffer either.

I felt pressure against my mind and my telepathy picked up stray thoughts. Something was going on in the hotel.

Something was very, very *wrong*. The people out there were terrified.

Screams filled the air and I jumped, startled.

Suddenly, something slammed into the door with a loud thud. The door shook on its hinges but held. Then, something slammed into the door a second time and it bowed inward slightly.

Tempestt moved away from the door, aiming her blaster at it. The weapon hummed as it powered up.

The "being quiet" strategy fell away in the next instance as Mona moved from the window and rose to her full height. "We need to get out of here."

"What's out there?" I asked and realized that my voice was shaking.

In the next instance I got my answer when a horrid screech-howl filled the air. Gonzo swallowed noticeably. "It's the arachnid demons."

My thoughts instantly turned to the monsters we'd first encountered when Jonathan (Ardet) had taken us to Nick's mansion. These monsters were part of Burton's crime syndicate. I could only imagine that they'd been the product of some experiment of his.

I turned my focus to the door, which wasn't going to hold much longer as the arachnid demon rammed itself into the door again and screeched. Mona threw her hands towards the door and hurled ice at it, reinforcing the door.

"That won't hold it off for long," she announced.

"We need to move," Tempestt said.

"There's no other way out," I said, noting that the door was the only way in or out of the room.

"They tracked us here, Zedo, just like you said," Tempestt commented, unable to look at me. "I'm sorry."

"It doesn't matter now," I told her, looking around the room.

"The place is swarming with those demons," Mona said. "We were headed back to our room when Lester burst in with some of his men and those demons."

Something slammed into the window, shattering the glass. Tempestt cried out and suddenly an arachnid demon was climbing through the window, dripping saliva from its mouth and bearing its fangs. Gonzo swore and hurled a yellow energy blast as it as Tempestt opened fire.

The demon screeched, and another began to climb over it before it took its last breath.

"We need to go up, not out!" Mona shouted, covering her hand in ice and hurling it at the broken window. She covered the window in a thick sheet of ice and turned to me. "Zedo, we need you to open the ceiling."

My eyes grew wide and I took a step back. "What? B-But how? I—"

Mona moved across the room to me. "You can control the elements, right? This building is made up of material from the earth itself! You can manipulate it! Burst a hole in the ceiling and get us out of here!"

I started to stammer, but she placed a hand on my lips to silence me. "Shut up, Zedo. You can do this. Just breathe."

I nodded and focused on the ceiling. I called energy to me and threw my arm in the air. I balled my hand into a fist and began to thrust it in the air, over and over—channeling energy into the gesture like a jack hammer. The space between my hand and the ceiling began to ripple as I poured power into the gesture.

Sweat beaded across my forehead and I repeated the gesture. An arachnid demon slammed into the ice and it began to fracture. Mona poured a new layer of ice on top.

I forced the materials of the ceiling to respond to my elemental manipulation.

"Hurry, Zedo!" yelled Gonzo as another demon rammed the door again.

I poured more power into the gesture and yelled. I ripped open a significant hole in the roof and since we were on the top floor of the small motel, moonlight spilled in from above.

"YES!" I exclaimed, proud of myself. Gonzo moved and patted me on the shoulder.

"Good job, amigo." He turned to the women. "Let's move, folks. That door and window aren't going to hold much longer." He flexed his knees and then fired his body up like a rocket and landed easily above us outside the hole I'd created and stepped onto the roof.

Gonzo looked around and then peered down. "It's alright up here."

"I can't fly, genius!" yelled Mona.

Tempestt let out a sound that resembled frustration and offered her a cradle of her linked fingers for her foot. "Come on, Mona! We don't have time for this."

"We're cheerleaders now?" said Mona, eyeing the younger woman's hands.

Tempestt rolled her eyes. "Mona—"

Just then, an arachnid demon slammed into the door again.

Mona moved without another word and placed her foot in Tempestt's hands and she was tossed straight up, letting out a yell of astonishment at the teen's strength. Gonzo reached out and grabbed Mona and pulled her onto the roof.

"Zedo, the space isn't big enough for both of you to fly up together," Mona shouted down. "Throw Tempestt up and then you follow."

Tempestt moved towards me and lifted her leg for a boost off but I shook my head. I gestured with a hand and raised the air in the room until a gust filled the room and lifted Tempestt off her feet. She gasped and then I pushed my hands up, forcing her into the air and through the hole.

Gonzo caught her and pulled her onto the roof.

An arachnid-demon blew the door off its hinges and several rushed into the room. I screamed and instantly threw my arms forward—hurling flames at the demons that were about to lash out. The flames sent the demons flying back and through the doorway. The flames burned the doorway and then the room caught on fire.

Before a new group of demons could break into the room, I gestured downward and formed an air cushion under me and then propelled myself up and through the hole.

I left the ground just in time because a half second later, five arachnid-demons burst into the room, screeching.

I arrived on the roof and landed. Smoke began to rise through the hole. The fire had caught and was spreading.

I moved to the edge of the roof and heard countless screeches and howls fill the air. Dozens of the arachnid-demons surrounded the motel.

They swarmed below us and I suddenly wanted to retch. The demons were hideous and worse was the fact that more than a dozen had dragged innocent people out of the hotel and had begun to feast on them.

But then I caught sight of six beings among the demons. *Lester* turned his eyes towards the roof and I knew instantly that he was looking at me. I couldn't hear him, but I saw his lips move and then he pointed at me.

Several of the demons turned to face us and began to scale the side of the hotel. I backed away from the edge of the room.

"I was afraid of that," said Mona.

"We need to get out of here," added Tempestt.

"We'll have to fly," Gonzo said. "There's no other way."

The arachnid demons were clawing their way up the side of the motel, which was slowly becoming consumed by the fire I'd started.

In the distance I could hear the faint sound of alarms; first responders were on the way.

Tempestt yelled out and opened fire with her blaster. I spun and caught sight of the first of the demons climbing onto the roof. Her blaster bolts slammed into two demons, knocking them off the roof and back into the hoard below, which began to consume their fallen brethren. I once again felt the urge to retch.

Gonzo hurled energy blasts, killing a few more. "We need to move!" he yelled.

"There's another building across the street!" Mona shouted. "Get us there and we can get down to the vehicle and—"

"And then what?" asked Tempestt. "There are at least fifty of those monsters down there! They'll catch up to us in a car! We should just fly and—"

"We need to move, NOW!" I shouted, hurling a burst of air at several demons as they rushed across the roof towards us.

Gonzo grabbed Tempestt around the waist and flew off, heading to the building across the walkway. I ran towards Mona and she grabbed me about the waist. I lifted us into the air and turned in mid-air to secure my hold on her arm, holding her tight as we flew over the lip of the roof.

Mona cried out and I looked over my shoulder. An arachnid demon had latched onto her. In the next instance, the demon had yanked her off me and had fallen back onto the roof.

"Mona!" I yelled, turning back. Five more demons had come onto the roof and were attacking Mona.

I landed and hurled flames at the demons.

A moment later, the rooftop access door flew open and five goons rushed onto the roof, followed by Lester.

I pulled Mona to her feet and tried to move her behind me, but she knocked my hand aside. She didn't need me to protect her and I grinned to myself. I liked that about her, too. Even now, facing all of this, she stood on her own.

I wondered if Gonzo and Tempestt had made it to the other roof. Were they safe? Were they battling the demons?

Lester moved towards us, his black hair pulled back in a short ponytail. "Do you fancy my Anansi demons?" he asked, gesturing at the corpses of the black, furry creatures.

So that's what they're called, I thought to myself. *Anansi demons.*

"You created these beasts?" Mona asked, her chest heaving in and out.

"My father," he answered, confirming my suspicions. "But truly, they're the product of The Blank."

I looked at him and frowned. "What's *The Blank*?"

He smiled, but the gesture didn't reach his eyes. "Wouldn't you like to know?"

I moved to attack him, but Mona held me back.

Lester's men drew their weapons and aimed them at me.

I heard screams behind me and turned to catch sight of Tempestt and Gonzo on the adjacent roof battling the Anansi demons. I whirled back around and faced Lester and his goons— they hadn't moved at all.

"I'm done playing games with you!" I shouted and threw my arms forward. I called upon my earth powers and chunks of the roof gave way and the goons fell through the roof and into the flames that were consuming the motel.

Lester took several steps back and raised his arms, shielding his face from the flames. Horror was etched on his face.

Suddenly, four more goons appeared on the roof.

I yelled, and power welled up—overtaking me.

In an instant, fire exploded from my chest and began to travel over my body, but it didn't burn my clothes. I gasped, astonished at my display of power, but it didn't matter. I couldn't allow myself to become distracted.

We were under attack and I wasn't going to let Lester get away. Smoldering embers rained down from my body.

The flames erupted from both palms and then shot out of my mouth. I aimed the full force of my powers at Lester.

Shock stopped Lester's men in their tracks, but not for long. I punched my fists forward and streams of flames engulfed four of the men and then through the environment around us.

Everything the flames touched were engulfed. Their screams filled the air, a chorus of wails.

The stench of burning flesh filled the air.

"Zedo!!" Mona shouted behind me.

I turned around and a vortex of flames shot from my mouth and she dodged it. I'd almost hurt her. I closed my mouth and tried to calm myself.

My heart raced. Mona pushed herself to her feet and glanced at me, eyes wide with horror.

"M-Mona, I'm sorry! I-I didn't mean to!"

Two of the remaining goons opened fire and I lifted myself into the air. I landed on a ledge twenty feet up and looked down at the destruction all around me. **I'D CAUSED THIS**, at least the destruction on the roof.

"We should take him out now, Zedo," said Mona, hurling ice beams at the goons.

"I wouldn't give you the satisfaction!" Lester shouted and then turned and took off running.

Mona and I gave chase, heading across the destroyed rooftop.

Lester jumped off the edge of the building and fell to the ground below.

Without a thought, I followed after him. Mona was right behind me, but I threw up a breeze that helped her land softly on her feet.

As I struck the ground, Lester was already racing in the opposite direction. The Anansi demons were closing in on us.

Seconds later, Gonzo and Tempestt flew overhead, having given up on defending their ground on the second roof top.

I cleared a path for us with fire and then forced the demons back as I manipulated the earth, splitting it beneath our feet and causing several demons to fall into a crevice of my creation.

Up ahead, Lester neared a building and jumped up, finding hand-and-footholds on bricks, window shutters, and railings until he reached the eave of the roof and flipped atop it.

I skidded to a stop as I watched him, amazed. The others rushed ahead of me, keeping an eye on Lester as he dashed across the rooftop and leapt towards the next building.

"What is that?" I asked, forcing my feet to move.

Even as Lester landed on the roof of the next building, his momentum barely slowed.

"It's a particular brand of obstacle course training called parkouring!" shouted Tempestt.

That must've become popular after I'd fallen into a coma. I lifted myself into the air and flew towards Lester and tackled him in mid-air as he jumped towards the next building.

He grunted as our bodies collided and we went through a fifth-story window of a brick building, scaring a hefty woman cooking dinner. Lester slammed a fist into my chest, which knocked me back. I loosened my grip on him and he slipped out of the embrace and then moved towards another window across the room and shattered the glass. The woman screamed and watched in horror as Lester sailed through the broken window.

I eyed her apologetically and then followed Lester through the window. Free falling through the air, I caught sight of Lester's form as he landed on the street below, glass falling to the ground all around him. A crowd of pedestrians parted on the street, and he made a run for it.

I'd lost track of my teammates, but I wasn't going to lose Lester. I chased after him, but his speed was faster than my own. I was surprised he wasn't tired, yet.

As I closed the gap between us and stretched out my hand, something slammed into me, knocking me off my feet. I yelled and hit the ground and then realized that an Anansi demon was on me. It snarled and tried to slam its powerful jaws over my forearm. I yelled and blew it away from me with a burst of wind and then fired a si' beam through its throat as I rose to my feet.

I dusted myself off and looked around, but Lester was nowhere to be found. I swore under my breath and tried to calm my breathing.

I heard footsteps behind me and turned to see my teammates racing up the street towards me.

"He got away?" Mona asked breathlessly. I nodded, and she groaned in frustration. "Coward!"

I turned to Tempestt and I guess my expression was a little harsher then I'd intended. She took a step back and held her hands up in mock surrender. "I'm sorry, Zedo. I really am. I didn't mean to—"

"We can't go to your home now," I told her. Then I looked at the others. "We need to get out of here and find somewhere else to go until we can figure out what to do."

"We need to kill Lester," said Gonzo and Mona nodded. "Either he's toying with us or—"

"He's testing us," I told them then thought it better to be honest. "He's testing *me*…at least that's what he said once." I shook my head. "It doesn't matter right now. Let's just focus on getting back on the road."

"I'll find us a vehicle," Tempestt said, her voice low in defeat. She shuffled down the street and selected a vehicle to hotwire that would fit our needs.

Gonzo moved off to help her.

I glanced at Mona and could tell she was furious. I opened my mouth to say something, but she held a hand up to silence me and then moved down the street, leaving me alone with my thoughts.

I ran a hand through my sweat-slicken hair and exhaled sharply. Behind me, Tempestt and Gonzo hotwired several motorcycles.

Within ten minutes, we were heading to Tennessee. Gonzo had decided on Memphis. We needed to keep moving until we could come up with a plan.

I'd never visited Tennessee before; it was filled with nature and beauty. This would be a new experience, like the rest of my new life. I think I would like this adventure, for all had changed in thirty years.

Only thing I wish I could've figured out was why Lester kept sparing our lives when he could've easily killed us…

Chapter 18:

Memphis

☙❧

The team and I rode on. We passed through Knoxville and did a little site seeing. For once, we got to be normal people—tourists—and not secret agents on a mission of vengeance.

I watched our backs and made sure that we weren't being followed. Soon, we were coming to our exit.

The speed limit increased and my eyes grew wide. "Look at the speed limit! It's two hundred forty!"

Gonzo, who drove in the lead, looked over his shoulder and the wind blew his dark hair backwards. "Go to auto pilot shutter mode!" he shouted.

As I pushed the necessary buttons, it became safer to travel and it gave the motorcycle more of a blocky form. Shields formed and raised like wind guards, turning the motorcycle into more of a cone-shaped vehicle. The two wheels disappeared and went inward, turning into vents that released energy to propel the vehicle forward. We went faster and faster until we reached speeds around 225mph! I was amazed at it all.

To my left and right, my teammates were red and blue blurs as they zoomed past me. I grinned and increased the speed of the cycle.

Soon, we arrived at a rest station. Tempestt approached me and I could tell that her heart was heavy. She apologized for the part she'd played in Lester tracking us.

I forgave her and she quickly changed the topic.

"Zedo, can I tell you something?"

"Sure." I looked at her. My heart quickly filled with worry as I could sense her anxiety levels rising.

"You know how I use my fighting skills to make up for my lack of powers?" I raised an eyebrow, curious as to what she was getting at. Tempestt smiled coyly. "Well, through fighting I have sharpened my abilities and I have gained something extraordinary." She told me that she'd discovered this gift while on the roof with Gonzo.

I didn't know that one could gain an ability just by attuning their senses to the world around them.

"I can use levitate," she said, beaming. She exhaled sharply and closed her eyes. A swirl of wind appeared at her feet—leaves were pulled into the tiny vortex— and she lifted herself five feet off the ground.

"Cool, levitation," Mona said as she walked by.

Tempestt fell, losing concentration. "I haven't actually mastered the ability yet." She blushed; embarrassed.

I helped her to her feet. "Don't feel bad. I haven't mastered my powers, either."

"Of course not," Tempestt replied. "You have a bunch of powers. That'll take awhile to get control of."

I grinned, and then went over to my motorcycle. Gonzo moved to walk beside me. "Where are you going?" Gonzo asked.

"I'm checking my cycle's systems. Trust me, I'm not going anywhere. I learned my lesson last time."

He rubbed his hands together. "Mind if I take a look?"

I shrugged, happy for the help honestly. "Be my guest. I don't really know what I'm looking at anyway."

Gonzo moved around the motorcycle while it was still in its cone-shape and pressed a button next to the ignition. A shimmer appeared around the vehicle and it began to shift its outward appearance. "Amazing!" he exclaimed.

My eyes grew wide as it shifted from the cone-shape, back to a motorcycle, and then turned into a small vehicle. "What did you do?" I asked, in awe of the morphing capabilities.

"I didn't do anything." He chuckled and clapped his hands together. "This is what we call a Morphicle. Basically, it's a vehicle that can morph into any car. It's like the newest type of public vehicles, but they cost a fortune like—"

"The kind Lester Burton has," I said.

"Exactly." Gonzo looked at me over his shoulder. "I bet he has a few." Gonzo moved to pop the morphicle's hood and looked at a small screen next to the engine. "Well, Zee, that's not all. It has a battle mode, where you can get weapons of any type to appear above the headlights. I'm guessing whoever we stole this from was in the military. This is definitely military-grade tech."

I shook my head in disbelief. Times had surely changed.

Gonzo seemed to be in his element. "And if that's not enough, you have a laptop and a GPS system that appears from the dashboard; plus, scanners that can determine potential dangers on the road. Hey, I'll be right back! I want to share my findings with the others."

He smiled and moved down the sidewalk to talk to the ladies. As he talked to Mona and Tempestt, I took the papers I'd received from United Affairs out of my pack.

After Gonzo talked to the ladies, Tempestt showed me how to use the laptop. With her help, I used something called a *'scanner'* and sent them back to United Affairs via something called *'email'*.

An hour later, we were back on the road. Halfway to Memphis Gonzo was pulled over, but Mona and I pulled over, as well to back him up.

"Is there a problem officer?" Gonzo asked, climbing off his motorcycle.

"License and registration," the officer demanded.

Gonzo frowned and set his mouth to lie. "Um, I just bought this motorcycle, sir. I'm having the company mail me the papers."

"Is there a problem?" Mona asked the man with the id badge that read Officer Daryl Shaw.

He immediately reached for his gun as Mona and I approached him. "Get back on your bikes!"

I froze in my footsteps, but Mona edged closer to the officer. "I'm sorry, officer, but I can't do that," Mona said.

He aimed his weapon at her. "Stop right there!"

I instantly moved into action. Mona took one more step and he opened fire, releasing three rounds.

Mona side flipped with no hands and landed, dodging the bullets. She threw her hair back and launched herself forward at the officer. She punched him several times then threw him aside.

"That was awfully foolish of you, officer," Mona said, throwing her hair back. "I was unarmed."

The officer slammed into the ground and pressed a red button on his wrist. "You're one of those freaks!"

I slammed my fist into his face—knocking him unconscious.

"I'm ninety-seven percent positive that whatever he just did wasn't a good thing," Tempestt said, her eyes on the red button on the officer's wrist.

"He's calling for back-up," Gonzo intonated.

My heart sunk. "Let's go," I told the others before I realized it. I turned and moved back towards my motorcycle.

Mona leapt onto her motorcycle and we rode off.

"Hopefully they won't notice us," Gonzo said, hitting a communications button that allowed his voice to fill the speakers of my vehicle and Mona's.

"He was wearing a body cam," Mona told him as she pressed a button on her cycle and it began to shift to a four-door sedan.

We rode onward and raced through traffic. I hope we weren't about to be confronted by state troopers.

Surprisingly, we reached Memphis a few hours later without incident. I couldn't help but think that trouble would find us, again…It always did.

Had the highway patrolman called for back-up or had the button he'd pushed been for something else entirely?

I bit my lower lip, perplexed.

What if he worked for Burton?

I shook my head and wondered what we'd gotten ourselves into. I needed time for peace and rest. I was tired of fighting and I needed answers to my other questions.

Burton wasn't the only issue at hand.

Gonzo led us to a simple hotel and we checked in, getting two rooms. As we settled in for the evening, I activated my laptop and checked out United Affairs. They hadn't received my information yet even though I'd submitted it electronically.

The next day, the team decided to tour the city. We started with Graceland, the estate of the late Elvis Presley. These days, it serves as a museum that became open to the public in 1982.

After that, we went to New Beale Street. Gonzo told me that the historic area had been rebuilt in 2015 after a fire had claimed much of the area. The streets were paved in marble now.

The buildings were much different then what I'd seen in books and magazines in the 80s.

That night, I moved outside of the hotel room I shared with Gonzo and stood on the balcony, gazing up at the moon. I exhaled sharply, the breeze that filled the air soothing me.

Suddenly, the door behind me and to the left opened and Mona stepped outside.

"Hey, there," she said, her voice warm. She moved towards me.

I grinned. "Hey, Mona. I just stepped outside to get a moment of peace."

Mona stopped in her tracks. "Would you prefer to be alone?"

"Not at all, I don't mind if you join me."

She grinned and moved to stand beside me on the balcony. She linked her arm through mine and I looked at her, surprised at the show of affection. She didn't seem fazed by it.

My heart began to race. Being this close to her made me nervous. She smelled *so good*.

Mona grinned to herself and glanced up at the moon. "Isn't it beautiful, Zee?"

I looked at her, unable to take my eyes off her as the wind rustled her hair. "She sure is."

Mona looked at me and smiled. "How do you know the moon is a *she*?"

I chuckled and looked away, blushing. I couldn't tell her I had a crush on her, could I? Did people still do that: admit they had crushes on people? When I was growing up you just slid a note across your desk that said, *'Do you like me: check YES or NO.'* Things had changed.

I exhaled and tried to calm my beating heart. "This is nice, Mona," I decided to say instead.

"What is?" she asked, glancing at me.

"Being normal," I replied. "We spent an entire day just being normal, no fights, no powers…just being *human.*"

Mona exhaled and placed her head on my shoulder. I tried not to tense up. She was so close to me. "I agree, this was nice…but it's just a distraction, Zedo." I could sense a hint of sadness in her voice. "Pretty soon, we'll be back on the road ready to tackle our mission. We need a plan though. We can't just keep aimlessly driving across the country. We'll never know *true* peace until Lester and his father are dead."

I looked at her and she lifted her head off my shoulder to lock eyes with me. "Does it have to be that way?"

"Do we have to kill them before they kill us?" she asked, but I could tell it was more of a rhetorical question then one she was posing. She looked away and laid her head back on my shoulder. "Let's not worry about that, right now. For just one moment, let's just be here in the moment…okay?"

I nodded, unable to say anything at all. I turned my attention back to the sky and watched the moon hang above our heads.

We stood there for a moment and watched the moon. We stood there, and in that moment, we stood there perhaps as more than friends...

Chapter 19:

Commotion

ೞ

Morning came, and we gathered our belongings. Soon, we were all packed up and prepared to leave Tennessee.

Mona seemed pretty happy this morning. I thought maybe she was happy about our time on the balcony, but she soon cleared that up when she told me that she'd talked to her former landlord and her apartment was back to normal—ready to be inhabited again.

She morphed the sedan back into a motorcycle and then latched it to the back of Gonzo's vehicle, which he morphed to a massive pick-up truck.

She looked over at me and for a while I felt a deep connection. Was I falling in love with Mona? I had never been in love before, had never even kissed a girl before, from what I could remember…. Was this what it felt like?

I would do anything for Mona. I would do anything to see her smile, to gaze into her beautiful eyes…

"Hey, Zedo," a voice called, pulling me from my thoughts.

I turned and caught sight of Tempestt. "Yeah?"

"You ready?" she asked, cocking her head. I nodded and climbed behind the wheel of my vehicle, which I'd morphed into a blue 2020 Mustang.

We were off but had no destination in sight.

In my heart, I knew that Lester wasn't about to stop sending his goons to test and try to end us. We needed to get a step ahead of him. I reached out with my senses and felt a pull towards the South.

I pressed the button that would link our three communications systems together.

"Gonzo," I called. "I need you to plot a course to Louisiana."

"Louisiana? What for?" asked Mona before Gonzo could reply.

I drove in silence for a second. I didn't know what it was. I just had a feeling, an inkling that we needed to be there. I just knew it. It's like something was simply drawing me there.

"I have a feeling we should be there," I finally told the others. "Just trust me."

"Aye aye, Captain," came Gonzo's reply. I heard him stroking the keys of his laptop. Seconds later coordinates scrolled across the screen of my GPS. I grinned and adjusted my vehicle's speed as we headed towards Louisiana.

Ten hours later, we stopped to rest in a little town just outside of Shreveport.

"I'm so hungry," Tempestt groaned, stretching her sore muscles. I nodded in agreement and closed the door to my vehicle.

"Perhaps we should grab a bite to eat and find somewhere to sleep for the night?" suggested Mona.

I opened my mouth to reply, but a chilling scream filled the night air. Our heads snapped in the direction of the scream.

"We shouldn't get involved," Tempestt said from where she stood next to Gonzo's truck.

"How could you say that?" countered Mona, shock filling her voice.

The screamed sounded again and I swallowed hard. "Daddy, stop it, please!" I heard several punches being thrown and a woman screamed.

"I'm not going to stand by while some woman is beaten," Mona said, then she took off running, following the sound of the screams. Without another thought, I ran after Mona.

"Come on!" I told the others.

As we rounded the corner, I caught sight of a man standing beneath a street light. At his feet was a woman. She sobbed—hand pressed to her cheek.

The man pulled his fist back, preparing to strike again.

"Stop!" I yelled, stretching my hand forward and firing a si' beam from the palm of my hand. The si' beam sliced through the man's shoulder—a flesh wound.

The man yelped and spun to face us. I gasped as realization filled me.

"I know this man!" I said. It was the man from the house: Edward Wong! At his feet, his daughter—Seay'—lifted her face and looked at me.

Seconds passed, silence and tension filled the air.

"It's YOU!" yelled Edward, his eyes glowing red. I took a half-step back. Was he possessed?

Had he followed us?! Was he another of Lester's minions?

"Step away from the girl," Mona said, moving in front of me. "I don't know who you are, but—"

Edward Wong reached behind him and drew a pistol from the small of his back. "Get back!" he shouted, aiming his weapon at Mona.

As Gonzo and Tempestt rounded the corner, he shifted his aim.

"Whoa, whoa," said Gonzo, skidding to a stop and raising his hands. He scooted in front of Tempestt, blocking her from harm.

"Put the gun down," I told Edward, my voice strong and sure as I eased to Mona's side.

Without warning, he opened fire.

Mona threw both her hands forward and fired ice beams towards Edward. The bullets hit the ice and froze in mid-air.

Edward's eyes returned to their normal hue and grew wide with shock.

I lifted myself into the air and threw my arm to the right, forcing the wind to rise and knock Edward off his feet.

"There is always a time when we lose our way…" I told him, watching his hands.

As the others ran towards Seay', I landed a dozen feet in front of Edward.

"We can help you."

He looked confused as he tried to sit up. As his eyes focused on me, he scooted away from me—seemingly terrified. "H-How did I get here?!"

I frowned. "You don't know how you got here?"

He began to pant, looking around. "Wh-Where's my daughter?"

"Father!" Seay' cried, breaking free from Mona's side.

"You're trying to take her from me!" Edward shouted, scrambling to his feet.

"What's wrong with him?" asked Tempestt. "He's a madman!"

Edward turned towards us and snarled, saliva dripping from his lips.

I began to generate a si' beam in the palm of my hand. "He's not himself. I think he's under some sort of mind control."

Edward lunged at me and I hurled the si' beam his way. The si' beam exploded on contact and sparks hit the ground—landing next to some kind of liquid.

Gonzo shouted behind me, but I couldn't decipher his words. In the next moment, a fire erupted and I realized the liquid wasn't water, but gasoline!

The fire began to spread, separating Edward and his daughter from the rest of us.

"Get out of here!" I told the others. "I can handle this."

"No, this doesn't make sense!" shouted Mona. "What the hell is going on?"

"I think he's under Lester's control," I told her. "Get out of here! Take the vehicles and go! I'll give you guys a head start."

"You don't have to tell me twice," said Tempestt, turning and running off.

"Do you think little Burton sent him to keep us busy until he can get here?" Gonzo asked, watching the flames.

"Could be," I replied, not taking my eyes off Edward as he paced back and forth beyond the flames—his eyes locked on me. "I don't want you all to wait around and find out. Go, I'll catch up."

"This is freaking ridiculous," Mona said, agitation in her voice.

"Look, I'm not going to put you all in danger just because—"

"Who do you think you are, Zee?" asked Mona, shoving me. I tore my eyes away from Edward long enough to look at her. "We're all adults. We know what we got ourselves into."

"Just go! Let me handle this! I know this man. I don't think he's—"

A snarl filled the air and I turned to the flames. Edward leapt through the flames, and as he did, he transformed into a massive Siberian tiger.

"Mona, go!" I shouted. She didn't argue and turned to run.

I called upon the force of my elemental powers and hurled a wall of air at the tiger. The tiger slammed into the wall and fell back. Blood ran down the shield and then fell to the ground as I disbursed the wall of air.

The tiger jumped to its feet and began to circle me.

"Edward, I don't know how you ended up here, or why you're attacking me, but I know this isn't you!" I looked around but there was no sight of his daughter. Where was she?

I could tell the tiger was about to pounce, but instead of pouncing, the tiger began to shimmer as if its skin was covered in light. The tiger began to transform and in seconds Edward stood before me, his chest heaving in and out.

"I don't know why you brought me here!" he yelled. I could hear such pain in his voice.

I frowned. "I didn't...I had nothing to do with you being—"

"Don't lie!" he yelled. "He told me you were after me!"

"*He?*" I cocked my head. "Who is 'he', Edward?"

"You're after me! You're hunting our kind!"

I held my hands up in mock-surrender. "Burton's lying to you, Edward. I'm not after you or your daughter."

He didn't seem to hear me as he began to walk towards me, dragging his left leg as if he was under the influence. "I am a beast, a super human, and you want all of us dead!!"

I called power to myself, drawing energy from the earth as I called upon that power. I slammed my foot into the concrete and it began to crack—causing a fissure to open up in the ground. Edward looked at the ground and stopped in his tracks.

"I showed my parents who I was," Edward said, but as I looked at him—fire all around—I could tell he wasn't really talking to me. His eyes were focused on something that wasn't there, possibly the past.

I looked around. Where was his daughter? Was she dead? Had the flames consumed her? Or had she been a projection?

I shook my head, NO, she'd been there. The others had seen her, too, but where was she *now*?

"I showed my parents who I was. I revealed my powers, but... they were frightened of me. My own *parents*!" Tears welled up in his eyes and his lip quivered.

"People fear what they don't understand," I told him, trying to figure out where this was going. Was he coming out from under Burton's spell?

"People have sense enough to run!" Edward shouted. "We're abominations; demons with powers!" He transformed back into the Siberian tiger and leapt into the air, roaring.

I quickly called energy to my palms and fired flames into the tiger's chest. As the flames slammed into the animal—knocking it back—I heard a mighty roar behind me. I turned to see a lion jump through the flames; Edward's daughter!

Before I could throw up a shield of energy, the lion was on me, sinking its claws into my chest. I screamed and a moment later, the tiger was attacking the lion.

I screamed out in agony, blood gushing from my wound. I hurled a si' beam into the lion's chest and it let out an tormented growl. In the next moment it fell off of me.

I rolled over and forced myself to my feet, my chest on fire from the pain.

The lion rolled and as it stopped, it shimmered and transformed back into Seay'. The tiger shimmered, and Edward's body appeared. He coughed, smoke rising from his body.

"Where, where am I?" Edward asked weakly, coughing.

"Edward?" I called.

"How did I get here?" he said, looking around, confused. Had he forgotten that quickly? We'd just had a similar conversation only minutes before.

Then, he caught sight of me and began to recoil. "I know you. You're Zedo Jeta! Y-You came to my house once."

"That's right," I said, moving towards him. I was still on my guard.

"How did I get here?"

"I don't know, but we're going to find out."

He looked over to his daughter and caught sight of her lifeless body. "Seay'!" He rushed to his feet and ran to her. A pool of blood was spreading about her mid-section. When he screamed out, I knew she was dead.

As I moved closer, I caught sight of burn marks on her chest where my si' beam had cut through her.

I had taken her life…*my* powers had taken her life… Even though her father had attacked her, he hadn't killed her… *I had.* I swallowed the bile that threatened to come up and realized that it was self-defense.

Even though the loss of life was tragic, she'd jumped into the fray and attacked me.

After a moment, I heard alarms blaring in the distance. First responders were on the way. Just then, the sound of tires screeching on concrete announced another vehicle and I turned.

Mona leaned out the window of my vehicle. "Let's go, Zedo!"

Suddenly, I heard the unmistakable noise of a helicopter. I turned my eyes towards the sky and Mona looked up, too.

Moments later, Gonzo's truck came around the corner with Mona's car trailing behind it. Tempestt rolled down the window and caught sight of the dead girl. We locked eyes and I nodded. Tempestt noticeably swallowed and I knew that she knew I'd killed Seay'.

It was necessary, Tempestt telepathically said. I exhaled sharply, but the pain in my chest didn't ease. I looked at the wound Seay' had caused and knew I'd need stiches.

The sound of the helicopter grew closer and all of our eyes turned towards the sky. Gonzo swore. But it wasn't just one helicopter. There were several and they were beginning to form a circle around us.

"Let's go!" Mona shouted again.

I looked over my shoulder. "He's coming with us."

"What?!" the others shouted.

"He's not safe by himself. Burton sent him after us and now, he's going to be a target…just like us." I looked at Tempestt. "Just like *her.*"

Tempestt sucked in a breath.

"I'm sick of hearing this broken record," Gonzo said.

I grinned somberly. "Like I haven't heard that before." I looked over my shoulder and lowered my voice. "Edward…"

"WE HAVE YOU SURROUNDED!" someone in the lead helicopter shouted over their PA system, their voice booming down on us.

I eyed Edward again, willing him to look at me. I reached out with my mind and spoke to him telepathically. *We have to go, Edward…I'm sorry.*

He didn't jerk away from my mental touch. He simply rose to his feet, unable to pull his eyes from his daughter's lifeless body.

"Edward, we have to go now," I repeated, my voice strong and clear.

"FREEZE!!" came the voice over the PA system. "Don't move or we'll open fire!"

"They're not playing around!" Gonzo shouted.

I reached out with my mind and shifted the wind, slamming a wall of air into the side of a helicopter. The wall of air sent the helicopter spiraling through the air and into the side of a nearby building, causing an explosion.

My eyes grew wide with horror. I hoped that building was empty.

"LET'S GO!" shouted Mona seconds before the other helicopters opened fire with machine guns.

I threw up a shield of fire to block the bullets—and hopefully melt them before they came towards me.

With one more look at his daughter, Edward sniffled and then forced his feet to move.

Leaving his daughter's body behind, he moved towards me and then past me as he headed towards the vehicles.

Are you sure this is a good idea? Tempestt telepathically asked me.

He was a pawn of Burton. I can't just leave him.

Are you sure he isn't still a pawn? And what are you going to do when he realizes you killed his daughter?

"I think he already does," I said aloud as I moved towards my car at a run. Mona opened the door and I glanced at Edward. "Sit in the front. I'll get in the back."

He said nothing but did as he was told. I climbed in the vehicle and he did, too, and then Mona took off just as an ambulance and fire engine pulled up but stayed a little behind as the remaining three helicopters gave chase after us.

"Can you do that again?" Mona asked. "The thing with the air?"

"We have to get them off our tails!" Gonzo said over our vehicles linked communication system. His truck zoomed past us.

I reached out the window and stretched a hand forward. Focusing, I caused the air to shoot forward and brought the second helicopter down, slamming it into the ground where it exploded in a mushroom of flame, shrapnel, and smoke. Two down, two to go.

"This can't be just Burton," Mona yelled. "Look at the markings on those helicopters!"

"They're government vehicles," came Tempestt's reply. "It's gotta be the CIA or homeland security or some other organization."

Mona pressed a button on the dashboard and suddenly a cannon popped up from the hood. My eyes grew wide in awe.

"You're going to kill them," Edward said from the passenger seat, his voice low.

"Duh, Sherlock!" she replied, pressing another button which caused the cannon to aim towards the sky. In the next moment, the cannon released blasts of green energy. I watched as the blasts sailed across the sky and struck the third helicopter, bringing it down.

"One more!" I yell.

"It's evading me!" she replied. Suddenly, she slammed on the brakes and I had to hold onto the seat in front of me to keep from being thrown into the front seat.

Before us, Gonzo skidded to the left and raced down a side street, and now we knew why. A half-dozen police vehicles were racing in our direction, lights flashing and sirens blaring.

Edward unbuckled, and his body began to shimmer. Moments later, he transformed into large bald eagle and flew through the window.

"What is he doing?!" Mona questioned as I climbed into the front seat.

I watched as Edward flew towards the last helicopter. He flew into the helicopter and grabbed the pilot with his talons.

Screams filled the air and I watched as he dragged the pilot out of the vessel and let him go in mid-air. The pilot fell to his death moments before the helicopter began to spiral out of control and crashed into the ground—bursting into flames on impact.

Edward soared across the sky and landed atop Gonzo's truck, his talons digging into the roof of the vehicle—denting it.

"Wow!" exclaimed Tempestt.

"And we're sure he's on our side?" Gonzo asked.

"I am now," Edward curtly replied.

The police vehicles swerved around the wreckage and I wondered what I could do. I climbed out of the car and pushed my palms in the vehicles direction—hurling si' beams at the tires. The front tires of the lead vehicle burst, and the driver tried to skid to a stop, but instead caused his vehicle to flip end over front, causing a wreck.

However, the others kept coming. I swallowed hard and flew upward, drawing energy towards me. I struggled to clear my mind, something was interfering.

I see you, Jeta, a voice said in my head. I froze instantly, gasping. I knew that voice. It was BURTON! It was unmistakably Burton's voice. He was *here* somewhere!

I looked down and caught sight of my friends in their vehicles. They were in trouble. Burton had telepathically contacted me as a warning. My telepathy was limited to people in close proximity to me or people with whom I shared a prior connection. So, where was he?

I shook my head. That didn't matter. What mattered right now was making sure my friends were safe.

I flew towards them—five police vehicles gaining on them.

I landed as Mona and Gonzo rushed past me. The police vehicles were still about a half mile behind us. I took a deep breath and exhaled.

I reached deep down inside of me and then reached outside of me and into the Earth itself. I reached for *power.* The Earth responded, and power came slowly, but surely.

Instead of using that power to attack, I let it gather inside of me until I felt it reach overwhelming levels like a sink that was beginning to overflow.

I held that power in place.

All of my powers responded differently. I suddenly felt warm and safe now. It was nothing like the energy I felt when I pulled power for my atmokinetic gifts or fire. Anger fueled fire and a deep hunger for change fueled the weather, but air and earth were vastly different. Earth power felt like peace and harmony and air power felt calming.

Finally, I focused my attention on the remaining police vehicles. I stretched a hand forward and the earth responded. Geysers of earth shot up from underneath the vehicles, piercing the vehicles like shish kebabs.

With the vehicles taken out of the picture, I flew off and headed towards my friends, landing atop my vehicle and climbing back in as Mona reduced the vehicle's speed.

"Crisis averted," Mona said as we rode off into the night.

For hours, we rode in silence. Edward was quiet, too quiet. He was grieving, yes, but even his thoughts were silent. As I listened in, I heard *nothing*. It was as if he was just numb to the pain.

The pain in my chest grew unbearable and I could feel myself breaking out in a sweat. "Mona…" I called, and I noticed she glanced at me in the rearview mirror.

Her eyes grew wide and then she turned in her seat. "Zedo, you're bleeding!"

"I—" And that was all I got out before I blacked out.

I woke up in my least favorite place, but I often called it home. That's right, I was at the hospital again.

They'd given me stitches, and my leg throbbed. I pulled back the hospital blanket and caught sight of a bandage on my left thigh. They'd shot me up with something, that was for sure.

I tried to sit up, but the pain was excruciating. I hoped Burton wouldn't send someone to attack me in the hospital; I wouldn't be able to protect myself anyway.

I wondered where the others were. Was Edward okay? Was he out of his numb mode?

I relaxed against my pillows, forcing my thoughts to slow down. I closed my eyes, but only for a moment as in the next instance, a knock sounded and the door to my hospital room opened.

Two men in suits entered the room, followed by a nurse who checked my vitals. The door closed behind them and I tried to sit up again, wincing as pain shot through my chest.

"Can I help you?" I said, my voice hoarse.

"What's your name, kid?" said the older of the two men. He was Caucasian and wore a brown suit with a striped yellow and navy-blue tie—tacky.

"Who wants to know?" I asked, giving him an attitude that was classic teenager.

"Detective McClain," he said, pulling out his badge.

"What? Is that supposed to scare me?" I said, my voice sounding stronger.

The detective rolled his eyes and tried again. "What's your name?" the detective asked.

"I'm Zedo Jeta."

He turned and whispered something to the gentleman beside him. I waited, not knowing what would happen to me.

Just then, I realized I should've lied. The pain meds were messing with me.

Detective McClain turned back around and said, "You are under arrest for the death of a Seay' Wong; and for other offenses in other states."

The two drew their weapons. They weren't regular guns but were sleeker in design and smaller.

I guess somehow, they found out about my exodus at the lab back in Michigan, but who was I kidding? My face had been splattered all over the news for weeks, as had Mona and Gonzo's faces. The FBI, Homeland Security, and no telling whoever else, was on our tail. Burton wasn't the only one that wanted us.

My team had left a lot of damage in our wake.

Even though the Secret Agencies were unknown projects, or so I was told, they'd found a way to spin the story to where it had looked like we'd stolen something from the government.

"I don't want to have to do this," McClain said, cocking his weapon.

"Put your hands in the air, now!" yelled his partner, whom he'd failed to introduce.

I didn't move. "I won't move, sir. I don't have a reason to."

"Do as we say!"

I cocked my head. "I can't. I have an answer for everything. See, if I don't want to, technically, I don't have to."

"You're resisting arrest," McClain said.

"You haven't tried to arrest me yet, detective," I sarcastically replied.

Finally, I was fed up. I gestured with my hand and slammed a burst of air into them, knocking them back and into the wall.

I threw the blankets off and forced myself to my feet. I instantly grew dizzy and forced that feeling aside, as well. I didn't have time for dizziness.

How long had I been out?

I grabbed the blanket and tore off a piece of fabric. In the next moment, I yanked the I.V. out of my arm and quickly tied the fabric around my forearm to stop the bleeding—treating the fabric like a tourniquet.

I stripped Detective McClain's partner of his clothes—he was more my size than the older man—and then I made my way towards the hospital exit.

"Where are you guys?" I said aloud and in my mind, telepathically searching for my friends.

Follow the sirens, came a reply from Mona. I grinned to myself and then left the hospital out the front door.

Two helicopters with searchlights aimed at the entrance were in view. I shielded my eyes as I stepped out into the night. As my eyes grew adjusted to the blinding light, I caught sight of dozens of FBI agents, police officers, and members of the local SWAT team surrounding the entrance or leaning against the hood of their vehicles—weapons raised and pointed at me.

"Awwwww!" I exclaimed, smiling. "I feel so special! Is all this for me?"

"Place your hands in the air!" someone said over a megaphone. "If you don't we will be forced to react!"

I was weak, but I was strong enough to get away. But I needed a plan.

"Zedo!" someone shouted, and I turned my head to the group of onlookers that had gathered behind the police barricades. Mona stood there with fear etched on her face. Thirty feet away I spotted Gonzo's truck; he leaned out the window. I assumed Tempestt was with him.

An eagle flew overhead, and I assumed it was Edward Wong.

I had to get out of here. I could hear myself breathing. This was too much. How could I get away without being shot?

I looked at Mona and when our eyes met, she nodded.

I swallowed hard…Innocents were about to lose their lives.

With a cry of pain from moving too fast, I threw my arms forward and launched several si' beams from the palm of my hand—aiming at the helicopters. The helicopters were hit and exploded on impact, momentarily distracting everyone present as flames and debris spread.

I lifted myself into the air and a moment later, shots rang out.

I flew with increasing speed and headed towards a nearby clearing.

I caught sight of Mona running towards the truck below me and Eddie—now in his human form—was a few feet behind her.

Where was my vehicle? Where was Mona's?! It was no longer attached to the back of Gonzo's truck!

But I couldn't worry about that now, I needed to get as far away from that hospital as possible.

Below me, sirens blared as the police and other vehicles began to chase me. I flew onward, trying to evade them.

Gonzo, hit the highway and I'll join you! I'm going up beyond the clouds to lose them, I thought towards him. I guess I was out of range because I didn't hear his reply.

Up, up, and away I went—flying higher and higher until I disappeared beyond the clouds. Luckily, it was a cloudy night, but up so high, I could see the stars.

I gasped in awe of the beauty before me and simply hovered forty thousand feet in the air. There were *so many stars* in the sky!

I wondered if life was really out there. Then, I recalled that Secret Agency IV had made contact with a life force in space and knew that there was indeed intelligent life somewhere out there across the stars.

I glanced back at the earth beneath me and realized I'd long lost sight of the vehicles that had tried to track me.

Slowly, but surely, I lowered myself back down towards civilization and searched for Gonzo's pickup truck on the highway.

Where were we??

In the final moments before I floated sixteen hundred feet above the city, I saw things I knew I'd never forget—myself back in the lab, Burton smirking and ready to end my life. The flash of the memory ended, and I shook my head, willing the memory to dissipate. I could never put the pieces of it all together, why *me?* What was so special about me that Burton had wanted to hurt me?

Or had it all just been mere coincidence?

I found myself examining jumbled images in my mind—raw memories that still threatened to overwhelm me. I realized I was still as terrified of Burton as I had been in those moments before I'd fallen into my 30-year coma.

I ran a hand through my curly hair as it fluttered in the wind and turned my eyes to the road beneath me, scanning for Gonzo's vehicle.

Finally, I spotted it on the expressway. I tried to clear my mind as I flew towards the vehicle. *Tempestt,* I telepathically called. I could feel her shock and surprise at being contacted. She momentarily recoiled from me.

I winced.

Jesus, Zee! You nearly gave me a heart attack!

Sorry. Tell Gonzo to pull over.

I landed on the road's shoulder and Gonzo pulled over, the headlights lighting my outfit.

Gonzo leaned out the driver's window. "Gang's all here, boss. Climb in!"

I grinned and moved towards the doors, climbing in behind Tempestt. Mona was already in the backseat. I looked out the rear window and caught sight of Edward relaxing in the extended cab.

"I'm fine back here," he said, before I could ask.

"Alright then," I replied. I looked at the others; we were an odd bunch: three former government agents, an assassin, and a doctor. The only two things we had in common was that we were all super humans and all on Burton's radar.

As Gonzo merged back into traffic, I looked at Tempestt. "How much trouble are we in?"

She bit her lower lip in a sign of regret and reached for the radio dial, turning it on.

Static sounded for a second before she found a station. A man was talking. We'd caught him in the middle of an announcement. "This just in. A teenager has attacked hundreds of officers on his own! He is believed to be one of the world's many super humans. The new bridge that was just completed seven weeks ago was destroyed completely in less than ten seconds."

I looked over to Mona. "What bridge? I didn't destroy a bridge."

She shrugged. "I guess they're blaming you for natural disasters, too."

The disc jockey continued his report. "It looks like the tax payers will once again have to foot the bill as the Mary Miller Memorial Hospital suffered under this teenager's onslaught, as well. Now whether this was accidental, or a downright terrorist attack is unknown at the moment. Until repairs have been made, please stay off of the New Sasado Ave and Central Boulevard. Sources have stated that it'll take around a quarter million dollars to repair the damage to the hospital. A half dozen lives were also lost during the attack. Everyone at 96.5 FM would like to send our thoughts and prayers to those families. This is Lane Henry, be safe out there."

Tempestt turned the radio off.

"Well, Zedo, it seems you're the talk of the town," Gonzo said.

I shook my head. "If Burton was watching or listening, he knows where we are now. He has eyes and ears everywhere."

"When we leave here, we'll be out of harms way," I told them.

Mona scoffed. "You said you had a feeling we needed to be in Louisiana. Are you saying that you no longer think that?"

I reached behind me and unlocked the hatch that would let me slide the rear window open. I ignored Mona's question and climbed into the back of the truck. I wanted to talk to Edward.

I sat across from the doctor. He looked so uncomfortable: knees to chest and his arms were wrapped around his legs. I couldn't imagine what he was going through... But then I could. I had lost my entire life. He had lost his daughter.

I cleared my throat. "Edward... how are you holding up?"

He looked up at me and his eyes were blood shot red. The death of Seay' was taking a toll on him. "Call me Eddie," he said.

I nodded. "How are you, Eddie?"

He shrugged. "As well as can be expected." He looked away, his dark hair blowing in the wind. "That monster took my free will away from me." He was silent for a moment, his eyes unfocused. I could tell that he was seeing it all over again in his mind's eye. "Lester Burton and his goons stormed into my living room a few days after you left. I guess they tracked you to my place. He told me who he was, who his father was, and what he could do. He threatened me and my daughter's lives. I couldn't tell them where you'd run off to.... I honestly didn't know. And when we refused to help him, he injected us with something. Must've been a mind control substance, because the next thing I remember is waking up in the street with you in front of me and Seay' dead…"

Eddie looked at me and tears were flowing down his cheeks.

I felt my heart sink. "Lester and his father are going to pay for what they did."

Eddie nodded and turned away. "I guess being a freak isn't all it's cracked up to be." He looked at me. "My parents were afraid of me. I guess it comes from my genes."

"I figured your parents were normal if you said they feared you…"

He shook his head. "See, I was born into a Mexican-Chinese family. My parents were far from an ordinary couple. If that wasn't bad enough, they had powers. My father was Chinese American and had the power to control any animal. It was really weird growing up around birds that helped repair your roof and raccoons that cleaned up or squirrels that set the table."

I was amazed. For me that would have been extremely great. I wondered why it bothered Eddie so much.

"My mother was Mexican American and her parents were furious when they learned that their only daughter was marrying a man of another race. They tried to relocate her several times to keep them apart, but my father always found a way to find my mom. My mom was an amazing woman. She possessed the ability of zoolingualism; she could talk to animals. When she came into her power as a teen, people in the neighborhood thought she were crazy and eventually ran my grandparents out of town. Eventually, when she ran away with my father, they settled in a town and found a house away from prying eyes. Somehow, I came out with the ability to transform into any animal I wanted to."

"You said your mother *was…*" I asked.

He nodded. "They're dead, Zedo. I only had Seay' left. They died when I was fifteen. I had just gotten my powers two years before. They tried their best to teach me how to control my powers. It was crazy going to school and accidentally transforming into a bear and scaring the entire class."

"It must have been horrible."

"It was horrible," Eddie confirmed. "I really didn't have any friends. We had to move because super humans weren't really accepted in that town. We eventually found a home in Iowa. My mom started to home school me for fear that I'd transform in a public school and attack people. One day my mom was out in her garden where a neighbor caught her talking to a dog. We started to get death threats and a few months after that, my parents were murdered by an organization now known as *the H.A.T.E.R.S*— Humans Against Terrifying Evil Repulsive Super humans."

"That's quite an acronym…." I was at a loss. I didn't know human/super human relations were that bad. "You didn't go to the authorities?"

"And tell them what?" he asked, anger in his voice. "What would I say, Zedo? 'Um, excuse me, officer. My mom and dad, who are super humans, were killed by the H.A.T.E.R.S.' Yeah, that would've worked." He waved my comment off with a dismissive wave of the hand. "I only survived because I transformed into a passerine-type bird. My mom made me leave…She told me '*esconder, mi amor! No dejes que te vean.*' But I shouldn't have left."

Eddie continued to tell me his story well into the night. I simply stayed silent and let him talk.

He'd had it rough. After his parents died, he was alone. Somehow, he managed to find his paternal grandparents and finished school. He went to college, double majored in psychology and biology, and then medical school afterwards. He'd succeeded in life more than he ever thought he would, going on to practice internal medicine at the local hospital. While working there, he met a nurse whom would become his future bride—Victoria Cole.

After several years of dating, he'd proposed, but he never revealed his secret until the night of their wedding. That night, Edward had transformed into her favorite animal—a golden retriever. She wouldn't believe it; she just wouldn't accept it. Several months passed by before she felt she could trust him again and eventually, she accepted his true self.

Nine months later, the couple welcomed a baby girl into the world, which they named after Eddie's mother: Seay'. Victoria became the infant's middle name.

When Seay' Victoria Wong was twenty months old, her mother was diagnosed with breast cancer.

Victoria Cole-Wong lost her battle with cancer when Seay' was five. Eddie relocated to a small town and raised Seay' as a single parent. Years later, I'd stumble into the Eddie and his daughter and change their lives forever...

By morning, we crossed into Texas and stopped to refuel and grab breakfast. I was famished.

The gas station we stopped at also doubled as a diner and in the middle of breakfast, I heard a snap-pop sound from behind us. Gonzo—who sat in front of me—looked up from his meal and his eyes grew wide. A humming sound filled the air behind me and everyone in the diner turned.

My heart froze and an icy coldness filled me.

There, standing in the center of the diner stood Lester Burton.

"He has a blaster," Tempestt whispered and I eyed the weapon in his hand. It was much like the weapon the detective had drawn in the hospital.

"You've been quite busy, Mr. Jeta."

"I told you they would find us," Gonzo said. Mona quickly silenced him. The others slowly rose to their feet and I slid out of the booth, facing Lester.

"Mr. Wong, you failed me," Lester said, eyeing Eddie. He then turned to Tempestt. "That seems to be a recurring issue with operatives I send after Mr. Jeta."

Tempestt took a step back and Gonzo closed the gap—blocking her from Lester's view.

"How'd you find us?" I asked, stepping forward. Lester cocked his weapon and I froze in place.

The patrons of the diner were antsy but didn't move. In the corner, a mother shielded her children as if anticipating a gunfight.

"We've been looking for you for some time now. I've had members of The Shadow monitoring news outlets. You popped up on our radar and I had our finest trackers to do their job. At least I can count on them." He eyed Eddie again. "It's so hard to find reliable help these days."

Eddie's jaw clenched. "You're the reason my daughter's dead."

Lester gestured at me with his silver blaster. "No, you have Mr. Jeta to thank for that."

I swallowed hard. Eddie shook his head. "I don't blame Zedo. *You* sent us after him when you took control of our bodies."

"Bore someone else with the details that led to her death," Lester said, yawning.

Eddie moved to confront Lester, but I held him back. "What do you want, Burton?" I asked him.

He eyed me, the light reflecting on his olive skin. "I want what I've wanted from the beginning: you to surrender. Stop running. It really is getting tiresome chasing you across this lovely country."

"That wasn't the question," Mona said. "What do you want *with* him...with *us*?"

He laughed. "My dear, no one wants you"—he nodded in Gonzo's direction—"or the mongrel for that matter. I just want Jeta. My father wants samples of his DNA sequence in order to reconstruct copies of him."

I swallowed again. "Burton wants to *clone* me? Why?" But deep down I already knew the answer.

"To use your clone's powers against the world, Zedo," Mona replied. She looked at Lester. "Let these innocent people go. This has nothing to do with them."

"My dear, this has nothing to do with *you,* either." He looked around the diner. "Get out of here."

Without another word, the patrons of the diner cleared out within seconds.

"We want your father dead," Gonzo said.

Lester smirked, his eyes glowing. "So do a lot of people." He took a step forward, his blaster still aimed at me. "You were one of my father's most successful projects," Lester said. "And since you survived, you have achieved more then we thought you would…More than we thought you *could.* Your powers could be *limitless.*"

"Imagine what Burton would do if he could clone you and your powers," Tempestt said from behind me and to the right.

"Exactly," Lester said. "Our army would be stronger than ever. No nation could stand in our way."

"Army?!" exclaimed Mona. "Y-You're building an army?"

Lester clicked his tongue. "See, I've gone and said too much." He grinned sinisterly and then gestured towards the exit with his blaster. "Leave," he ordered. "I just want Jeta."

I looked over to Gonzo and nodded. Lester watched as Gonzo and the rest of the team walked out. As they passed by, Mona placed her hand on my shoulder, squeezed once, and walked on.

"She's a keeper." Lester whistled. "Did you see her body? She's curvy in all the right places." He eyed me with curiosity. "Is she yours?"

"Women aren't property." I moved towards him and he lowered his blaster. "They're people...and your father didn't make me. He can't have my DNA." I stood within two feet of him; I could feel his breath on my face. "I won't give you what you won't."

"Then I'll just *take* it."

Without warning, I headbutted him and he fell to the floor, cursing as blood gushed from his nose. I flew up and through the glass roof, glass falling to the ground.

Lester opened fire, but it was too late. I was out of range.

I heard him scream my name, but I was already focused on calling my atmokinetic powers to bare down on him.

I manipulated the air and created strong winds, causing warm and cold air to collide. I lowered the temperature in this area and raised it outside of the zone. I stretched a hand upward and affected the atmosphere—forming a tornado.

I forced the developing funnel down from the sky and into the diner. Within moments, the violent machine tore through the building structure.

I hoped the citizens had all cleared out in time and hadn't stayed behind to watch the encounter.

Clouds swirled around, and parts of the sky grew dark, forming a greater storm.

I tried to balance the weather as I flew away. I searched for Gonzo's vehicle and landed on the extended cab. This time, Mona rode in the back, her auburn hair whirling around her face.

"What happened back there?" she asked. I turned towards the chaos I'd caused just to deal with Lester. When I didn't answer her, she shoved me in the shoulder and I looked at her. I expected the rage I felt to be reflected in her eyes, but instead I saw nothing but sadness. "What did you do?!"

"I had to take care of Lester."

She didn't say anything but leaned against the frame of the truck as it rode on. We sat in silence for a few moments before she spoke again. "He is right about one thing."

"And what is that, Mona?" I asked, facing her.

"We have to stop running." She moved her hair out of her face. "Zedo, you can't keep using your powers like that everywhere we go. It isn't safe. You could've killed people and—"

"I understand, Mona," I said, cutting her off.

"No, you don't." She shook her head. "You were asleep for thirty years, Zedo. You don't know what the world is like. Everyone isn't accepting of super humans. Every time *we* use our powers and there's an audience, it reflects on *us all*."

Gonzo pulled over on the side of a dirt road. Everyone climbed out of the truck as we decided on what our next course of action could be.

We were no closer to finding Burton than we had been on Day One. I said we needed to take the fight to them, but the others had other concerns.

For hours I had to defend using my powers to such an extent and explain myself. It was three against one; Eddie had refused to speak since he'd only recently joined us.

I just didn't understand why I had to answer to them. Weren't we all on a mission for vengeance? What did it matter how I used my powers?

Which would be better, getting killed because you didn't use your powers or using your powers and surviving?

Chapter 20:

Uncharted Territory

cs⦿so

I talked to Eddie after the argument had died down. He was still the newest member of our team, but it seemed like he had been there since the beginning. I needed to know someone was on my side.

Argument aside, he was beginning to forget the past and let go of his grief, and just like me, he was ready to focus on the future. We needed to find Burton and end this.

Maybe then we'd all get some peace.

A few hours later, we passed a torn sign that read *"Old Oklahoma."*

Frowning, I wondered why it was called Old Oklahoma. Had I missed something?

The land was vast but scorched and widely deserted. Buildings had collapsed in on themselves. Debris was everywhere. The streets were overrun with weeds and soon became rocky due to the concrete being cracked and long taken over by nature. This place was a wasteland.

The sky grew darker though the hour wasn't late.

"What happened here?" I asked, in awe of the devastation..

He pressed a button on the dashboard and a beep sounded. "Hey, Siri, where are we?"

The virtual assistant system within the truck began to speak, its voice feminine. I wondered if '*Siri*' was an acronym. "You are entering Oklahoma, now known as new Uncharted Territory. In the year 2013, the largest factory in the state known for manufacturing weapons for the government to conduct chemical warfare exploded and polluted the skies with detrimental toxins. The state of Oklahoma had to be evacuated and quarantined. The explosion destroyed most of the ozone layer specifically in this area and left high levels of radiation in the atmosphere. Approximately 17,324 lives were lost and over 14,000 citizens were critically injured."

"Radiation?" Mona said, her voice low—barely above a whisper. "Perhaps we should turn around."

"We're after Burton," said Gonzo. "We're already going to die. We might as well continue on."

Tempestt slapped his arm and he grinned. "That's a horrible joke."

He shrugged, and Siri continued on. "New forms of land have formed since then and new plant life has grown. Civilians are not allowed to return to explore the terrain or to see the extent of the damage. Any civilians found within the state's limits will be prosecuted for trespassing on restricted government property and charged to the highest extent of the law."

"But if the state is radioactive, who'd come charging in after civilians?" asked Eddie as he climbed into the truck and squeezed in between Mona and I. "Sorry, the wind feels…weird out there."

"Oklahoma has turned into both a huge graveyard and a ghost state," the system finished.

"I can't believe that this is Oklahoma. I visited this place when I was ten," Tempestt said.

"Tem, this place has been deserted and destroyed for seven years," Mona said.

Suddenly, lightning struck the ground in front of the truck and Gonzo slammed on the brake. We screamed and my seatbelt bit into my shoulder.

A gale force wind slammed into the side of the truck and sent us flipping over.

I screamed and next to me, Mona braced herself—placing her hands on the ceiling.

"Hang on!" Gonzo yelled as we slammed into the ground, but we didn't stop rolling. Glass shattered, and I closed my eyes.

I called upon my powers, trying to calm the wind, but I couldn't. Something was fighting against me.

Suddenly, the truck stopped rolling. We'd landed on our side.

"Everybody okay?" I asked, trying to slow my racing heart.

"No," groaned Gonzo as he unbuckled himself.

A groaning noise filled the air then the truck lurched. We began to sink. "Quicksand," Eddie said.

"Or it could be mud!" said Tempestt. "Let's not assume quicksand."

Just then, rain began to hammer down on the truck in blinding sheets.

"Alright, everybody out," I said.

"No, what about my hair?" Mona asked me.

"Mona get out of the truck!" Gonzo yelled, kicking his door open. He hoisted himself out of the truck and reached down to help Tempestt out and into the waiting storm.

Eddie climbed out next, followed closely behind by Mona. I was the last out and utterly shocked by how the weather had changed in an instance.

But I shouldn't have been surprised. We were in a toxic wasteland. The atmosphere had been ripped to shreds and there was no such thing as normalcy here.

"It's just mud," said Gonzo. "Eddie, can we get a little help here?"

Eddie's skin shimmered and he transformed into a rhinoceros and rammed the truck. It rolled over and landed right side up.

The truck was battered, and the windshield was shattered, but other than that it seemed fine.

"What the hell happened?" Mona asked, brushing her wet hair aside as wind and rain raged all around us.

But before we could answer, a loud rumble echoed across the land and the ground quickly cracked and opened up—swallowing us.

I couldn't tell how loud I screamed as we fell through the earth.

This was truly Uncharted Territory and it seemed as if the Earth was alive and looking for victims. We had no warning.

I could see lava underneath us as the earth continued to open and move us through the asthenosphere; and then came the excruciating heat.

My eyes grew wide. I tried to fly or call upon another power, but all of them seemed to fail me—even my power to control the earth!

I caught sight of boiling lava and we were falling fast.

"Gonzo! Zedo! Do something!!" screamed Mona, who couldn't fly.

"I can't do anything!!" Gonzo shouted. "Eddie?"

He tried to transform but couldn't seem to either. "Something's blocking our powers!"

The intense heat was overwhelming. I felt the hair on my arms began to burn away. *This is* it, I thought to myself. I was about to die.

I looked at Mona and she glanced at me. There was this look in her eye that made me think she'd wished we had more time to explore the feelings we hadn't even talked about having...

Suddenly, I watched as her auburn hair began to change— turning jet black, the same shade as Tempestt's.

"Mona, your hair!" I yelled.

She grabbed at her hair—which was being blown by the wind—and her eyes grew wide. "What the—?"

The excruciating heat had changed her hair.

I reached out with my mind and began to push against the barrier that blocked our powers.

I recoiled at a touch of evil and realized that it wasn't the Earth fighting us, but *someone*.

I tried to calm myself, despite our impending demise. "EARTH!" I shouted, forcing energy to expand all around me. Suddenly, the force that had held us exploded and before my eyes I saw energy shatter like glass.

Next to me, Gonzo gasped for air as if he could feel his powers returning.

Tempestt yelled and suddenly stopped falling. She floated on air—her power of levitation had returned!

"GUYS!" Tempestt shouted, her black hair blown by the heat. The edges of her hair seemed to burn away shortening her hair from waist length to elbow length in the matter of seconds.

I reached for Mona and caught her hand and then forced air beneath our feet like a cushion, slowing our descent.

Eddie screeched and transformed into his eagle morph and Gonzo began to propel himself upward, flying.

Mona wrapped her free hand around my waist and buried her face in my shoulder, sobbing.

Slowly, but surely, we moved away from the pit of boiling lava!

As we moved towards the surface, I realized someone stood at the mouth of the crater that had sucked us in.

My vision cleared and I caught sight of Lester. He smirked down at us from the mouth of the crater. He was dressed in all black— per usual. Thunder sounded and lightning flashed behind him.

His eyes glowed with a poisonous green.

Tempestt was the first out of the pit, and she levitated towards Lester, attempting to kick him. Lester simply swatted her away with the flick of his wrist.

Tempestt went flying through the air and skidded to a stop as she slammed into the ground.

Gonzo fired a yellow energy blast but Lester deflected that, too.

Eddie grew in size until his eagle form grew to the size of an elephant! I didn't know he could do that!! Lester fell back, his eyes wide with shock. He threw his arms up to shield himself, but Eddie grabbed him with his talons and flew off.

Mona and I burst through the crater and I landed next to Gonzo. Placing Mona on the ground, I took off without another thought—flying after Eddie and Lester.

A fork of lightning burst from the sky and slammed into Eddie! Eddie screeched, and Lester howled.

"Eddie!!!!" I shouted, flying faster as he released Lester and began to fall from the sky.

He continued to fall from the sky—unconscious—but Lester seemed to catch himself in mid-air and then flew off.

I reached out with a hand and called the air to my aide— letting it catch Eddie and slow his fall until it lowered him to the ground.

I realized that Gonzo wasn't too far behind me; I didn't know he'd flown away from the others. "No, stop! HELP HIM!" I shouted behind me, as I flew to catch up with Lester.

Gonzo dove towards the ground as I increased my speed.

"LESTER!" I shouted.

Lester stopped flying and floated in mid-air—the rain still coming down in sheets and soaking us.

Lester began to clap, "Well done. You did it. You caught up."

"This needs to end, Lester! You're not going to get what your father sent you here for! I won't surrender, and you've got to stop running."

"You first," he said, lowering himself to the ravaged ground. I followed him.

We landed in the town square of a long-deserted village. I moved towards Lester, walking through the deserted village.

Totaled cars were piled up on either side of the sidewalk. Many of the vehicles were just burned-out shells of their former selves.

The buildings, upon a closer look, weren't just wooden. Some were concrete and the ones nearby—the ones still standing, at least—were covered in scorch marks. Had some sort of fire destroyed this town during the event that destroyed this state?

My shoes crunched against the broken glass and then squished as I passed through mud.

The wind howled through the broken windows and I turned my attention to Lester, who stood in the center of the town square, his chest heaving in and out.

"Take me to your father," I told him.

He cocked his head. "Are you surrendering?"

"I'm making a demand. I won't allow him to manipulate me. He can't clone me, but I *will* kill him for what he's done."

"You're out for revenge, Jeta," he said, more of a statement than a question. "Tsk, tsk, tsk. Don't you see, you can't win. You can't beat my father."

"Why not? Is he like us? Is he a super human?"

Lester didn't answer, not right away. But the silence was all I needed to confirm my suspicions.

"If you won't tell me, I'll let your mind do the work."

He opened his mouth to protest, but I stretched a hand out and called upon my telepathy and mentally took hold of his mind.

I slammed into Lester's mind like a battering ram and took control of it with psionic energy. I heard him gasp for air and his eyes began to bulge.

I'd never used my powers in such a malicious way, but the power felt seductive…I liked it.

Lester's arms flopped to his side and he fell to his knees. My powers were assaulting his mind with brute force.

I closed my eyes as I focused on infiltrating his thoughts. I gagged as toxic memories poured into my mind from his.

In my mind's eye, I saw his memories as black and green energy flowed between us.

Lester moved in front of a mirror. He looked very much like he did now in the present. He ruffled his hair and then turned away from the mirror and headed down a long, poorly-lit corridor.

He was scared; his heart hammered against his rib cage.

He moved towards a large set of black double doors guarded by two men dressed in battle garb with pikes in their hands.

"I've come to see the Shadow Leader," he said, trying to sound strong, though it was evident he lacked confidence in his body language.

The guards pulled the large black doors apart and permitted Lester to move into the large chamber beyond.

Before him, on a throne, sat a man dressed in a cloak—the hood pulled low to cast his face in shadow.

"Father," he called out, his voice trembling.

"You've come back empty handed…AGAIN," the man on the throne said, his voice dripping with disdain. "You're a failure in every way."

Without warning, the man threw his arm forward and flames burst from his palm.

Lester didn't have time to protect himself. The flames slammed into Lester, hurling him across the chamber and into the far wall.

Lester cried out, begging for mercy.

The memory shifted, blown away in a haze of gray smoke to reveal a new setting.

Lester moved into view. He was a child, dressed in a dingy t-shirt and shorts. "Papa?" he said aloud.

The man turned and back handed him. Lester fell to the floor and began to sob.

The memory shifted again, and Lester was atop a building. He moved to the edge of the roof. Tears flowed down his face and the wind rustled his hair.

He peered over the edge and then stepped back.

"I can't do this anymore," he said aloud. "Forgive me."

He moved to jump off the roof, but someone grabbed him from behind, pulling him to safety.

"No!" Lester cried. He broke away from his savior and turned to find a woman with a bald head and dark eyes glaring at him.

"You're WEAK, Lester!" She shouted. "No wonder the master hates you so much! You're always trying to off yourself! Suicide is for the **weak***! Grow a pair!"*

"You don't understand, Desdemona!" he shouted.

The woman snarled. "I understand that you are a disappointment!

Lester wiped his eyes. "I'll never—"

I was pulled from the memory as a fist slammed into the pit of my stomach and I was thrown backwards and into a nearby building. I slammed into the brick wall and fell to the ground. Several loose bricks fell on top of me.

"Noooo!!!!" Lester yelled, shouting like an animal.

I gasped and then coughed. The punch had knocked the wind out of me. I forced myself to my feet and realized I was back in my own body.

My head still throbbed from the memories I'd seen.

Across the square, Lester stood, his eyes expanded in shock, legs spread as if he were trying to keep himself on his feet.

"What did he do to you?" I asked, sympathy filling me. For the first time, I saw Lester as human.

Lester screamed and rushed towards me. He was out for blood.

I threw my fist forward and fired a si' beam, but he dodged it. I fired another, but he just kept coming.

Lester yelled and lashed out, tackling me. We slammed into the ground and I tried to throw him off me, but that didn't work.

I threw up my arm to block him, but that didn't stop him from slamming a fist into my rib either. I gasped, pain erupting in my chest.

Lester rolled to his feet and kicked me in the side and I writhed with pain. The tip of a small, wedge-shaped blade appeared from the top of his boot and my eyes bulged.

I barely had a chance to brace myself when the blade slammed into my ribs and sent a blazing jolt of pain deep into my body.

"NEVER—" He kicked again, sending more pain into my body. "—VIOLATE—" He kicked again. "—MY—" He kicked yet again. "—MIND!" Lester kicked once more, this time catching me near a kidney.

I howled in pain and a wave of anguish rolled through my body. I tried to roll away and found myself rolling in my own blood.

My vision was spotty, and I heard someone yell my name. Lester was yanked backwards by a hand and flung across the town square.

I looked up through my blurred vision and caught sight of Gonzo standing over me—having just pulled Lester off of me. He hurled a yellow energy blast at the man and then took off running after him.

In the next moment, Tempestt was at my side. She dropped to the ground, fear etched on her face. "Oh, God, Zedo! There's so much blood!"

"Get out of the way," said another voice and then Eddie filled my vision. Eddie pressed a hand to a wound and I screamed out. Tempestt took a step back, a hand pressed to her mouth.

"What are you doing to him?" Tempestt asked.

"I'm a doctor," Eddie told her.

The rain fell on my face and further blurred my vision. I turned my head as Eddie tried to treat my wounds and caught sight of Gonzo and Lester engaged in a fist fight.

Across the town square, Mona stood on the sidelines, hurling ice beams at Lester, but he evaded them.

"Hold on, Zedo," Eddie said, but I felt like I was fading fast. "He's losing too much blood."

I heard a clap of thunder and then Mona swore. "Where is he?!"

"H-He just *disappeared!*" came a reply from Gonzo.

"We have to get Zedo out of here!" Tempestt cried, running towards them.

Suddenly, I felt energy build up and I turned my head towards the sky. Rain droplets fell into my eyes and I blinked them away.

My powers were calling out for help and I could feel my very essence interacting with nature. That was the beauty of having elemental powers—I was *connected* to the elements. I was connected to earth, air, fire, and water. I was connected to the mind and the weather.

"Back up," I whispered. Eddie looked at me. Thunder sounded, shaking the ground. He looked at me and then looked at the sky. He frowned and then turned his eyes towards me one more time. "Step back," I told him, my voice weak.

He rose to his feet and stepped back.

"What are you doing?" Mona asked, rushing towards him. She shoved Eddie. "Help him!" She shoved him again. "You're a doctor!"

"He told me to step back!"

The world around me responded to my need to be healed. Lightning ripped across the sky and then forks of lightning began to strike all around me, flashes of white, blue, and purple.

Tempestt screamed and jumped back.

They gave me a wide berth as the forks of lightning searched for me—blind as a bat.

"I'm *here*," I said, talking to the weather. The winds howled, and thunder clapped again.

Four forks of blue lightning fell from the sky and slammed into my body! I gasped, but I didn't feel pain.

Every nerve was lit within my body. In that moment, when the forks of lighting struck my body, I felt *infinite*!

The lightning supercharged my cells and they began to mend. Nature was healing my body.

My body glowed, and my wounds began to heal themselves. I gasped, and my eyes flew open and began to glow with blue energy.

I rose to my feet. The others looked at me with a mix of bewilderment and fear.

I now knew why Burton wanted me so badly. My powers were immense. I could commune with the very earth on so many levels. If he cloned me and made an army using my DNA, he'd be unstoppable.

Evil would be unstoppable.

I stretched out a hand towards the others. "*Come*," I said, and though I'd spoken low, the earth echoed my voice and it resounded with a mighty BOOM.

The others recoiled.

The wind whispered to me and I heard a single word on the breeze: *Michigan*.

Did that mean we needed to return to where it had all begun?

I had to follow my instincts. If the Earth wanted me to go to Michigan, then that must be where the answers were.

Was Burton there? Was it all going to end now?

"Come," I said to the others and this time my voice sounded like my own.

Tempestt was the first to move towards me. She placed her hand atop mine and the blue sparks of electricity that had rolled across my body began to move over hers. She jumped but wasn't shocked.

She looked over her shoulder, her hair blowing in the wind. "It doesn't hurt. It just tickles a bit."

"I won't hurt you," I told the others. I know my powers scared at least one of them…Mona.

Slowly, but surely, the others moved to place their hands atop mine.

The blue sparks moved across their bodies and I turned my eyes towards the dark clouds above. My powers had deepened, and I felt a change in me.

I trusted the weather like one trusted their best friend. I talked to the weather. *"Michigan."*

Lightning fell from the sky.

"Zedo!!!!" shouted Mona.

I locked eyes with her. "Don't let go," I told her, and I could see my reflection in her eyes. My pupils glowed a light blue and sparks flew through my curly hair.

The massive fork of blue lightning slammed into us, but there was no pain. A blinding flash of white light encompassed the area.

Our bodies were reduced to pure energy. I felt my body elongate as we were pulled back into the sky with the lightning bolt.

The others screamed, or at least what I'd perceive as a scream. My body vibrated with energy and then the energy rolled off me.

I could tell that we were moving at speeds that rivaled the speed of light, but I couldn't see anything. My vision was filled with the blinding white light.

However, I could tell that we were quickly transported out of Oklahoma—the Uncharted Territory—riding a wave of lightning.

Chapter 21:

I'm Going to Find You

CRO

The sky opened up, thunder sounded, and lightning fell from the sky—depositing us on our feet on the sidewalk.

Civilians jumped back as the lightning slammed into the ground, denting the cement. I blinked and realized that it was raining here, too.

The others appeared at my side, soaked and dirty from the battle.

"Where are we?" asked Gonzo.

I looked up and caught sight of the revolving globe with the words "United Affairs" on it. I grinned to myself. The universe was ready to deliver some answers to me.

"I don't get it," said Eddie. "Why'd you bring us here?"

I looked at him. "I didn't... the lightning did."

He frowned. "But didn't you—"

I walked off before he could finish, climbing the stone steps that led to the entrance.

Mona caught up to me. "Zedo, why are we here?"

"Honestly, I don't know, Mona. The universe brought us here, I didn't. All I know is that the weather told me to come here."

She stopped in her tracks and looked at me. "The *weather* told you?" she said with skepticism in her voice.

300 | A c r o s s   t h e   S t a r s

I shrugged. "My powers are growing."

She bit her lower lip. "I'll say." Without another word, she moved in front of me and pushed open the glass door, getting out of the rain.

The building was alive with activity. At the reception desk sat the triplet security guards. I grinned to myself. This was going to be interesting.

They looked up in unison from their individual tasks and spoke, finishing each other's sentences.

"I—"

"—am—"

"—sorry," the third man finished. "Mister—"

"—Sashar—"

"—is—"

"in a meeting," finished the last brother.

The others stood behind me and I cocked an eyebrow at them.

"Thanks, all of you," I said. "I'll wait." I walked towards the elevator without waiting for them to give me clearance.

The others fell into step behind me.

"They're going to raise the alarm," Tempestt said, eyeing the guards, who glanced at us defiantly.

"We're here for a reason," I told her.

"Care to share with the class?" Gonzo asked. "This doesn't make sense, Zedo."

I ignored him, and we rode the elevator up to Mr. Sashar's floor. As I stepped off the elevator, I turned to the others. "I don't know what to expect in there, but—"

"You brought us here to find out about your family, didn't you?" Mona asked.

I shrugged. "All I know is that the weather whispered 'Michigan' to me. I don't know why, but this is important."

"I disagree," Mona said, crossing her arms over her chest. "We have a mission, Zedo. This is selfish."

"I have to agree with her on this one," Gonzo added, looking uncomfortable. "I'm sorry, bro, but this wasn't part of the plan. We need to focus on finding Burton."

"I was brought here for a reason...I need to follow this through."

Gonzo opened his mouth to speak, but Tempestt placed a hand on his shoulder. "He just needs a minute." She looked at me and nodded. "Right, Zee?"

I nodded and telepathically thanked her for helping me.

Mona's jaw clenched. "We'll give you ten minutes, Zedo...and then we're out of here."

"That's more than enough time," I told her and then turned and headed down the hall to Mr. Sashar's office.

I don't know if the others remained in the hall or went back to the lobby. Right now, I needed answers. Everything else could wait.

Soon, I arrived at Mr. Sashar's office door and walked in without knocking. Mr. Sashar sat behind his desk and instantly looked up. Three individuals sat in the room before his desk and turned in their chairs to see who'd interrupted the meeting.

"Zedo?" Mr. Sashar said, rising from his seat and moving towards me.

"Mr. Sashar."

"I'm in a meeting right now, young man. Come back later," he whispered to me. "This is highly inappropriate."

"I can't," I said aloud. He gestured for me to lower my voice, but I didn't. "See, I came from Oklahoma to Michigan to get this information. There's a reason why I'm here."

He chuckled and then looked at the others and they laughed nervously. "You came from Oklahoma? Yeah right. No one can enter the Uncharted Territory. Well, you're going to have to go, now," he told me.

"Who is this young man?" asked a lady in her mid-fifties. She wore a periwinkle pants suit and had short red hair that had been cut into a bob.

"Zedo, these are my colleagues. I am in the middle of a very important presentation. Now '*Mr. Coma*' you're going to have to leave right now before I call security."

I looked at him and grabbed him by his collar and lifted him off the ground with strength I didn't know I had. He gasped and grabbed for my hands as his colleagues rose to their feet, shocked.

"What are you doing?!" he asked, his eyes bulging. "Put me down!"

"I'm calling security," the woman said, circling to Mr. Sashar's desk. She reached for the phone, but I fired a si' beam at it and the landline exploded. The woman yelled and jumped back as sparks filled the air.

"Step back," I told her, and she obeyed.

"He's one of those *freaks*!" exclaimed the other man in the room. He was an older white guy dressed in a dark blue suit.

I turned my glare on him and he took a step back, wary of me. I then turned my attention back to Mr. Sashar. "You're going to do as I say. And one more thing, don't *ever* joke about the things I've been through in my life! I've been through hell! I've lost thirty years of my life!"

The others in the room began to murmur amongst themselves. I lowered Sashar to the ground. The others rushed out of the office.

I threw Sashar over his desk. "Get me the information I need! NOW!" I ordered.

"Okay. Okay, just don't kill me. Please, don't kill me. I have a family."

"Get the information!"

He rumbled through papers and disks. Finally, his hands stopped on a stack of papers. "H-Here." He handed me a single disk and a small stack of papers. His hands were shaking. "The disk is two sided. The papers give you the rest of the information," he said nervously. "Now leave!" he shouted.

"I'm not finished."

"What is it?" Fear filled his eyes. "I don't have anything else for you!"

"Give me your weapons."

He froze. "What?"

I grinned. "Give me your weapons, now. Like right now. I'm not playing with you."

He rolled his eyes and reached behind his back and lifted his shirt. He handed me his blaster and the words *Chase 3000* were engraved on the side of it.

"What is this?"

"It is an upgraded prototype of a blaster. It's not on the market yet." I aimed it at him and he began to back away from me— hands raised as if that would protect him. "Be careful with that! It doubles as a stun gun."

I kept the weapon aimed at him, and slowly backed out of his office. Is this why I'd been brought to Michigan, to receive information about my family?

Was this information more important than the hunt for Burton?

I turned and rushed to the elevators. I figured that he wouldn't try anything and would be too scared to react, but I was wrong.

"We have a code nine emergency!" said a voice over the building's intercom. "Code nine. Calling for building lockdown."

Sirens began to wail, and I groaned in annoyance.

Metal panels began to cover the doors of the offices and the windows as well.

As I dashed for the elevators, metal slowly covered all of the passageways and exits; the entire building was being put on lockdown!

"Zedo!" came a voice from behind me.

I turned to see Mona standing at the end of the hall. "Aren't my ten minutes up? What are you doing here?"

"Saving your butt. What else is there? Come on, we don't have much time," she said, pointing to the metal panels closing off the area. She turned, and I ran after her.

We soon reached an uncovered door but as I reached for the handle, the emergency exit door was quickly covered in metal.

I flexed my palm and fired several si' beams at the metal and it quickly burned away a spot. I soon kicked the door down and we entered the stairwell.

As Mona and I raced down the stairs, we finally came to the ground floor and flung the door open before it was covered in metal, as well.

I heard feet on the stairwell behind me. "Where are the others?" I asked as we turned one final corner and entered the lobby.

Mona and I froze in place as right before us were hundreds of officers with their weapons pointed at us.

"Put your hands in the air right now!" one of them ordered over a megaphone.

I looked up to see Sashar staring down at us. Then, metal covered his window—protecting him.

I turned to look at Mona. "I'm going to get us out of here," I whispered.

"What do you plan on doing?"

"Mona, you have to trust me. Do you trust me?"

She looked into my eyes and nodded. "You haven't led me astray, yet. I trust you."

I grinned.

"Surrender or we will be forced to shoot!" yelled an officer.

"Put your hands up now!" came the shout of another.

I closed my eyes and obeyed, lifting my hands in the air.

"What are you doing?" Mona asked.

"Getting us out of here," I replied and a moment later, the winds began to pick up as I shifted the air in the sky above the building. A swift breeze filled the lobby from the opened doors.

I reached out for power and it came willingly. "I call upon the power of weather and the power of air." I created a violent windstorm with speeds rivaling that of a category 2 hurricane.

The dozens of officers in the lobby were lifted off their feet and began to yell as the wind carried them about the lobby.

Mona grabbed onto my arm to steady herself. "Zedo!" she yelled.

I opened my eyes. "Where are the others?"

"I sent them to get a getaway vehicle."

I nodded and threw in a couple of bolts of lightning in order to shatter the unbroken glass.

The sky grew dark.

Someone opened fire, but with the winds rivaling speeds of 120 mph, there was no telling who was struck by that bullet.

As I lifted Mona and myself into the air, I caught sight of the security officer triplets.

"This—"

"—can't—"

"—be good!" they said.

I balled up my free hand and jabbed my fist into the air, forcing the wind upward—blowing the roof off; providing us with an exit.

Mona and I flew through the whirlwind, our hair was blowing about our faces. Together, we flew out of United Affairs and landed several blocks away from United Affairs.

"Over here!" came a voice from behind us.

Mona and I turned and caught sight of a yellow Hummer. Once again, Gonzo was behind the wheel. "Zee, Mona, come on! We have to go. First responders are on the way."

Mona ran towards the vehicle.

I turned towards the remains of United Affairs and with a flick of the wrist, the storm ended.

I patted my back pocket. I had gotten what I'd come for.

"Where to now?" Gonzo asked after we'd been driving in silence for a while.

"Pull over," I said.

The others looked at me. "Why?" asked Mona.

I sighed and rubbed my eyes in irritation. "Please."

Gonzo pulled off the road and into an abandoned parking lot.

"What is it, Zedo?" he asked, noticing I had the papers I'd received from Mr. Sashar in my hand and had been reading. The others turned in their seats to glance at me.

I flipped through the first two pages again. "There's an address here. The address belongs to my father's sister, Kelsey. There's also information in here confirming my father's name was Troy Jeta. I know from my visions of the past that I'm biracial, though I always kind of suspected that."

Tempestt frowned. "Wait…you brought us to Michigan to retrieve data on your family?"

"You're trying to find them?" asked Mona.

"This is the opposite of what we should be doing!" Gonzo exclaimed. "I know you missed thirty years of your life, Zedo, but we need to focus on the here and now. We need to find Burton."

I remained silent, my eyes glued on the pages.

Eddie cocked his head, studying me. "What? No way." I looked up and our eyes met. I saw realization dawn on him and I quickly looked away, ashamed. "You're going after them."

Mona looked from Eddie and then to me. "What? Zedo, no! If you think you're about to leave us, you've got another thing coming! You're trying to find them on top of this mission, aren't you?"

"We can't get side tracked right now," Gonzo added.

I finally looked up, folding the papers up and stuffing them back into my pocket along with the disc. "Yeah, I'm seriously considering it. I have to know who I am."

Mona sighed in frustration and rubbed a hand across her forehead. "You're Zedo Jeta, leader of this team—a team *you* created by the way—and a former agent of Secret Agency XII that fell into a coma at the hands of a madman bent on global domination. Oh, and did I mention that you possess extraordinary powers like none I've ever seen before?"

"And let's not forget that you teleported us hundreds of miles through lightning!" added Gonzo.

"I'm still not over that one," said Tempestt, shaking her head in amazement. "And, you converted an assassin into a good girl." She grinned and looked at Eddie. "You even found us a doctor for when we get banged up."

"That was accidental," said Eddie, glancing out the window as memories of how he'd come to join us filled his mind.

I shook my head. "I know that part, but nothing else. I need to know. It's important to me."

"I agree that it's important," began Mona, "but it isn't as important as our initial mission. Zedo, we need to find Burton and end this wild goose chase. I can't believe we're even debating this."

"We're not debating this," I answered.

"He's already made his decision," Eddie said. An awkward silence filled the air and Gonzo looked at Eddie then turned his attention to me.

"Zedo?" Gonzo called with worry in his voice.

"I need to do this. There was a reason the weather spoke to me and said we needed to go to Michigan." I dug into my pocket and pulled out the documents. "*This* is why I was told to go back to Michigan. I have to believe that fate is leading me to focus on this now."

Tempestt dropped her head. When she spoke, she sounded like a child who'd just lost her best friend. "And what about *us*?"

I swallowed hard. "We haven't really accomplished much trying to find Burton. There's been a better chance of them finding us then the other way around."

"And we know Lester and his goons can find us," said Tempestt.

"I feel like we're screwed," I told them. "I feel like we've already lost, and no one has gotten around to telling us…"

"I disagree," said Mona. "We're not going to lose."

"This is all my fault," I told them, looking away. "If I hadn't been so hellbent on revenge, we wouldn't have lost so many…"

"We wouldn't have lost my brother." I looked up and met Mona's gaze.

"Or my daughter wouldn't have died," added Eddie.

I felt a lump rise in my throat. "And I'm sorry for that. Truly, I am…I need to focus on this."

"Then their deaths were all for nothing," Mona said. "You're giving up on the mission because of this sudden urge to find your identity."

"We need to regroup anyway," I told them, looking around the Hummer at each of my team members.

"Lester is responsible for those deaths," Gonzo said. "We all knew what we were signing up for when we met up with Zedo, except Eddie." He glanced at Mona. "We knew from the beginning that we weren't all going to survive this mission."

"So, you're saying we—"

"Continue on with the mission," I said, finishing Mona's sentence. "I'll catch up, I promise. But I need to do this."

She nodded. "If you want to go, I won't stop you."

"I don't *want* to go, Mona! I *need* to!"

"I know what it is like to have limitations," Eddie said, gazing out the window—his eyes unfocused. "I know what it's like to have pieces of you missing."

I nodded. "It seems as if we *all* had troubled childhoods and our lives suffered. But at least you got to live your life. Burton took that from me. He took my life from me!"

"But you signed up for the agency!" shouted Mona.

"I was a kid! I didn't know what I was getting into! I shouldn't have been there in the first place! It was all a mistake! I never got to grow up and experience life. I was trained to be a machine. I never had a chance to experience love. I never got to go to the prom. I barely even remember my first girlfriend. I don't know anything about me. I don't know who I am! I feel like a stranger in some guy's body."

The car filled with silence once again and Tempestt placed her hand on mine. "Do what's best for you, Zedo. We can hold the fort down for a while."

"I can't believe this," Mona said. She opened the door and climbed out of the Hummer.

"What are you going to do?" asked Gonzo.

I looked down at the papers in my hand and then looked at the window, catching sight of Mona pacing back and forth on the sidewalk.

"I'm going to find my family."

Chapter 22:

Please Clap Your Hands

CR&O

I let out a deep sigh and closed my eyes for a moment. When I opened my eyes, I cleared my throat. "Mona's apartment is ready for her to move back into, right?" Gonzo nodded. "I'll search for my family and regardless of if I find something or not, I'll meet you all there in a week."

"Sounds like a plan," Gonzo said, nodding. "It'll take us about fourteen hours to get back to her city."

"We'll set up our base there and get to work on finding Burton," Tempestt added. "Seven days from now, you'll arrive, and we'll go from there."

I nodded in agreement. "What can happen in seven days?"

"A lot," Eddie answered, finally pulling his gaze from the window. "But I agree, if you were urged to Michigan for those documents, then you need to follow through."

"We'll be fine for seven days," Gonzo told me. "Mona will be pissed, but she'll be fine. We know you're not abandoning us."

I nodded and looked down at the documents in my hand. On the first page was my mother's name: *Kelly Re' Ridge.* Underneath my mother's name was a snapshot of my birth certificate with my date of birth listed as June 29, 1975. Both of my parents' names were on the birth certificate, along with their races.

At that moment, I was hit with a vision of the past—my ability of retrocognition kicking in.

In my mind's eye, I saw a woman, crying in prison. She began to scream into her pillow. There was a tiny, barred window in her cell and through it I caught sight of the moon. It was the middle of the night.

She lifted her head and I instantly recognized this woman. She was the lady from my previous vision—my mother.

A female guard approached the cell and hit the bars with her nightstick.

The guard turned around and yelled for the cell door to be opened; and as soon as it did, she walked in and threw Kelly to the ground. The guard began to beat her until she stopped her screaming. Bruises covered Kelly's upper body.

When Kelly lifted her hand to strike back, the guard punched her—blackening her eye.

The female guard continued to beat Kelly into compliance and blood spilled onto the cold concrete—gushing from Kelly's broken nose and busted lip.

Two male guards raced towards the cell and pulled the female guard off the inmate.

One of the male guards dashed back to his desk to call for help. Kelly lied on the ground bleeding in the meantime.

When help finally arrived in the form of medical personnel, Kelly was handcuffed and taken to the infirmary.

Guards stood by her door as she was treated and recovered.

As she lay in bed, she silently cried and rocked back and forth.

The guard who had called for help moved towards Kelly's infirmary station. He nodded at the two guards flanking Kelly's room. It was obviously that he was the lead correctional officer.

With fair skin and dark brown hair, the man was handsome and stood at 6'2" with an athletic build. He appeared to be in his mid-30s.

As he walked into Kelly's room, she also noted that he was bowlegged.

This male guard checked on Kelly often, even after she left the infirmary.

After she was released from the infirmary and returned to her cell, the guard still came to visit. Often, he'd simply stand by her cell and talk about poetry—which happened to be a favorite of Kelly's. Sometimes he'd even recite some of his own poems for her.

If she was in the yard, he'd take a stroll with her, much to the dismay of the other guards. They weren't supposed to show interest in the inmates, but this particular guard fancied Kelly despite the reason she'd been locked up.

A few years later, Kelly was released from prison and to her surprise, that same guard stood waiting for her at the gate. He smiled, flashing his perfect teeth, and Kelly rushed into his arms—kissing him for the first time.

Finally, after years of flirting and stolen moments, they could be together. It was such an odd story, but Kelly had found her redemption in jail in the form of this man: Adam Rozel.

He took her by the hand and the two walked to his black jaguar.

After he took her shopping for new clothes, Adam took her to a hotel where he'd reserved her a room where she could rest, shower, and remain until she got back on her feet. After she showered and changed into a simple outfit, he then took her a beauty salon.

By the end of the day, she looked very much like her former self, with her hair layered and cut into a blunt bob.

Within a few months, Kelly found a job at a local diner waiting tables.

Eight months after being released from prison, Kelly and Adam relocated to Tallahassee, Florida—Adam's hometown—and settled into a relatively comfortable life.

However, she never stopped wondering what had become of her children. She never revealed to Adam that she'd been a mother. She wasn't aware of how much he knew when it came to why she'd been sent to prison.

She didn't even know if she could find them.

A year later, in January of 1984, Kelly Re' Ridge and Adam Rozel tied the knot in front of close friends and family in a small church in Tallahassee.

Nine months later, on October 3, 1984, the couple was blessed with a healthy baby boy, which they named Adam Rozel Junior, after his father.

When their son was seven months old, the three Rozels moved to Arizona where they settled in a cozy suburban home.

Around this time, Adam Sr. found a job as a deputy sheriff in the nearby district.

Kelly became a full time stay at home mom and settled into a drama free life absent of super human abilities. Now, she focused on a normal life.

Nearly two years after Adam Jr. was born, Kelly gave birth to a set of twins, identical girls, which they named Ashley Marie and Rachel Rena Rozel. They were born on May 15, 1986 at 5:43 pm.

Now with three children to care for, all under the age of two, Kelly found herself juggling a life she wasn't quite prepared for.

Adam began to slowly withdraw from the family, staying out at all times of night and leaving a tired Kelly at home to care for the children.

When Kelly caught Adam with two other women in their home in '88, she packed up the children's clothes and they moved to motel thirty miles away from their cozy neighborhood.

Around this time, Kelly's health began to slowly decline.

After five months away from home, Kelly and Adam tried to reconcile and she moved back into the family home. Adam promised to never commit adultery again.

Instead, he picked up a new and awful habit. He began to indulge in binge drinking.

Kelly didn't want her second marriage to end in disaster. Instead, she fought to keep it afloat.

In 1988, she convinced her husband to go to rehab.

That following year she found herself pregnant again. In January of 1990, she went into preterm labor at 30 weeks.

Kelly lost a great amount of blood during childbirth and the baby went into distress. The baby was stuck in the birth canal with the umbilical cord wrapped around his chest, cutting off his air supply and almost chocking him to death.

Before being rushed into surgery for an emergency C-section, Kelly passed out from the pain. The child was ripped from her body and the doctors went to work on reviving him—he'd been pulled from his mother's womb blue.

The baby was revived, and Aaron named their fourth child Todd Andrew Rozel.

Kelly's health went on to further decline in the months following Todd's birth. However, she soon recovered and began to live each day to the fullest.

In 2001, Kelly took the kids to New York City and while they were there, chaos broke up.

She hadn't used her powers in over twenty years, but now was the time. At 8:46a.m. on September 11th, Flight 11 crashed into the north face of the North Tower of the World Trade Center. Kelly and her kids were only a few blocks away, exploring the city.

Kelly turned her eyes towards the World Trade Center and caught sight of fire and smoke. Around her family, dozens of hands pointed to the sky as people gasped and yelled.

Kelly's mind began to race.

"Mom?" called sixteen-and-a-half-year-old Adam Junior.

She looked at her son, then her other three children. "Take your brother and sisters back to the hotel. I'll be there soon."

"Mom! What's going on? What happened?" asked fifteen-year-old Rachel, braces gleaming as light reflected off them.

Kelly moved towards her daughter. "Listen, I need you to go with your siblings. Go back to the hotel, lock the door, and I'll be right there."

Ashley—Rachel's twin—stood nearby with eleven-year-old Todd at her side.

Rachel's eyes grew watery, but she took a step back towards her older brother.

*Kelly quickly hugged her other daughter and youngest son. "I love you all, dearly," she told them. "Now, **GO!**"*

Adam Junior turned and led his siblings back towards the hotel and Kelly turned without another word and moved against the crowd, heading towards the World Trade Center.

She had powers and she could help. Even if she was out of practice, New York City needed her help.

Moments later, a second plane appeared and slammed into the South Tower.

For a brief moment, Kelly froze in place—shocked by the devastation. America *was under attack. "The Shadow's back?" she said aloud, wondering if the great dark enemy had returned.*

Then, she forced her feet to move. She didn't have time to wonder who this great evil was. She just needed to help.

She began to run and then was in the midst of emergency personnel. A massive evacuation was under way, but she needed to get inside the building and help.

"Ma'am, come back here!" someone yelled as Kelly slipped through the barricades. People were running all around, trying to evacuate. Bodies fell from the sky like raindrops.

Fear gripped her heart and the faces of her children filled her mind—all of them.

"Forgive me," she said aloud, wishing she could hold all of the babies she'd been gifted with, even the ones she hadn't seen since they were toddlers…

And with that, she rushed into the South Tower.

That day, Kelly Re' Ridge-Rozel and dozens of others lost their lives when the South Tower collapsed at 9:59a.m.

The vision shifted, and Adam Rozel Senior came into view.

Adam was left in tears as he watched reports from New York City. Believing his family was dead, he drank himself into unconsciousness.

Eventually, he woke to dozens of missed calls from his children. They were alive and on September 15th, he reunited with them at the airport when they were finally allowed to return home.

Though his children were alive and well, he fell into a deep depression at the loss of his wife.

In 2002, after a night of binge drinking and overcome with grief, Adam Sr. stormed into his eldest daughter's room. She looked so much like Kelly. Her lips were pink just like hers. Her hair was long, like Kelly's had been a few years ago when she was pregnant with Todd.

He needed Kelly. So, in her absence, he took Rachel.

That very night, Adam Jr. ran away from home, sickened by what his father had done to his sister. Enough was enough for him.

Rachel, traumatized and too fearful of retribution, suffered abuse at the hands of her father for another eighteen months. Her twin, Ashley, tried to fight her father off Rachel but failed and instead fell into silence. Ashley often took Todd out of the house during the nights their father took Rachel's body.

Why had no one gone for help?!

Shortly before her eighteenth birthday, Rachel Re' Ridge discovered she was pregnant and knew that things had to change.

With help from her sister, Rachel went to the police and reported the sexual abuse. After that, her sister took their little brother, Todd, and disappeared.

Adam Sr was charged with aggravated assault, statutory rape, and incest.

To this day, he remains in prison.

On December 15, 2004, Rachel gave birth to her son, Joey, after twelve hours of labor and found herself utterly alone in the world.

The vision ended, I screamed and bucked against my seat belt.

"Zedo!" someone shouted, grabbing me.

I yelled, my vision blurry.

"It's okay, it's okay," someone said, grabbing me.

My vision cleared, and I realized Mona stood before me. She held onto my arms, trying to calm me down. I slowly calmed down and tried to get my breathing under control.

I reached up and touched my face. It was wet with tears. I'd been crying.

"Where were you?" she asked. "Are you alright?" Worry was etched on her face.

I looked down at the papers and a tear fell onto the paper.

I immediately felt sick to my stomach from both sensory overload and a deep sickness at what I'd seen. I opened the door to the Hummer and vomited.

Once the contents of my stomach were emptied, I felt sobs rise. I climbed out of the Hummer and suddenly felt like I couldn't breathe.

I was having a panic attack.

Tempestt and Eddie climbed out of the Hummer and moved towards me.

"Breathe, Zedo," said Eddie, a hand stretched out towards me.

I shook my head and backed away from him. "Oh!" I cried, and tears fell. "It was *horrible!*"

"What did you see?" Gonzo asked, moving towards to me.

"He's having a panic attack," Eddie noted as I hyperventilated.

I fell to my knees and then pitched forward on all fours. Eddie knelt next to me and rubbed my back. "There, there, slow breaths, friend."

My heart broke for my mother. My heart shattered to pieces for my half-sister. I couldn't even imagine what that must've been like for her.

Though I'd wanted to clap my hands in celebration for finally getting some answers in the form of the documents, what I'd seen in the visions ruined all of that.

My family was a mess…

Tempestt pulled the papers off the backseat and walked towards me, reading them. "Zedo, there's so much information about your family." She tried to hand the papers to me, but I moved away from her—retreating from the pain those documents inflicted on my mind.

"What's wrong with him?" Gonzo asked, confusion etched on his face.

Tempestt placed a hand on my shoulder, but the papers were in her grasp. The papers brushed against my skin, triggering another retrocognitive vision!

For his horrible deed, Adam Sr. was abused in prison by guards and taunted by his cellmates for his crimes; beaten within an inch of his life.

Across the state, Rachel played with a little Joey at the playground in the trailer park she lived in. People called her white trash because she lived in a trailer park, but it was the best she could do. She was nineteen and a single parent barely making ends meet.

Her son was all that brought joy to her life. He was growing up and almost one now. It had been hard for Rachel and her son to survive, but she refused to give up.

She was more worried about him than herself; he was her motivation to live.

She feared the day Joey would ask about his father. How could she tell him his father was in jail? How could she tell him that his father was actually his grandfather?

She couldn't live with herself if she ever told him.

When the time came several years later when he finally inquired about his parentage, she'd lied.

Rachel told Joey that his father died in a car accident on the way to the hospital to see him the day he was born.

The vision shifted and I suddenly found myself in a hospital within a birthing room...

On a humid summer day in Mississippi, a pale skinned young woman of fifteen with chestnut colored hair and thin lips gave birth to quadruplets. On the wall on the other side of the room, a calendar was marked July 5, 1904.

After the teenager gave birth to the babies, a nurse moved down the hall to the hospital's waiting area and informed the father.

*Together, the young mother and her mate named the four boys Moore, Michael, Scott, and Charles. Their names were written at the bottom of their beds as they slept in the nursery with the given surname '**Re' Ridge**.'*

The seventeen-year-old father watched his sons sleep and he was filled with a plethora of emotions. How could he provide for four children? They'd only been expecting one.

The couple wasn't wealthy by any means, but they were able to get by.

Mr. Re' Ridge was from a family of farmers and was grateful for four healthy sons that would one day be able to help him tend to the land and animals.

Many years later, the eldest of the quadruplets—Moore—was the first to marry. His wife had a son and they named him Moore Martin Re' Ridge Junior.

Moore Junior eventually married and had a daughter, which he named Alexis; Alex for short.

Alexis married a gentleman named Paul Jackson. When Alexis gave birth to a daughter, they named her Kelly Marie.

When Alexis and Paul's marriage ended, Alexis changed her daughter's name from Kelly Marie Jackson to her maiden name Re' Ridge.

Kelly grew up in Michigan with her mother.

She began dating in middle school and met her second boyfriend in tenth grade. Though it was uncommon to see interracial couples in her neighborhood, Kelly refused to let people's opinions keep her from Troy Jeta.

They dated until they graduated from their respective high schools.

During their freshman year in college, Troy proposed to Kelly. The couple wed on the last day of the Spring semester—May 25th.

On June 29, 1975, Kelly gave birth to fraternal twins. She and Troy named the two boys Zedo—the oldest by five minutes—and the other Zahdo Jeta.

On their anniversary—which also coincided with the release of Star Wars: Episode IV- A New Hope— in 1977, Troy began a lengthy affair with a co-worker. Kelly found out from a friend when that same friend caught Troy kissing the woman at a restaurant.

Less than six months later, their marriage ended in a bitter divorce.

On a bright morning, Kelly arrived at her ex-husband's new residence and a huge argument erupted. In the end, Troy and his mother, Brenda, were murdered and Kelly was imprisoned.

They boys, Zedo and Zahdo, were separated and they took on different lives with their new foster parents.

I suddenly fell back into my body and jerked away from Tempestt. She jumped back, confusion etched on her face.

I gulped down a breath of air.

"Zedo, what did you see?" Tempestt asked.

I held up a hand and pointed at her. "Keep that paper away from me!"

Eddie looked at Tempestt's hand. "The document is triggering visions."

I nodded and eased against the brick wall behind me, slumping to my feet.

"Let's give him some space," Mona said, backing up before she turned and walked away.

Chapter 23:

Wicked Predictions

ॐ

I couldn't believe it. I saw my early life. I saw my mother's life. I saw the history of my maternal family before my eyes.

I looked at my hands and they were shaking. My head throbbed in pain from the sensory overload as my brain tried to process it all. It had all happened so fast, and all I'd done was touch their names on my papers.

I knew my mother had powers similar to my own—at least when it came to emitting energy from her palms—but was that all she could do? Was she the first in my maternal lineage to show abilities?

And what about my father's side? Did he have powers, too? Was that why they'd gotten married, or was it primarily because they loved each other?

Did my paternal Grandma Brenda have powers?

I needed answers.

I'd seen both of my parents so clearly in my vision. I kind of looked like a lighter skinned version of my dad. He had a thick, medium afro and warm mahogany skin.

What had he been like? It would've been nice to have grown up with a father…or a mother, despite Kelly's second marriage being so tumultuous.

But regardless of what my mother had done in her past—including murdering my dad and grandmother—she had died a hero. She died trying to save lives.

Perhaps that was what I needed to do, too, instead of seeking revenge against Burton…Maybe I needed to be a hero, too.

I needed guidance.

There's no telling how different my life would've been if I'd grown up with parents.

Just then, my thoughts turned to my twin. Where was Zahdo? I knew I had at least one half-sibling I could find—my younger sister, Rachel—but what of my twin brother?

After a moment alone with my thoughts, I rose to my feet and moved to where my teammates had congregated on the other side of the abandoned parking lot.

I dug the disc out of my pocket. "How can I see what's on this disc?" I asked, raising it to show it to the others.

"Are you sure you want to?" asked Gonzo. "You freaked out from what the papers triggered."

"He's right," said Mona, ever the pessimist. "We don't truly know the extent of your powers, Zedo. Every time we go into a conflict, we find ourselves surprised by yet another ability."

"We're not talking about some fight breaking out," I retorted. "We're talking about data. Sure, my powers seem to be growing, but—"

Eddie took the disc from my hand and turned it over in his. He then pointed behind us. We turned around and I caught sight of a florescent sign that said, 'Internet Café.'

"Well aren't you just the helpful guy," joked Tempestt.

We made our way across the street. Mona and Tempestt grabbed coffee while Eddie and I plopped into seats in front of a flat screen computer. Gonzo had opted to stay with the Hummer.

Eddie slid the disc into a slot on the side of the computer and the screen turned black before it lit up with a bright light.

All of the eyes in the café turned towards us. I blushed in embarrassment.

Eddie reached to pull the disc from the slot when the screen darkened and then a green dragon appeared on the screen, but the disc wouldn't budge. "We have to get it out now. It's a dragon virus."

"GET THAT OUT OF HERE!" said an employee who ran towards us. "You're going to expose all of our network to hackers." The employee reached to yank the device out when the large, green dragon opened its mouth and spoke.

"Zedo Jeta."

I froze, and the employee stepped back, shocked. "What the—?"

"It isn't a virus," Eddie said in awe. "It's a message."

"Well, it sure looked like a virus to me," said the patron who sat next to us.

"You won't find the answers you seek," the dragon said, addressing his statement to me.

"Why not?" I said, answering it.

Eddie chuckled. "I doubt it's interactive, Zedo. It's not going to—"

"It isn't time, yet," the dragon replied, proving Eddie wrong.

Eddie's jaw dropped but he quickly shut it.

The dragon began to circle the screen, whipping its tale back and forth. "You have much to do before your true history will be revealed."

"Why?" I asked. "Why can't I know my history now?"

"Your destiny hasn't been fulfilled," the dragon answered. "You must wage war against The Shadow. Days and nights must pass. You will face the Shadow Leader. Many will fight at your side over time, but only *you* can bring about the end of the Shadow Wars with blood and bone."

I swallowed hard. This wasn't the first time I heard the words 'The Shadow', but *war*. No, that wasn't right. The dragon had said *"wars"* plural! That meant that things were only going to get worse.

"What is he talking about?" Eddie whispered.

I shook my head but didn't take my eyes off the dragon. "Is The Shadow Burton's organization? Is he going to attack the United States?"

"He's going to attack the *galaxy,*" the dragon replied.

Clearly, everyone in the internet café had been paying attention because I heard a collective intake of breath.

"When is all of this going to happen?" Eddie asked. "Are we talking immediately or—"

"The wars will wage when the wars wage," the dragon said. "One hundred twenty-five years from now, you both will be on the forefronts of war."

My eyes grew wide. "How is that possible?"

Eddie quickly did mental math. "That's the year 2145. How could either of us be alive then?"

The dragon roared and Eddie recoiled, as did most of the people in the café. But I didn't.

I chill ran down my spine. 2145 was a long time away, but to hear that I'd be fighting for over a hundred years wasn't comforting.

"You must travel across the stars, Zedo Jeta…Your journey has just begun. You won't know *you* until the galaxy knows peace."

"I won't know who I am until—"

Suddenly, smoke began to rise from the screen and the dragon disappeared. In the next moment, the screen imploded, and I jumped back. Patrons screamed.

"You're going to have to pay for that!" yelled the employee as Eddie and I raced out of the internet café. Mona and Tempestt were right behind us.

"What the hell was that about?!" demanded Mona as we climbed into the Hummer and Gonzo pulled out of the parking lot.

"I have no idea," I said, perplexed. "What did it mean by 'you won't know *you* until the galaxy knows peace'?"

"It means we need to focus on Burton and take him out *first*," Mona said. She looked at me. "I heard the dragon, Zedo."

"Everyone did," I corrected.

Tempestt turned to face me. "Clearly, he's a threat."

"But to the *galaxy*?" asked Eddie. He shook his head. "I didn't know that there were more inhabitable planets out there."

Gonzo laughed. "You thought we were all alone in this big universe?"

"Where've you been all these years?" asked Tempestt. "Living under a rock?"

Eddie blushed with embarrassment. They didn't know that he'd cut himself off from the world at large, but I did.

I glanced out the window, because just like Eddie I didn't know that there was life out there. I didn't know that, across the stars, there were other worlds with civilizations at risk.

How bad was Burton? I thought we were dealing with a global criminal. Clearly, I was wrong.

This was a bigger issue than I'd thought.

We drove in silence for a few hours before we pulled into a rest stop a quarter to eleven.

I climbed out the Hummer and caught sight of a large boulder near the building that housed the traveler restrooms.

I climbed onto the boulder and exhaled, relaxing against it. I slowly leaned back until I was flat on my back and laced my hands behind my head. There were so many stars in the sky tonight.

I wondered about the hundreds of worlds out there across the stars.

I heard approaching footsteps and turned my head to see who was coming. Mona approached and when she saw me looking at her she stopped.

"Sorry. I didn't mean to disturb you."

I sat up. "No, it's no problem. You aren't disturbing me. Come on. Come sit with me for a while." I helped her onto the boulder.

She sighed as she relaxed and then I laid at her side, once again looking up at the star filled sky.

"What do you think your life will be like in the future…like once this is all over?" she asked me, staring up at the sky.

I thought about it for a moment before I answered her. "I want to find my family, go back to school, and graduate. Once that's all done, I'd like to settle down and start a family. I want to continue my life the way it would have been… Well, the way it should have been." I let out a deep sigh. "Realistically, if I hadn't fallen into a coma, I probably would've ended up as a secret agent. Maybe my powers would've come naturally, and I'd be sent out on missions as a spy."

"We both know that it would've been that way," she replied. "We never would've had a chance to have normal lives."

I moved my head until she filled my vision. "Perhaps we would've led normal lives after being free from the agencies."

"I don't think they ever would've let us be free…Even now, I'm on a mission for the agency. I'm not free."

"But you've known love…You're not some slave to your agency, Mona."

She opened her mouth to respond, but just then Gonzo ran up to us—interrupting. "You guys ready?" he asked.

I sat up and exhaled. I looked over to Mona and she grinned sadly. I felt that we'd just missed another chance to express ourselves; our feelings.

I helped Mona rise to her feet once I got up. We slowly headed back to the Hummer. I playfully nudged her in the rib and she did the same. I chuckled softly.

"What will your life look like after all this is over?" I asked her.

"Oh, I don't know, Zedo. I haven't thought that far ahead, yet."

"Maybe you can fill me in on your answer some time."

She tucked a strand of hair behind her ear. "Maybe by then I'll have an answer for you."

Chapter 24:

The Academy

CB&O

We climbed back into the Hummer and hit the road. Something told me that Mona had more to say to me and I knew for sure that there was more I wanted to say to her.

However, I was unable to say anything. I couldn't find the words.

I sat in the passenger seat and looked over my shoulder. I caught Mona's eye and she grinned at me. I grinned back at her and then turned back around, glancing at the crescent moon.

Maybe some things were better left unsaid.

As I glanced at the moon, the topic that kept coming to mind was that of *The Shadow.* If Burton was part of it, then surely Lester was, too.

I shook my head. This was getting too complicated. I had awakened from my coma prepared for revenge. Now, I was told by a computer program that I was destined to save the galaxy.

But how accurate was the program? Was it the truth? Or was it just a fallacy told to occupy me and distract me from my search of the truth?

How had Mr. Sashar from United Affairs known to upload that to the disk?

I pulled the documents about my family from my pocket and rubbed my forefinger over my mother's name. I wondered what life would've been like if I'd been raised by her…

I caught flashes of light from behind my eyelids and I felt my mind wake. My eyes fluttered, and my foggy vision cleared. I'd fallen asleep without knowing it and the sun was rising in the distance.

I looked to my left and caught sight of Mona in the driver's seat. I sat up and she realized I was awake.

"When did we switch drivers?" I asked, still groggy.

"Well, good morning to you, too," she said, grinning. "We switched drivers about six hours ago. You were out cold."

I rubbed my eyes and glanced around. I quickly realized that we weren't on the highway anymore. We were approaching a massive complex made of futuristic skyscrapers.

My jaw dropped in awe of the buildings before me. I looked at Mona. "Where are we?" I asked, my voice filled with wonder.

Suddenly, Gonzo's head appeared in the spot between the driver and the passenger seat, startling me. "We're *here*!" he exclaimed.

"Where's *here*?" I asked.

"We're at the academy," Mona said. "It's kind of like the school Gonzo went to."

"Yeah," he agreed. "It's kind of like that…but so much more."

We passed through a gate made of silver that gleamed in the light. Mona pulled into a parking lot filled with hundreds of vehicles.

After we all climbed out of the Hummer, I glanced around—trying to take it all in.

Mona moved to my side and nudged me playfully in the rib cage. "Welcome to the Lightway Academy of Ashton."

The academy was composed of steel buildings and three brick buildings. It became obvious that the brick buildings were much older and that the steel skyscrapers had only been built in the past decade or so.

Maybe it was just my imagination, but it felt like something positive was calling out to me. I felt safe here. I felt like I'd arrived at sanctuary.

Vines ran up and down the sides of the central brick building we were now approaching. It seemed to stretch out for a couple of miles and was about seven stories high with smaller four-story buildings on either side of it. In the distance I caught sight of several weeping willow trees.

The windows of the brick building were made of mosaics.

I brushed my hair away from my forehead and once again, my mouth dropped in admiration of the building's beauty.

We moved towards the central brick building and before us, the thirty-five-foot-tall wooden door opened and out walked an old man.

Mona suddenly beamed and ran towards him—her newly altered jet black blew in the breeze. It still amazed me that being in the Uncharted Territory of New Oklahoma had changed her hair from auburn to black.

The old man smiled and opened his arms and embraced Mona. He was dressed in a navy-blue robe with billowy sleeves that put me in the mind of a mage.

"Were we expected?" I asked Gonzo.

"Mona called ahead while you were sleeping," he told me and I nodded.

After Mona pulled out of his embrace, she turned and introduced us one by one. "Everyone, this is Dr. Brandon Webster."

He took me by the hand and shook it, his grip firm. "It's a pleasure to meet you all."

"Dr. Webster trained me back when I was in the agency."

"Yes," he agreed, "but that was before I defected and came here for sanctuary among the Lightway."

I frowned, confusion filling me. "What are the Lightway?"

"Not '*what*', my boy," he said, grinning. "But *who*. Lightway are super humans that have aligned themselves to the light and fight on behalf of those who cannot. They commune with light energy and dedicate their lives in service to the universe."

I had so many questions, but now wasn't the time. Dr. Webster turned and led us into the academy, Mona at his side.

Beside me, Tempestt gasped and oohed at everything that impressed her. But in all honesty, so much about this place impressed me, too.

Beyond the main foyer there was a massive curved stairwell that led to the upper levels.

Children, teens, and adults moved about the building and seemed so content with their life here.

I never knew that there were so many of us.

As we moved through the hallowed halls, Dr. Webster gave the rest of us a brief history of the academy, which had been named after its super human founder—John Corsair Ashton.

"This academy was designed for super humans," Dr. Webster told us. "It was created to help super humans learn how to control and use their gifts for the good of all mankind. The academy's founder believed that humans and super humans could coexist and thus welcomed what many would deem as '*normal*' humans to visit the academy and even seek employment here."

"Dr. Webster was one of those humans who decided to come work and learn from super humans," Mona said, grinning as she looked at the old man. Clearly, she adored Dr. Webster.

"People not only came here to receive training in how to control their abilities, but also to seek an education if they were unable to find peace in the public or private school systems."

"Just like H.I.T.S," said Gonzo, grinning.

Dr. Webster looked at my friend and nodded. "Yes, just like that institute, but our focus is a more liberal education, rather than just the applied sciences and technology."

Dr. Webster made a left and led us down a corridor decorated with portraits of super humans using their abilities. I stopped in front of a portrait that vaguely looked like my grandmother Alexis—Kelly Re' Ridge's mom—but it couldn't be her...could it?

I pulled myself away from the portrait and caught the end of the doctor's sentence. He then coughed and continued. "The leaders of the Lightway Council on Tewey gave the founder, Lightway Supreme Master Ashton, permission to start the academy."

"I still can't believe there are planets outside this solar system," said Eddie.

Dr. Webster looked over his shoulder, frowning. "Where've you been all your life, living under a rock?"

Tempestt laughed and I nudged Eddie, laughing, too. Eddie blushed in embarrassment at being asked that question for a second time.

The doctor pushed open a set of double doors and we walked into a massive chamber. "Yes, there are more planets than the ones in this system. Life *does* exist outside Earth and this solar system."

"What do you do here, doctor?" Eddie asked the doctor, changing the subject.

Dr. Webster looked over his shoulder. "These days, I teach galactic history, but back in the day I taught power control."

The room we entered was decorated in massive paintings of men and women dressed in armor with rapiers in hand. The blades of the rapiers glowed in various colors.

Mona told me the men and women were Lightway and they held acesabers in their hands. Busts of academy leaders lined the walls, too.

Dr. Webster led us to a sitting area on the far side of the room and we settled in for a conversation. "So, Mona, tell me. What brings you to the Lightway Academy of Ashton?"

Mona opened her mouth to speak, but I interjected. "Before she even answers that question, tell us about Mona."

She turned to look at me and glared. The doctor clapped his hands together and laughed a hearty laugh.

"Well, the young Miss Mona Lisa-Flynn was one of our students who never truly committed to any one program. She would drop in from time to time but never became a full-fledged Lightway."

"There was no way I could complete my training here *and* be a secret agent," Mona told the doctor.

He tapped her hand affectionately as if to say, '*I know.*'

The doctor clapped his hands together again and glanced at the five of us. "So, I'll ask again. What brings you to the academy?"

In unison, my four teammates glanced at me, but only Mona spoke. "Doctor, my friend could use some of your help…"

I opened my mouth to speak, but Mona beat me to the punch.

"He's a super human, but his powers are beyond anything I've ever seen." The doctor looked at me, but I suddenly felt bashful. "He possesses the abilities of elemental manipulation, atmokinesis, telepathy, flight, and retrocognition."

The doctor's eyes grew wide with each ability being listed. He looked at me. "Is that all?" he said sarcastically, but with a playful grin on his face.

"I can also emit little beams of energy I call si' beams," I told him.

"That's a lot of power for such a young fella. How old are you, thirteen?"

"Forty-five," I informed him, and when shock filled his face I quickly explained that I'd been in a coma for thirty years and my body seemed to be frozen in time.

The doctor rose to his feet and the rest of us did, too. "I've never heard of so many powers in one person."

"Can you perhaps help him focus his powers?" asked Mona.

"Now, hold on there," I said, stopping Mona. "My powers aren't out of control. I can do just fine without—"

"No offense, Zedo," said Gonzo, "but we all talked about it while you were sleeping." I looked at the others, but they wouldn't meet my gaze. "We're all a little uneasy about your powers, man... I mean, you're a juggernaut! But you don't have full control and you know it."

"You're *scared* of me?" I said, shock filling my voice.

"We're not scared of *you,* Zedo," Tempestt said, moving towards me. She placed a hand on my forearm. "We're scared of your powers."

I slowly pulled away from her and I could see that the gesture had hurt her, but right now I didn't care.

"So, instead of letting me search for my family, you all decide to drop me off at super human daycare?"

Mona shook her head. "We need to focus on Burton, Zedo. Everything keeps pointing to that."

Gonzo placed a hand on my shoulder, but I slowly shrugged it off. "Look, buddy. Stay here with the Lightway and the teachers for a while and get some training. We can still stick with the original plan."

"Yes," agreed Mona. "But instead of meeting in a week, stay here and get some training for the Lightway. We can meet up at my apartment in a few weeks and track down Burton."

I shook my head. "You don't get to make those calls for me, Mona." I took a step back. "It doesn't work like that." I suddenly felt so betrayed. I looked at Eddie, but even he seemed to be unable to meet my gaze.

I turned to leave, but the doctor called out to me. "Young man, it seems that your friends have your best interest at heart. You don't want to be a danger to yourself or others."

I whirled around and suddenly a strong breeze swept through the room, blowing their hair back and rustling their clothes. "I'm not a danger to ANYONE!"

"Clearly," the doctor replied, sarcasm dripping in his voice. He adjusted his wind-swept clothing and rose from the couch he'd been sitting on. He moved towards me and I tried to remain calm. "Stay, Zedo. Let us help you." I clenched my jaw, irritated. "At least let me finish giving you a tour…If you don't want to stay after that, I'll understand."

I sighed in frustration and nodded curtly.

Mona moved towards me and kissed me lightly on the cheek. *Judas,* I thought.

"We'll see you in a few days, Jeta." And with that, Mona headed towards the exit. Gonzo was next. He squeezed my shoulder and nodded at me and then followed Mona out of the door. Tempestt hugged me and then Eddie patted me on the back.

And just like that, my family was gone…. My friends were gone…My *team* left me. They'd abandoned me just like my mom had.

They abandoned me…and I'd never felt worse in my life.

Dr. Webster led me out of the room and we headed out to the garden. "Mona gave a pretty extensive list of your powers."

"Yeah," I said. I wasn't in the mood for light conversation. As soon as I figured out where I was going from here, I was out of here.

"That's Joel," he said, pointing to a young teen with red hair and fair skin.

I realized Joel was standing next to a few of the plants. "What's his power?"

"He's a chlorokinesist."

"Meaning?"

"That means he can create, shape, and manipulate plants."

Joel ignored us as we watched him. Instead, he stretched his hands out and a vine wrapped around one of his forearms and lilies appeared from the buds.

Dr. Webster gestured to the garden around us. "He created most of the plants here. It was his own special project, but now he tends to the garden to give us all something beautiful to look at and appreciate."

I took a step towards Joel and he looked at me. He stretched a hand out and one of the vines moved through the air towards me. I stretched out a hand and suddenly felt my earth powers hum within me. I touched the vine and it responded to my touch, coiling around my forearm and presenting a purple lily to me.

"It likes you," Joel said, eyeing the vine as it twisted in mid-air and then folded in on itself until it just floated around Joel.

I grinned and then moved back towards the doctor. Perhaps this place wasn't so bad after all.

"You control the elements, Zedo," Dr. Webster said. "You could potentially control any of these plants. But it's more than just *control*."

"It's an honor to interact with nature," I told him. "I don't take my powers for granted, and I don't abuse them."

He held up his hands in mock surrender. "No one said you did, Zedo."

"It sure feels like it," I muttered under my breath.

"Come," he said, beckoning me after him. "Let me show you more of the academy."

We exited the garden and headed into one of the smaller buildings.

"To our left," he said, pointing, "is Andrew Davidson." I caught sight of a young guy with a curly afro similar to mine.

He was white and wore glasses, but seemed young, like me. He stood at the front of the class. "He's a genius and teaches one of our technology classes to eleventh graders."

"So, he's a student here?" I asked.

The doctor shook his head. "He's a professor here. He has the ability of enhanced intelligence. He came into his powers prematurely but managed to graduate from high school at the age of ten, and then graduated from college at twelve. By the time he was sixteen, he also held two doctoral degrees. Now at nineteen, he's joined the staff here at the academy to teach others just like him—super humans."

"I'm impressed," I admitted. "You house a lot of talent."

"We really do, Zedo. I think you'll like it here."

I shook my head. "You misunderstand, doctor. I'm not staying."

He looked at me. "And why is that? You don't think you belong here?"

"It's not that. I have a more pressing matter to attend to."

"What could be more pressing than controlling your powers and understanding them better?"

"Finding my family and better understanding who I am better," I answered.

He looked down at his watch. "There's so much more to see, but we don't have the time."

"Why not?" I asked, my forehead creasing.

"We have to start testing your powers."

My eyes grew wide. "Test my powers? Bu I—"

"Come now, Zedo. Show me what you're made of." He led me to an elevator and he pressed a button that took us to the lower levels.

The elevator opened on the bottom floor and led into a massive laboratory.

I stopped in the doorway, frozen by fear and memories of 1989.

The last time I'd been in a lab, things hadn't turned out so well for me. My heart thumped inside my chest and then I felt my chest grow tight. My anxiety levels began to rise.

When the doctor realized I wasn't behind him, he turned and motioned for me to follow him.

I swallowed hard. I wasn't some defenseless kid anymore. These days I had multiple powers at my disposal.

I wasn't going to fall victim again. I could defend myself now.

In that moment, I decided to not be afraid anymore... No one was going to hurt me, at least not this way, ever again.

I forced my feet to move and passed several work stations until I stood beside the doctor, who now was engaged in a conversation with a beautiful brunette.

"Zedo, I'd like to introduce you to my daughter and assistant, Phoebe Webster."

"It's nice to meet you," she said, grinning and shaking my hand. I smiled politely and gazed around the lab, taking in my surroundings.

I noticed that I instantly started looking for the other exits but stopped myself.

I turned my attention back to Phoebe and her father. Phoebe was about 5'5" and wore glasses. She looked to be in her mid-twenties and wore simple slacks and a sweater vest over a white blouse. Her hair was pent up in a simple style.

"Zedo, we're just going to run a few tests," Dr. Webster said. He gestured at a nearby machine. "This particular machine will measure your energy output." He pointed at another. "The other will catalogue your abilities."

"Why do we need to catalogue my powers?" I asked, growing suspicious. "I'm not staying. There's no need to—"

"It's simply academic," the doctor replied, holding up his hands to stop me from worrying. "You're in safe hands here, Zedo."

"It's not your hands I'm worried about," I replied under my breath.

"You're worried about the machines?" asked Phoebe. I slightly nodded, and she smiled warmly at me. "Don't worry about them either. I'm a technopath. I can control technology with my mind. So, it not only makes me the perfect assistant in a lab, but also your new best friend."

Phoebe turned and walked down a flight of metal stairs. She slowly lifted her left hand and two devices lifted off the ground and moved to another table. She gestured with her right hand and one of the two machines beside her powered on.

In the next moment, she turned and looked up at her father. "We're good to go, daddy."

Dr. Webster gestured for me to lead the way down the flight of stairs. I moved towards Phoebe and she led me to an oval shaped platform.

"Stand here, please. This is a power grid. When you use your powers on it, it'll transfer the data to the machines and then to the computers upstairs."

"Where will you be?"

She gestured back to the level the stairs led up to. "We won't even be four hundred feet away." She placed a hand on my shoulder. "You're *safe* here, Zedo."

And with that, she turned and headed back up the steps to stand beside her father.

"What will I do?" I asked, looking up at them from their control station.

"We'll monitor the powers you use and see how long you can hold out," Phoebe said.

My eyes grew wide. "Hold out from what?"

She chuckled and answered, "You'll see."

Just then, the brightness in the lab increased and I shielded my eyes.

I heard a churning sound and then darkness surrounded me from above. I looked up and my eyes grew wide with shock as a huge chunk of the ceiling fell. I stretched my hands forward and called upon my aerokinetic powers to use the air to hurl the chunk of the ceiling aside. Undoubtedly, I'd used more air pressure than I'd expected because the chunk split and fell on both sides of me.

As the chunks landed with a thud, they turned to black-and-white static and disappeared. My eyes grew wide.

"What the—?"

"A projection, Zedo," Phoebe said, stroking the computer keys in front of her. She didn't even look up until after she'd finished her sentence. She smiled again, trying to ease my worry. "Everything will be a simulation, Zedo—a projection of my power to manipulate the machines. I told you, you're safe here."

I nodded and then looked at Dr. Webster. He nodded, and I called energy to myself.

In the next moment, two static projections of guards appeared, and they opened fire. I flew upward and then hurled si' beams at them. The si' beams slammed into the guards' chest and they disappeared.

The walls around me began to close in me and I called upon my earth powers to shatter them into static nothingness. Then the walls seemed to immediately reappear.

I looked at Phoebe and she smirked. I grinned and glanced at the walls. This time the four walls had ten-inch thick nails and broken shards of glass embedded in them. The walls launched the objects and I had to use my powers to destroy them—spinning and flipping through the air.

I wrapped energy around me and then pushed it away in the form of flames from my palms.

I landed and inhaled sharply.

Above me, in the control station, I caught the ending of Phoebe's sentence to her father. She spoke in a lowered voice, but I could still hear her as I flew around the lab, destroying her projections.

"Look at this, father," Phoebe said as new readouts appeared on the screen before her.

Dr. Webster moved over to the readout screens. His jaw dropped, and he smiled.

"Are you *seeing this?!*"

"Yes, Phoebe, I see it," he replied, placing a hand on the screen to enlarge the image.

Phoebe shook her head. "The machines must be broken or something... These levels aren't possible for most of our beginners to achieve."

"You sound shocked, Phoebe," Dr. Webster said, turning around and looking at her. "Zedo is no beginner."

"Well, yes, I'm shocked, dad. He has *multiple* powers. I assumed those si' beams and flight were all, but he just used fire and air and earth-related powers, too. I haven't seen these kinds of readouts in any of our students here. I haven't even gotten these kinds of readouts from the masters of the High Council on Tewey."

"He's outdoing anyone else across the stars," Dr. Webster said, and then he looked at me as I landed on the sensory pad, panting. "He's doing about as well as I expected."

"What did you expect, exactly?" I asked, moving towards the stairs that would lead me to the control station. I wiped sweat from my forehead.

"I'd expect nothing short of game changing levels from the offspring of Kelly Re' Ridge," Dr. Webster said.

I froze in my steps. "Y-You knew my mother?"

Phoebe looked at her father, shock etched on her face. "Kelly?" Phoebe asked. "Zedo's one of her children?"

"Yes." Dr. Webster kept his eyes locked on me. "And to answer your question, Zedo, *no*, I didn't know your mother…but my father did."

"How?" I asked, moving up the final steps to stand before them. My mind began to race and I recalled the portrait of my grandmother Alexis. I *knew* that was her! "My mother trained here…didn't she?"

Dr. Webster nodded. "For a short while when she first came into her powers. Your grandmother, Alexis, studied here briefly, as well."

"I wondered why I saw a portrait of her here."

He grinned. "You saw that, did you?" I nodded and the doctor ran a hand across his forehead. He glanced at his daughter. "Phoebe, would you give us a moment?"

She nodded and walked away.

I found it such a huge coincidence that Mona had been trained by a man with links to my own family—the family I was trying to find.

"Zedo, there's so much about your family that you don't know."

"I've been trying to find them. But how'd you know I was related to Kelly?"

"You look so much like her," he said and turned to walk towards another computer.

I wondered how accurate his words were. I was biracial. Did I really look like my mom? It was hard for me to even detect similarities sometimes. I felt that I took more after my father than my mother.

"Zedo, you come from a long line of beings known as the Ones."

"What?" I asked, frowning. "The what?"

He stroked a few keys and an image of Kelly as a child popped up. She had a toothy smile plastered on her face and was missing her two front teeth. She was dressed in dirty overalls and her brown hair was in pigtails. At her side was my grandmother, young and slender with a smile etched on her face.

"Sometime in the early 2000s we had most of our photos uploaded to a mainframe." The doctor faced me. "This is a picture of your mother and grandmother. Zedo, you're an heir to the line of Ones."

"But what does that *mean*?"

He shook his head. "It's not for me to say, Zedo. You'll have to travel across the stars to find your answers."

"But if you know now, why can't you just tell me?"

He shook his head again. "I don't have all the answers, Zedo. If I did, I promise I wouldn't hold out on you. All I can say is that you are destined for great things, just like your ancestors."

I rolled my eyes. First the green dragon from the disk had talked about my destiny and now the doctor was, too. Why couldn't they just tell me up front what I was destined to do?

What in the world was a 'One'?! One what? One man? One super human? What?

I was supposed to join the others in a few days, but a few days turned into me changing my mind. I learned so much at the academy and against my better judgment, I decided to stay.

My teammates had been right. I was a little rough around the edges when it came to my powers. So, I stayed and trained with

Lightway Masters—guardians of peace and defenders of the galaxy—and honed my powers.

My days started before sunrise with Master Tammy Waters—a woman in her mid-forties with the ability of geokinesis. She could manipulate elements derived of the earth, like me. By 8 in the morning, I joined Master Joseph Grande—a descendant of someone called Ariana—down by the river to practice my aquakinesis.

My air lessons with Master Joan Lee took place after lunch, and then I went to class. Not only was the Lightway academy a place where super humans could hone their skills, but it was also an accredited school. I quickly dove into my studies and took hold of my education. I was determined to get my GED.

After school, I had pyrokinetic lessons with the gruff Master Aaron Braxton.

My life had changed drastically, and I'd have to thank Mona whenever I saw her again. My goals in life had shifted. Yes, I still wanted to find Burton and watch the life leave his eyes, but I also wanted things for myself; personal goals.

I wanted to graduate, I wanted to train, and one day, I wanted to become a Lightway. However, that last goal would take years as I'd have to be apprenticed to a master first and spend years under their tutelage.

I wasn't ready for that level of commitment just yet.

Throughout my stay at the Lightway Academy of Ashton, I'd grown both mentally and physically. Even my spirituality had been pushed with meditation.

I loved this place.

Autumn arrived, and I watched the leaves change colors and fall.

Dr. Webster had promised to help me find a member of my family and after ten weeks at the academy, he called me to his office.

On November 14, 2020, Dr. Webster handed me a single piece of paper.

My heart raced. This year had gone by so fast. So much had happened in just ten months. I'd come out of my coma, I'd made lifelong friends in Gonzo, Tempestt, Eddie, and Mona, and so much more. I'd enrolled back in school and now I was finally getting answers.

I opened up the piece of paper and on it was one piece of information. My heart leapt for joy.

On the sheet of paper was my younger sister's name, place of employment, and home address.

"Zedo," began the doctor, "I know what this means to you, but you really should stay and complete your training. Stay and finish school."

"I'll come back, doc." I ran my finger across the sheet of paper. I was going to meet my sister.

"Zedo…you and I both know if you leave, you won't come back for some time…"

I looked at Dr. Webster. He was right and we both knew it. If I left now, it would be ages before I would be able to return to the academy.

I still owed my friends my allegiance and I'd already stayed here much longer then I'd intended.

"Well, I guess I'm headed to Vegas."

Chapter 25:

Rachel and Joey Rozel

❦

Dr. Webster didn't try to stop me. I would be leaving the next day and made sure I said goodbye to the masters that had trained me and the friends I'd made during my stay at the academy.

Master Braxton gave me $2,000 and told me to stay out of trouble. I thanked him and the next morning, Dr. Webster drove me to the airport, having booked me a flight the previous night.

I arrived in Vegas and hailed a cab, heading to Rachel's place of employment. I didn't even know if she was at work today, but I'd stay there until I saw her.

I didn't know how I was going to introduce myself. I didn't even know if she'd be open to talking to me.

I've given up everything to come here on a whim.

I needed this. I needed to know who I was. I needed to know the siblings my mother had created. I needed to know.

The cab pulled up to a diner which looked much like any other diner I'd visited with my teammates. I paid the cab driver in cash and then gazed up at the sign that read *Joe's Diner*.

I moved into the diner and looked around. It was crowded with tourists as it wasn't too far from the Vegas strip.

"Sit wherever you can find a spot," a voice said. I looked up and caught sight of the person the voice belonged to.

I froze. Before me was my younger sister—though she looked so much older than me due to me still being frozen in the body of my teenage self.

I stood in that doorway for a moment and felt my breath hitch.

Rachel Rozel looked so much like our mother that I almost thought I was staring at Kelly's ghost for a moment.

"Excuse me," said a voice behind me and I moved out of the way. I realized that I was blocking the entrance.

I moved out of the way and watched Rachel as she moved from table to table, refilling drinks and taking orders.

I eased into an empty booth and looked at the menu. My throat suddenly felt dry.

What was I going to say?

Rachel moved towards me and pulled a notepad from the front of her black apron. Her chestnut brown hair was tousled and shoulder length. She wore a white shirt with "Joe's Diner" across the front.

"What can I get for you?" she asked seconds before she looked up from her notepad. "Oh, my God. Jimmy, what are you doing here?"

I looked at her, confused. "I'm sorry?"

She laughed and shook her head, blinking the comment away. "I'm sorry. You look so much like my nephew James. I thought you were him for a second."

So, I had another nephew out there named James and he looked like me. I wondered which of my half-siblings he belonged to.

"I'm sorry about that. What can I get for you?" she asked, still shaking her head and laughing at herself as she prepared to take my order.

I stuttered for a second as I tried to come up with something.

"Mom, what table does this go to?" said a voice.

Rachel looked at me apologetically. "Give me a second. I'm sorry." She twisted her body and looked towards the kitchen. I turned as well and caught sight of her teenage son, Joey. "Table seven, Joey! Didn't you read the order slip?"

The lanky teen with dark hair shrugged his shoulders and moved to the other end of the diner.

Rachel turned towards me and exhaled. "I'm sorry about that. It's my son's first day on the job."

I wondered how old Joey was now? I quickly did the math in my head and realized that he was almost sixteen.

Rachel looked at me, waiting for me to order. I opened my mouth to speak, but food items didn't come out.

So instead I said, "My name is Zedo Jeta. I'm your half-brother." She looked at me, frozen. She simply stared at me. After a

moment of silence, I decided to say something else. "Kelly Re'
Ridge-Rozel was my mother."

Without another word, she turned and walked away. She
headed towards the kitchen and shouldered her way past her co-
workers. Joey looked at his mother and could tell she was upset.

He looked around the diner, trying to figure out where she'd
come from. He caught sight of me and frowned.

For a brief moment, I felt a presence brush against my
mind—telepathically searching for something—and then the feeling
passed as quickly as it had begun. In the next moment, Joey turned
to follow his mother into the kitchen. The swinging doors closed
behind him.

I rubbed my chin for a second and realized that Joey had
tried to probe my mind. He was telepathic, just like me. I wondered
if Rachel knew.

I absentmindedly glanced out the large window and caught
sight of Rachel and her son briskly walking across the parking lot.
They were heading towards a beat-up car.

I realized she was trying to leave. I rushed out of the diner
and ran across the parking lot.

"Hey!" I called, moving across the parking lot.

Rachel didn't turn around, but Joey did. He stopped and
turned towards me. "Who the hell are you?" he asked. "What did
you do to my mom?" He balled up his fist, but his mother grabbed
his arm and pulled him back.

"Let's just go, Joey," she told him. "Now."

I had to do something. I couldn't let her leave. "I felt you touch my mind, Joey."

They stopped and looked at me. "What did you say?" Rachel asked. She looked at Joey and he turned red in the face. I realized in that moment that he hadn't told his mother that he was a super human.

I wondered how long he'd known.

I took a step forward and looked at Joey. "You tried to read my mind. You're telepathic."

"How'd you know?" he asked. "People can never tell when I—"

Rachel looked shocked. "You didn't tell me you could—"

"I'm telepathic, too," I told him. "I'm a super human, just like you."

"Who the hell are you?" he asked, and Rachel swatted his arm.

"Watch your mouth, young man." She looked at me. "Leave us alone. I don't know who you are, but—"

"I'm your half-brother," I told her. "I know you don't believe me but let me explain."

"That's impossible," she replied, looking defiant. "My mother's been dead for a long time. You look to be about the same age as my son."

I stretched out a hand. "Let me show you," I told her. I'd never shared my thoughts with another person, but I figured I could.

If I could read minds, shouldn't I be able to turn that power outward and share my thoughts with another?

Joey took a step towards me. "You're not touching my mother."

"I'm not going to hurt you…either of you."

Rachel bit her lower lip. I could tell she was nervous and unsure. Joey looked at me and I felt him brush my consciousness with his own. He looked at his mom. "He's telling the truth. He's not going to hurt us."

Rachel looked at her son and seemed to relax a bit with his reassurance. She took a step forward and touched my hand. Her hand was trembling.

She was nervous, but so was I.

I closed my eyes and focused and pulled the memories of my visions of the past back to the forefront of my mind.

As the first flashes of memory filled my mind, I felt Joey place his hand atop mine, too. I felt a buzzing sensation across my skin and the hairs on my arm rose as energy vibrated within me.

A flash of light glowed between our hands and I saw the memories in my mind's eye. Rachel gasped and then Joey did, too, and I knew they were seeing what I was seeing.

I showed them the memories of me, Zahdo, and Kelly when I was a toddler. Then I flashed forward to memories of Kelly with Adam Senior when she was pregnant with Rachel and her twin sister. I shifted the memories and tried to keep them happy.

Unfortunately, I couldn't steer away from the memory of Kelly's trip to New York City with her children in 2001.

Just then, Rachel yanked her hand away. She was gasping. She placed a hand over her mouth.

Joey swore, his eyes wide with shock.

I looked at my hand. It still pulsed with energy. I couldn't believe that I'd opened my mind to not one, but *two* people and they'd been able to see my memories.

"It's *true*," Rachel said, shock and disbelief still in her voice.

"But *how?*" asked Joey.

I looked around and saw that some people were leaving the diner and staring at us. "Perhaps we can talk about this elsewhere?"

Rachel looked around and then nodded, noting the people. "Did you drive here?"

I shook my head. "I caught a cab."

She nodded at her run-down car. "Climb in." She moved towards the driver's side and climbed in. Joey eyed me and then climbed in the backseat.

"Get in the front," he said as he rolled down the window. "There's no way I'm letting you sit behind me."

I did so without a word and Rachel pulled out of the parking lot. We rode in awkward silence for twenty minutes. I glanced at Rachel out of my peripheral vision. She continuously rubbed her forehead. I bet a headache was forming.

The car smelled like cigarettes and burgers.

I felt another mental nudge from Joey and turned in my seat. "Can you stop trying to read my mind?"

His eyebrows rose up. Rachel pulled her eyes off the road for a moment. "Joey? Wh-What are you doing? Stop."

"I'm trying to figure out if this is for real."

"I told you I'd tell you everything. You don't have to invade my mind to learn the truth."

He crossed his arms over his chest and glared at me. "Then start talking."

I exhaled and eyed Rachel. She looked at me, eyes filled with curiosity.

I turned around in my seat and began from the beginning. I told them how I'd grown up in the foster system until I'd run away and enlisted in the system until I was pulled into Secret Agency XII.

I told them about Burton and falling into a coma. I told them about waking up in January 2020 and all that had happened.

I wanted to skip over details about putting together a Vengeance Team and all of the things we'd been through, but thought better of it. I decided to share that, too. I picked back up with Mona and the others dropping me off at the academy and how I'd been searching for my family since I'd had visions of the past.

By the time I got to the point of my story about arriving in Vegas, we'd pulled up to Rachel's house.

We climbed out of the car and I looked around. Rachel lived in a trailer park, but I wasn't going to judge her. I didn't know her life. All I knew was that she was my mother's daughter and had been through *hell* and still managed to wake up every morning.

"Joey, go on in and let me talk to Zedo."

"Mom, I'd rather—"

"Joey!" She whirled around and exhaled. "Please…go into the house and let me talk to Zedo. I'll be in soon. And don't think we aren't going to discuss your new power, young man!"

He stood there for a moment as if trying to decide if he was going to obey or not and then he looked at me. "I'm watching you." I said nothing but had received the message. He turned and headed into the trailer, slamming the door behind himself.

"He's very protective of you," I said.

She nodded and tucked a strand of hair behind her ear. "Yeah, he's always been my little bodyguard."

I made sure that he wasn't lingering in the doorway. "Does he…" I cleared my throat. "Does he ask about his father?"

Her eyes darted back and forth from the trailer to me. Her eyes were so empty, so very alone. "How'd you know about that?" She didn't sound angry. She just sounded broken.

I told her how when I'd been shown the past, I'd also seen bits and pieces of her life after our mother had died.

A tear ran down her face and she angrily wiped it away. "I'm fine," she lied, so quietly that I'd barely heard her. She didn't meet my gaze and a dry breeze swept through the trailer park. "No, he doesn't know."

I nodded. "I'm sorry that happened to you, Rachel. I really am—"

"Why are you here?" she asked, her voice filling with irritation. She crossed her arms over her chest.

I was taken aback. "I...I wanted to know you. I've been searching for my family. I've been trying to learn about who I come from and—"

"Our mother's dead. I haven't talked to my brothers or sister in years. We don't have a family. It's broken. Senior made sure of that."

I just stood there. A silence filled the distance between the two of us, but I suddenly realized that I understood her. "I understand you, Rachel. No, I don't know what it's like to be in your shoes, but I know what it's like to be broken."

She began to cry again. "Well, at least you can get your revenge."

"Didn't you?" I asked. "Adam Senior's in prison now."

"But he's still alive!" she yelled, her anger bursting forth. "He took my innocence! He took away my choices in life! He's the reason I have no life!"

"But you have Joey..."

Her breath hitched, and she wiped her tears. She pressed a hand to her mouth and gulped in air. "Yes...I have Joey."

"I don't want anything from you Rachel. To be honest, I wish I could help you. I guess...I guess I just hoped to have a relationship with you. You're my only connection to Kelly...to our mother. I've lost so much and I'm trying to put the pieces of my life back together."

She nodded and moved to sit on the steps of her trailer. She patted the steps next to her and I took a seat next to her. "It's weird having a brother that's older than me but looks like he could be my son."

We both laughed, and Rachel leaned against the steps. Weariness came off her body in waves.

"What do you think your life would've been like if Kelly hadn't died?" I asked her.

She sighed heavily and immediately answered; she didn't need to think about it. "Happier."

Wow.

That hit me hard; one word, but so much depth. So much meaning.

She looked at me. "But we can't go back in time. There's no need to dwell on the past. All we can do is keep breathing and move forward. I just know I have to keep breathing...for Joey's sake...and for my own."

"But what about—"

"No, Zedo," she said, shaking her head. "I can't talk about the past. Let's talk about the future... You're out of your coma now. You have time now. Time is on your side now. You can forget about that Burton business, forget about vengeance, and live your life."

I thought for a moment. What could my life be like now? I'd learned that there were worlds across the stars. There was a whole universe out there that I could explore... Perhaps I could explore it now.

But then again, I couldn't let my friends down. They were waiting for me. They'd *been* waiting on me for some time.

"I can't begin to live my life until Burton is dead."

She sighed. "Beyond that, Zedo. What do you want your life to be like beyond revenge?"

"To be honest, Rachel, when I was a kid, I wanted a different life. I wanted to be an actor. I wanted to make action movies and be a star. I wanted to fall in love before I was too old and maybe be a father. I wanted what everybody wants: a happy ending."

"It's not too late for that. You're frozen in the body of a fifteen-year-old for crying out loud! Finish school and go to college! Live your dreams. You're a good-looking kid. I'm sure you can break into acting."

I shrugged my shoulders. "Maybe." I had things on my list that still needed to be checked off. Before I could begin to think about my future, I first needed to take care of some things from my past.

I'd met my sister and laid down the framework for building a relationship with her. Perhaps I could get Joey in contact with the academy, so he could receive some training.

"Just be careful with your thoughts around Joey," I told her. She bit her lower lip and I instantly knew what she was thinking without probing her mind. "One day he's going to want to know, though..."

"I hope that day doesn't come anytime soon," she replied, weariness filling her voice. "I'll try to keep my thoughts clear of it, but sometimes I see my father in his expressions. It's unnerving."

I was about to say something, but Rachel beat me to the punch. "Are you hungry? I never got a chance to take your order before you dropped your bomb on me." She rose to her feet and dusted herself off.

I rose to my feet, too. "Yeah," I answered. "I'm starving."

She opened the door and led me into the trailer.

After dinner, Rachel provided me with a blanket and a pillow and I slept on her couch. That night, I dreamt of Lester and of my friends. They were locked in a fight and seemed to be losing. Lester hurled Gonzo through a wall and slammed his fist into Tempestt's rib cage.

He snarled and slapped Mona aside. Then, he spun and flew towards Eddie—who was in a rhino morph.

My eyes flew open and I gasped. My heart was racing, and I looked around. I was still on the couch in Rachel's trailer, but my mind had been elsewhere. Had I just experienced a nightmare…or had I seen a glimpse of the future?

Were my powers growing yet again?

I tried to relax but I couldn't. I was officially wired and needed to check on the others. I needed to find my friends. I needed to make sure they were okay.

But the thing was, I hadn't gathered any numbers. I didn't know how to contact them.

The only thing I knew was that we were supposed to meet at Mona's apartment.

Perhaps I just needed to go there. Perhaps I should just go to Mona's apartment and hope for the best. I couldn't let my nightmare become real.

I had to do something. I'd been away from the hunt for Burton for too long. I had to get back to the others and focus on the mission.

I got off the couch, found a pen, a piece of paper, and wrote Rachel a note. I would be back to check on her and Joey. This wasn't the only time I'd see them.

They were my family…I'd found them, but now I needed to be with my other family—the one I'd found with a common purpose.

I took my wallet out and left Rachel half of the money Master Braxton had given me back at the academy. Hopefully $1,000 would help Rachel. She needed it more than I did.

I walked out of the trailer and closed the door, making sure it didn't slam shut. It was still dark outside, and a chill was in the air. Daylight was still a few hours away, but I couldn't put this off.

That nightmare had been a warning. Lester was coming for my friends and they had no idea.

I had to get to them. I had to help them. We needed to end this. Perhaps I'd take care of Lester and Burton would be forced to come after us.

Maybe then, we'd get our revenge. However, before any of that could happen, I needed to get across the country and to Mona's apartment.

I'd teleported through lightning once and wondered if I could do it again but wasn't sure how to make that happen.

I didn't have time to figure out how to get the lightning to help me, so I leapt into the air and flew off. I flew with urgency at speeds rivaling that of a 747.

I'm coming, you guys, I thought. The wind whipping my hair as I flew onward. *Hang on, guys. I'm coming.*

Chapter 26:

Vengeance

ᏣᏌᏍᏍ

After hours and hours of flying, I was exhausted. I lowered myself from the clouds and caught sight of a plane flying in my direction.

I grinned and landed atop it. I called upon my ability to control the air and forced it to hold me in place as the plane flew across the country.

November 16, 2020

I plane-hopped several times until I reached Mona's city.

I took to the skies again and landed just outside of Mona's apartment. I instantly noticed a change in the air. It was colder hear and I felt like a weight was pushing down on me.

The sky had darkened and clouds swirled about overhead. I wondered if it was going to storm.

As I approached Mona's apartment building, I noticed several men dressed in dark red robes. One of the men shifted and locked eyes with me.

My jaw clenched. *Lester.*

So, I'd been right. Lester was here. The neighborhood was silent. No one was outside. It was still—soundless. Not even birds whistled.

Something was definitely wrong.

"He's here," I heard the man say. The four men converged on my position and tried to circle me. I didn't give them that chance.

"Before you even try something, let me just say this. None of you have to die. Leave now. Lester isn't worth it."

"We don't work for that idiot," one of the men said. He had a cut across his brow that was still bright red; it was recent.

"We work for the Shadow Master," another said.

"Your death is imminent," the third said.

"You're wrong," I replied, "but even if it was, it wouldn't be dealt by your hands."

Without warning, the four men lashed out. I back flipped and tried to gain some distance, but they were on me instantly.

I hurled a si' beam at one then ducked under the fist of another. The third tried to slam his boot into my chest but I blew him away with a burst of wind.

Adrenaline raced through my veins and I called on my powers to keep me alive.

These were trained warriors, not the mindless lackies Lester usually kept at his side.

I hurled flames into one of the men and he was reduced to ash. My eyes grew wide with shock!

They weren't human! My flames weren't hot enough to reduce bone to ash! They were otherworldly!

A fist slammed into my jaw and I fell backwards. Pain washed over me, and I flew upward to gain some distance.

My vision swam, and I suddenly realized that they hadn't followed me. They couldn't fly!

I flexed my fingers and tried to come up with a plan. Their eyes stayed locked on my position.

I looked at Mona's apartment building. If these goons were here, then so were my friends.

Rage boiled inside me and fueled me. I wasn't the type to go down without a fight. These three goons stood between me and Lester.

I pulled energy towards me and called upon my earth abilities. I hurled myself at the ground, landed, and sent the energy outwards. The earth responded, shooting chunks of the ground upward like geysers.

One of the goons was caught in the cement geyser and was reduced to dust. I spun and hurled flames at another one of the men but he evaded the flames.

These last two goons weren't going down easily.

I looked around but didn't catch sight of the second survivor. Where had he gone?

The goon in front of me had Asian features and lashed out, his hands extending like claws. My eyes grew wide and I tried to evade him. His arm flew overhead, and I slammed my fist in his jaw.

He yelled and then reached for me. I swung my other fist, igniting it in flames. The fist missed its mark and instead the goon spun out of the way. I moved quickly, becoming a blur as I flew upward and then back down.

The goon wasn't ready. I knocked him aside and brought my foot down on his throat, crushing his windpipe. I then ignited my fist in flames again and slammed my fist into the man. He was instantly reduced to ash.

Three down, one to go.

Suddenly, I was tackled from behind and slammed into the ground. My face hit the concrete and I yelled. My face felt warm and sticky. I realized I was bleeding—some of my flesh had been ripped off by the impact.

I screamed and rolled, throwing the last goon off me. I jumped to my feet and wiped my face. The pain was excruciating.

I suddenly thought of Mona—not as someone to swoop in and defeat my foe—but just in general. Her face filled my mind's eye. If anything had happened to her while I'd been out here fighting these four guys, I wouldn't forgive myself.

In that moment, I realized that I'd missed her. I then realized that if something had happened to her, I would be devastated. I'd be sorry because I'd been unable to tell her...to tell her—

A fist appearing out of nowhere brought me back to reality.

The goon had attacked again, materializing out of thin air. "He can teleport!" I exclaimed.

Not only could his fingers turn into razor sharp claws, but he could teleport, too! This wasn't going to be easy.

I heard a whooshing sound and turned. He'd tried to sneak up on me, again, but that wasn't going to happen.

As he swiped a hand full of razor-sharp claws towards my face, I howled with full fury and called down a bolt of lightning. Just as his hand was about to connect with my face, the bolt of purple lightning slammed into his body.

The goon screamed as he sizzled and then exploded in a burst of ash. I relaxed for a moment as the smell of burnt flesh filled my nostrils.

I spat blood and wiped a hand across my face, feeling a mixture of sweat and blood.

I was tired, but it wasn't over yet. No, the fight had only just begun.

I moved towards Mona's building again and walked through the iron gate that led into the apartment complex.

The door that led into her building was closed. I was still furious. I stretched my arm forward and flexed my fingers towards the door. I blew it off its hinges with a burst of superheated air. It flew across the hall and slammed into the far wall with an impact hard enough to be felt in Texas and embedded itself in the wall.

I moved into the building and realized that the halls were darkened—not a single light was on. Had the power to the building been cut off? Is that why it seemed deserted?

I felt a drop fall unto my neck. As I looked to the ceiling, I could see water stains and drops falling. I frowned. I heard the sound of flowing water and looked down. Water flowed freely out of the apartment.

Was the entire building flooded?

I began to generate a si' beam in my palm as I made my way through the building.

I was on guard. I didn't trust Lester to not have more goons lurking around the building.

Surely, he'd come with more back-up then four men.

I moved deeper into the building and the water levels rose higher, now covering my calves.

Mona lived upstairs, and I glanced up the central stairwell.

As I made my way up the stairs, the water receded, until I simply treaded in ankle-deep water. My classic Chuck Taylor shoes were already soaked and squished as I moved about the building.

Suddenly, the lights flickered on and I froze, dread filling me. Then the overhead lights exploded—showering me with sparks.

I shielded my head and moved up the stairs faster.

This complex seemed to be abandoned. I hadn't found a single person. And by the time I arrived on Mona's dark floor, my thoughts were confirmed.

I moved down the hall, my heart racing faster and faster as I approached her door.

Something moved in my peripheral vision and I turned my head. To my horror, a body floated on the water and moved down the hallway.

I jumped out of the way as the body was carried down the hall and to the steps.

On Mona's level, the water seemed to rise again and fall over the stairwell like a waterfall.

What was going on?

I moved down the hallway and stood before Mona's door. I stretched out with my mind and tried to use my telepathy, but I hit a wall. Something, or better yet someone, was blocking me.

I touched the gold doorknob that was attached to Mona's door. The lights flickered, and I looked to the floor. Water found its way through the slit under the door. A disturbing chill went down my spine.

Water wasn't just coming from Mona's apartment, but from them *all*!

I turned the knob to open the door, the door was unlocked but the door wouldn't open.

I repeated the same move I'd completed to get into the building in the first place. I flexed my fingers and slammed a wall of air into the door, blowing it off its hinges. But instead of flying backwards, the door was propelled forward by a wall of water.

Water raced past me, knocking me off my feet. I screamed and was swept away by the flood!

The water moved like a raging river as it coursed through the apartment building. I heard glass shatter and water began to spill out of the building.

I called upon my aquakinetic abilities and wrapped myself in a bubble of water. I gasped as air filled my lungs.

I rose to my feet and watched from within the water bubble as the water began to recede. As the water levels reached knee-level, I dropped the water bubble and moved into Mona's apartment.

As I entered what used to be Mona's apartment, I saw that a couple of her chairs had been broken. A huge feather lay on top of what was left of her shattered television.

I pushed my body through the freezing water. Three of her windows were broken and wind whistled in, chilling my body; it was Autumn after all.

Water continued to drip from the ceiling.

"Ah, you came back," said a sinister voice.

I jumped and turned around. Behind me, sitting in a chair was Lester. He sat with his legs crossed—presenting himself as the perfect gentleman—and was utterly dry! His clothes weren't soaked like mine were. I envied him for that.

It was fall and I was soaked in water. My body shivered, but I tried to ignore it.

Behind Lester, the shattered window let wind in and rustled the wet curtain at its side.

Lester was dressed in all black, his hair rustling in the breeze.

"Lester," I said. I looked around. I didn't see my friends. Where were they?

As if reading my mind, he uncrossed my legs and spoke. "You're looking for them, aren't you?" He smirked. "I can't believe my father chose *you*... You're *pathetic.*"

"Your father is going to die by my hand," I told him.

With that, Lester's jaw clenched, and he seemed genuinely taken aback. He rose to his feet. "He can't be stopped. I don't care if he wants you alive. I grow weary of taking orders."

"Then you're welcome to join him, Lester. Just die."

He cackled and then his eyes began to glow red and his voice grew deeper and distorted. "NO! *YOU DIE!*"

He slammed his hands together—the clap resounding off the walls with a sound like thunder—and a shockwave swept through the apartment, shattering the remaining windows and buckling the walls.

The shockwave slapped into me and knocked me off my feet. I went flying across the apartment and slammed through the wall and into the next apartment.

In the next moment, Lester was on me. He grabbed my throat and squeezed hard.

I gasped and clawed at his hand, trying to pull his hand off me. I felt my energy drain and realized that Lester was draining it! He was pulling power from me.

He rose to his full height and lifted me off my feet until I dangled in mid-air. "You're *weak*, Jeta!"

And with that, he threw me aside like a rag doll. I hit the wall and crumbled to the floor, gasping for air. My body slumped into the remaining water.

Lester turned to the wall and gestured with his hand and a burst of superheated air blew the wall apart—shattering it into chunks of wood and bricks.

My eyes grew wide with horror! Lester had drained my energy and had then copied my ability to control the elements!

Lester's body began to twist and contort—my powers were incompatible with his own. But he wasn't going to let that stop him! He reached for the sky and I felt the weather respond to him.

I forced myself to my feet and felt the air vibrate as Lester manipulated the weather. The sky opened up and I felt the weather shift.

A funnel cloud began to descend from the sky and my ears popped. The air was shifting too quickly. The weather was being ripped apart and grew unstable.

The funnel touched down with a loud thud and slammed into a nearby apartment building with a sound like a freight train slamming on brakes.

Lester yelled, and I screamed as the power exploded and the tornado began to unleash its fury on the neighborhood.

The tornado turned and then hit the apartment complex, ripping the roof off! The floor above us split open and I could see the floor above me as floor boards were ripped from their foundation and sucked into the vortex that was the tornado.

Suddenly, I caught sight of Tempestt! She was screaming and holding onto a door—her body angled towards the tornado as it tried to suck her into it.

"Tempestt!!" I cried, launching myself into the air as I flew towards her. "I'm coming!"

She seemed to hear me and turned in my direction. "Zedo!!" she yelled. "Behind you!"

I turned to catch sight of Lester flying towards me. He'd unleashed this natural disaster and now it had a mind of its own.

Lester slammed into me and we went hurtling through the air, twisting and turning as we exchanged blows. Lester flexed his fingers and claws appeared—claws similar to his goon that had attacked me earlier.

Lester could copy others' abilities! He was a bigger threat then I'd realized.

His claws flashed, and I managed to get my arm up to defend my eyes—which he was aiming for.

I didn't feel the cuts he created, perhaps I was numb to pain right now, but I did see my skin open. I began to bleed.

Agony rolled through my body as he struck me with another fist. I dodged a table that was being pulled into the tornado.

I needed to get some distance between Lester and me! And I needed to get to Tempestt.

Lester came at me again—his right hand extended with the claws emitting from his fingertips—but I knocked his arms aside and slammed my fist into his sternum.

Lester was knocked out of the sky and slammed into the ground below, just outside of the apartment complex. I dropped from the sky and landed inside the apartment adjacent to Mona's.

I inhaled sharply and looked down at myself. I was covered in cuts and bleeding from several wounds. My clothes were still soaked in water, but I wasn't cold anymore. Adrenaline was coursing through my body, in addition to the pain, and had cancelled out the feeling of being cold.

However, everything still seemed to work. I was glad nothing was broken. I looked around and wondered where the others were. The tornado had torn apart the apartment building next to us and began to grow in size.

Below me, Lester was beginning to climb to his feet. I quickly called energy to me and it came instantaneously, welling up from the ground, falling from the sky, lifting up from the water, and wrapping around me from circuits that still crackled with energy. I combined the air and water with the fire from the sparks and earth from the floor boards and hurled all four forms of the elements at Lester.

He screamed and tried to throw up a wall of superheated air to protect himself, but it wasn't enough. The glowing force of energy detonated and tore through him.

Lester screamed and was forced down into the ground so much so that his body slammed through the earth and landed in the complex's basement.

I reached towards the sky and called lightning down then hurled a bolt towards the basement and into Lester's body!

He screamed—the sound echoing—and I watched as he began to convulse as the lightning hammered into him a second time.

Just as the weather had once come to my assistance, the tornado Lester had created came to his. Just as the lightning had allowed me to move through it and teleport to Michigan, the tornado absorbed Lester and then imprinted him with it.

Lester's face appeared among the funnel. I gasped and spun around, but Lester's eyes followed me wherever I turned! He frowned, and his glowing red eyes glared down at me.

"Zedo!" someone shouted. I looked up, expecting to see Tempestt, but instead, I caught sight of all of my friends!

Gonzo held his left side and had a black eye, but he stood next to Tempestt. Mona leaned over a half-broken banister—her black hair blowing in the strong wind—and our eyes met. "Give him hell, Jeta!" she shouted. I then caught sight of Edward. Blood flowed from his busted lip.

They all looked worse for wear.

I flew towards them and landed next to Eddie. He clasped me on the back.

"Is he dead?" asked Gonzo.

I shook my head and brushed my hair aside. "This isn't over yet."

Mona limped towards me. "What took you so long?" she asked.

"Thank you will suffice," I said, grinning.

She hugged me tight. "I'm glad you're here now," she whispered.

"Me too," I whispered back. As I pulled away, I moved towards Gonzo, but was yanked backwards and pulled down and then through the wood panels of the flooring.

Down, down I went. As I tried to use my strength to stop, I realized I couldn't. Lester forced me into the ground and I slammed into the cement foundation.

Lester chuckled, his voice still distorted and then he leapt from the tornado and floated on the air.

"You're not going to win here!"

I glanced up at the others and nodded. The only way we'd get out of this alive would be to attack together as one unit!

Eddie transformed into his giant eagle morph and swooped down and reached out with his talons. Lester spun and fired a si' beam into Eddie's wing.

The eagle cried out and Eddie morphed into his human form and fell towards the ground and slammed into the ground.

"Eddie!" cried Tempestt as she levitated across the air.

I hurled si' beams at Lester just as Mona and Gonzo launched ice beams and energy blasts, respectively.

The three remaining able-bodied members of my team and I lashed out at Lester, but he was able to defend himself against us.

Mona hurled an ice beam at him and one beam sliced through his arm. Mona then rushed forward and slammed her fist into his face before she generated an ice shard and stabbed him.

Lester hurled flames at her and she fell backwards, moving behind a wall to protect herself.

The sight of the apartment building around us was appalling. It was a ruin; the tornado had ripped it apart. It was barely recognizable as the place I'd arrived at barely an hour ago.

Lester snarled and yanked the ice shard out of his abdomen. "Is that all you've got?!" he shouted. "You send a bird and an ice witch against me, Jeta?!" he laughed. "You're pathetic!"

I let out a war cry and lashed out, but he vanished. A second later, he reappeared several feet behind me. Before I could turn around, Lester stabbed me in the back.

I screamed out and Gonzo hurled a yellow energy blast at him.

Lester slammed into the remains of the partial wall and his body was submerged under the water that still flooded the base of the apartment building.

As he resurfaced, he gestured with his hand and hurled wind at Gonzo—tossing him into the tornado. The tornado spit Gonzo out—hurling him through a window and through two rooms before he crashed into a bathroom on the thirteenth floor.

Next, Tempestt came towards Lester. Lester lifted himself into the air and Tempestt levitated in his direction. As she kept her focus, she fought him in the air, kicking and throwing punches at the man that had once sent her to kill me.

I flew to her aid and called upon my aquakinetic powers. Water flew through the air and wrapped around my forearm like a whip. I swung my arm and the water-whip slapped Lester aside.

As Lester was knocked aside, he reached out and grabbed Tempestt's leg and threw her into the ground.

Tempestt slammed into the ground and rolled to a stop. Mona rushed to her side, climbing over debris and tried to shake her awake.

Eddie limped to their side, holding the shoulder that Lester had shot a si' beam into.

As I turned to see where Lester was, he was gone.

As the tornado Lester had created continued its rampage, it invited two more twisters to join it. Lester was out of control! He was manipulating the weather way past its limit.

I finally caught sight of Lester. He stood on the half-destroyed roof—arms outstretched towards the tornadoes he'd created.

I had to stop him. I stretched out both of my hands and drained the last reserves of my power to control the tornadoes. The forces of nature responded and began to swirl around me.

As the disastrous trio swirled around me in a circle, I closed my eyes and sensed their very being.

Lester screamed—his rage echoing in the air as the wind howled.

As the trio combined as one and formed an F5 tornado, they wrapped around my arms and I directed my arms towards Lester.

He screamed out and tried to shield himself, but the great beast sucked him into the eye of the storm. As he yelled out in agony, we could hear his bones popping.

The tornado began to pull Lester apart.

Suddenly, the tornado backfired and exploded—a shockwave hurling me through the air. I slammed into the trunk of an oak tree and fell to the ground. I gasped for air, drained and in pain.

Lester reappeared before me, his clothes half torn off and some of his flesh was missing. Blood was everywhere. His face haunted me as half of his left side was missing, however, he wasn't dead.

His chest heaved in and out as he heavily breathed. He popped his left shoulder back into place and spat blood.

"Why won't you die?!" I shouted, forcing myself to my feet.

Gonzo grabbed Mona and flew towards us while Eddie stayed at Tempestt's side.

Lester held up a hand and Gonzo and Mona slammed into a wall of compressed air. They hit the ground and stood there, horror etched on their faces.

"This is between the two of us, Jeta."

"I agree," I said, focusing all of my concentration on a plan.

"All I've ever wanted to do was please my father."

"That's never going to happen," I told him, my chest heaving. Pain was trying to pull me under, but I wouldn't give in.

Mona and Gonzo used their powers as they tried to break through Lester's barrier.

I reached towards the sky and thunder sounded. The sky opened up and rain began to come down in a downpour.

My energy reserves were basically depleted, but I pulled from my own life essence. A surge of energy coursed through my body and I called three bolts of red lightning from the sky and they slammed into my palm.

The smell of charred flesh filled my nostrils. I glared at Lester and hurled all three of the bolts at him. They slammed into Lester's sternum and Lester screamed as he was simultaneously burned and electrocuted alive.

"This isn't my end, Jeta! Someone will finish what I've started!!!!!" Lester shouted right before the lightning exploded. I was hurled backwards, but Mona caught me.

I glanced up just as Lester's body hit the ground. His eyes were open wide and the same went for his mouth. He began to glow with a black hue and slowly was reduced to black smoke that scattered to the four winds.

It was over.... I had defeated Lester. The rain still came down as hard as ever, but at least the tornado began to subside.

The destruction of this community was infinite. Soon, these people would have to rebuild and start their lives all over.

Mona helped me lie down among the debris and Gonzo moved to our side.

"It's over," Gonzo said, looking at the remaining ashes Lester had left behind.

"No," Mona said, looking at him. "It's just beginning."

My throat was extremely dry. I opened my mouth and let some water droplets fall in. "Burton's still out there...somewhere," I said.

Eddie appeared over a mound of debris, Tempestt in his arms. She was awake and had a hand pressed to the back of her head.

I suddenly heard the sound of sirens in the distance. First responders were on the way.

"No more running," I told them.

"No more running," they said in agreement.

The truth of the matter was, I was too weak to run even if I wanted to.

Eddie, Tempestt, and Gonzo relaxed against a chunk of upturned asphalt as Mona helped me to my feet.

I wondered what she thought of me.

I had to face the truth. I liked her... a lot. I wondered if she liked me, too. I wish I had a piece of paper to write on, so I could slide it to her.

I looked at Mona as emergency personnel arrived and ran about, searching the rubble. She stared in the distance. Gonzo and the others were talking amongst each other, recounting the battle.

Even in the pouring rain she looked beautiful to me.

I took a deep breath, suddenly conscious that I probably only had another few seconds to be alone with her, to say something that I'd felt for a while. I wasn't afraid to say it... not anymore.

"I think I like you," I told her and then shook my head. "No, I *know* I like you, Mona Lisa-Flynn." She didn't look my way; maybe she hadn't heard me. I cleared my throat and spoke louder. "I like you, Mona... I hope you don't mind."

She suddenly looked at me and grinned, almost despite herself. She was covered in dirt and grime from the battle, and soaked in rain, but she'd never looked more beautiful to me.

"I don't mind at all, Zedo," she replied, leaning towards me.

My heart fluttered and then I leaned in, too, closing my eyes and then our lips met in what was my first kiss.

It seemed as if, at that exact moment, I could hear fireworks going off.

The world had frozen, and everything had stopped. The entire universe was at ease!

What was she thinking? Was she feeling the same way I did?

I wondered if this meant something. Were we supposed to start a relationship now? I pushed the thoughts aside and focused on the moment.

Our lips moved, and she wrapped her arms around my neck and I pulled her closer to me—my hands on her waist.

Slowly, but surely, we pulled away and Mona smiled. I chuckled and looked at her, blinking against the rain.

The rain slowly began to stop, and the clouds parted, revealing the sunrise.

Mona leaned her head on my shoulder as we watched the sun rise on this new day, November 17, 2020.

I wondered what the new day would bring. Now that Lester was dead, we were one step closer to finding Burton.

Though I thought all these things, I tried to remain in the present. We needed to regroup and come up with a plan. I was exhausted, but our work had just begun.

Was Burton on Earth, or across the stars?

Wherever you are, I thought to myself, *I'm coming for you.*

To be continued...

Concept Art

When I initially reached out to my brother, LaNorris, to discuss him bringing my characters to life for the cover to give everyone a visual, I had to share my concept art. I'm not a great drawer, but I knew what vision I wanted to go for.

I'm amazed that he truly stuck to the concept art when he brought Zedo Jeta, Mona Lisa-Flynn. Gonzo Daniels, Tempestt, Eddie Wong, and Lester Burton to life.

*** <u>About the Author</u> ***

Jay, as a child, discovered that his life could be a whirlwind of adventures by simply opening a book and reading. To this day, reading is still his favorite thing in the world, followed closely by watching movies. He still has a fondness for fantasy, sci-fi, and fiction, which is probably why he writes for those genres.

When Jay DeMoir isn't working on his next book, he's usually binge-watching old tv shows on DVD or making music or teaching young minds.

Jay DeMoir is not only an alumnus of the University of Memphis, where he received his BA in Communications (Film& Video Production) and minored in English Literature and Psychology, but also an educator. During the day, he's a Middle School English/Language Arts teacher and currently seeking his master's degree in education.

Another hat he wears is that of CEO of a multimedia company 'House of DeMoir Productions.' Jay DeMoir is also a filmmaker, registered screenwriter, and musician that has seen his stories brought to life as web shows, documentaries, and musicals.

Jay DeMoir would love to hear from his readers. Feel free to contact him via:

Goodreads: Jay DeMoir

Twitter: @JayDeMoir

Instagram: @jay_demoir

Email: houseofdemoir@gmail.com

Made in the USA
Columbia, SC
18 May 2022

60533486R00238